"Hold on to your hat, this story has action written all over it."

"The writing is superb, the hero is a yummy alpha, the heroine strong and likable, lots of steamy sex, and nonstop action. What's not to like?"

HUSH

"Addictively readable. . . . Testosterone-rich, adrenaline-driven suspense. . . . Packed with plenty of unexpected plot twists and lots of sexy passion."

"Gripping. . . . Fast-paced and loaded with action."

"Hot and steamy. . . . The sexual tension is magnetic."

"Adair is a master of pulling together exciting adventure and burning passion to make a spine-tingling read!"

BLACK MAGIC

"Plenty of sex, and a hero who always comes to the rescue."

"A hot new adventure."

"A very sexy adventure that offers nonstop, continent-hopping action from start to finish."

HIDE AND SEEK

"Cherry Adair stokes up the heat and intrigue in her adventurous thriller."

"Outsize protagonists, super-nasty villains, and earthy sex scenes."

"Gripping, sexy as all get-out."

"A reason to stay up way too late."

KISS AND TELL

"A sexy, snappy roller-coaster ride!"

"A true keeper."

Also by Cherry Adair

Afterglow
Hush
Black Magic

Available from Pocket Books

CHERRY
ADAIR

RELENTLESS

POCKET BOOKS

New York   London   Toronto   Sydney   New Delhi

Pocket Books
A Division of Simon & Schuster, Inc.
1230 Avenue of the Americas
New York, NY 10020

This book is a work of fiction. Any references to historical events, real people, or real places are used fictitiously. Other names, characters, places, and events are products of the author's imagination, and any resemblance to actual events or places or persons, living or dead, is entirely coincidental.

First Pocket Books paperback edition April 2013

POCKET and colophon are registered trademarks of Simon & Schuster, Inc.

For information about special discounts for bulk purchases, please contact Simon & Schuster Special Sales at 1-866-506-1949 or business@simonandschuster.com.

The Simon & Schuster Speakers Bureau can bring authors to your live event. For more information or to book an event, contact the Simon & Schuster Speakers Bureau at 1-866-248-3049 or visit our website at www.simonspeakers.com.

Manufactured in the United States of America

10 9 8 7 6 5 4 3 2 1

ISBN 978-1-5011-1009-2
ISBN 978-1-4516-8433-9 (ebook)

RELENTLESS

❦ ONE ❧

Ex-MI5 special intelligence operative Connor Thorne extended his hand without getting up from behind his desk. "Give me the leash. Fluffy will be in your arms before dinner."

"Awesome." His prospective client, Someone-or-other-Magee, pushed the bridge of black-framed glasses up her nose as she sat down across from him, bringing with her a fragrance of warm cinnamon that made his hormones sit up and take notice. Her gaze dipped, briefly, to his mouth and lingered there until Thorne felt his heartbeat in his lips. An unexpected, unwelcome response shuddered through him as a frisson of awareness arched between them.

Bloody hell. Long-lashed doe-brown eyes returned to his. "Who's Fluffy?"

The watery light, shining into his office from the large window behind him, highlighted her wild, dark curls and clear complexion. Wholesome and hopeful. Neither of which appealed to Thorne in the slightest.

She wore a long-sleeved white T-shirt—not too loose, not too tight. The soft fabric skimmed enticingly over small, plump breasts and tucked into dark-washed jeans. Gold hoops at her earlobes shone through loose, curly, bitter-chocolate-brown shoulder-length hair. A delicate chain around her slender throat glinted in what passed as sunlight in Seattle in June.

Her purse, a small brown leather affair, looked like a camera bag and was clutched like the Holy Grail on her lap, as if it held state secrets. He probably should've glanced at the file handed to him by Maki at the front desk, but since this kind of "find" was child's play, Thorne hadn't bothered. She'd tell him her tale of woe, he'd hold whatever *it* was, and he'd tell her where to find it. Next.

With one slash of a boning knife, and a couple of bullets, he'd gone from one of MI5's most trusted operatives to *this*. "Don't you want me to find your cat?"

She gave him a sparkling look from those big brown eyes, clearly enjoying a private joke. "I'm allergic."

Of course she is, he thought, unamused. "Dog, then." *Something small and yippy, named Baby.*

Her pretty mouth pinched as if she were biting back tears, or suppressing a smile. "Deathly afraid of them."

Pissed off and not really sure why, he found his patience, what little he had, abruptly ending. "Are you a librarian or a nursery school teacher?" He imagined her surrounded by sticky hands and adoring gummy smiles.

"I'm guessing from your tone that you don't hold

teachers or librarians in high esteem? How do you feel about photographers?"

"Photographers?"

"I'm a commercial photographer. Mostly print ads for agencies. Diapers, shoes, jewelry, that kind of thing. It pays the bills." She cocked her head. Miss Magee wasn't nearly as sweet and wholesome as she pretended to be. There was a definite bite in her tone when she said sweetly, "I hope you don't find that as offensive to your sensibilities as teaching?"

"What you do for a living is immaterial. I'm attempting to ground the conversation." Find that equal ground that allowed people like her to trust that someone like him could find her missing pet. Or ex-lover or piece of jewelry or whatever it was she wanted from Lodestone.

Light duty. He'd been instructed by a team of MI5 doctors to take it easy. No running, chasing, falling down, or getting shot at. One year, they'd ordered. No excuses or exceptions. He wouldn't like the consequences if he didn't comply, they'd warned.

He was complying, goddamn it.

Thorne left rainy London for rainier Seattle, and somehow managed to make it to day forty-three. He was bored out of his mind. He'd rather deal with the oddly intriguing Miss Magee than contemplate if he'd ever be fit for duty again. Permanently in the mood to shoot something, socially unacceptable in his present position, he schooled his features to appear as polite and affable as he could manage.

It took effort. No offense to the curly-haired woman

in front of him, but he just didn't relish jobs where bullets weren't a factor. It was a shortcoming he had to live with. Temporarily. Desk duty, or being crippled for life.

"What *do* you want me to find?" Because, goddamn it, he'd find it. Whatever it took. At least he'd earn his paycheck from his friend Zak Stark, and not freeload during his recuperation.

Tucking her hair behind one ear, she pointed at the thin file folder on his desk. The one he hadn't bothered to look at. He'd seen her in the waiting room, and labeled her Nursery School Teacher, Lost Cat. Proving that one shouldn't judge a book by its cover, no matter how Librarian Spinster looking.

"Give me the CliffsNotes."

"I want you to find a tomb."

Bloody hell. "I don't do tombs."

Her eyebrows vanished beneath her bangs and she blinked behind her glasses. "You . . . don't *do* tombs? What does that mean?"

Her bangs needed cutting; they were constantly in her eyes. "It means, Miss Magee, that if it's a tomb you're looking for, I don't find them."

Her stare was a little too direct. "Why not?"

"Because I don't like heat, or sand, or going to places I find unpleasant." *Not unless I'm fully armed and have some asshole bad guy in my sights.* It was in a desert that he'd received his injuries. Thorne was in no rush to go back.

Only 322 days to go, he thought bitterly.

"How . . . limiting." She pushed her glasses up her nose again. "Isn't it your job to go wherever the client needs you to go?" She paused, and when he didn't respond, said, "Who says the tomb I want found is somewhere hot and sandy? Maybe it's the tomb of the Unknown Soldier in Hietaniemi cemetery in Helsinki? Or the tomb beneath the Arc de Triomphe in Paris? Or—"

Terrier, meet bone. He repressed a sigh, a groan, and the words *fucking hell.* "Do you have a general location?"

Her fingers tightened on her purse. "Egypt." She cleared her throat, and just in case he was hard of hearing repeated firmly, "Egypt."

Bugger it. *Magee? Egypt?* He joined some dots, and didn't like where they led. Fuck. He resisted cursing in any or all five languages, and opted for a teeth-clenched, polite "Did you bring me something?" While Thorne didn't believe in coincidences, some people did. Anything was possible. He hoped that wherever his logic was leading him, it was dead wrong.

"Like what?" Her lips twitched. "A Bundt cake?"

Thorne's back teeth ground together. "Like something I can hold so I can tell you where your tomb is."

She leaned forward in her chair, avid curiosity sparkling in her eyes. "Right. That thing. How does your superpower work?"

"I'm *not* a freak." Even if that's what he considered himself in his heart of hearts, he didn't have to admit it out loud. And he sure as hell didn't have to sit under her suddenly too-interested microscope. "What I do is referred to by scientists as a well-developed sixth sense." Which had materialized full-fucking-blown after he'd died on the table and been brought back to life eight months ago. He started to rub his thigh under the desk, then realized what he was doing and placed both hands on the desktop. A *desk*, for Chrissakes!

"Oh." Leaning forward, she contemplated him for several moments. "How does it work for you?"

He leaned back. Her subtle movement made him feel . . . invaded. Ridiculous. He'd killed men twice her size with his bare hands without a single flutter of his heartbeat. Why should this slip of a woman with her Bambi eyes rattle him? She didn't, of course; she was just the most interesting thing to happen to him since he'd started working for Zak. Which just showed how restricted his life had become.

"I hold something and can tell you where the person who had it last is located."

Her brilliant smile stole his next smart-ass comment. Her teeth were white and straight, except for her eye-teeth, which were just crooked enough to charm him. If he were a man who was enchanted by teeth that needed braces. The smile, which lit up her whole face, was like an electric shock jolting his body. It took her from pretty to stunning and caused an unwelcome, and annoying, chemical reaction in his body.

"Perfect!" she told him cheerfully. "They told me to bring something connected to the tomb when I made the appointment. But I couldn't figure out how the box would help you—" She dug in her bag and withdrew a chamois-covered item about the size of a ring box. She gave him an inquiring look.

"Put it down, and slide it over." Not because her placing it in his hand diluted anything, but Thorne wasn't ready to stand just yet, and for reasons he refused to explain to himself, he didn't want to touch her.

Opening the bag, she dropped a small gold box covered in hieroglyphs into her palm. Clutching the purse to her middle and the box in one hand, she rose to lean over the desk and nudged it forward. His response to her nearness was immediate and visceral. His head swam with the enticing fragrance of her cookie-scented skin. He could drown in her chocolaty eyes—goddamn it. The woman was as tempting to his palate as she was to his senses. Enough of this crap. Redirecting his attention, he picked up the small box. It was light in weight and heavy in ominous undertones.

For fuck's sake. Sand. Desert. Egypt. The goddamned trifecta. And then—

512946010355149598317637251.

A superfecta!

The numbers scrolling through his head made him set the box on the desk. Not quite as fast as if it had burned his fingers with a flaming blowtorch set on high, but close enough.

Not Egypt. But only slightly less repugnant. "This comes from London."

"No," she assured him firmly as she resumed her seat. "It's from the tomb of Queen Cleopatra, which is somewhere in Egypt, I believe."

He flicked open the lid. "It's empty."

"I know. Whatever was in it was lost. Can you use your superpower to find where it came from?"

Thorne picked up his GPS, although he didn't need confirmation. He punched in the coordinates he was seeing in his head, then turned the device to his new client. "The Natural History Museum, London."

She bit her lip, her expression pained. "Can't you go *further* back than that?"

There was an imperceptible shadow dancing right behind the London GPS location. Try as he might, Thorne couldn't read it. "Apparently not."

Her shoulders slumped. "Damn. Damn. Damn."

"No charge."

Her gaze shot to his face. She was not amused. "Well, of course not. I hired Lodestone to find a tomb, not a museum."

"Then bring me something from the tomb and I'll tell you where it is." He drummed his fingers across the tabletop. If he couldn't shoot something, was it too early for a drink?

"If I could do that then I wouldn't need you to find it, now would I? This is all I have." Her expressive eyes welled.

He checked the clock. Noon? Good enough. There was a bar a block over. "Are you going to cry?"

"Maybe. Yes." She sniffed. A tiny tear, magnified by the lenses of her glasses, shimmered on the edge of her long, dark lashes. "Probably." It fell, glistening as it slid over her rounded cheek, beneath the frame. "This was pretty much my last option. I'm so disappointed and frustrated."

Who wasn't? They only came to Lodestone when they were desperate enough to try anything—even something as out of the park as sixth sense locating. "Why's this tomb so important? Are you an amateur archaeologist?"

The answer he wanted to hear was no, she had nothing to do with archaeology and was just curious. Or it was a bet—or any bloody thing that wasn't related to who and what he knew she was about to tell him. The tears were about to fall in earnest, if that trembling lower lip was any indication, and she looked so forlorn, Thorne figured he'd give her a minute before shuffling her out of his office and sending her on her way. He should call his shrink and report progress. Six months ago he would've kicked her out in the first thirty seconds. Yes, progress indeed. The desk job was making him soft. Christ.

"My father's an archaeologist." The tear dripped off her stubborn chin, leaving a shiny trail on her cheek. "August Magee."

And there it was. Dots all joined and tied in a big fucking red bow. Which was why, he was damned sure, his new boss and soon to be ex–good friend, Zak Stark, had given him this assignment just before conveniently hieing his arse to some jungle in South America for months on end to build an adventure camp for pre-parolees.

The tie-in between Miss Magee, London, and Egypt was so blatantly obvious as to be laughable. Too bad he was rarely amused.

Thorne's father was one of the professor's largest benefactors. What he knew of the professor was precious little. But he did know the man liked his booze, and had a propensity to lie. Did *she* know who *his* father was? "Go on."

"The tomb of Cleopatra has been my father's life's work for over twenty years." Tears apparently forgotten, she was now all earnest sincerity. "He finally discovered its location three months ago."

"He's 'discovered' that tomb—what? Five or six times?" Thorne pointed out dryly.

"Oh, damn," she sighed, drawing his disinterested gaze to her small, plump breasts. "You really *do* know of him. Seven times. But the seventh was—"

He redirected his attention. She had a soft, delectable mouth slicked with glossy pink lipstick, and just looking at those shiny lips made him hard. And annoyed. Thorne wasn't in the market for a lover at the moment, and he doubted the luscious Miss Magee was the one-night-stand type, even if he was. Pity, but there it was. "Look, Miss Magee—"

"Isis."

Of course it was. Trust a crackpot archaeologist like August Magee to stick his kid with the name of an Egyptian goddess. "Let me be brutally frank here, *Isis*. Your father's reputation precedes him. He was archaeology's darling more than a decade ago, but he has a problem with veracity. He's cried wolf more often than not. And frankly his drinking hasn't done him any favors." He pinched his fingers together as if holding a shot glass and tipped it back for illustration. "If the tomb *really* exists, and if this time the find is genuine, then he's going to need evidence before he's believed. Having you do it for him probably won't do the trick."

"He has Alzheimer's," Isis said flatly.

Thorne stared at her for a moment, waiting to see if there was anything else. Satisfied there wasn't, he got to his feet. Not that he was walking anywhere. But he rose so she'd take the hint and leave. "Then it would appear you're screwed." His leg protested as if a great white shark had seized his thigh muscle between its teeth. He gripped the edge of the desk, keeping his expression neutral with effort, even though his knuckles were turning white. "Sorry I can't help you."

She beamed those big, tear-drenched eyes up at him like a surface-to-air missile with complex target tracking. "Please."

Gut tight in reaction to her soft plea, he resumed his seat. "All I can tell you is that whatever was inside the box is somewhere in the museum in London. While my skills are pretty specific, the best I can do is give you the general location of what you're looking for. Finding it could possibly take you months, if not years. There are in the neighborhood of seventy million items there."

She frowned. "How could you *possibly* know that?"

"My father is one of the benefactors of the museum. The *Egyptian* section of the Natural History Museum in London, in fact." Thorne was going to hand Zak his arse on a platter five minutes after the emotional Miss Isis Magee departed. He was supposed to be recovering, not dealing with emotional-baggage-laden weepy females.

"The Earl of Kilgetty is your *father*?" Her eyes went wide and she slid to the edge of her chair. "That's terrific. He'll be a big help. And I know every single artifact my father donated to the museum, right up to the last piece. We can go through the exhibits. Hands on. I *know* we'll find something that'll lead us to Egypt and Cleo's tomb."

We? "Unless you have a mouse in your pocket the answer to that is a resounding no. I have absolutely no desire to return to England under any circumstances." For two excellent and compelling reasons that were none of her damned business. "Moreover, I loathe Egyptology, as many people in authority would be delighted to tell you."

"My cousin Acadia assured me that Lodestone finds anything, anyone, anywhere." There was now more than a bite to her words. "I believed her assurances that you were as good at this as Zak is."

Ah. Her *cousin* Acadia. Zak's lovely new bride. Suddenly all the puzzle pieces fit neatly into place. A small detail his friend had conveniently omitted before clasping him on the shoulder and telling him to "Take it easy" while he was out of the country.

"Well?"

Bugger it! "Is your photograph under the word *tenacious* in the dictionary?"

She sat back, crossing her long legs. She was wearing strappy purple sandals, and her toenails were painted an unexpected fluorescent pink. "I *know* that my father finally found Queen Cleopatra's tomb. I believe it so much that I've liquidated all my assets to prove it. I've sold my condo, Mr. Thorne. And my car. And cashed in my stocks. I'll do anything to prove once and for all—to *everyone*——that this time he did it. *Will* you help me find the tomb?"

Fuck. He understood high stakes. She was gambling everything on a roll of Lodestone dice——Thorne owed Zak. His capitulation had nothing to do with Isis. Life was for the living, not the dead. Thorne leaned back, steepling his fingers. His thigh throbbed, his chest ached like a mother, and he didn't need a sixth sense to tell him he was going to regret this. "Start at the beginning."

CONNOR THORNE HAD A tightly coiled intensity that Isis found both mildly disconcerting and strangely compelling. He smelled delectable. Not cologne, but clean skin and some kind of outdoor-scented soap. Feeling an irrational need to touch him, she wished he'd offered her a handshake. He wasn't her type at all, but that didn't prevent her from feeling the tug of attraction. Either that, or it was the taco she'd hastily consumed for lunch before coming to the Lodestone office.

Having the window at his back was probably strategic, because it cast his face in shadow and spotlit her. He gave the appearance of strength without being musclebound. He was a large man, broad shouldered, probably tall although he hadn't fully stood up so she wasn't sure. Isis preferred men on a smaller scale, and a little easier to handle. He didn't look like he could be handled at all.

His eyes were hazel, more on the green side; his dark hair, close-cropped in an almost military style, looked as soft and sleek as a seal's pelt. Unlike his hair, his features appeared to be carved from granite. His mouth was bracketed by twin grooves. Isis doubted the man ever smiled. The expensive-looking dark suit he wore accented the breadth of his chest, emphasized by a crisp, pale blue open-necked dress shirt. The charcoal suit had probably cost as much as her car. Or would have, if she still had it.

He had a beautifully shaped mouth, and Isis had to use concerted effort to maintain eye contact. Just looking at him elevated her pulse to pleasant levels of anticipation. "First, what should I call you?"

His mouth thinned as he surveyed her out of cool, dispassionate eyes. "Thorne."

Boy, was that an accurate description of the man or what? "Just Thorne?" The placard beside his office door said CONNOR THORNE. Connor suited him nicely, but then, so did Thorne. He was very prickly, and they'd barely exchanged a dozen sentences.

"Just Thorne; let's not mix it up."

"Right." Having people calling him *Thorne* was just giving him positive reinforcement to be so prickly. But since she wasn't in charge of his psyche, Isis let it go. She settled back and recrossed her legs.

He looked, so he wasn't totally unaware of her.

Isis considered herself fearless. Spiders and snakes had never bothered her, but she wouldn't want to bump into Connor Thorne in a dark alley.

"Assuming that's fine . . ." he prompted after a long moment, and she shook her thoughts back into the present. Her predicament, not whatever shadows her own psyche wanted to paint around him.

"Several months ago my father put together a team of the best archaeology students and interns he could find." Selling everything of any value to finance the dig. Nobody had wanted to fund him. He'd jumped ahead of himself one too many times, leaving himself without any allies other than the Earl of Kilgetty and herself.

Isis didn't have any money to give him, and Thorne's father, the Earl, had cut off funds when he realized his patronage was going into a deep, dark hole. The money had been like pouring millions of gallons of water onto the Egyptian desert.

Isis watched Thorne's eyes to see if he was truly listening. The tears had worked, but she could tell he wasn't a man who would fall for that more than once. The waterworks hadn't been hard to pull off. She was at the end of her emotional rope, and a good, cleansing cry would be terrific right now. Some women thought crying was a sign of weakness, but Isis considered it a release valve for pent-up emotional pressure.

She'd save that indulgence for when she left his office.

Thorne leaned slightly to the side, resting an elbow on the arm of his chair. The light behind him cut a dark shadow over one slashing cheekbone, and she suddenly wanted desperately to get a shot of him backlit by the runnels of rain hitting the window, the Seattle skyline a hazy backdrop. The whole scene was soft and gray and rather melancholy.

But not him. Thorne was right in the middle, vibrant and larger-than-life.

His green eyes boring a hole through her façade.

There was no law to say—even in the middle of her crisis—that she couldn't enjoy the view. And the fact that the attraction didn't appear to be reciprocated didn't lessen her enjoyment looking at him. That just made it easier.

Everything she'd owned now belonged to Lodestone International; the price of Thorne's help. But they were just *things*. And things were replaceable.

The only item of value she hadn't liquidated was her three-year-old Canon 5d Mark II camera, which she was never without.

So it was a good thing looking was free. Not that she could afford even that after she'd paid the hefty retainer and tried to budget the daily expenses of keeping her father in a comfortable facility. Comfortable meant hellishly expensive. He had no insurance. Zak and Acadia weren't aware of her financial difficulties, and Isis preferred to keep it that way. Yes, as a last resort she could ask for help. But for now, she still had options. She'd known three months ago that the money—his, and hers—would run out.

She'd debated doing the sure thing and keeping him there for another three months. Or opting to take a wild, crazy gamble and use some of her carefully hoarded funds to pay Lodestone to find her father's treasure. There was only a month left before she had to find other accommodations for him. Twenty-eight days, to be precise.

Connor Thorne was her Holy Grail *and* Hail Mary.

And if she happened to enjoy looking at him, that just made things easier.

His English accent, coupled with the deep bass of his voice, made her stomach feel light and fluttery, and made her heartbeat speed up pleasantly. He might have the personality of a kumquat, but he was incredibly sexy to look at. Her artist's eye wanted to photograph him against a rough wall, with a spear in his hand. In nothing more than a drape of a loincloth. The thought tempted her to smile. She had to settle for him fully clothed in his office. Ah. Imagination was a wonderful thing, and best of all, free.

For some perverse reason she enjoyed his pithy sarcastic responses. While she talked he kept his gaze on her face. She liked that. He might think she was full of BS, but he paid her the courtesy of looking at her, even if he was thinking about getting the oil in his car changed.

The energy humming off him was almost tangible, even though he was perfectly still. His eyes looked quite green as he steadily watched her. Observed her. "And?" he prodded not all that patiently as she considered the best way to bounce outside light to reflect off his face.

Right. The point. "Prior to that, he'd spent a year in Egypt with Dylan Brengard—that's his assistant—searching and confirming. To make sure that when he published again, he had all his *t*'s crossed and his *i*'s dotted." Because she'd threatened her beloved father with dismemberment if he was once more touting his find without sufficient proof—the actual tomb, ready to be opened and photographed.

"Miss Magee—" He caught himself. "Isis. I know you want to believe that he really did find the tomb this time, but the reality is that he'd 'found' it a half-dozen times before. And each time his peers and the international press became less and less gullible. He has Alzheimer's—wouldn't it be best for everyone if you allowed the media to forget as well? Surely in his condition, he can't be as bothered by this as you seem to be?"

Not acceptable. She'd heard the same song and dance a dozen times, and she wasn't having any of it. Not when she'd paid, and paid well, for his services. "There were fourteen of them on the dig. Some he'd rehired from various other expeditions. Half of them were new, fresh, eager to prove what he believed. He phoned me on the afternoon of the nineteenth day. He was almost incoherent with excitement."

She put up her hand as he started to tip back his hand in the drink salute again. "No, he *wasn't* drunk, Mr. Thorne. He was happy, jubilantly so. He told me they'd found the tomb. *Really* found the tomb. In the Valley of the Scorpions." Not strictly true, but that had been her conclusion after he'd returned home.

"Not the Valley of the *Queens*?" When she shook her head, he continued with a hint of skepticism, his tone Sahara dry: "That's an area of more than a hundred square miles. Was he more specific?"

"No. He felt strongly that if the information got into the wrong hands, someone with more resources would try to scoop him before he could get inside and document what he found." She wrapped her fingers around the amulet her father had had made for her in a bazaar in

Luxor in the good old days, when he'd been riding fame and glory for all he was worth. "*Everyone* on the team saw the entrance; a couple of them dug far enough inside to retrieve some small artifacts. He had all the tools and supplies they needed. They were going to start digging the next morning."

"And did they?"

Isis hesitated, because this was the tricky part. "The team returned to their camp for the night. They'd gone just far enough inside the tomb to ascertain that it was Cleopatra's. My father assured me he had some small artifacts to show he was right——"

"Why do I hear a giant *but* coming?"

"He was found the next afternoon, dehydrated and disoriented and with a scalp laceration, indicating he'd been hit with a blunt instrument and left for dead. The entire team had been brutally murdered." The thought of it still gave her goose bumps. "The authorities said by local tribesmen."

"It didn't strike you as odd that out of all those strong, able-bodied members of his crew, he was the only one left alive?"

Not at the time. "I was just happy that he *was* alive," she admitted. "I had no reason to question it then. At first, after I brought him home, he remembered absolutely nothing. He'd suffered blunt head trauma. He didn't even recall that he'd gone back to Egypt. It took several months for the memories to start coming back. He remembered leaving the group at dusk while they were preparing the evening meal. He said he wanted to go back to the tomb to take more pictures. He swears he took a bunch of images before the light went.

"He remembers getting into the Jeep and riding back to camp. His memories after that are spotty. He recalls coming back into camp and smelling the meat burning for the evening meal. He remembers seeing everyone lying about as if they'd taken a nap where they'd fallen— only there was so much blood. Then he doesn't remember anything else. He swears someone struck him on the head. Sometimes he remembers being pulled from his vehicle. Other times he swears someone was lurking at the dig. His injuries substantiate that he was hit, hard, but obviously not where he was at the time the attack happened."

"And when the authorities went to the location? Did they find the tomb?"

Isis took a deep breath, knowing that what she said just reinforced the unbelievability of the story. Mystery killers, kidnappers, tomb espionage? It sounded like something out of a movie, even to her. She was losing Thorne, fast.

Tears again? Nah. That was a trick that'd only work once.

"My father and his dead team members were found at the Dafarfa Oasis, two hundred miles from where he'd told me he'd been. There isn't a tomb there for more than a hundred miles."

"And did the authorities find who'd murdered all those people?"

"No."

"Any leads?"

"Not as far as I know."

Thorne made a condescending sound deep in his throat. "Not to put too fine a point on it, that's a terrible track record for anyone, even to a loving daughter. Given the professor's penchant for hyperbole, why do you believe him this time when he's lied at least half a dozen times before?"

"He didn't lie." *Exactly.* "He didn't have all the information. And this time is different—because *this* time I have a picture to prove it."

⤳ TWO ⤳

Five hours later they were airborne.

The 747 from Seattle to New York and on to London was full, everyone crammed in like sardines. The first-class cabin was more spacious, but Thorne still felt like he'd been shoved inside a tin can. The air smelled of the steak they'd had for dinner, and a faint, underlying scent of Isis's ginger cinnamon soap. The cabin lights were dimmed. Thorne's light was off. Isis, sitting between himself and the window, had a halo where her light shone on her hair.

She'd changed at Zak's place into pale blue jeans and a long-sleeved red T-shirt, and wore dangling red and gold earrings that kept tangling in her hair. As much as it annoyed him—tempted him to untangle the glinting metal plates, touch her hair—Thorne kept his hands to himself. The urge to touch her was already ridiculous and required a good deal more discipline than he'd anticipated.

"How will your skill work when we get to the museum?" Isis asked quietly.

Business. That was safe. "You suspect where your father was when he was attacked, right?" She nodded.

"I'll touch the things you sent to the museum to complete his exhibit, and see if there's a location match."

Her eyes widened behind her glasses. "You do remember that there are thousands of artifacts in the collection, right?"

More than aware. "It's a long shot, but it's the only shot we have." And given all that rubbish about assaults from mystery figures and murder, the quicker this was over, the better.

Even if a small part of him did settle into the instinct of years of training. In, out, put the bad guys down.

If there were even any bad guys.

"You won't have to touch *everything*," she countered, with what seemed like mild amusement in the dim light. "It's thirty years' worth of work. I can sort and eliminate things by obviously wrong locations and unlikely dates. That'll cut down the time, won't it?"

"Sure." From ten years to five. Finding the right matching location, while not knowing what type of artifact would hold the GPS location, was akin to searching for a thief in a prison.

"I'm glad I can help you help me. I hate sitting around waiting, don't you?"

Yeah. One of the things at the top of his list. He shifted in his seat so he could straighten his legs, and she moved her feet to give him more room. "You can stretch out some more if you like."

"I'm good." As good as it was going to get, anyway. He'd let the flight attendant take his suit jacket and cane, and had rolled up his sleeves in deference to the stuffiness on board, despite the air blowing down on him. It wasn't cooling his unwelcome attraction to Miss Magee any.

She looked up at him, eyes earnest behind her black-framed glasses. Her breath smelled sweet from the Diet Coke she was drinking. Thorne didn't drink sodas, but he wondered absently what it would taste like on her tongue if he kissed her. Which, of course, he was absolutely not going to do.

Curling her legs up under her on the wide leather seat, she pitched her body closer to his. Her closeness, and the subdued lighting in the cabin, made the situation far too intimate and made Thorne want to bury himself in her heat and cinnamon scent. She licked her unpainted mouth as if she were reading his thoughts. "Were you in an accident?"

"Yeah." *I accidently walked into Boris Yermalof's boning knife.* He watched the attractive flight attendant bringing around coffee. It was natural to think of the Russian when he was on his way to London and talking about Egypt. The bloody Russian was the reason Thorne had been banished to Seattle in the first place. The chase through Egypt eight months ago had ended in Israel, where his two partners had been brutally butchered, and when Thorne had avoided being gutted like a fish, it was more by accident than design. Everyone considered his survival a miracle.

He resented being put in a holding pattern when all he wanted to do was track Yermalof down and do unto him as the Russian had done unto Thorne's partners. Twiddling his thumbs wasn't Thorne's thing. Babysitting a deluded big-eyed cutie while he served out his sentence was proving more challenging than he had time for. The fact that he was supposed to be recuperating didn't make it less of a problem.

Isis predictably asked, "Was it a c——"

Without turning to look at her, he said unambiguously, "I don't talk about it."

"If there's anything I can do . . . ?"

"No."

The flight attendant smiled and flashed her cleavage over the small tray holding china cups. The rich scent of Sumatra eradicated—for the moment—the smell of Isis's skin. Thorne turned to glance at her.

"Do you want coffee?" He wasn't a man who chatted. He didn't want to be her friend, and he didn't want to fucking *bond*. London. Hopefully he'd find something that would satisfy her. He'd go back to Seattle, where the weather suited his mood, and she could go . . . wherever the hell she wanted to go. None of his business.

"No thanks. I probably shouldn't have drunk those two Diet Cokes." She reached up and turned off her overhead light, then pulled the thin blanket across her lap, up over her chest. "I want to sleep so I'm fresh when we arrive."

She was plenty fresh. He took a coffee, ignoring the woman lingering at his side until she pushed off. "Good idea," he told Isis. The coffee was hot and black. Not French press, but drinkable. He drank it in two gulps, then placed the cup and saucer on the wide space between their seats. It wasn't a wall, but it marked his space from hers.

Isis wiggled down in her seat, curling up to get more comfortable, her elbow pushing his cup dangerously close to the edge as she shifted, trying to balance her head on her hand.

Mentally shoring the barriers, he moved the cup after all. Now he couldn't pretend that he wasn't looking at her instead of the discarded cup. Eyes closed, Isis was close enough for him to see the way her long lashes cast shadows on her creamy cheeks, and feel her warm breath against his upper arm. She didn't look very comfortable but her discomfort was none of his business. If she woke up with a stiff neck that was her own fault.

She wasn't asleep. He could practically hear her mind working.

He knew he wouldn't find what he was looking for without her help at the museum. She at least knew which decade of artifacts and paperwork to check as a jumping-off point. He didn't want to go; that was a given. But he'd performed numerous jobs for queen and country that he hadn't wanted to perform. Sometimes a man had to shut the hell up and just do what had to be done. His father was one of two people in London whom Thorne had no desire to see, but to get Isis and himself into the back rooms of the museum, he needed his father's help.

Bloody hell. He'd then owe His Lordship a favor. No good deed went unrecorded in the Earl's ledgers.

Still, with Isis's tenacious assistance, he could make the trip quick and relatively painless. If anything in the professor's artifacts was from his recent dig, Thorne would give Isis the information she needed and send her on her way. He didn't need to go to Egypt with her. Just point her in the right direction.

She wanted the mythical tomb of Cleopatra? If her father had been in the Valley of the Scorpions and that's where the tomb was, he'd find the connection.

She'd leave; he'd go back to Seattle. The end.

She'd have her answers, and he'd forget about the curly-haired woman who batted her long lashes from behind smudged glasses.

He'd learned something else about his client—besides that she was as tenacious as a Rottweiler. She was a tight-wad who made every penny work twice, once for each side. The heated conversation between them at Sea-Tac Airport had drawn a small crowd of amused onlookers. It was only when he informed her with all the superior arrogance of his ancestors that with his bad leg, sitting in steerage for nine hours was completely out of the question, that she had partially acquiesced. He could go first-class. She'd go coach.

Thorne purchased two first-class tickets and told her to shut up and enjoy her heated nuts.

"You can talk to me," she said drowsily, without opening her eyes. "I'm not asleep."

He slipped off her glasses. Her mouth tightened at the unexpected contact. Not disgust; more like surprise. Thoughtful, he folded the earpieces and stuck the glasses in his shirt pocket, beside the photograph she'd given him—reluctantly—back at the Lodestone office. "How long have you been living with the Starks?" He'd taken her to Queen Anne Hill to pack and was not surprised that she'd directed him to Zak's house.

"A month. They've been kind enough to let me camp out there while I regroup."

Thorne could smell her hair and skin—cinnamon. She'd twisted her curls up on top of her head, and her face unframed by all that hair was pure and sweet. Opening her eyes, she gave him a drowsy smile. There were humor and charm in her big brown eyes and sensual mouth, elements oddly more insidious than overt sex appeal.

He removed the picture from his breast pocket. "Tell me what you see."

She didn't take the piece of paper from him, just touched his hand to bring it closer. An unwelcome frisson of awareness zinged up his arm at her touch. The speed with which she withdrew her fingers, the way her mouth did that tightening thing again, indicated she'd felt the same thing. *Bollocks.* He was a grown man, and she was the first woman on his radar in too long. "Need your glasses?"

"No, I see fine close up." She straightened to push her fringe out of her eyes. "It was taken in the evening. Seven or eight, I'd guess. You can tell by the angle of the sunlight." Her arm brushed his when she pointed. "This is clearly a tomb entrance. See the way the earth slopes, but the size of the rock is not uniform to its surroundings? That was backfill. This section here is undisturbed. This section here, where the team started to dig, is darker where the rocks and soil were excavated. The photographer was my father. He always manages to insert himself into pictures." There was a wealth of love and amusement in her quiet voice.

"Usually it's his thumb; this time it was his shadow. He sent this from his phone soon after he took the picture."

"Who do you think this is?" Thorne pointed to a shadow off to the left.

"I thought it looked like a second man standing with his back to the light. But I blew up the image in my lab several months ago, and it's too hard to tell. It wasn't clear enough to make out if it's a person or a rock formation. And when I spoke to him he said he'd left everyone back at camp."

Because a man with Alzheimer's would remember. "Probably rocks, then," Thorne said easily, tucking the photograph back into his pocket behind her glasses. Or the man Dr. Magee claimed struck him on the head. Thorne's gut told him it was the latter. That complicated things. He'd rather hoped recovery would be easy. He suspected Isis Magee was like crabgrass: insidious and hard to get rid of. But if someone had indeed attacked Professor Magee, Thorne couldn't let her go off in search of Cleopatra's tomb alone.

Bloody, bloody hell.

"Try to sleep," he told her, reaching up to adjust the air nozzle. "Tomorrow's going to be a long day." Probably long and hellish as well as hellishly long.

Isis pushed back her seat to recline more fully and gave him a small smile as she snugged the thin blanket to her chin. "I'm equal parts excited and terrified," she murmured as her lids dipped lower and lower.

Unfortunately, Thorne thought as he watched her eyes flutter and close, *I feel exactly the same way.*

London

ISIS LOOKED UP AT the imposing Georgian edifice with its warm brick façade and neat rows of blank-eyed sash windows. The building looked rigid, precise, and boringly symmetrical. If this was a hotel, there wasn't even a discreet brass nameplate outside the glossy black front door.

The sun was shining, but the chill in the air caused her to snug the collar of her red Windbreaker up around her ears and stuff her hands deep in the jacket's pockets. She'd thrown together her clothes for the trip based on digging through dusty antiquities in the museum and, hopefully, for a trip to Egypt, where the temperatures in June hit the high nineties. Not for fancy hotels or London's chilly version of summer weather.

Jeans, T-shirts, underwear, socks. Two pairs of shoes. Her camera bag, which doubled as a purse. Although she was rarely without her Canon, she'd left it locked in the hotel safe for this "quick" trip. Too bad; she'd like to take some angled shots of the building, which looked like a buttoned-up virgin on her wedding night. The thought made her smile.

She didn't care much about what she wore, but her silent companion was dressed in another beautifully cut business suit, which he'd changed into at the hotel, where they'd stopped long enough to drop off their luggage and wash up.

His clothes shouted armor. His crisp blue and white pinstriped shirt was open at the throat; his short dark hair ruffled in the breeze like the pelt of a seal. He looked deceptively at ease. But her artist eye saw the slight tension in his shoulders, and the grim line of his mouth.

Connor "Just Thorne" wasn't casual or particularly approachable. In fact, he was a bit on the surly side and hoarded his words as if they were currency. Which was too bad, because Isis bet he'd be fascinating if he opened up. She spent her life getting silent things to speak, at least in her photographs. He'd be no different. She would search to find just the precise angle, and the form of lighting, that would reveal the story.

What drove the man?

What kind of accident had caused the limp? Why wouldn't he talk about it? She wanted to pry him open like the clam he was. She wondered, as she glanced around, just what kind of crowbar would be necessary to pry inside his secrets.

He hadn't clued her in to whom they were seeing or why, other than a brief mention that his father had something to do with the museum they needed to visit.

He rang the highly polished doorbell, the sound echoing discreetly inside.

"Where are we?" They'd already checked in to the hotel, and one wouldn't ring a doorbell at a hotel in any case. Trying to guess where they were and why they were there, she glanced around at the neatly trimmed boxwood hedges surrounding a beautifully manicured Stepford-perfect flower bed filled with deep purple salvia. Bright red petunias would look better than the stick-straight salvia, she decided.

There wasn't a bend or a curve to be seen. Everything was precise, straight, uniform. In fact, she bet that whoever was in charge of the plants had cut back any stragglers so they were exactly even in number on each side.

Before he could respond the door was opened by a distinguished, *unamused* man with snow-white hair and a beak of a nose. He wore a starched black suit so stiff it appeared to have the hanger still in it. Isis buried her instant levity, wondering if the man was aware he'd caricatured himself. "Master James," he said in round, self-important tones. "This is something of a surprise."

"To all concerned," Thorne replied dryly as the man stepped back to let them inside. "Is His Lordship at home, Roberts?"

The butler glanced down his nose at Isis for a moment, his nostrils flaring, as if he smelled something unpleasant. "I'll inquire, sir. Shall I bring tea to the yellow room?" The butler held himself with stiff dignity.

"Coffee and a diet cola. Heavy on the ice."

"Certainly." Roberts half-bowed and went right, while she followed "Master James" to the left. Roberts, she noted, disappeared like magic, and it was only her imagination that had her smelling sulfur in the air, which otherwise bore the scent of lemon polish and flowers.

Wowza! She'd been in hotels smaller than this place. "Your name's James?"

He picked up speed, his hard-soled shoes and cane landing slightly uneven, staccato strikes on the marble floor. "*Thorne.*"

"Okay by me," she said easily, looking around with interest as she trailed behind him. Tension rolled off him in almost visible waves. Isis closed the gap between them in a probably misplaced sense that he needed someone to stand with him. She kept her tone light as she tucked her hand into the crook of his elbow and adjusted her steps to match his. "My father always said, 'A child with many names is a child loved.'"

He didn't shake her off but made a derisive noise under his breath as they circumvented a large wood and marble table with an enormous floral arrangement dripping from a blue and white vase half as tall as she was. That many hydrangeas and Casablanca lilies couldn't possibly get enough to drink, they were crammed in so tightly. "Not in every case," he said coldly, finally disengaging from her hold to slip his hand in his jacket pocket.

Ow. "This is your parents' home?" Isis asked in exaggerated hushed tones as their shoes clicked loudly on marble the color of beach sand and the tap of Thorne's cane echoed in surround sound off all the hard surfaces.

"Already amused, I see." Thorne let her catch up to him again in the vast entry hall. He wasn't letting the grass grow under his feet. Whatever the reason for the cane and slight limp, the man moved fast. She had to trot to keep up.

She couldn't imagine a child scampering through the halls or sliding down the magnificent curved teak banister. Not that she could imagine Thorne as a child, either. Feeling his unbearable tension as if it were a living thing in the too-still, unbearably grand house, she forced a small smile. "I was just thinking I'd like to get Roberts into a room filled with white Persian cats and photograph his reactions. I bet fluff never lands on that suit of his—it has super-repellent on it, doesn't it?"

His lips twitched. "You have a very interesting mind, Isis Magee."

She would have loved to linger, because the place was magnificent in an overly gilded, museumy kind of way, and her fingers itched for her camera. She got the quick impression of miles of pale marble, busy wallpaper, and gold . . . *everything*; of potted palms and large portraits of stern-faced people in period costume, as she hurried to keep up with Connor's long-legged, if slightly uneven, strides.

"*House*. Not home. But yes. Rosebank House is their primary residence."

The "House" seemed too tame a name for the palatial mansion. "Did you grow up here?" Isis asked, doing a quickstep to sync her steps with his.

"Third floor, corner bedroom. I fled the scene on my eighteenth birthday and never looked back."

His fingers brushed hers as they walked. A pleasant little zing of electricity ran up her arm. He didn't appear to notice. She wondered with amusement what he'd do if she slipped her hand into his. She liked touching him. Liked the smell of him, and the look of him. Resisting the impulse to twine her fingers with his, she said, "I suspect this house casts a long shadow."

He gave her a surprised look. "Long and extremely . . . *heavy*. This way."

The room he ushered her to was not yellow, but rather a pale Wedgwood blue complete with white plaster accents and an enormous crystal chandelier. Everything in the room looked expensive—as if there should be a velvet rope preventing visitors from entering. Even though James Connor Thorne, or Connor James Thorne, or Just Thorne, was a thoroughly modern man and should've looked completely out of place in a room filled with baroque furnishings and silk upholstery, he appeared quite at home. But then Isis suspected he'd look at home wherever he was. He had self-confidence to spare. It was very sexy on him.

She took it all in, her eye for detail cataloging the furnishings as if she were preparing for a photo shoot. He crossed to the fireplace to stand beneath a large painting, circa seventeen hundreds. The stiffly posed man exuded self-control and moral strength. Like Thorne, he stood, one hand in his pocket, his expression grim as he stared defiantly at the artist as if to say, "Hurry the hell up. I have things to do and people to kill."

"He looks . . ." Isis observed. *Surly and extremely unhappy.* "Important," she finished.

Thorne flicked a glance upward. "That was painted by Joshua Reynolds."

"How many Thorne relatives back is this guy?" She crossed the thick area rug to inspect a portrait of a man in formal dress of the period. He had a strong face and piercing green eyes, and his hair was powdered and tied back. He wore a long, wide-collared lime-green frock coat over a silver waistcoat, a froth of white lace at his throat and wrists. His hand, with an enormous emerald ring on it, was on one hip as if to say, "So there, you peasant."

"Garrett Thorne, sixth Earl of Kilgetty. My great-great—" He paused and gave her a wry smile. "Many greats back. The story is he had two wives, and two mistresses. A pair in town and the other at his country estate."

She narrowed her eyes at the portrait. "Yes, I can see the exhaustion on his face." Smiling, she noted, "You don't look remotely alike."

"Your refreshments, sir. His Lordship will join you in half an hour." Roberts placed a silver tray containing a gorgeous silver coffeepot and paper-thin china cup, a carafe of soda and a glass, and a plate of cookies on a side table before bowing himself out.

"I'm surprised it isn't *two hours.*" Thorne poured her soda into the glass. Using the silver tongs, he chose two delicate, lacey cookies and placed them on the china plate. Isis could've eaten a horse along with the cookies, but she politely took her drink and plate and went to sit gingerly on a slippery powder blue brocade sofa with crocodile feet.

If it were her sofa—which it could never be, because it was quite hideous—she'd paint its toenails fire engine red. She carefully put the plate of buttery cookies on a nearby side table. The fabric would probably stain just by one's *thinking* about eating a cookie while seated on it.

Thorne stood beside the massive Carrara marble fireplace, filled with scentless white roses and Queen Anne's lace. How on earth could he exude sex appeal while holding a teacup with little red flowers on it? He'd propped his simple black cane to the side of the fireplace and stood with his feet a little apart.

Isis wondered how such an unbending man could make her think of sex all the time. Not just sex, but hot, messy sex, sweaty-skin and twisted-sheets sex. Resting her palm on her throat she felt her rapid heartbeat, caused by just looking at him and imagining . . .

He's not the One, she reminded herself. She suspected Thorne would be quite happy to take her to bed. And she was pretty sure the experience would be mind-boggling.

Too bad she wasn't willing to risk sleeping with him and losing her heart to a man who she doubted had commitment on his mind.

Safer not to complicate their relationship and risk him not helping her on her quest.

Even though he was wreaking havoc on her senses, and firing her imagination, she'd lust in private and put on her game face for the duration.

"Why would he make you wait so long?"

"He's sure to be thrilled to see I'm back."

The sarcasm dripping from his tone made it clear the comment was facetious. She took a sip of her drink, then held the glass between her hands on her lap. She was in no position to judge father-child relationships, but it seemed he and Daddy Dearest didn't see eye to eye. "I'll take a wild leap here and say you don't get along."

He picked up a small jade elephant, then returned it to the end of a line of five others in descending size on the mantel. "I was the Great Disappointment."

She looked at him over the rim of the cut crystal glass housing her humble Coke. "No siblings to disperse the brunt?"

"An older brother, Garrett." His fingers briefly whitened on the edge of the carved marble mantel. "He died on his twenty-first birthday."

She absorbed the undertones, and her heart felt what she saw in his eyes before he masked it. "I'm sorry. Were you close?"

"Extremely. We—"

"James." The man's voice was cold and crisp. Isis looked over her shoulder, fumbling with her glass and the slippery seat to get to her feet as the Earl of Kilgetty greeted his son.

Thorne didn't walk over to greet his father, and his father came only a few steps into the room. Neither extended a hand to shake. Thorne put his cup and saucer on the high mantel and turned back, his face expressionless. "You look well, Father."

"I can't say the same for you. I thought you'd gone to live in America."

"Seattle, yes. This is Professor Magee's daughter, Isis. Isis, the Earl."

The Earl and his son were the same height and shared the same hazel eyes, but on the father the color was muddier and less interesting. He looked stern and unkind. Bitter. Isis had the irrational urge to rush over and stand beside Thorne in solidarity. It would've helped if he'd introduced his father by the way Isis was supposed to address him. My lord? Your Earliness? Hell.

"Pleased to meet you," she decided was good enough. The Earl gave her a cool, disinterested look, his gaze flicking from her sneakers up her jean-clad legs and over the open Windbreaker, then landing on her wildly curling hair. He didn't look impressed with what he was seeing. Too damned bad.

"How is August?"

"I'm afraid he has Alzheimer's," she said. "I suspect his condition was exacerbated by the attack he sustained on his last trip to Egypt." She'd come to terms with her father's illness, and her voice no longer broke as she shared the news.

"Yes," the Earl said vaguely, with all the interest of one looking over yesterday's newspaper, then turned his attention to his son. "Your mother is in Paris shopping. I'm sure she'll be sorry to have missed you."

"I'm sure she won't give a damn," Thorne returned flatly.

"That's uncalled-for." His father's thin lips disappeared in disapproval. "Why are you here?"

"I'd like you to contact the museum and have them grant us access to Professor Magee's artifacts."

"To what purpose? This is an odd time to show an interest in Egyptology." He tucked his fingertips into his jacket pocket like the man in the portrait nearby, as if he were posing for his own portrait.

Thorne's eyes narrowed. "Have I ever requested a favor of you? Can't you just do this because I ask?"

"They're preparing to exhibit Magee's discoveries. They will be available on the ninth of next month. You can see everything then with the rest of the public."

Ouch.

"This is a time-sensitive matter," Thorne said tightly. "I've already spoken to the museum. They won't grant us full access. You, however, are not only on the board, you're their biggest sponsor. Make the call."

Thorne's father glanced at Isis. "Forgive me, Miss Magee, but your father has had . . . *issues* in the past. His drinking became a serious problem, and his veracity came under question with each preposterous claim. It was only with the help of my public relations people that I was able to smooth the path to this exhibit, and restore some verisimilitude to a career spanning thirty years. I don't want any adverse publicity to taint the exhibit at this juncture. What do you hope to find?"

"W—" Connor started to say hotly, but Isis cut them both off.

"With all due respect, that's my father you're talking about." Isis placed her glass on a spindly table with a sharp click. "We're asking you to pick up the phone and make one call. If that's beyond your capabilities, the name Magee still holds some weight. We'll get what we need with or without you." Her teeth ground together, and she held on to her temper by a thread. Her response was knee-jerk, probably rude and uncalled-for, but her father's situation was already a sore spot for her without this sanctimonious man casting aspersions.

"The first time you bring a woman home, and she's not only American, but as uncouth as her father. Congratulations, James. You have once again sunk to meet my low expectation." If his tone could have gotten any icier, it would have frozen half of England in one go. "I'll make a phone call. Roberts will see you out. I'll tell your mother you stopped by." His expressionless eyes flickered from his son to Isis. "Miss Magee." The Earl of Kilgetty turned on his heel and walked out of the room.

∝ THREE ∽

"That went as well as could be expected," Thorne muttered wryly, opening the door of the taxi almost before it came to a full stop in front of the house. Isis threw him a hot look before getting inside and slipping silently across the seat. He slid in beside her and gave the driver the address of their hotel.

"I'd apologize and claim His Lordship wasn't himself, but that's exactly who he is, and neither of us makes any pretense otherw——"

Isis shocked the hell out of him when she flung her arms around his neck and pressed her mouth to his. Her lips were moist and warm, slightly parted, and more comforting than lustful. But Thorne had enjoyed that encounter with his father even less than she had, and if she was offering comfort, he wasn't a man to turn down such an enticing offer.

Whatever the reason, he hadn't been the one to make the first move. There was absolution there.

Wrapping his arms around her, he pulled her in, angled his head, and feasted on her with deep, greedy kisses, like a drowning man gasping for air in a monsoon.

She gave back in equal measure, gripping both hands in his hair, pressing against him as she dived right in with verve and enthusiasm.

Adrenaline surged through him, and he was already hard. Unbuttoning her jacket, Thorne slid one hand inside, cupping the small, heavy weight of her breast. Her nipple was hard through the thin cotton of her T-shirt, and she arched her back to press her breast hard against his fingers. She whimpered as he rubbed his thumb over the hardness, feeling the pucker of the areola through the thin satin of her bra and toying with her nipple. She shifted beside him, her tongue dancing with his, her teeth scoring his lower lip, sucking on it until he thought he'd come right there in the back of the taxi.

His dick pulsed, and he pulled her across his lap without breaking contact. The vibration of her moan, low in her throat, went through his body like the hum of a tuning fork. Her fingers tightened in his hair. He cupped her arse, pulling her hard against where he needed the pressure. It didn't help—made it worse, in fact, and more unbearable.

Combing his fingers through her silky curls, Thorne held her head steady as he invaded her mouth. The taste of her drove him mad. Lemon cookies and cola. Comfort and reprieve. He skimmed his other hand under her T-shirt to the softness of her midriff, just above her jeans. Her skin was like rose petals, cool and impossibly smooth.

The kiss was wild and bordered on rough. It was the kind of kiss long-term lovers shared, not the touch of two virtual strangers.

His fingers slid under the thin barrier to find bare skin. Thorne had never in his life been so aroused at the mere touch of a woman's breast. The feel of her bare skin made him want to strip her naked so he could see all of her. The weight of her breast fit his hand as if made for him. Her sweet breast rose and fell erratically in the cup of his fingers. Thorne was stunned at his visceral reaction to her. Yes, God yes, he was physically attracted to her. He wasn't made of stone. But there was something more—what the Spanish called *la ñapa* and the Louisiana French called *lagniappe*. That little bit extra. She was dangerous to his equilibrium.

Shivering, she murmured low in her throat, and without stopping the kiss, firmly gripped his wrist and removed his fingers from her breast.

His chest ached and he realized he'd forgotten to breathe as his hungry mouth devoured hers. Reluctantly he lifted his head, sucking in great drafts of air as she did the same. Skin flushed, her eyes were closed, long dark lashes smudges on her cheeks as she fought to catch her breath.

He had to put a stop to this, now. In a minute. In an hour. Fuck it, tomorrow.

Thorne pulled her back again, already missing the slick texture of her mouth and the way her body responded to his touch. Crushing his lips to her, he swept inside and found her tongue waiting there for him. Isis didn't receive passively; she wasn't afraid to give as good as she got. Her hand gripped the back of his neck, making him shudder.

"We're 'ere, gov. Want me to take another turn around the park?"

APPARENTLY THAT IMPULSIVE I'm-sorry-your-father-is-a-jerk kiss in the cab had scared off "Just Thorne" because he'd dropped her off at the hotel two hours ago and disappeared.

Too bad, because Isis wanted—rather desperately—to kiss him again, preferably not in a moving vehicle. She presumed he'd come back eventually. She very much looked forward to locking lips with Thorne again. He was a fabulous kisser.

The hotel was way too damned expensive, but he'd typically overridden her protests about the unnecessary cost. At this rate, given Lodestone's exorbitant fee and Thorne's per diem, her small budget for expenses would be eaten up before they found what she was looking for.

Dressed in jeans and a pale blue T-shirt, her feet bare, Isis stared out of her hotel window, enjoying the sight of the darkening evening sky, the city lights twinkling in a beautiful sparkly blanket as far as the eye could see. She hadn't been to London in several years, and she was eager to get out and explore before they got down to some serious work at the museum the next day.

No matter how pricey the hotel, she didn't want to spend the evening alone in her room. It gave her too much time to think. She was worried about her father. His health hadn't been good since he'd returned from Cairo, and while his Alzheimer's prevented him from being aware she was gone, she liked to check on him every day. Had she missed something? As confused as he was about the circumstances of his "accident," had he given her clues to Cleo's tomb that she hadn't picked up on? Her father loved puzzles, and the more obtuse and confusing the better.

She'd searched his apartment in Seattle a dozen times looking for anything that might lead her to his last find. Isis believed that he'd discovered Cleo's final resting place this time. He'd found his life's work, and it was a cruel irony of fate that now he didn't remember exactly where he'd been.

No one would believe he'd done what he'd promised. It was up to her to close the circle of her father's brilliant legacy while there was still time.

Before his death. And before someone else claimed the historic discovery for themselves.

Where the frick are you, "Just Thorne?"

He was from London, so she presumed he had friends there. Was some girlfriend reaping the benefits of *her* warm-up? The thought annoyed her no end. Holding the drapes aside, she swore under her breath. He was no monk. And she'd made her position clear—he was well within his rights to do whatever he pleased with whomever he wanted to please.

That didn't mean Isis had to like it.

Blasted man.

She'd showered, ordered the cheapest thing on the room service menu, and eaten a solitary and too early dinner. The evening stretched out before her like a thick blank notebook.

To hell with him. She was in no mood to watch a movie at inflated hotel rates, and she had, as her grandmother was wont to say, ants in her pants—although she was pretty sure Nana hadn't meant it in quite the same way. Or maybe she had; her Nana had been a spitfire until the day she died last year, at ninety-two.

Yes. Ants in her pants. Hot to trot. Horny.

She hadn't meant the kiss to get that heated that fast. She'd offered a comforting hand, and he'd taken it as the offer not of her arm, but of her entire body. He was an awesome kisser. First-class. And Isis imagined he'd be an equally spectacular lover. God only knew, she wanted the infuriating man, but they'd known each other five minutes, for goodness' sake. One of them had to be sensible.

She could be sensible while she was kissing him, Isis decided. She could allow herself to lose her head a little with him, but she decided not to qualify exactly how much and how far a "little" kiss would take her.

But she was *not* going to sit waiting for *any* man in a hotel room when she was in an exciting city that was just waiting to be explored. The swanky room was all about the large, inviting bed. The farther away she was from beds when with "Just Thorne," the easier it would be for her to maintain a safe distance. He was temptation personified, but as much as she was intrigued and as much as she wanted to kiss him some more, they had a business relationship. She didn't want to muddy the waters when she'd invested everything she had on the chance that he could tell her where to find Cleo's tomb.

Sex, no matter how tempting, was out.

Pulling her red Windbreaker out of the closet, Isis grabbed her camera bag and slung it across her body. It doubled as a purse, and was rarely out of her sight. Tucked in next to her precious Canon 5D Mark II was some walking-around cash, a credit card that was almost maxed out, and her keycard. She let herself out of the room and headed for the elevator.

Jabbing the button, she shook her head. He'd kissed her into complete delirium, leaving her hot and bothered, then practically shoved her out of the cab before she knew what hit her. The fact that she'd called a halt a nanosecond before that was immaterial.

Before she realized that he wasn't getting out with her, she was looking at the back of his head as the taxi sped away.

She touched her mouth as the elevator dinged. "Chicken."

Picking up a London street map in the lobby, she set out to explore the city. Isis kept to main thoroughfares, and happily window-shopped for several hours. The brightly lit shops beckoned, but she didn't buy anything, just looked, and smelled, and tasted. She popped into an ice-cream shop and ordered a banana split, inhaling it while talking to a young mother and her two ice-cream-smeared little boys.

She took hundreds of pictures—of buildings, and people, and flower boxes and anything else that struck her fancy. When she was taking photographs she totally lost herself. She finally realized how much time had passed, only because her feet were starting to hurt. The shops were starting to close and there weren't as many people on the street. It was too early to go back, so she decided to see the comedy she'd been dying to see at a fifties-style movie theater a few blocks from the hotel.

It was well after eleven when she let herself into her room and kicked off her shoes. She frowned just inside the door as she tried to remember where the light switch was. She was sure she'd left the light on before she—

The bedside lamp flashed on. "Just call me Thorne" was lying on the bed, hands stacked behind his head. "Where the bloody hell have you been all night?"

Isis gave him a cool look. He looked delicious, his hair rumpled, a pillow crease across his cheek. "Would you like to rephrase that?" she asked pleasantly as she put her bag on the desk and started removing her coat. His cane leaned against the back of the chair.

"Where have you been, and with whom?"

"Camilla and Charles invited me for dinner. I hated to say no." She walked to the narrow closet and hung up her coat and scarf. "And how did you get into my room? I locked the door when I left."

He sat up, swinging his bare feet to the floor. He had huge feet, even for a man over six foot three. Just looking at his feet turned her on. "To go *where*?" he demanded tightly. "You didn't bother leaving a note, or a phone message. For all I knew, you were abducted."

Isis sat in the chair by the desk, out of his pacing path, and shot him an amused look. He was mad. She could see that as he limped-stalked, limped-stalked. But his anger was over-the-top and totally illogical. "Really?

By whom?" She toed off her shoes. Damn, her feet were cold. She rubbed them together as he prowled.

Raking his fingers through his short hair, he glared at her.

Amused, she grinned. Her smile slipped a bit as she said casually, "I might ask the same question. Were you with a woman?" She didn't like the idea that her Thorne had been out carousing with another woman, but she was hardly going to tell him that. Nor, quite frankly, did she want to claim ownership, even to herself. He wasn't hers. Would never be hers. She cocked her head, considering how she might just borrow him for a while.

He arched a brow. "If I was, it would have absolutely nothing to do with you. We're here on business, remember? We go to the museum tomorrow; maybe we'll find something, maybe we won't. If we do, I'll give you the location. I'll go back to Seattle and you can go and find this tomb that no one has any interest in."

No longer amused, she felt her entire body bristle at his condescending, supercilious tone. "That suits me just fine. The museum opens at ten. We'll leave the hotel at nine forty-five."

He closed the gap between them in two long strides to close his fingers around her upper arms and lift her out of the chair.

"All I could think about for the last five hours was the taste of you."

"You don't sound particularly happy about it," Isis muttered as he pulled her onto her toes.

He slid one arm around her waist, his hand gliding up

her back, easing her forward in small degrees, until she was molded to him, thigh to thigh. His body couldn't lie. He was *very* happy to be with her. "I don't do flowers and romance." His fingers slid inexorably up the furrow of her spine until he tangled his fingers in the hair at her nape.

She gave him an exaggerated look of shock. "Color me not in the least bit surprised." A little dazed at the powerful sensations coursing through her, she felt her lips curve. "I'll add that to the list. Number two: don't do romance. Check. I already have that you 'don't do tombs.' Got it. Anything else you don't do?"

His eyes looked very green and extremely annoyed as he yanked her incrementally closer until not even a breath came between their bodies. "Why the hell did you kiss me?"

"I wanted to." The more annoyed he got, the more amused she became. "You looked like you needed a kiss. You liked it. I liked it." *A lot!* "We're both adults. Why not?" She noticed the nerve jumping in his jaw and the pulse racing at the base of his throat. She placed both hands on his chest and felt the thud-thud-thud of his heart beneath the hard muscles of his chest, through the crisp cotton of his starched shirt.

"You can't just kiss a man senseless, then walk away."

His skin was scorching hot through the fabric. She kept her hands still, though she wanted to glide them all over him in exploration. But for now, simply touching him was enough. She enjoyed the sizzle and pulse of the electricity arcing between them. She didn't have to act on it to enjoy the moment. She liked the feel of him. The smell of him. The complexity of him.

The knowledge that there couldn't be, wouldn't be, anything beyond attraction and momentary satisfaction was at once tempting and a strong deterrent. She *wanted* an emotional connection with a lover. As far as she could tell, Thorne wasn't the kind of man who'd connect with a woman with anything more than his libido.

That wasn't enough for her, no matter how badly she craved his touch, No matter how much she wanted to fall into bed with him. Emotionless sex wasn't what she wanted or needed. No matter how loudly her body screamed otherwise. "We *were* in a cab," she pointed out reasonably as he stroked her back, which was in no way soothing, nor did it help her resolve. Her breasts felt heavy, and the ache in her very center pulsed with every heavy heartbeat. "You chose to drive off into the sunset without a backward glance." That wasn't really fair to say, but it was fun lobbing the ball back into his court just to see his eyes narrow and glitter.

"Clearly a tactical error." His gaze was hard, his intent crystal clear. Either he was going to kill her or kiss her senseless. She couldn't wait to find out.

She rose on her toes, leaning in so their mouths were closer. Was his heartbeat a little erratic? She thought so. Hers certainly was. He'd been drinking brandy. She smelled it on his breath and wanted to taste what he'd tasted. "Wars have been lost on less," she murmured against his mouth. He smelled so good, she was drunk on it. Brandy and starch and the unique smell of his skin combined to make her dizzy with longing.

He said roughly, "Damn it, Isis—" Then groaned as he crushed his mouth on hers.

Her mouth opened willingly, letting him in, tasting the tang of brandy on his tongue. Heat flared at every pulse point as she slid her hands up his chest and around his neck. His hair was too short for her fingers to tangle in the strands, but she cupped the back of his head, urging the kiss to deepen, loving the slick tangle of tongues and the hard edge of his teeth on her lower lip. Her muscles turned to water. Seething, hot water that melted her bones and flushed her skin.

He lifted his head, his breath fragmented as he dragged in air. "You must *stop* kissing me, Isis Magee." His lips skimmed her mouth, trailed to her jaw as his arms tightened around her with steely strength. The words were hardly out of his mouth before he swooped his mouth back on hers and took the kiss from hot to incendiary. It was a kiss unlike any Isis had ever had, and had only imagined earlier that day in the cab. She'd thought that was hot. But this was no-holds-barred vertical sex, even though their hands were in noninflammatory places.

"Okay." She pressed her damp mouth against his hot neck so she could get a few breaths. "Sure." Felt the hard, rapid pounding of his pulse in the cord of his neck, and took a little bite, then laved the wound with slow sweeps of her tongue, tasting salt and need and wanting more. "Fine."

She disengaged, then thought better of it, and reached up and kissed him on the mouth again. Faster this time, but no less satisfying. "You have to go now."

"Go?" He blinked her into focus. "Go where?"

"To your own room. I'm not having sex with you tonight, Connor James Thorne."

"You've got to be— Why the bloody hell not?"

"Because you're just not ready for me."

THEY ARRIVED AT THE museum precisely at ten and were taken into the bowels of the building to the large room housing Dr. Magee's contribution, which was being readied for exhibition in the Egyptian wing.

The Earl *had* made the call, and his request had opened the door, literally. They had until closing to be alone with Professor Magee's artifacts. Given the sheer volume of the task, Thorne had better move fast.

He surveyed the walls lined with shelves and drawers and visually divided the room into zones as he removed his suit jacket and hung it over a chair back. Thorne's one indulgence was clothes. He favored custom shirts and suits, and this Fioravanti had been hand-delivered to him just before he left London several months before. Not quite the correct garment to wear in the basement of a museum, but it was what had been close at hand when he'd dressed this morning.

There must be thousands of objects, small and large, and boxes and boxes of papers and files. Everything neatly cataloged.

The prospect of finding anything connected to the mythical tomb was daunting. Especially since Thorne didn't believe said tomb even existed in the first place.

Hot, sweaty, hard-driving sex was what he needed, Thorne thought as he watched Isis's shapely jean-clad arse bent over a box. With her. Get it out of his system and off his mind. The woman blew hot and cold, making him insane, and they'd barely known each other two bloody days.

Instead of waiting to have breakfast together, she'd eaten at the tearoom across the street. So when he, being a team player, knocked on her door to escort her down at eight in the damned morning, she informed him she wasn't hungry.

So now, hours later, he was starving, and she, perversely, wasn't hungry at all. She was also too damned cheerful. Without cause.

Her pale blue jeans accentuated her long legs and tight butt, and a canary-yellow long-sleeved T-shirt outlined her breasts to the point of distraction. As usual her glasses were smudged. Itching to take them off her face to clean them, he reminded himself he was not the woman's nanny. The reality was, he didn't trust himself to touch her, even casually. She was maddening, pure provocation disguised beneath innocuous, innocence-scented skin. Isis might smell like a damned cookie, but just looking at her brought out a primitive me-Tarzan, you-Jane need to strip her bare and take her right there on the cement floor.

She shouldn't be so enticing, and Thorne was damned sure that once he'd had sex with her, he'd go back to normal.

But all he could think of was how it would feel to rip

off her clothes and feast on her pale skin. How it would feel to slam into her wet heat and feel her legs wrapped tightly around his waist.

Her wild curls were held on top of her head this morning with some lethal-looking stick, but half of her hair had already sprung loose, and dark spirals danced around her face as she worked. She needed tidying up. But that would require he touch her. Not going to happen.

She'd left the hotel with glossy pink lips, which had been sexy as hell, but now Thorne realized her unpainted mouth was even sexier. Her big brown eyes looked bigger subtly smudged with color, the black-framed glasses making her look like a sexy schoolteacher.

Despite his foul mood, which he made no effort to conceal, she remained as smiling and friendly as the girl next door.

But there hadn't been a girl next door, and no girl next door smelled as mouthwateringly sensual as Isis Magee. She wore perfume guaranteed to drive him insane in such close quarters. Was cinnamon even a perfume? Spice and sex. He wished he could open a window to dissipate the pheromones. Go to a larger room. Another continent. Instead he was stuck in the small, Isis-scented room for the duration.

His debt to Zak Stark was going to be marked PAID IN FULL.

"How should we go about this?" Isis asked, looking around, suddenly misty-eyed as she saw her father's life's work collected in one place. Or because—God only knew why women cried.

"By not bursting into tears because you miss Daddy," he told her unsympathetically.

She blinked back moisture and gave him a tremulous smile that nibbled a little hole in his heart. "You're absolutely right. We'll honor his legacy by finding Cleopatra's tomb and showing the world just how brilliant he is."

Or spin their wheels, find absolutely nothing, and prove Magee was indeed a charlatan. "Right. Let's get to work."

"Did you know all Ptolemaic queens were called Cleopatra or Arsinoë or Berenice?"

No, and neither did he care. What had she meant last night, anyway? He wanted to demand an answer to the "You're not ready for me" statement. But to ask meant he was thinking about it, and he didn't want her to know he'd given her rejection a moment's thought. Damn her. It was some kind of psychological game she was playing. Well, he wasn't a player. Either she wanted him or she didn't. It was only sex, for God's sake.

He could, and damn well *should*, get his itch scratched somewhere else. Sex was nothing more than a physical release. Hell, he could take care of that on his own.

"She was queen of Egypt, but Cleo wasn't Egyptian." Isis took a pile of papers out of the bottom drawer of the cabinet and settled them in her lap to look through. "She was the last of the Macedonian Greek dynasty that ruled Egypt from the time of Alexander the Great's death to about thirty BCE. She co-ruled with her father when she was about eighteen, then married her much younger brother, which is a big *ew*, but that's how it was done in those days."

Putting the papers back in the drawer, she closed it and swiveled on her behind to survey a pile of nearby boxes. She didn't appear to have a system, but it kept her out of his hair. Apparently she couldn't work without chitchatting, and he half tuned her out.

"Pharaohs married siblings to ensure rulership, but her kid brother had powerful guardians, and when they got wind she was trying to get rid of him, they instigated a revolt and expelled her from Alexandria. Where were you last night anyway?" she asked, without a segue.

Thorne glanced up with a puzzled frown. Where was the connection between Cleopatra and his absence the night before?

Annoyed with himself—a., for caring, and b., for having to look at her—he scowled. The woman got under his skin and burrowed there, whether he wanted her there or not. If he had to be here, if he had to be here with *her*, why couldn't she be plain and plump? The old adage about men never making passes at girls with glasses was bullshit.

He wanted to make more than a pass, and that was the problem. She wasn't the kind of woman who'd go for a quickie, and he wasn't in the market for anything more. Not his thing. Never would be.

It would help his dick if he remembered that soon he'd be neck deep in an important op at MI5, and females would be the last thing on his mind. At least ones with home and hearth in their eyes, no matter how mind-boggling their kisses.

Isis dragged a box by the flaps across the cement floor. She'd made a fortress of boxes and paperwork across from him. She plopped down cross-legged in the center, not minding the cement floor, and pulled the box closer, then dug out a small notebook.

He'd checked in at Thames House, home of MI5, to see if they'd any new intel on Boris Yermalof. The man had made a fine attempt at amputating Thorne's leg with an extremely sharp boning knife, and then, because Yermalof was all about overkill, shooting him in the chest. The answer was no. Yermalof was still in the wind.

But the bounty was still on his head, and the strong suggestion was to return to Seattle posthaste. Then he and his coworkers had gone out for drinks. Very civilized.

None of it was any of her damned business. And what the hell did she do? *Bathe* in cinnamon and ginger? He tasted the light fragrance of her on his tongue. *Goddamn it.* "If you plan on *reading* every damned scrap of paper your father donated to the museum, we'll be here for the next ninety-nine years," he told his client briskly without answering her question. "All we're looking for are papers and/or artifacts from the last two years, remember?"

It was all there, in one claustrophobic, dust-free room until tomorrow, when the curator and a team of assistants would start moving artifacts to one of the seven Egyptian galleries upstairs to ready the displays for the well-publicized opening the following month. The Natural History Museum in London housed the world's largest and most comprehensive collection of Egyptian antiquities, and the Earl had been instrumental in obtaining, at his own expense, thousands of priceless pieces to add to their vast collection.

He'd championed August Magee for years, and Thorne knew his father would be damned if anything took away even a glimmer of his glory for bringing the fabled Egyptologist's lifelong discoveries to the museum. The exhibit, he'd read last night, would comprise Professor Magee's entire collection of artifacts and environmental remains from his excavations. Thirty bloody years' worth of crap to look through.

"I have to read the papers to find dates," Isis told him, flipping through another small notebook. "I have this box full of small items, but I have no idea which comes from which dig. And you didn't answer the—"

"Let's speed things up a bit." Her mouth, wide and mobile, always looked on the verge of smiling. *What did she have to smile about?* Thorne thought, annoyed. Annoyed, more with himself for noticing the sparkle in her big brown eyes and her secret amusement, than at Isis. Clearly cinnamon was a secret nerve agent that caused normally prosaic and sensible government operatives to have the impulse control of an adolescent.

"Write down the locations of his digs for the past *five* years." She'd given him two years; now he needed to widen the search if he didn't want to be in here with her until they were both as dry as the antiquities they were pawing through.

"Here—" Thorne removed a small notebook and his

favorite Montblanc from an inner pocket of his jacket and handed her both. He hovered a breath from her lips. He wasn't going to kiss her, but the memory of last night's kiss lingered. The taste of her, the fragrance of her skin, the heat as he'd sunk into the heat and flash of their kiss— Fuck it. No. He shifted his head to avoid contact, but their hands brushed as the pen changed hands. The graze of her fingers gave him what felt like an electric shock that zinged all the way up his arm and resonated in the lizard part of his brain, which was helpless to resist her allure. Fortunately, he was made of sterner stuff than his hormones. He withdrew his hand. The hand that wanted to independently touch her skin and tangle in her hair. The hand that wanted to curve around her breasts and discover just how soft her skin felt.

Body flooded with heat, he gritted his teeth and kept his tone even and cool with effort. "I'll use this"—he held up a handheld device similar to a GPS, but government issue—"and we'll know where he was. I'll compare artifacts to digs. Anything that doesn't match up might—and I stress *might*—be from the tomb at the mystery location."

This, he knew, was an exercise in futility. He'd humor her for today. Tomorrow he'd return to Seattle with or without her.

She chewed the corner of her lower lip, the pen poised over the pad as she tried to remember. "The Hor-Aha dig was 2008 and well into 2009. That was near—can you show me a map?"

Thorne removed the map he'd procured from his office last evening, unfolded it, and spread it on the floor in front of her. When she leaned over it, he had a glimpse of the lightly tanned swell of her breasts. Jesus God. He was as randy as a schoolboy. He rolled his chair far enough away so that parallax hid her attributes from his avaricious view.

He'd endured Boris Yermalof's brand of retribution with more equanimity than dealing with Isis Magee. She affected him more than she should. More than he wanted her to.

She glanced up to give him an inquiring look. "Do you usually carry a map in your pocket?"

"I carry whatever is required for the job." Be it a map or an Uzi. He had to roll the chair closer to see where she was pointing on the large unfolded map. He inhaled cinnamon, which made him dizzy, which in turn annoyed him. The smell of her wasn't seductive in any way, shape, or fucking form. Someone should send a memo to his dick. "Give me my pen back. I'll write down the coordinates."

She did so, and he managed not to brush her fingers with his, and even managed not to inhale the warm scent of her skin. Waiting until she moved away to take a breath, he wrote down the approximate location of each of the professor's findings. In this case, approximate was good enough. He didn't need to go there, just eliminate each as he touched the artifact. Whatever remained unaccounted for, would, in a perfect world, be the tomb of Queen Cleopatra. Since Thorne knew how damned imperfect the world was, he wasn't holding his breath.

"Is that it?" he asked when she'd finished identifying

where her father had been for the past five years. That should be far enough back.

"Oh! Wait, I think he helped a friend on the Neferirkare dig for a few weeks three years ago. It's right . . . here." She pointed at the location on the map, then met his gaze. "Yes. That's everything."

There was a gap of a few months where he'd been stateside, and then the months he'd spent nailing down the location and ostensibly found the tomb.

Ready to go to work, Thorne made a makeshift desk from a stack of boxes, then placed his map, GPS device, notepad, and pen out. He sat down to make some notes, glad to get off his leg for a minute or two. It ached and burned.

Two seconds later Isis walked her chair right up beside him. "Now what do we do?" Thorne didn't get it. He'd lain in a swamp in Central Africa, oblivious to the stench surrounding him as he out waited his quarry. He'd smelled his partner's blood as well as his own when Yermalof had tortured the crap out of them. Why the bloody hell couldn't he ignore the fragrance of this woman's skin?

"*We* do nothing. *You* feel free to read whatever you like to your heart's content. I'll touch an item and eliminate it. The faster I go, the faster I—we—can get out of here."

"I know a way to speed things up," she told him, leaning forward so that his entire body clenched in response to her closeness. "We can eliminate anything bigger than a bread box. The artifacts he brought back will be small." She gave him a cheeky smile, which chipped another flake from the rock of his heart.

He stared back at her for a beat or two—debating—then decided that if he put his mouth anywhere near her mouth, he'd be screwed. He'd been hired to do a job. He'd do that job. No more. No less.

That meant no fraternizing with the client.

No touching.

No inhaling.

Absolutely no kissing.

"Small enough not to declare when he came through customs? Then they wouldn't be here," he pointed out, trying to get out of her gravitational pull, but without success. "The museum wouldn't countenance—"

"Small enough to have in his *pockets* when he was knocked out. He had handfuls of small rocks and things in his pockets, notes and little bits of pottery. I didn't really look. The museum asked that I send them *everything*. I just tossed the last bits and pieces into a box and shipped it. I'll look for the box. Maybe they haven't had a chance to go through it yet."

"Right." He checked the map a couple of times, broadening the latitude and longitude for each location to be eliminated, then got to his feet, pulling on the white cotton gloves given to them when they'd been let into the storage area. She was sitting far too close. He'd been attracted to a lot of women—some even at first sight. But never like this. *Attraction* was a mild word for it. He was in a state of semi-arousal all the time. Uncomfortable as hell. "You can go shopping if you like. We can meet back at the hotel later." Where, given half a glance of encouragement, he'd have her naked and flat on her back in minutes flat. Mutual satisfaction guaranteed.

No. Fucking. Fraternizing.

What did he need to remind him? A two-by-four across the head? There was somewhere a lot lower where a hard blow would be more effective. Unfortunately, he was far too conscious of that region of his body already.

"I didn't come all this way to go shopping," she responded cheerfully. "What?" she asked, when he gave her a pointed look.

"You're blocking my workspace," he said briskly, wondering how long before she realized this was a hopeless task and called it quits.

She grinned. "You do your thing, and I'll see if any of his papers give us a clue." He waited for her to roll her chair back across the room, then observed her graceful return to her cross-legged position among the boxes.

She left a drift of spicy cinnamon in her wake.

↶ FOUR ↷

Isis adored her father. But Holy Mother of God, the man loved writing notes. Copious, rather dry notes, hundreds and hundreds of pages of them, many of them accompanied by extraordinarily bad sketches. She read until her eyes crossed, then persuaded Thorne to take her to lunch in the cafeteria, since they weren't allowed to eat in the storage rooms.

He'd been taciturn while they ate, then hurried her back downstairs. "I really appreciate how dedicated you are to helping me; it's very sweet of you," she told him as they walked downstairs. His slight limp and the use of the cane didn't impede his speed, and she suspected that without his injury he'd take the stairs three at a time and leave her in the dust.

He paused midstep to raise a brow. A muscle jerked in his jaw. *"Sweet?"*

She smiled at his clear distaste at being called that. *"Kind of you."*

"I'm neither sweet nor kind. You paid for my services, I'll do my best to ensure you get your money's worth."

"Does your leg hurt?" She knew it *hurt*—she wanted

to know to what degree. Isis was pretty sure he wouldn't be so bad-tempered and surly if he weren't in pain.

He glanced at her as they reached the landing. A group of teachers and a gaggle of schoolkids clattered past them, and they stepped aside to let the herd pass. "No," he told her succinctly when they resumed their descent.

She was worried about him standing for hours, but the only way she could get him to sit down had been to insist she was hungry so they could go upstairs to the cafeteria.

They unlocked the door and turned on the lights. "Why is your injury such a big secret?"

"It's not a secret. It's none of your business."

"Apparently," she said, unoffended. Her father was grumpy a lot of the time because he was distracted, or hungry, or too hot. "Too personal?"

Thorne took a fresh pair of cotton gloves from the box by the door. "Is *anything* too personal in your book?" he asked, pulling on a glove while giving her a less than friendly look.

He had nice hands. Big and strong-looking. The bright overhead lights shone on several scars across the back of his right hand before he pulled on the other glove. Part of the same accident?

"How did your brother die?"

"Jesus—"

"I just wondered if your injury and your brother's death were linked, that's all."

A muscle jumped in his jaw, and his eyes looked black.

"Garrett was swept overboard m——the family yacht. There was a squall, he . . . died."

"That's terrible." Her heart ached for him. What a tragedy. She stopped what she was doing to look at him. He continued working as if she weren't there.

"We were alone on the *Breeze*."

"God. That's even worse. You must've fought so hard to save him."

"I did. Other people didn't see it that way. He was the heir, and I was glad for it. He liked everything that entailed. It worked out well for everyone."

"And then he died, and now you're the heir." Neither Thorne nor his father appeared to be very happy about it.

"I have absolutely no interest in being a wealthy dilettante. I have a job. I pay my own freight. If you're going to chitchat and waste my time, you can go back to the cafeteria and read a guidebook while I work."

Isis turned an imaginary key against her lips. "Just Thorne" was not amused. He went straight back to the drawer of artifacts he'd been touching before they left for lunch and before she'd started asking questions.

She too pulled on a pair of gloves. Being an only child, she couldn't fathom what it was like to lose a sibling. Hideous, she imagined. "How much older was Garrett?"

He was quiet for so long, Isis thought he wasn't going to answer. "If I tell you will you shut the hell up?"

"How do you get to know someone if you don't ask questions?"

"*One* ruddy question. Choose wisely—it'll be the only one you get."

"How old was he?"

"Twenty-one when he died. And bonus answer? He was seven minutes older than I."

"Dear God. You were twins." The distance between Thorne and his parents now became a little clearer to her. They blamed Thorne for his brother's death.

"Are you going to dog my footsteps for the rest of the day?" he demanded with a scowl as he rested his hand briefly on each item in a wide drawer, multitasking by giving her an irritable look as he did his work.

The question had been rhetorical, and since she could almost smell brimstone in the room, she backed off. "I like watching you work," she told him easily. She liked looking at him. His shirt still looked crisp and fresh; he looked like a man on a mission, with those sleeves rolled up his muscular forearms. He had a nice straight nose, almost Roman, and his ears lay flat and neat against his head. Very sexy.

The planes of his face were hard, but she liked the soft look of his military-short haircut, and the no-nonsense, almost fluid way he moved. Even though he was a large man, and even with the limp, his movements were almost graceful. He was aware of the space he took up and filled it to capacity. Isis found it very sexy. He intrigued her.

Wanting to reach out to feel if the dark hair on his muscular forearms was crisp or soft, she instead folded her arms around her waist and said, "You have a very delicate touch for a man with such big hands." She leaned her butt against the cabinet next to where he worked. "Are the scars on the back of your hands from the same accident?"

He didn't look up as he touched a gold and glass scarab bracelet she vaguely remembered her father letting her wear when she was about five or six. It had been way too big, and heavy on her wrist, but she'd loved the colors of the glass beads. Thorne moved his hand to a solid gold pendant studded with lapis lazuli. "What about 'I don't talk about it' do you not understand?"

"Now, see, you never actually said that. *Implied*, perhaps, but not *stated*."

He turned a steely look on her. "I have two things to say to you. Both are statements. One: I do not now, nor will I ever, discuss my injuries with anyone, and you in particular. Two: if you want this done, then you have to leave me the fuck alone to *do* it. Is that clear enough for you?"

Lord, the man was cranky. But it was hard to be pissed off at a guy with a bad limp wearing white cotton gloves. "I could sit over there and read my father's diaries. Would that help you concentrate?"

"As long as you don't talk, or breathe, or hum."

"I'll breathe just enough to keep me conscious in case you find something," she told him cheerfully, backing up with both hands raised as he gave her the evil eye.

It was companionable working silently among her father's things. Thorne was pretty fast as he opened a drawer, ran his hand slowly over each item, and moved on to the next. Starting to get sleepy from the inactivity, Isis took out her camera and framed some shots of him as he worked. Without looking over at her, he snapped. "Three: no pictures of me."

Unoffended, Isis put her camera back in the camera bag and picked up one of her father's ubiquitous small black notebooks, flicking through what were mostly rough sketches. It took her a moment to recognize what she was looking at.

"Oh, my God! Of course. Damn it, why didn't I think of this before?" She jumped to her feet, not waiting for his response. "My father was always paranoid that someone would steal his notes and trump him on his discoveries. When he wanted to keep things close to his chest he'd draw a *tyet*, the hieroglyph knot of Isis, somewhere on the page. He always left himself cryptic clues to jog his memory."

"Let me see that." Thorne held out his hand. He'd taken the cotton gloves off, and Isis had a moment to admire how strong-looking his hand was, before she gave him the book. Normally she wasn't that fond of people telling her what to do. She'd pretty much raised herself, running wild in whatever camp her father was digging in during the summers, and living with her aunt in Seattle during the school year.

She could either choose to be thoroughly annoyed by his crappy bad humor or else be sympathetic and give his overbearing personality a pass while he was helping her. Besides, honey was more attractive than vinegar. Isis considered his crankiness almost part of his charm, because he did it with such grim deliberation. The more he pushed, the more curious she became, so if he thought that by being rude, she'd be turned off, he was sadly mistaken.

His eyes ran over one page, then another as he flicked through the book. "This doesn't tell us any—" He stopped talking so abruptly, Isis took a small step toward him, putting a hand on his wrist with concern. His skin was hot to the touch. "What is it?"

"*Cairo*. Not just a general direction. I know specifically where he had this diary last."

SIX HOURS LATER THEY landed in Cairo. The city was hot, muggy, and filthy for most of June through August. Even the locals fled the fly-ridden city for cooler climes, not that anyone could tell from the insane traffic, a mixture of vehicles with engines, vehicles that were animal powered, vehicles that were being pushed, and pedestrians who considered they had right-of-way—everywhere. Driving in Cairo was a contact sport and no one was chicken.

It was in the mid-seventies at ten at night, but the daytime temperatures would rise to the nineties, and the thick, odoriferous air still held high humidity due to the city's location in the Nile delta valley.

After Isis flatly refused to hire one of the more reputable—and high-priced—taxis, he'd agreed to a local cab company and negotiated the fare from sixty pounds to fifteen.

"Brace yourself," he warned as they lurched out of the taxi line and did a wheelie out of the terminal at breakneck speed—miraculous considering the vintage of the vehicle.

In passable Arabic, Thorne gave the driver directions to the Zamalek region, where he'd booked them into the Marriott hotel while waiting for their flight from Heathrow. Isis would protest the cost, but he didn't give a shit. He wanted a clean bed and a decent night's sleep. His leg hurt as if fire ants were crawling in and out of his thigh. He'd been crouching and standing on a hard cement floor at the museum for hours, followed by a six-hour flight in coach. He'd pay for the rooms himself, which would please his pinchpenny client.

The ubiquitous black, white, and rusty taxi had no springs—either on the chassis, or beneath the blanket—and probably flea-covered seats. They were lucky there were bloody seats at all. They passed through the security checkpoint, where Thorne signed their names in the book, showed his fare receipt, and proceeded without incident.

They passed a burning car, and the thick, oily smoke filled the vehicle, making Isis cough. Thorne silently handed her his handkerchief and she pressed it to her nose.

She was way too bloody *perky*. Too cheerful, too . . . fresh and appealing in an annoying, girl-next-door way that made his teeth ache. None of that had any kind of adverse effect on his dick, which liked her a great deal. Of course, he hadn't had sex in almost a year, which would account for his irrational attraction to a woman he wouldn't have given the time of day to a year ago.

He had a preference for tall, bosomy blondes who disliked commitment as much as he did. This woman was all up in his face as if, by paying Lodestone's fee, she had a goddamned right to ask him questions that were none of her bloody business. She smelled wholesome, not sexy at all. *Like something one should eat,* he thought with irritation. Well, yes, there was that, Thorne thought wryly.

Out of sorts, and anticipating staying that way for the duration, Thorne braced one hand and his good leg on the seat back as they screamed around a corner, narrowly missing a pack of ragged kids darting across the busy street. The kids scattered like buckshot.

Isis shouted, "Thanks." And Thorne realized too late that he'd slammed his forearm across her chest to prevent her from being thrown through the windshield. He removed his arm, but not before he felt the imprint of her soft breasts as a tingle on his skin. *Bloody hell.* He glared out his window.

Cairo was, to Thorne, the seventh level of Hell.

He'd never encountered such brazen flies. They were everywhere, and no amount of encouragement dispersed them from clothes or skin. They just stuck around for the free ride.

"I haven't been here since last year." Isis held her hair at her nape to lean out the window. Thorne grabbed her arm and drew her into the relative safety of the interior of the taxi. She wore a pink T-shirt, and his fingers clamped on bare skin. Silky soft, satin smooth, lightly tanned, bare skin.

Releasing her arm, he shifted as far to his corner as was possible without riding outside the vehicle. No touching, he decided.

He imagined he could smell cinnamon. *Nonsense.* The windows were open, blowing muggy Cairo-stinking air around them. He was delusional because he didn't want to be here. *Here* reminded him of eighteen hours in surgery, a month in traction, more months of physical therapy. *Here* reminded Thorne of Boris Yermalof. A sharp boning knife, high-velocity bullets, bone fragments, and metal rods. Plates and pins and the possibility of fucking-well hobbling for the rest of his life.

Here was exactly where Thorne did not want to be.

He didn't like heat. Or sand. Now he could add cinnamon to the list.

There were no working streetlights in the city, making it a free-for-all, with every man for himself as they slalomed through the busy thoroughfares without the benefit of the horn. Most people didn't bother with headlights, either, so cars came out of the darkness at breakneck speeds. The only good thing Thorne could say about the taxi was that the brakes worked. Worked *loudly,* but functioned. Which was imperative since the driver used them often, with no warning, and accompanied by a litany of yelling, screaming, and arm waving.

Thorne didn't care for the pungent stink of the streets, or the dust clogging his nose, or the lunatics sharing the road, but Isis was wide-eyed and happy as hell to be risking whiplash. One step closer to her goal.

He'd forgotten that he'd promised himself to send her on her merry way once he found a jumping-off point for her in Cairo.

He'd leave her tomorrow, head back to Seattle.

"I'd like to go straight to the location," she told him, looking around eagerly. With the temps in the seventies, it was downright tropical compared to a London summer, which compared favorably to a Seattle summer: chilly.

Warm, dry wind from the western desert blew in through windowless openings, sending Isis's cinnamon-scented hair across his face. She'd changed into a breast-hugging pink T-shirt tucked into her jeans before they'd left the London hotel. Her strappy sandals revealed the fluorescent pink polish on her toenails. If Thorne didn't have a shitload of things to worry about right then, he could become quite fixated on her pretty feet. As it was, he had more pressing concerns.

Since leaving London earlier that evening, he'd had a fucking itch on the back of his neck. The kind of itch that warned him he was in someone's crosshairs.

Returning to London before the Boris Yermalof investigation was resolved had been a mistake of monumental proportions. And it wasn't as if he hadn't been warned.

"We won't find anything at this time of night in the dark," he told her, keeping an eye on the driver's fly-speckled rearview mirror to watch the traffic behind them.

The driver seemed oblivious to the swinging ornamentation hanging in the middle of the cracked windshield, which was adorned with a Christmas tree air freshener so old it curled at the edges, and a dozen dangling *hamsa*, palm-shaped five-fingered protection amulets. One would think his view impaired. Or maybe that was why he slammed on his brakes every few hundred yards whether he needed to avoid the car in front of him, a pedestrian, or animal, or nothing at all.

Twenty people could be following them, and Thorne wouldn't know it, as the headlights behind them zigged and zagged between other vehicles like Indianapolis 500 racers gunning for the checkered flag.

"We'll find the place first thing in the morning," he assured her, watching as a closed-panel white van crept up on their left.

He rested his hand on the weapon in the small of his back. Thanks to MI5, he'd discreetly brought the weapon with him from Seattle.

"At least let's drive by and see what we're dealing with," Isis pressed. "My father left clues in some odd places. We don't know what it is, but can see *where* this one is, and perhaps plan a strategy for tomorrow."

She might've let him know about her father's proclivity to leave clues. But even though Thorne had the notebook, he had still run his hands over every artifact in every fucking drawer for eight hours.

The notebook was all he had to show for an extremely long day. Thorne was not in the best of moods.

It took twenty-five hair-raising minutes to get to the souk Khan el-Khalili, where his mental GPS indicated the book had originated. The souk was of course empty, the stalls closed for the night, but the fragrance of cooked meat and spices still perfumed the air, coupled with the stink of urine and wet dog.

"Satisfied?" he demanded, not masking his irritation as he ordered the driver to continue on to the hotel.

"It was worth a shot. I'm not surprised my father left a clue in the Khan. That shop is owned by an old and trusted friend, Beniti al-Atrash. He sells carpets and small replica——" She stopped yammering to shoot him a sympathetic glance. "Oh, God. It's your leg. Here, let me do that for you."

Thorne didn't realize that he was massaging the tortured muscles with one hand until Isis pushed his gripping fingers aside and laid both slender hands over his spasming muscle. "Oh, Thorne . . ."

Her hands were small, but strong, and she seemed to know what she was doing as she massaged the muscles firmly. "My aunt used to get excruciating muscle spasms in her butt," Isis told him, her attention totally focused on his leg as her hands kneaded the hard muscles with determination. She glanced up. "That's not too hard, is it?"

The massage felt far from therapeutic. He grabbed her wrist. "Move up a few inches and tell me yourself." He resisted the temptation to move her hand over his dick, which had come to life the second she touched him. Or, more likely, it had been semi-erect since he'd met her back in Seattle. "Don't look so shocked, darling. You're the one with her hand on my crotch. Do you *want* to screw in the back of a taxi?" His voice was intentionally harsh. "You certainly give every indication it's what you want to do. If so, I'll be happy to oblige you. But you might want to wait for a clean bed at the hotel."

Her fingers curled against his thigh like lotus petals closing at night as she gave him an assessing look. "Were you this mean before your accident?"

"I was this mean from the day my mother stuck a silver spoon up my arse. This is who I am, Isis. Don't dick around with my dick. I'm a man, not a boy. Give me a scintilla of encouragement and I'll have you naked with your legs spread before you can say 'You're not ready' in that sweet, reasonable tone. Do I make myself cl—"

The crunch of metal erupted—front and back, simultaneously—as they were rammed from behind and shoved into the car in front of them. The rear-end collision flung them violently into the front seats. Isis screamed. Thorne's arms shot out—one to brace her, the other to prevent himself from being jettisoned into the front of the cab.

Horns honked, people yelled, metal crumpled, and glass shattered.

"Out! Get out!" Thorne yelled, grabbing her by the wrist and dragging her out of his side of the crippled vehicle. Five cars, including the white van, hemmed them in. The van had shoved a black Honda into them, collapsing the small car like a concertina. The Honda driver, a young man in overalls, was climbing out of the passenger-side window with the help of several bystanders who'd raced to the scene. There didn't appear to be anyone in the white van, which was slewed across the road, blocking traffic in both ways—much to the ire of the drivers and passengers of a dozen vehicles backed up in each direction.

Their cabdriver, arms waving, demanded restitution from anyone who'd listen.

"Are you hurt anywhere?" Thorne demanded, tightening his grip on her wrist and dragging her away from the scene. Adrenaline surged through him as he saw the back door of the van slam open. A man jumped out, spun around, looked for—

Skin pale in the lights from a nearby fruit vendor's stall, Isis straightened her angled glasses on her nose and shifted her camera bag strap, which had twisted around her neck. She blinked, trying to absorb what had just happened. "Wait, we can't leave—"

A bullet whizzed over their heads.

"Go! Go! Go!" Thorne hoped to hell she didn't have whiplash as he jerked her into a low, flat-out run.

THORNE'S FINGERS CLAMPED LIKE steel bands around Isis's wrist as he dragged her through the labyrinth of small streets and dark side alleys of the souk at a full-out run. A few startled people jumped out of the way to eye them curiously as they ran by.

Isis had no idea if anyone was actually chasing them, and looking over her shoulder wasn't an option. It took three of her strides to match one of his, and that was with his bad leg.

It required all her concentration to keep one foot in front of the other as she blindly followed his lead, her camera bag bouncing against her hip. Thank God she'd worn it across her body. Everything of value was in it. She figured anything left in the taxi would be long gone by the time—or if—they returned to the scene.

Intermittent pools of dirty yellow light helped illuminate the cobbled streets, but the winding alleys stayed black as the night. *Thorne must have eyes like a cat*, she thought as they passed a pile of discarded baskets, to avoid all the shadowed obstacles in their path.

"Why are we running?" She tried to pull back, to slow down, but he gave no quarter and just kept moving, almost pulling her arm from its socket in the process. Her chest heaved; her heart galloped painfully behind her ribs. Black spots danced in her vision and sweat caused her glasses to slide down her nose.

Her lungs were on fire by the time Thorne jerked her into a dark, narrow doorway. "Stay put." He gave her the once-over, shoving her against the wall before her knees buckled. "I'm going back to see who's following us."

"No! Wai—" He melted into the shadows, something solid and dark in his hand. His cane? Her breath lurched. A *gun*? No . . . why would a Lodestone agent have a weapon? Where had it come from? And how in God's name had he gotten it through customs?

Questions burned and she clutched the side of the doorway with trembling fingers. Guns upped the ante. Weapons meant serious business.

Did the accident have anything to do with her father's find? "Oh. My. God." Isis fell back against the wall. "No. That's *insane*. It can't be . . ." Rubbing her upper arms where sudden goose bumps of apprehension pebbled her skin, she took a shaky breath. Someone had been willing to kill her father's entire crew, leaving him for dead. They wouldn't stop there. But it seemed too far-fetched to think the traffic accident had anything to do with what had happened to her father more than three months ago.

The two couldn't be related—could they? Wrapping her arms around her middle, she stayed in the shadows and told herself not to let her imagination run wild. It was highly unlikely the people who'd almost killed her father had somehow ascertained that she'd show up in Cairo months later.

She wished she hadn't insisted on going to the souk in the middle of the night rather than the hotel. The accident had been just an accident. Fender benders were a dime a dozen in this part of the world. That hadn't been a shot she'd heard, it was a car backfiring, and Thorne hadn't had a gun, it was the light shining on his cane.

That all made more sense than her silly overactive imagination. Taking a shuddering breath, she released the death grip she had around her waist and breathed in and out slowly. *Crazy sauce.* Thorne's crude observation in the taxi, the reaction she had to him physically, and her overactive imagination had taken her on a crazy detour. She needed rest. And protein. And chocolate.

Isis took the opportunity to catch her breath, her eyes trained into the darkness, alert to a danger she couldn't identify and wasn't sure even existed. Whatever—or *whoever*—was after them, her body was still in flight-or-fight mode despite her pep talk. Her rapid heartbeat pulsed behind her eyes, and sweat trickled down her temples and between her breasts. Her jeans and cotton shirt clung to her damp skin like a shroud. Plucking the shirt away from her chest with one hand, she pressed the fingers of the other into the stitch in her side, and leaned forward to ease the pain.

Her eyes adjusted to the darkness, and she could make out the bulky shapes of closed stalls across the alley. She saw a large rat skitter by her hiding place, its eye glinting briefly in the light. Isis grimaced. Give her a spider any day, but beady eyes, twitching whiskers, and evil, scritchy little pink feet grossed her out.

She pressed back against the door just as the rat swung its beady red eyes in her direction. If that thing ran into the doorway near her practically bare feet, she was going to lose it. "Get lost!" she said, more mouthing than making a sound. "Go on. Shoo!"

The sound of someone approaching, breathing hard, shut her up fast. The scrape of a shoe coming from the direction Thorne had disappeared in made her sag with relief. Good, he was back. She almost stepped out of the doorway, but thank God something held her back. She froze as two shadows ran by. This time there was no mistaking the fact that both men were armed. She pressed against the door at her back and tried to become invisible.

Minutes later, Thorne called her name softly as he approached out of the darkness. Despite his limp, his steps were a lot quieter than those of the two men who'd run past. His fingers unerringly manacled her wrist and he gave a little tug to get her feet moving. "Let's go."

"Two men, armed, ran that way." She indicated south, knowing his cat eyes would see the gesture.

"I doubled back to follow them. Now we're behind them. At least until they figure it out. Ready?"

Apparently he didn't have a "slow-start" button. He went from zero to sixty, hugging the walls as they ran. The sounds from the main thoroughfare beyond the souk were muted, and only a handful of people witnessed their passing as they clung to the shadows.

"You don't have to hold on to me like a bag of laundry. I'm running as fast as—"

"Quiet."

Really? Isis was tempted to say "Fuck you!" and take her chances. This was getting ridiculous. She had no idea where they were, who those men were, or why they were running. But maybe they could stop and ask some questions? Or maybe Mr. Macho-Take-Charge could take half a second to explain what was happening and why, without issuing terse orders and dragging her around by the arm, willing or no.

"You know—"

"I don't care. Shut up and keep moving."

"Go to hell!" Isis muttered as she kept moving.

Thorne used her wrist as a fulcrum to keep her slightly ahead of him. The deeper they went into the market, the fewer people they encountered, until they seemed to be alone on the planet, and still he moved quickly through the oppressive darkness.

He yanked her into another deep, dark, smelly doorway. Slamming his muscled forearm across her chest, he pinned her to the studded metal door as if she'd break free and sprint off on her own at any minute. It took several minutes to catch her breath and be capable of speech. At least it seemed as if this time, he wasn't going to leave her and run off alone.

"Who's chasing us. And why? Thorne, we have to find the authorities and—" She gasped, trying to keep her voice to a whisper, but her breath was so labored it was hard to even speak. Things were pretty lawless in Egypt, but she and Thorne weren't locals, and they could be put in jail on a whim. The thought wasn't comforting.

His chest rose and fell against her breast. He wasn't out of breath, but she wondered how he'd run so effortlessly with his leg, which had been painful before he'd run a marathon. "This is insane. Why do you have a gun? Why do they? Who *are* these people?!"

"I'd rather err on the side of caution," he told her cryptically, his voice soft and very close. Insanely, the smell of his clean sweat made her insides contract, which under the circumstances made Isis aware of how loudly his pheromones were shouting to *her* pheromones.

They appeared to be on the same frequency, which had never happened to her before in her life. It was fascinating. And as soon as she could suck in a breath that didn't burn like fire, as soon as her manic heartbeat settled down, she'd sit down and examine the feelings. But right now, all she wanted to do was survive the evening.

"How on earth can you find your way around a strange place, and in the dark, no less?" She hated the wheeze in her voice. Yoga? She needed Pilates.

"Memorized the map." His breath ruffled her hair, and Isis resisted the urge to lean against him for a minute or two or twenty. "I think we're clear, but keep an eye out for strangers."

Despite the obvious severity of the situation, she smiled in the darkness. "Seriously? We're in a foreign country. *Everyone* is a stranger. What—"

"We'll find a taxi five blocks over. Move fast, and stay close. Ready?"

Like I have a choice. "Sure."

They slowed to a brisk walk, but that didn't feel like much of a break to her rubbery legs. Her breaths were finally controlled as she spied the minarets of al-Azhar Mosque above the rooftops of the souk.

By the time they emerged from the narrow street and approached the pedestrian underpass, Isis saw that he *was* carrying a weapon. "Hey," she said, bringing her eyes up from the gun to Thorne's grim face. His expression scared her a hell of a lot more than the big black gun in his hand. "W—"

"Bloody hell." He pulled her up short in the deep shadow of an old gnarled sycamore tree on the grassy verge. The warm breeze brought with it the pungent smell of urine, causing Isis to wrinkle her nose.

"The lights in the underpass should be on. Stay here for a minute. I'll go—"

This time it was she who did the wrist grabbing. "No thanks. I'll go with you. I feel too exposed out here, and if anything happens to you, I'll be stuck here alone."

After several heartbeats, he agreed quietly, not sounding particularly happy. "All right. Hold on to my belt so we stay together, but my hands are free. If we encounter anyone, fall to the ground and keep your head covered until I give the all-clear. Got it?" His eyes glinted. "And if we should run into any action, don't bloody well help me."

"God, no. I'll run like hell and leave you in the dust." *Chauvinistic ass.* He managed to make her blood boil in so many ways, and not all of them were good. "Let's get this over with."

She didn't need to hold on to him going down the steep stairs, but once at the bottom, she slid her hand into the back of his jeans to grip his belt. The heat of his skin through the damp fabric of his shirt gave Isis a crystal-clear image of them rubbing their naked bodies together. The picture was so clear, so visceral that her nipples peaked, and she pressed closer to his back, as turned on as if he'd touched her.

She enjoyed the sensation, if not her lousy timing. The nerve-racking darkness and the eye-watering stench got rid of the image pretty fast. Eyes moving from side to side as she strained to see any threats in the gloom, Isis kept pace and acknowledged the duality of her responses to the man. As annoying as he tried to be, she was still turned on by everything about him. Go figure.

They entered the dark mouth of the tunnel. She'd only been inside once, many years before, and tried to picture it in her mind's eye as they walked. A curved ceiling, lots of cracked, dirty white tile, cement floor, a jog at the end . . .

There was enough light from the entrance to illuminate partway inside—but from there the rest of the tunnel disappeared into thick darkness. The close confines smelled strongly of body fluids and greasy french fries. There were American-style fast-food places everywhere in Cairo, and people the world over littered.

Their shoes echoed alarmingly as they crunched on the gritty floor. The air was still and close, and did nothing for her sweat-dampened skin, or her recurring jitters.

"Down!" Thorne yelled, reaching back one-handed to rip her fingers free from his belt. A shot ricocheted through the space, causing Isis to flinch. Then another. She dropped flat on her stomach on the filthy floor, then rolled out of the way as booted feet converged and the sound of flesh meeting bone mingled with men's grunts and guttural curses. She rolled into as small a ball as possible and covered her head with her arms—which was insane, because her forearms weren't fricking *bullet*proof.

⫷ FIVE ⫸

Thorne was ready for them—in fact, he fucking well *welcomed* them. He'd had enough of this bullshit of running around in the dark with his head up his arse. His lips curled back in a snarl as he got off a shot at the guy on his left, which was answered by a hoarse shout, followed by a bullet coming from his right. Close enough to feel the heat and hear the buzz as the shot whizzed by his ear, then ricocheted farther down the curved walls. The sound echoed in the close confines of the tunnel, mingling with the explosion of shattered tile and cement behind him.

He spared a quick glance to assure himself Isis was out of the line of fire. She was down on the ground, pressed tightly against the wall, head buried in her arms.

He counted four men but suspected there might be more. Thorne spun to face the closest gun, parried the first blow with his forearm, and used his weapon hand to slam into an eye socket. The man howled, grabbing him by the wrist, and wrenched his arm back. Thorne followed the momentum of the twist, extricating himself, kneed the guy in the balls, and followed through with a right cross.

It would be nice to get some questions answered, but these guys were clearly the brawn so he saved his breath. Feeling a rush of displaced air, he spun around as someone ran up behind him. Parrying the thrust of a knife with a chop of his arm, he felt the thin, white-hot line cut in his skin. Fuck, he hated knives. The man topped Thorne by a good six inches and was at least fifty pounds heavier, all of it fat, but he moved fast. Only a quick, fast-shoe shuffle had Thorne dancing inches out of reach before the man grabbed him around the throat. He spun and fired a shot almost point-blank into the man's chest. The warm scatter of blood hit his face before the guy dropped.

"Who sent you?" Thorne demanded, shooting out his fist as a third guy, robes flapping, came at him with some sort of cudgel.

Someone else grabbed his arm, trying to wrench it out of its socket. Pain radiated up into Thorne's neck as he leaned into the wrench. His fingers went numb, and the Glock he was using fell uselessly to the ground. Fucking hell! There was too much action to even consider dropping down to look for it. Thorne spun, rammed his elbow into someone's jaw, and heard the snap of breaking bone and a grunt of pain. He danced back to avoid another knife, slipped on a pool of blood, and righted himself with a flip in midair before he went down.

Another attacker seized upon his disadvantage and with a wild cry leapt at him. Thorne grabbed his wrist, wrenched the knife from his fingers, and did a round-house kick with his bad leg to the guy's head. Boot met cranium with a sound like an exploding watermelon. The guy dropped.

So his leg *was* good for something. Good to know.

Fatty was back and sucker-punched him in that nano-second's distraction. Thorne's breath went out in an agonized rush of air. But he'd been hit worse, and he repelled Fatty's buddy, Robes, by slamming his palm into the bridge of the guy's nose where there was bone, not soft cartilage. The crunch was satisfying, but he didn't have time to admire his handiwork. They kept coming, more and more of them, like thugs out of a clown car. One down, two more entered the fray.

Fuck. It was like fighting a goddamned mythical hydra. Cut off one bloody head and two more took its place. A second gut punch elicited a harsh exhale as Thorne staggered backward. Broken ribs, he was sure. No time to feel it. Striking out cobra-fast, he sliced the side of his palm into Fatty's windpipe. With a gurgle, the man tottered, clutching his throat as he dropped to his knees.

Robes came at him again. Thorne's philosophy was, if an opponent wasn't standing, he wasn't fighting. As Robes got close enough, Thorne grabbed the front of his loose garment, pulled him in, and at the same time stuck out his leg. The guy ran right into the obstacle, went down with a girly shriek, and lay on his belly panting.

Thorne let a short guy get close enough that he could smell the cigarette stink of his breath, Thorne's eyes watering at the man's powerful body odor. *Jesus.* He should kill the guy just for stinking. He hauled back and delivered a lower-rib shot, using the guy's own forward momentum to make the blow memorable. The man's gun went one way, the guy the other, but he managed to stagger back upright like a Weeble, then came back in, head lowered like a bull fixated on a red cape.

Thorne let him come, keeping the others in his peripheral vision. Stinky was in their way, so he had at least a couple of seconds to maneuver while their shots were blocked.

Stinky was breathing hard and ragged. Couldn't get his lungs filled. Thorne compounded his problem by pummeling his rib cage, specifically his vulnerable short ribs, until the man's breathing became even more labored.

Having sustained a similar beating from his friend Yermalof, Thorne knew how bad the guy hurt, and just how badly the guy's chest must be screaming for mercy every time he tried to drag in a breath. Grabbing a fistful of Stinky's thick, wiry hair, Thorne brought the guy's nose down sharply and his own knee up hard. The sound of crushed cartilage and bone was extremely satisfying.

Flinging him aside, he ground his foot down on the guy's wrist. A kick jettisoned the knife aside as it fell uselessly from the man's numb fingers. For good measure Thorne gave the man a little tap on the side of the head with the toe of his boot.

He heard the man behind him seconds before he felt the breeze of a blunt instrument skimming his ear. The blow struck hard to his shoulder, hard enough to drop him to one knee.

He was up fast, but in the intervening few seconds, there was a wild cry, and Isis launched herself out of the darkness to attach herself like a spider monkey to the guy's back. Arms and legs wrapped around the man's torso, she hung on for dear life as the man tried to unseat her.

Jesus. If it hadn't scared the crap out of him, Thorne would've laughed.

The man cursed colorfully in Arabic, whirling like a dervish with a determined woman clinging on his back, scoring her nails into the flesh of his face. She was trying to pull him off center with her weight. The man staggered and cursed, trying to pry her legs from around his waist, but she was determined and her ankles were dangerously locked together over his dick.

The diaphragm was a prime target, and Thorne made sure when he hit the guy there, he hit hard enough for every bit of air to leave the man's lungs. It had little impact.

"Off!" Thorne yelled at Isis. He saw her eyes glinting in the darkness, then she lifted one foot and slammed her heel down with unerring accuracy directly into the man's groin.

The injured man gave a bloodcurdling scream and doubled over to clutch his balls. Thorne's balls contracted with him. Isis was on her feet and several steps out of range when the man's eyes rolled back in his head and he was down.

"Good job. Let's get the hell out of here while the going's g—"

He shouldn't have been so goddamned self-satisfied,

because he felt a rush of air. There was someone he hadn't seen. The man rushed him, knife gripped as an extension of his arm.

"Grab my gun on the ground behind you!" he yelled to Isis. "Hell. *Any* fucking gun! *Move!*"

He and New Guy danced around in a circle, stepping over sprawled bodies as the knife wielder slashed. Thorne kept his distance while also maintaining his balance. He spun to block another attack on his flank, saw just in time Isis's wide eyes, and grabbed his weapon from her proffered hand. In one smooth continuous move, he turned the weapon on his attacker and fired.

The sound reverberated and echoed down the length of the tunnel. And then there was nothing left but pulsing silence.

Boom. Done. Only the adrenaline remained.

"You all right?" he demanded, crouching to feel for Stinky's and Robes's pulses at the same time. Both out, and unfortunately alive, as Isis walked around each man doing God only knew what, bending to pick things up off the floor.

"To say I'm more scared than I've ever been in my life is an understatement," Isis snapped, voice shaking. Thorne heard the shimmer of anger there, too. She was holding it together, but he suspected that wasn't going to last.

"Here, do something with these."

These were three guns and a heavy wooden object meant to splatter his brains on the walls. Thorne took the weapons and stuck them in his belt.

"Let's not stick around to ask questions."

"Or call an ambulance?"

"Or call an ambulance," he repeated dryly. The underpass had stunk before——now with various new body fluids leaking all over the place it was no wonder Isis had her palm over her face. Thorne slid his arm around her waist and propelled her from the tunnel at a trot.

They emerged into the street, where there were lights and people. Still, he kept his eyes peeled for more trouble as they sprinted toward the mosque, where he knew they'd find a taxi, even at this time of night. "How you holding up?" Adrenaline was leaking out of him, and he was aware of the agonizing pain in his thigh, the sharp sting of the deep cut on his arm, and the bruising ache of broken ribs.

"Oh, I've never been better," she assured him, sarcasm thick in her voice. Her eyes looked dark and huge in her pale face. Snapping open her camera case, she removed her glasses and shoved them with some force onto her face. She was filthy, but he didn't see any blood on her. Her respiration was erratic, and a pulse throbbed hard at the base of her throat. She turned her head to give him a hard look. "We'll be arrested when people see you covered in blood like this."

"Trust me, no one will even blink." He kept to the shadows of a stand of trees looking for a cab. Looking for more trouble. He'd look for answers later.

"Hang on . . ." She rummaged in her bag, which somehow hadn't been dislodged from her shoulder despite her recent activities. Isis handed him a wad of tissues and a tiny bottle of hand sanitizer, shoving them into his chest. "Here. Do the best you can. I can't afford to bail either of us out of jail right now."

Thorne cleaned up as best he could, the alcohol in the sanitizer providing a bracing sting in his cuts and abrasions as he scanned the vehicles passing and weighed their options.

How had Yermalof found him?

More important, did Yermalof know about Isis? Or had his men just been instructed to take *him* out? Were they even Yermalof's men, or had they been followed from the airport by opportunistic thieves?

He spotted a cab and stepped out of the shadows to wave it down. After stuffing Isis inside, he got in, too, slamming the door and giving the driver the name of their hotel.

Thorne kept watch in the rearview mirror as the cab pulled into the street. He considered if the attack had really been ordered by Yermalof.

"What . . ."

He shook his head. Not in the cab, and not until he had some definitive answers. She nodded a silent agreement. Smart girl. A chill cooled the sweat on his skin.

This hadn't been a random group effort. He'd been followed from the airport. Followed from London? Boris Yermalof had friends in low places all over the world. Especially here in Cairo.

Thorne knew going to London might reactivate Yermalof's directive. Now he knew. Fucking hell.

What the hell was he going to do with Isis?

"We landed less than an hour before the accident. Since I'm not stupid enough to believe that everything we've just gone through could be *random*, who could possibly know we're here?" Apparently she could only hold her silence for thirty seconds.

He slid the glass partition shut between the driver and themselves and lowered his voice. "The van that hit us followed us from the airport. They knew we were coming in on the flight." His tone was grim, and his eyes constantly flickered from the rearview mirror to the side mirror and back again.

Something struck him as off. Yermalof was nothing if not chillingly efficient. Sending that many men to rough him up wasn't the sort of message Thorne expected his archenemy to deliver. Good old Boris was a direct man and liked to inflict maximum pain. Personally. He'd waited eight months to come out of the shadows? He held one hell of a grudge, and the truth of the matter was, the *Russian* had won the last round.

Those guys, while fairly adept, hadn't been as skilled as Yermalof's usual men. Thorne would either be dead or back in the Russian's clutches if that were the case. The thought brought bile to his throat.

"How long till we get to the hotel?" Isis demanded tightly, eyes glittering. She looked a little green and swallowed convulsively. The adrenaline was definitely wearing off.

"Ten minutes. Are you going to puke?"

"Probably," she said in a small voice. "Don't worry, I'll try and wait until I get to my room."

She didn't make it.

WRAPPED IN A HOTEL robe, Isis opened the door on the second knock. "Sorry about that," she said immediately on seeing Thorne standing there. He'd obviously showered, too, and he was wearing clean clothes. The black T-shirt stretched across his broad shoulders and skimmed his flat abs. Black jeans, and even new shoes.

He'd been busy *shopping* while she'd huddled naked on the edge of the bathtub, fingers shaking so bad she couldn't turn the faucet. Residual tremors still shook her frame. Nauseous and in shock, she'd forced herself to stand under the jets until her stomach settled and she could hold on to the soap.

Clean, but naked beneath the robe, she eyed her ruined clothing heaped on the floor beside the bed, and her camera bag on top of the comforter. The only not-sucky thing to come from the evening was that her three-thousand-dollar camera had survived the running and mayhem unscathed. *That* she could not afford to replace. It was a miracle her camera made it through, which mattered more than a pair of jeans and a shirt. She pressed her hand to her belly.

There was always a first time for her iron stomach to let her down. Violence and death apparently was her sticking point.

Thorne filled the door frame, solid. She felt like a wet

noodle. "How are you feeling?" she asked, studying his stoic face for clues.

"Fine." He finger-combed his damp hair back off his forehead. Just another day in the life of Connor James Thorne.

She tightened the belt around her waist, conscious of the rasp of the terry cloth against her naked breasts. "Nice clothes."

"I brought some for you." He lifted the shopping bag at his side. Just when she thought he was an insensitive male, he redeemed himself and then some.

"Thanks. I couldn't put those on." She indicated the general direction of the mound on the floor behind her and stood back, allowing him room to enter. Tempted to fall into his arms and borrow his strength, Isis curled her bare toes into the short nap of the carpet instead. "I've never been up close and personal to that kind of violence before. It's different on TV." She was sure she'd hear fists against bone and see pools of blood in dark alleys in her nightmares for the rest of her natural life.

He paused, as if he wanted to say something but then changed his mind. "You look better," he observed, his gaze inspecting her from her wet hair to her toenails. "Color in your cheeks."

"Sorry if I embarrassed you." She wasn't really, but thought it was a polite way to open the conversation. She had so many questions, her mind was going a mile a minute. Luckily, when she'd been violently sick on the floor of the cab, she'd missed him, but only by a hair. The cabdriver had been vocally furious, but she'd been too sick to be embarrassed. Too terrified to care.

"You didn't," he told her shortly, his limp more pronounced as he moved a few steps inside and closed the door behind him. Isis was acutely aware of his sex appeal and of the bed taking up most of the room behind her. He lobbed the shopping bag onto the foot of the bed from where he stood, without even looking. "As for the driver—a hundred American could buy him a new car. Don't worry about it."

Since he wasn't moving farther into the room, she didn't, either, but the narrow opening between the bathroom door and mirrored closet was forcing her to stand closer to him than she felt comfortable with and gave her a fantastic view of his backside. Isis was confused and disgusted with herself. Men had *died*. How could she be even remotely aware of Thorne's body, his very alive body, when things could've fallen apart so easily? He could have died. *She* could have died. And what the hell was going to happen when the authorities discovered the bodies in the underpass?

"First thing in the morning, we have to report both the accident and the men who attacked us, and see if anyone retrieved our luggage from the cab."

Not that she was looking forward to reliving their experience, nor going to the local authorities, who could just as easily accuse them of both crimes. They hadn't shown any concern for her father when they'd found him wandering the desert alone and injured. In fact, at first they'd accused him of murdering his crew himself. Isis shuddered and rubbed her upper arms, more for comfort than warmth.

"Already done."

How long had she been in the shower? She locked gazes with him. "You should've told me. I would've gone with you." And hated every second of it, but she should've been with him. She at least owed him the courtesy of standing beside him since he'd gotten her through the incident alive. "What time do we have to go in for questioning?"

"We don't. It's all squared away."

She gave him a narrow-eyed look. Moves like that took bribes. Expensive bribes. "Thorne, I can't afford baksheesh. I told you, I'm doing this on a shoestring—"

"You didn't mention that, actually," he pointed out dryly. "But don't worry about it. I assure you, it's taken care of. I know people."

Isis bit back a sharp reply. He'd saved her life tonight, and his leg must be killing him. Maybe his royal lineage got him places she couldn't go, like the museum. She blew out a breath, determined to be fair. "Your networking skills are impressive. Remember that I hired you, and that I'm responsible for expenses, okay?"

Heavy bribes—baksheesh—were the cost of doing business here. Everyone expected them, especially the authorities. They weren't in her budget.

"I told you not to worry." He stared at her as if that was all that needed to be said.

She lifted her chin in defiance. Okay, *three times* was enough. She needed to reestablish the ground rules.

"Seriously? You work for me. I think we'd better establish who's the boss, and who signs your paycheck." Isis dropped the finger she'd pointed at him and stuck her hand in her pocket. Anger was good. Healthy. Much better than finding his arrogance sexy.

"*Zak Stark* signs my paycheck, and while we're here, *I'm* the boss. If you don't like it, feel free to hie your pert arse back to Seattle and wait for my report." His British accent became more clipped and pronounced and she got the feeling he'd prefer it if she left.

"You can be such an ass." She said it without rancor. He was who he was. And it was clear he wasn't going to change his tune just because . . . what? She was Isis Magee? A paying client? Her lips almost twitched as she realized she was giving herself a pep talk. *Right?!*

"So I've been told." He stuck his fingertips in his front pockets. Loose, but controlled. "We have no idea who those men were, or if they'll come after us again."

"The ones you left alive and still able to walk, you mean?" she demanded, matching his sarcasm. She refused to believe the police had let him get away with murder. Even if it had been warranted. There was more to Connor Thorne than met the eye. She had to stop letting his appeal distract her.

"Yes, those. And whatever friends and relatives they want to cut in on the deal."

Reality check, Isis Cleopatra. She fell back against the bathroom doorjamb with a thump. "You *don't* think it was random, do you?" Oh, God. She'd been hoping her suspicions were wrong. It was hard to maintain her anger at him, even when he deserved it, when she had withheld what might be relevant information. Now who was the ass?

"Thorne—I— Those men— The accident. The ambush. I think they might be the same men who attacked my father. I'm sorry. I had no idea I'd be bringing you into danger. Not that you weren't amazing at defending us. But now that you're in danger I think you should go back to London, or Seattle. I don't want you to get hurt because of me."

He raised a dark brow that spoke volumes.

Her cheeks heated. She didn't want him to go. But she had no right to ask him to stay. He could've been killed tonight. She could've been killed tonight. She walked farther into the room, but he didn't follow her, so she went back to where he stood reflected in the mirrored doors of the closet. One Connor Thorne was enough for any woman. Two was overkill.

She stuck her hands in the deep pockets of the robe and forced herself to maintain eye contact. Confessions sucked, especially when she was the one in the wrong. "I think those men might have been after me. You were in the way, which is why you took the brunt of the attack." Guilt gave her a pain in her midsection as she considered what happened from this point of view. Not random. Deliberate. Her fault.

Isis saw her too-big eyes, huge in in her pale face, reflected beside him. Her wet hair was slicked back off her face and moisture dribbled down her throat, tickling her skin. Thorne said nothing. He towered over her petite frame, and even though he was only a foot or so taller, he was big, broad, and incredibly masculine.

"My father didn't make up his attack—I think even you have to believe that after tonight." Not an ounce of empathy was evident on Thorne's face as she spoke. "I'm not going to let a bunch of thugs scare me off. I'll hire some bodyguards. Tonight's events convince me more than ever that my father found Cleo's tomb—" She sucked a painful breath into her aching chest.

God. What a mess. What a scary, insane mess.

"Someone wants to discredit him. And now I think those men knew I was here to find it—"

"Before you confess to masterminding the entire attack yourself"—he paused and sent her a look verging on kind—"this is Cairo. It's possible the attackers followed two rich Europeans from the airport with the express intention of robbing us."

"What thieves would go to that much trouble to attack two tourists? I'm not dripping in diamonds, and you . . ." She waved her hand at his nice but not too nice black-on-black ensemble. She stumbled over her words and caught herself from calling him gorgeous out loud. "Or, we could be close to uncovering a clue to the whereabouts of the tomb, and those people were sent to stop us," Isis insisted stubbornly, distracted by the path his eyes were taking as he followed a drop of water that trickled from her hair down her throat.

"Stop us from—*what* exactly?" He put his hand on the door handle and gave her a politely inquiring look that held a trace of heat. "Arriving at the airport and taking a quick drive through the souk?"

She cinched the belt around her waist and wished she'd ignored her repugnance to re-dress in the bathroom. Even though she was decently covered from throat to ankles, *she* knew that *he* knew she was naked underneath.

"My father was well-known here. At one point his reputation was unimpeachable. People know the name Magee. Many people in antiquities know me, or at least my name. Maybe they've been watching the airport to see if my father came back. You have to at least entertain the idea that we're on to something, and those men may have tried to stop us from getting close to the tomb."

"I'll add the info to my list." Thorne's gaze was fixed on her mouth.

Was he actually listening to her, or just looking? The terry cloth abraded her nipples as she shifted. "You have a *list?*" He was sex on a stick, Isis thought, annoyed with herself. It was impossible to concentrate on what was important when her body was hyperaware of him all the time. She wished there was an off switch for a few hours so she could think straight. "What kind of list?"

His warm hand slid under her hair and his fingers closed around her nape without him seeming to have stepped closer. She certainly didn't step back.

"I never rule anything out."

Her vision blurred, her insides melting as his thumb lightly caressed the base of her skull. It wasn't that she didn't want Thorne to kiss her—God only knew she did, and badly. "About these men—"

"Don't want to talk about them right now."

"Then about my father—"

"Definitely don't want to discuss him now, either."

"But—"

He brushed his other thumb over her lower lip, effectively boxing her in. Her lips throbbed with anticipation. She sighed as he took her mouth in a deep, slow kiss that mated their tongues in a slick, hot dance.

Isis liked to have the upper hand, and he was taking that away with his persuasive, marauding lips. When she was in control, she could stop. Not easily, but she could. When he took that away from her, she was helpless to resist. He was taking the balance of power from her, and she shouldn't like it. Shouldn't want it—but God help her, she did.

She opened her eyes to see the darker outer ring of green around his irises. *Abandon hope all ye who enter here.* Isis broke the lip-lock and had to clear her throat before she managed to say, "This isn't very professional." It sounded a whole lot more breathless and inviting than she intended.

His hand slid down her back and around her waist and he drew her up on her toes with his palm on her back. "Not in any way, shape, or form," he admitted with a breath from her lips. The penetrating green eyes saw right through her bravado, saw right down to the part of her that was naked, willing, and wanton. It would be foolish to claim she didn't want him when her desire for him was evident in every atom of her body.

He brushed her lips with his and murmured, "You should lodge a complaint."

"You don't *listen* to complaints." Isis slid her palms up his chest, feeling the tensile strength of solid muscle. She bracketed his face with both hands as he angled his head, pulled her in tighter, then parted her lips with his tongue. His jaw was rough, he hadn't shaved, his skin was warm, his mouth decadently pliable. Stroking his cheeks with her thumbs, she hummed her pleasure as she ran her stiffened tongue over the roof of his mouth.

Thorne shuddered. She let her tongue soften, slinking over his to prowl along the hard edge of his teeth. His fingers tightened on her back.

He was a Master Kisser. And Lord help her, Isis was a woman who loved kissing. But he took it to a whole new level, to uncharted reaches. She loved the slip and slide of meshing tongues, and the firmness of smooth lips. She loved the heat, and the textures. She loved hurtling into the unknown. For her, a kiss wasn't necessarily the endgame or a prelude to bigger and better things. A kiss was its own entity, to be savored and enjoyed while it lasted.

A hot, trembling need swept through her body, filling every cell with want. They'd fight for supremacy—later. For now she sank into the kiss and enjoyed every moment of it. He tasted of whisky, smoky and powerful, but more profoundly, he tasted achingly, wonderfully *familiar.*

By the time their lips parted, they were both breathless. Isis dropped her head to his chest as she waited out her crazy heartbeat and breathlessness. Her lips buzzed deliciously. "Wow. That was . . ."

"Yeah." His breath blew hot on the crown of her head.

Isis stepped out of his arms and smiled up at him through a haze of lust. She had to clear her head. "I'll get dressed. Thank you for bringing me— What did you bring me?" Her body hummed.

"Something to wear tomorrow."

"Was the boutique open? What time is it?" Well after midnight.

"The hotel staff opened the shop for me briefly so you would have something to wear. You can choose what you like in the morning."

Like any woman, Isis loved new clothes, but her thrifty side insisted they might get their luggage back, and if not, then she wasn't willing to pay the exorbitant prices at the upscale hotel boutique. "Not at those prices I won't."

"Don't worry about it. I'll pay."

"No, thank you. I'll pay my own expenses. And would you please stop telling me not to worry?"

His chest rose and fell and her fingers ached to touch him. "There isn't a snowball's chance in hell of ever seeing those suitcases again. Probably stolen before we came to a full stop after the accident. Fortunately I had our papers and passports on me."

Isis stared at his lips as he spoke. She was mesmerized. How could a man so controlled kiss like a bohemian? It was great news, but it still wasn't an answer. "And a gun, apparently." She gave him an even look. "How did you manage to get *that* through customs?"

"I have a permit."

Connections and money—a life much different from hers.

"I know some little shops in the souk. When we go to see Beniti, I'll take a quick detour to find something suitable." And cheap. "I can't believe this." Isis put her hand to her belly. "I think I'm actually hungry."

"Get dressed." He jerked his chin toward the bathroom. "The dining room is open for another half hour." Hot green eyes held hers. "Unless you'd rather stay in and order room service?"

∝ SIX ∾

The Israelis were just as eager as Thorne and MI5 to capture and prosecute the Russian tomb raider who for more than a decade had been stealing priceless antiquities and spiriting them out of Egypt and Israel to sell on the black market.

Thorne's arrival in London must've alerted Yermalof's people to his return from the dead.

Thirteen months earlier, Thorne and fellow MI5 operatives Lynn Maciej and Troy Ayers had followed Boris Yermalof's trail through Cairo into Israel. It was on Israeli soil that the kidnapping of Maciej had occurred. Seven members of the Mossad were killed in the resulting bloodbath that night.

With the aid of the Israelis, Thorne and Ayers tracked Yermalof to an oasis just outside Cairo where he was holding their female partner. What the sick fuck had done to her still turned Thorne's iron stomach. He'd seen a lot in his job, but that . . .

The Russian had extracted his pound of flesh for their audacity in hunting him down like a dog. Not to mention the sales he'd lost due to MI5's months-long, relentless pursuit.

He'd committed atrocities on Maciej before Thorne and Ayers had arrived. The trap had slammed shut behind them. Gut shot, Thorne had been incapable of defending himself—although God only knows he'd tried. The bastard used his knife to slice him from knee to balls. Thorne's stomach roiled. Experienced enough to know just how much pain to inflict and still keep a man alive, the Russian had kept them all in excruciating pain for hours. Yermalof enjoyed his work and had made it last. When he thought he'd ensured Thorne would die from blood loss, he'd turned to work on Ayers.

Bleeding like a sieve, Thorne had hung on to consciousness by a thread as he watched, through dazed, slitted eyes, the excruciating deaths of his partners. The memory of their screams, pleading with Yermalof to put an end to their agony, still fucked with his ability to sleep through the night. The Russian had laughed as he strolled out of the stifling warehouse, believing them all dead.

Three Mossad operatives had hauled Thorne's arse out of there and carried him miles to medical help, then evaced him to a hospital in Tel Aviv before he was shipped back to London.

He'd put in a call to his field officer at Thames House in the early hours of this morning to read them in. MI5 was willing to step in *if* the connection to Yermalof was confirmed.

Suspected, not confirmed.

Thorne considered Isis's confession that the incidents the day before had something to do with her father. Maybe. But most likely not. As far as he knew, no one was aware that she was in Egypt.

No. Yermalof had clearly followed him from London. Now he knew he had to get Isis back to Seattle with a minimum of fuss.

He was reminded by MI5 that he still had months left on his medical leave of absence, and that Yermalof had last been seen with his mistress across the globe in Argentina. In other words, basically, "Fuck you for your years of service to Her Majesty the Queen."

With a second call to friends in high places, Thorne had procured a car and some extra muscle. Accompanying the armor-plated, bulletproof-glassed, four-wheel-drive vehicle was a well-armed Mossad driver. Both waited outside the hotel for them that morning. Doug Heustis, a big guy with white hair who looked like someone's kindly grandfather, didn't warrant a second look. But Thorne knew his sharp eyes missed nothing. A good man to have at his back. Professional.

"What happened?" Thorne asked him after a firm handshake. "You get demoted?" Heustis had been one of the men who'd hauled Thorne to safety the last time he'd been here. The man was instrumental in saving his life. If there was anyone Thorne owed a debt of gratitude, it was this man.

Heustis opened the door for Isis, then shut it to walk around the front of the vehicle with Thorne. "Drew the short straw for babysitting duty, Thorne. You can't seem to keep your butt out of trouble."

"It's a skill," Thorne said as he opened the back door. "Keep your eyes and ears open. We seem to have gained a fan club."

"Will do."

It was nine in the morning, and already heat shimmered on the streets and made the air thick enough to chew. Isis, wearing a new eye-popping orange T-shirt and loose-fitting white cotton pants, turned in her seat to look at him. Her glasses, as usual, were smudged.

"You owe me seventeen more answers," she told him, as Heustis drove them to the souk without further comment. Oblivious to where Thorne's thoughts were, she wanted to take responsibility for something that had nothing to do with her. But if he told her that neither she nor her father had anything to do with this, he'd have to tell her about the Russian.

She was scared enough as it was.

No. He'd make up some bullshit story, put her on a plane bound stateside, and hunt down Yermalof like the demented bastard that he was.

He used both hands to remove her glasses by the earpieces, then she waited, a smile curving her lips, for him to clean them on the hem of her shirt. Lifting the soft cotton exposed a smile of pale skin and her belly button. Thorne wanted to kiss her right there. Hell's bells, he wanted to kiss her all over. He handed her back the clean glasses, drunk on cinnamon.

"If you stop *touching* them," he admonished with more

annoyance than the act warranted, "you wouldn't have fingerprints blurring your vision."

"Thanks." Sliding them back on, she managed to leave a thumbprint right in her field of vision. "I'll make a note of that. Although *that* wasn't an answer."

Last night over a late-night dinner he'd answered the questions he wanted to and evaded the rest. Isis was determined.

He was motivated to keep the truth to himself. Isis's concern gave him a convenient excuse to hire a driver/guard. While she was busy confessing to a nonexistent crime, he had to protect them both from Yermalof.

Thorne was good, damned good at what he did, but even he wouldn't be able to fend off a half-dozen professional assassins if that's who they decided to send next. Not with his leg, not with Isis with him. Taking on a gang of cutthroats worked in movies, but real life didn't have a director to yell cut, or a stunt double to take the bullet. If the attack *had* been instigated by Yermalof, screw Thorne's ego. He'd take all the backup required to protect Isis until he saw her safely on a plane.

He had feelers out to see if Yermalof was anywhere near Cairo. Yermalof or one of his unsavory friends. If such was the case, he'd lead the son of a bitch as far away from Egypt and Isis's business as possible.

"How do you feel about marriage?"

That came out of left field. He was pretty sure she wasn't proposing marriage on such short acquaintance. "I have no feelings for it one way or another. In the short term, it's a fine institution. For some."

She twisted in her seat to face him, causing the seat belt to divide her breasts, which drew Thorne's attention somewhere he didn't want to look. "Not for you?"

He thought of his father, an emotionally cold, granite statue determined to master his universe, and his mother, calm and blank when medicated either by booze or pills. Certainly he was destined to bow to the same genetic coding. Few marriages, if any, could survive that. He changed his depth perception so she was slightly out of focus. "No."

She cocked her head. "What if you meet the perfect woman for you?"

There was a snort from the front seat.

"My dear," Thorne told her coolly, "there are hundreds of women perfect for me. If I married them all I'd be a polygamist. I have yet to see a marriage that endures. It's an antiquated institution that leaves financial ruin in its wake, or two very unhappy people who 'stay together for the children.' I don't like failing at anything, and I'm not stupid enough to go into something where there's a disproportionate chance that I'll fail."

"That's because you're a salesman."

He blinked her back into focus. "A sales—why on earth would you say that?"

"Because you aren't the type of man who'd come home from work every night. You'd be off on some perceived adventure, and forget you even *had* a wife."

"Probably. All the more reason not to get something I'd be so careless with. I suppose you hanker for marriage, a white picket fence, kids, and a minivan?"

"I *do* want to get married. Sooner rather than later. I like the idea of a sweet little house somewhere in the burbs, and a husband who comes home to me every night. Call me sentimental and old-fashioned, but that's what I want. I enjoy my job as a photographer. Quite a lot, actually. But it isn't a career, and I can't make money taking pictures of cloud formations or sunlight on a snapdragon petal. I get my creative yaya, but those images don't pay the rent."

"So you want to marry for financial security, then?"

"I want a man who considers motherhood a full-time job, which it is. I'd work until the children came along, then I want to be a stay-at-home mom. I spent most of my life traveling between my aunt and my father, living in a cramped apartment or a tent. I want roots. Stability. To spend the rest of my life with someone I love, someone who loves me. I'd like to have three children—two boys and a girl, or the other way around. I'm dying to make school lunches and belong to the PTA. I can't wait to drive my daughter to soccer practice and my sons to dance classes, or vice versa."

His lips twitched, because she'd barely taken a breath in that litany of wants. It was good to want things. Better not to expect them. "If you're so gung ho about marriage, then why are you still single?"

"Because I've had two lovers, and I sincerely believed each to be the one. But it turned out that both were the ones *before* the one."

"What's the point? The next can just as easily be yet another one before the one."

"Maybe. I might not have a great track record, but I'm willing to keep trying."

"I'm not opposed to you trying with me until you find that elusive *one*."

"That's very kind of you, but I'll pass," she told him cheerfully, eliciting a muffled cough from their driver. "My future husband is out there. We just have to find each other."

"I hope for your sake you stumble across this paragon, and he gives you everything you think you want." Oddly, the thought annoyed the hell out of him, although Thorne couldn't for the life of him figure out why. She was a free agent. None of his business beyond him doing the job he was hired to do. She could trot off and marry whomever she bloody well pleased, and good luck to her.

"So do I," she told him, sounding like she meant it.

And probably regret it after the honeymoon period was over, he thought sourly, grateful to see that they'd arrived at the parking lot behind the mosque.

"Park over there; we'll walk it." Thorne ignored the ache in his leg, as well as his client's chirpy confession about true love, puppy dogs, and fucking rainbows somewhere over a suburban soccer field. He was grateful all around for the reminders to be cautious.

Heustis parked the black sedan under a tree and popped the doors.

Thorne slid out after Isis, so she was sandwiched between the two men. The driver fell back a few feet. Isis moved closer to Thorne as they entered the underpass. It looked different during the day—not better, just different. At night he'd only smelled the filth; now he could see it.

Once again she was wearing her camera bag bandolier-style, slung across her body, the strap bisecting her breasts. The brown leather saddlebag, about the size of a small loaf of bread, bounced on her hip.

"Want me to carry that for you?"

"No, I'm good, thanks. I never let this baby out of my sight. And thank God I *don't*, because after yesterday's drama, I'd be out three grand, with no recourse." She nudged his arm with her shoulder. "Why's the driver following us?" she stage-whispered, taking a double step to match Thorne's stride, then slipping her hand into the crook of his arm as if she had every right to do so. At least his gun hand was free.

"He wants to buy an area rug for his kitchen."

Isis laughed and squeezed his arm against the soft swell of her breast. Honest to God, the woman was a menace.

"Now you owe me eighteen answers," she told him cheerfully. "You can't avoid paying up forever, you know."

Avoidance was his middle name. Thorne merely gave her a dour look, which she answered with a smile. God, she had a pretty smile. And God help him, he liked the taste of it, too. The woman was tying him in knots with apparently little effort.

He faced forward and concentrated on not limping. He was man enough to know he needed to buy another cane.

The only sign of what had transpired the night before

was a large stain on the cement, which could be anything from chocolate ice cream to someone's spilled brains. He guided Isis around the dried blood and hastened their steps. "Tell me about Beniti al-Atrash."

"My father's known him for more than thirty years," she told him, willing to be distracted from her interrogation at least for a little while. "He has a stall and also a small shop, which back against one another: one high-end, the other touristy trash. He sells carpets and small antiquities." She sent him a sideways laughing glance. "Some genuine, most imitation knockoffs *pretending* to be genuine. He's been at the same intersection for as long as I can remember. His son Husani and I had a thing one summer many years ago." Her smile was sweetly wistful. "He's married now with two sons."

"A thing?"

"Oh, a hot romance. He was an older man—fifteen to my thirteen. It was a magical time. Husani taught me the fine art of kissing."

Thorne didn't want to hear about a "magical time," even if she'd been a kid. The kissing part he appreciated. "Remind me to thank him if I see him."

"He works for his father, so you'll probably meet him. God, I love this place." She spread her arms, inhaling deeply. "I smell citrus, and hundreds of spices, and leather. Do you like the smell of leather?"

"Only if it's used in bondage." He shot her a glance and smiled when her cheeks flushed. "No? Don't knock it till you've tried it." Inhaling, he picked up a noseful of body odor, piss, and strong Egyptian cigarettes. She lifted the camera from around her neck and paused to take a series of shots of a cat sprawled on a blanket in a fruit stall. Totally unhygienic.

He wanted to take her to meet her friend, see if they could find a clue to Cleopatra's damned tomb, then take her to the airport. He'd assure her he'd stay behind to look. Look for the Russian. What she didn't know wouldn't hurt her, and her father didn't know what he'd had for breakfast that morning, so he wouldn't be affected by her not finding the tomb one way or another.

She passed to cast him a curious look. "What's the matter?"

"We don't have time to take pictures."

"Go ahead, I'll catch up with you." She made some minute adjustment to the expensive camera.

Thorne kept his eyes moving, looking at faces in the milling crowd, watching body language, when he'd much rather be watching her. "We'll wait. Make it snappy."

She grinned, the camera to her face. "Punny." Looking through the viewfinder, she twisted the lens. "God—the sun's wrapping his whiskers perfectly . . ." Holding her breath, she squeezed off a series of shots, then moved a few feet to the left. "Just *look* at the colors." She deftly manipulated the camera to get what she wanted. "The oranges and the ginger cat are beautiful. Look how relaxed he is exposing his fat belly to the sun and how his coat and the fruit bring out the rich purple of the blanket."

He looked at it again. Cat. Oranges. Blanket. He still didn't get it. "You're an artist." Thorne watched her frame the next shot. How odd, he thought, watching the harsh sunlight tangle in her dark hair and bathe her pale skin with warmth. Listening to her, one could assume she worked with her father and had no other life. They'd spent every moment of the past several days in each other's company, they'd kissed, and yet he had no idea that her photography was a job as well as a passion. He realized he had no idea what she did when she wasn't hunting clues to a nonexistent tomb and taking photographs of products for ad campaigns.

"I didn't have the stomach for premed to become a proctologist," she said with a grin, showing her crooked eyeteeth and dancing lights in her big brown eyes as she secured her camera in the small bag on her hip. "There's Beniti's stall; come on." Grabbing his hand, she pulled him along. Thorne had never met a woman so touchy-feely. Isis Magee was vibrant and full of life. She woke his dulled senses when he was fairly certain he liked them just the way they were.

A tall man, wearing loose-fitting dark pants and an olive drab T-shirt, stood with his back to them. Isis went up behind him and wrapped her arms around the man's waist. *"Sabah el-kheir,* Uncle."

The man turned swiftly, anger written all over his face. The guy was barely a few inches over her five four, and to Thorne's eye, supremely unattractive, with a pronounced nose and black eyes. He couldn't be more than thirty. The moment he saw who'd grabbed him, his expression lightened, but he took Isis firmly by her upper arm and hissed. "Isis, little bird, what are you doing here?"

"I came to see your—"

"Come with me." He propelled her in front of him and Thorne's pulse jumped a notch.

She turned to look over her shoulder. "I'm with a friend—"

The man's black eyes sized up Thorne as he asked Isis, "You trust this man?"

"Trust him—of course."

"Then come. Both of you. *Quickly.*"

Thorne indicated to Heustis to wait outside and stay alert. The warning was unnecessary.

The guy, clearly not the older man he'd expected, was holding Isis's arm in a death grip, and she practically had to run to keep up with him. Thorne followed hard on her heels, right behind her through the densely crowded shop filled with small carpets and a hundred statues of cats, pyramids, and sphinxes.

They reached a dimly lit back room. No sunlight reached this far inside, and the small space was hung with carpets and bolts of cloth. The oppressive heat wasn't helped by the brass brazier with a pot of *shay bi na'na* in the middle of the room. The strong smell of the mint tea permeated the humid air.

"Husani al-Atrash, this is Connor Thorne. He's helping m—"

"Today is a day for visitors from the past." The urgency left Husani's voice as he gave Isis an inquiring look. Thorne read tension in the guy's body language and rested his hand on the Glock in the small of his back under his black T-shirt.

"What can I do for you, little bird?"

"I actually came to see your father."

While wondering who the other visitor had been, Thorne looked for exits. There were several. Possible weapons were all over the place, not to mention Isis's being in too close proximity to the man who'd taught her to kiss like a favorite royal concubine. Six feet. Casually he stepped between them as he looked around. For all he knew the guy was going for a fucking weapon.

"He was attacked in his home early this morning." Husani started moving small closed baskets from a large pile in the far corner. He turned to glance from Isis to Thorne, then went back to his housekeeping. "He is now in the hospital."

Isis blanched. "Oh no! Is he all right?"

"Like the professor, my father, too, has a hard head." He turned with a small smile that didn't reach his eyes. "Concussion, scrapes, and bruises. They're keeping him for observation."

"Which hospital? I'll go and see him."

"Kasr El Aini, in Garden City—I am sorry to tell you that we believe the attack had something to do with Professor Magee."

Isis leaned against a waist-high pile of carpets, then took a deep breath as she met Thorne's eyes. *See?* her eyes telegraphed. *It* was *about my father.* She looked back at her friend. "Why do you say that?"

"Two men came yesterday asking for a papyrus for Cleopatra's tomb."

"There was a *papyrus*?" Isis's brows lifted. If there really was such a thing it would be all that was needed to prove her father's claim.

"Not that I know of. But we have not heard this name since the professor's accident in the spring. Then my father's attack in his home. Two men asked when last my father had communications with the professor. It has been months since your father was here last."

"He's in a . . . He has Alzheimer's. He doesn't remember what happened that night at the tomb."

Husani frowned, stroking his bearded chin. "Your arrival has apparently set off an unfortunate chain of events, little sister. Cairo is not safe for you."

"We were attacked last night when I came here to see your father. Husani, do *you* know where the Queen's tomb is?"

He shook his head and started moving the baskets with more gusto. "I do not. But then you know how much your father favored puzzles. Especially since the community didn't believe his wild claims."

"Do you believe he found her tomb?"

He paused and glanced at Isis over his shoulder. "I believe that my father, a man who has never lied to me, believes this is so."

"Do you know where it is?" she asked again.

"I do not, nor does my father. But you must leave Cairo, Isis. These men are dangerous."

Thorne opened the camera bag and took out the small black notebook. "Does this look familiar?" He held it for the other man to see.

"Yes. We sell them here at my stall. The professor purchased many to jot down notes. Is this one of his?"

"Not sure," Thorne prevaricated. He didn't trust anyone.

The Egyptian met his eyes and merely gave a small nod before turning to Isis.

"Your father left two items with my father for safekeeping. Here."

"Thank God." Isis breathed deeply, then held out her hand. "We were hoping he'd left a clue of some kind. What's this?" she asked as the other man laid a length of wood across her palm.

"It's a broken piece of a walking stick. Don't ask me the significance, for I do not know."

"Seriously?" Isis took the carved stick and handed it to Thorne. "Not only is it broken, but a walking stick like this is mass-produced and sold at a hundred stalls here alone." Frustration laced her words.

Thorne took it, hoping she wasn't about to burst into tears. "The stick and carvings are machine made, probably in China. Nothing special about it that I can see."

She looked hopeful. "Maybe it's hollow and he's written me a nice letter explaining everything."

Thorne twisted and inspected. "Not hollow."

"Husani, what do the glyphs say?"

"A poem for long life and prosperity."

"Of little value?"

"Of no value at all, I'm sorry to say, little bird. It makes no sense to me, either, but my father informs me that the professor was very specific that he hold this, and the box, until he returned and to give them to no one else."

She held it out to Thorne. "Can you get anything from this?"

"Bought somewhere close by. I don't see any significance."

Isis blew out a breath and handed it back to her friend. "Would you mind if I leave it here with you? I have no way to carry it safely, and I don't want to lose it. Obviously it has some sentimental value for my father. I'll take it back to Seattle. Maybe seeing it will jog his memory." She paused. "What box?"

He handed her a small boxy reed basket about the size of her palm, crisscrossed with a length of grubby ribbon. An equally dirty white business-sized card was tied on top. Thorne reached over to pinch the paper between his fingers, acknowledged the stream of GPS numbers suddenly running through his head, and flipped over the card so both he and Isis could see the *tyet*, the hieroglyph knot hastily sketched on one side. He turned the card. The other side was blank.

Isis carefully untied the thin ribbon, stuffing it in her camera bag absently so she could lift the lid. The bright light in her eyes dulled. Inside was a ratty silk tassel, the kind that could be found on millions of Turkish rugs worldwide.

"Damn it, Daddy," she muttered under her breath, her disappointment evident from the slump of her shoulders. "Couldn't you just write me a note like a freaking normal person?"

"DYLAN CAME TO SEE me this morning as well," Husani told Isis with a frown on his smooth features as he handed her a small cup of mint tea she didn't want, then poured another for Thorne. "What's going on, Isis?" he asked after handing Thorne a cup. "Does your presence, and that of your old friend, have anything to do with my father's attack?"

Dylan? Her heart fluttered. "What did he want?" A small alarm dinged. The attack after their arrival in Cairo, Beniti's attack, and now *Dylan* had visited Husani?

Thorne cocked a dark brow in her direction. He had very expressive eyebrows. "And he is?"

"My father's assistant."

"Little bird's fiancé," Husani said at the same time.

"Dylan was never my fiancé," Isis quickly denied. "We dated. He wanted more; I wanted less." Zero chemistry, nothing like what she and Thorne created together. "What did he want, Husani?" she repeated.

"To speak with Father."

Her nape tingled with apprehension. It was plausible. Dylan, being an Egyptologist, and having worked for her father for years, knew Beniti al-Atrash. They came to her father's old friend when they wanted honest workers to go on a dig, or needed supplies whose prices hadn't been jacked up to the skies.

Why *wouldn't* Dylan visit him if he was in Egypt? But why would her father's assistant pick this time of year to excavate when the heat index was killer and most of the locals who could afford it left the city?

She adjusted the strap between her breasts, the weight of the camera comforting against her side as they talked. "What did he want?" She opened the bag and shifted things to accommodate the small box. It was a tight fit to close the bag. "Did you tell Dylan that Beniti is in the hospital?"

Husani shrugged. "No. When he found out that Father was not here, he said that Professor Magee sent him."

Isis curled her lip. "He did not."

Implacable, unflappable, Husani added, "He claimed your father sent him to retrieve the object he left behind on his last trip."

Her arm brushed Thorne's as she touched her camera bag. "The stick and the box?" His innate strength lent her courage. "Did he ask for them specifically?"

"No, which raised my suspicion. When I inquired as to what the item might be, he prevaricated, then admitted he didn't know what had been left. I informed him I had no knowledge of such an article, and he departed." Husani shrugged as if he had no control over the whims of fate. "He was not pleased."

Dylan "not pleased" was as petulant and whiney as a hormonal teenager. Isis shot a look at Thorne. "Dylan's fishing. He wasn't here that last time with my father, so he shouldn't even know about this."

"I figured. This adds another new player, doesn't it?" Thorne took his phone from the front pocket of his jeans. "What's this Dylan's last name?"

"Brengard." Isis's fingers tightened around the lid of her camera case. "You don't think he was the one who sent those men last night, do you? That doesn't sound like something Dylan would do. He's . . ." Weak. A follower. "A pacifist. Well, maybe not that, but he doesn't seem the kind to condone violence." He'd taken her rebuff with a shrug.

Isis knew unequivocally that if and when Thorne decided not to be as patient as he was pretending to be, he'd take and not ask. She just wanted to make sure to let him catch her when he was ready.

He gave her an indecipherable look as he punched in a number on his phone. "If there's enough incentive people will do anyth—" He stopped abruptly at the sound of a skirmish outside, whipping his gun from under his shirt at the small of his back and subtly stepping in front of her.

Heart in her throat, Isis peered around his arm, hearing running footsteps approaching, accompanied by shouts of anger.

Hell, not again—

❧ SEVEN ❧

Thorne and Husani both leveled their weapons toward the swinging curtain at the entrance to the inner sanctum as the driver pushed his way through the carpets hanging from the ceiling.

"Company," he said quietly and succinctly, his eyes intense and focused. He too carried a very large black gun.

Who the hell *was* Connor Thorne?

"Back door?" Thorne demanded, addressing Husani.

"I know the way," Isis told him, forcing the basket down so she could latch the camera bag. "Are you coming, Husani?"

"I will greet the visitors," he said grimly, tucking his gun into the back of his loose pants. "Go, little bird!"

"Thank you! This way." Isis pushed between hanging layers of fine kilim rugs. The stall backed up into Beniti's small shop, which faced the alley in the next block. Thorne stayed on her heels and the driver brought up the rear.

"Get the lead out," Thorne told her briskly as they moved from blankets, textiles, and plastic sphinxes to more expensive faux artifacts.

"We can go through here, and then through the next shop, and then out a side d—" Her words were cut off by the sound of a gunshot. She spun around, slamming into Thorne's hard chest. Isis braced a hand over the steady beat of his heart. "Husani!"

He grabbed her upper arm. "Let's go." Twisting her around, he propelled her between crowded display cases, intricately inlaid tables where she'd played as a child, had haggled behind the counter as she got older, and stolen her first kiss as a teen. *"Move!"*

They emerged through a narrow side alley crowded with tourists. The noise was jarring. How would they know who was after them in the crush of humanity? In the teeming mass of people someone could come right up and shoot them, knife them—*whatever* them—without being observed until it was too late.

Sweat beaded her brow, and her heart raced erratically with the adrenaline surging through her. She stayed close to Thorne, slipping her hand into his, grateful when his strong fingers tightened around hers as they pushed through the shoppers and tourists.

As they walked, Isis scanned the faces of the people surging around them like waves around a rock. Suddenly, instead of a million bits of color and potential photographic vignettes, she saw a thousand different threats. Everyone was suspect. Everyone looked potentially dangerous. One-handed she adjusted her camera around her neck, making sure it was safe if she had to run again, glad that *this* time she wore tennis shoes instead of strappy sandals.

"Back to the car?" She raised her voice to be heard over the noise of people haggling, shouting over loud music, normal conversation at higher than normal volume. This circus atmosphere, the colors and smells, the sounds of Egypt—all the things she loved now presented a threat. Thorne's fingers tightened over hers, and he gave a little tug. "Turn left."

Isis pointed right. "But the car's that way." Or not. She had her father's crappy sense of direction. She'd played in the labyrinth of the souk for years, but getting lost then had been an adventure that always led to pleasant discoveries and surprises—and a safe return to Beniti al-Atrash's shop, escorted by other shopkeepers who knew her and her father.

"We have another vehicle parked on the other side. Yes," he said to the driver, clearly in answer to something she hadn't heard. The guy melted into the crowds surging around them. Thorne kept her moving, although it wasn't a simple task to navigate the onslaught of shoppers and laughing, playing children filling the narrow streets.

Only someone intimately familiar with the souk could navigate the congested labyrinth with his certainty. If he'd studied a map of the area as he claimed, he must have a photographic memory, because his steps never faltered, and they were never obstructed by a dead end.

He walked quickly down what looked like a blind alley, but pushed through T-shirts hanging in wild disarray from the ceiling of a small stall. They emerged into one of the narrow car-lined side streets running alongside the bazaar. The vehicle, a filthy Jeep with tinted windows, was parked nose out. He activated the door lock from half a block away and popped the door, almost shoving her inside before rounding the front and getting in himself.

The car started with a deep throaty roar and they were off. He didn't drive crazily, although doing so probably wouldn't attract any more notice than did the rest of the drivers on the congested roads. He eased into traffic with aggressive confidence while she dug in her bag for a wad of tissue. Sweat ran down her temples and collected between her breasts.

"Want a tissue?" She glanced over at him. He hadn't even broken a sweat, and there was no sign of the gun. Unfazed and completely alert. She caught her breath. "I have some sanitizing towelettes as well if you—"

"Tell me about this fiancé."

She wasn't that vain, but she was damned if she'd wipe off her last vestiges of makeup if she didn't have to. She blotted her forehead with a tissue, then opened the camera bag and pulled everything out to get to the small pack of hand wipes in the bottom. She meticulously repacked everything neatly before opening the package. The astringent smell of antiseptic filled the car. "Dylan isn't, and never was, my fiancé." She wiped her hands, then the back of her neck, enough to cool her for a few minutes until the air-conditioning kicked in.

The skin around his eyes warped into a network of fine lines as his eyes narrowed. "That's not what your friend Husani seemed to think."

She adjusted the vent to blow directly on her face.

"He wasn't even a boyfriend. He was my father's assistant, and we dated off and on, and more because we were the only game in town than anything else."

"And yet here he is, right where you happened to be."

His tone, underlain with suspicion, made her skin prickle, and an unhappy swish curled through her stomach. Isis tried not to be an alarmist. Just because trigger-happy people had chased them—twice—didn't mean Dylan was part of some nefarious plot. The men in the underpass the night before had beaten the crap out of Thorne, not her. Her reaction was just a knee-jerk reaction to what was going on.

"It's not such a stretch," she told him, trying to be reasonable instead of reactive. "This is where his work is, after all. He worked for my father for years, but he's probably working for someone else now."

"Let's find out who." He lifted his hip to remove his phone from his pocket.

He didn't greet whoever answered the phone, merely gave his name, paused, and then said, "Give me a full report on a Dylan Brengard—who he's working for, and when he arrived in Cairo. Give me dates. Any intel on my old friend?" Pause. "Yes," his voice was curt. "I am. And I will." He didn't say goodbye, just shoved the phone back into his pocket.

"Who was that?" Isis demanded, resting her bent knee on the seat as she turned her whole body to face him. The time for his prevarication was over. Clearly Connor Thorne was not just some private eye. His connections went deeper than that, and his incredible fighting and defense skills screamed military. She wanted answers, and she damn well wanted them now. "*What* old friend?"

He blatantly ignored her question and fired off one of his own in return. "How many years did Dylan work for the professor?"

"Damn it, Thorne! Answer *my* questions first."

"*Your* questions aren't a matter of life and death."

"You're full of crap! You just don't want to answer me. If you refuse to answer any of my perfectly reasonable—and, I might add, *pertinent*—questions, then how can I be the judge of that? For all I know you're the bad guy and you're doing all this to scare me into . . ." She had no idea *what* because she was so mad her mouth was going faster than her brain.

". . . leading you to my father's discovery." She finished, knowing she was being illogical, and not giving a damn. He was *infuriating*.

He tore his eyes away from the road for one moment to glance at her. "*You* hired me, remember? I have no bloody interest in what two days ago I was pretty damn sure was your father's pie in the sky. Answer my questions, and when I'm sure we're safe, I'll answer some of yours. How long did you date Dylan?"

"Off and on for two summers. I spent quite a bit of time with my father here because I was commissioned to do a coffee-table book. He was here. I was here. We went to dinner, the movies when we were in town. Normal dating stuff." She glanced at him. "Now one of mine. Who are you and who do you really work for? Because you have skills you didn't learn from a mental GPS tracker."

He passed four cars at eighty miles per hour before answering. "I work for Lodestone."

Then Lodestone was more than just a company that found people and things. "Is that who you just called?"

He hesitated, eyes locked on the road. "MI5."

"MI5? What's that? A branch of the IRS?" She frowned. And why would he have *them* on speed dial? No one *wanted* to talk to them.

"British Secret Service."

"You're a *spy?*"

"No. I'm a Lodestone agent here to help you find a tomb."

Isis didn't know what to believe.

Traffic came to a sudden crawl. An accident involving three cars and a herd of camels blocked most of the road. While the men and the camel owners argued loudly and gestured with swinging arms and waving hands at one another, all the cars pressed into one narrow channel, bumpers kissing as they wound around the melee. An errant camel swung its back end into the roadway, nearly blocking their progress. Thorne stomped on the brakes, forcing Isis to brace herself against the cracked vinyl dashboard.

"A spy?! Seriously? So all this running, chasing, shooting, beating people to a pulp is child's play to you?"

He cursed under his breath and locked gazes with her for a moment. The intensity stole the air from her lungs.

"It's never child's play, and I'm not here in that capacity."

"Well, actually, you are," she pointed out—reasonably, she thought—"since we've done little else besides running and shooting since we got here. Is that how you hurt your leg?"

"Do you ever stop asking questions?"

"As soon as I get answers. That usually shuts me up for a while."

"Describe Dylan." His tone was curt, short, all business.

A spy, for God's sake. It was hard to wrap her brain around that. "He's about five eight. Shoulder-length caramel-colored hair, he favors ponytails—says it's sexy—has light brown eyes—"

"What the hell kind of color is 'caramel'?" he demanded, easing onto the verge and navigating past the stalled cars, animals, and wandering people by driving off the road and onto the sand.

"A warm brownish blond. I have a picture if you—"

He held out an imperious hand. He didn't snap his fingers. That was implied. With a sigh Isis got her phone out of her bag,

She scrolled through the images, then placed the phone in his hand.

"I saw this guy twice," he said. "Yesterday at the airport, and today as we were walking to your friend's shop."

"You think he followed us." It wasn't a question. If Thorne had seen the car, it had followed them. She was just giving herself time to assimilate all the information.

Thorne's grip on the wheel turned white-knuckled, as if it were that or throw a punch at someone. His gaze flicked up to the rearview mirror and he frowned. "I don't think it. Does he know about these cryptic clues of your father's?"

"I shouldn't think so. My father was really paranoid

someone would beat him to the punch. He trusted Dylan more than he did most people, but much as I love my father, he's a pretty selfish guy. I don't think he would've told even Dylan about the clues."

"Why wasn't the professor's assistant with him when he discovered the tomb?" Thorne navigated a small herd of goats and a woman standing on the roadside watching the cars inch by. A seven-minute trip had so far taken twenty.

The heat made her back sweat, and her shirt stuck to the hot vinyl seats. The cheap cotton T-shirt was probably staining her sweaty skin Halloween orange by now. She didn't know how Thorne normally got answers out of people, but she had the distinct feeling he was grilling her. "How do you know he wasn't?"

The hard, piercing gaze was back, reaching in, stripping her down to her bare bones. The look said he wanted answers and he'd wring them out of her one way or the other. "You said your father was the only one left alive."

"Dylan had food poisoning bad enough to be hospitalized. My father started the dig without him."

Thorne veered off the main road, taking them deeper into narrow streets. "When was that?"

"A few days before the dig." She saw the two enormous stone lions flanking the entrance to the Kasr Al Nile Bridge, which connected downtown Cairo to Gesira Island and the affluent Zamalek district. "Where are we going?" She doubted it was to the Egyptian Opera House or the Cultural Center.

He ignored her question, which nonresponse was getting more and more damned annoying. "Here or stateside?"

"Here." She needed him, and wanted him, but his shitty attitude about not answering any of her questions had to freaking stop. "Thorne, this is a *partnership*, remember? I don't like being dragged from pillar to post without explana—"

He held up a finger, cutting her off as he used the phone again, requesting confirmation of Dylan's hospital stay. "Hospital?" he asked her.

"I have no idea." Nor did she care. *Dylan* wasn't relevant. "But it was one in Cairo."

Thorne relayed the information. He put the phone away. Isis glanced beyond the frenetic cars, all of which wanted supremacy of the road. They'd reached the outskirts of the city. "Where are we going?"

"I got a read off that tassel. The basket was bought from the souk, but the silk tassel comes from one of these houses."

"I hope you can be more specific," Isis observed dryly. "I can't imagine my father knowing anyone who might live in this neighborhood. This is pretty high-end. Princes, diplomats, wealthy expats."

"Sponsors?"

Isis looked at the shady, tree-lined streets, upscale restaurants, and expensive art galleries they passed. "I know the names of some, but not all. He talked about some of them, I met a few at fund-raisers—I don't recall anyone from this elite neck of the desert." But then her father occasionally took money under the table for "special projects," something they'd argued about when she'd first discovered the practice. For a large donation, priceless antiquities found their way into private collections. He'd stopped telling her after she'd challenged him on the illegal practice. She loved her father, but he wasn't smart enough to be a crook and get away with it. She'd been terrified he'd be caught and jailed. He'd promised he'd never do it again——but she couldn't swear he hadn't.

"How the hell does your father expect you to follow such vague clues?"

"The clues weren't left for me to follow; he had them to jog his own memory." Isis sighed, exasperated. "Maybe he knew his mind was going . . ."

Thorne tapped the steering wheel. "This is it." He turned off the palm-tree-lined street onto a narrower road lined with tall oleander trees covered with white flowers, underplanted with bright red and deep purple petunias behind strips of meticulously maintained emerald-green grass. It wasn't until they came to the tall, black wrought-iron gates of a villa that Isis realized they were on a private road.

Sunlight glinted on the gate's gold embellishments and the high fences she could glimpse behind thick shrubbery. But it wasn't all the gilding Isis took note of; it was the red eyes of all the cameras trained overtly on their vehicle as they drove slowly through the entrance. She bet there were plenty more surveillance cameras she *couldn't* see.

"Curiouser and curiouser," she murmured. "How are

we going to gain entry? We don't know who lives here, or how they might be connected. Dad hated to be out of his element, so I can't picture him coming to a place like this." Or ripping a tassel off some multigazillionaire's prized carpet undetected.

"He had a lot of quirks for a guy needing investor backing."

"I know." She let a small laugh escape. "You should've seen him, though, once they showed up at the dig. He'd stand with his feet planted, wearing that ridiculous hat, and insist they feel the grains of sand fall through their fingers as he painted a picture of life here thousands of years ago."

"A salesman."

"Be it a hole in the ground, or a tomb, he has—he had—a way with painting a picture that investors loved." At least at first. Then they'd pretty much gotten sick and tired of his bullshit, and the money had dried up.

"That tassel came from this location. So either your father visited here, or someone from here gave it to him. Either way, this is the clue we're following because it's the only lead we have." Thorne opened the window and put his arm out to press the buzzer. Four cameras situated along the fence narrowed their lens apertures, zooming in on them.

"What is your business with Dr. Najid?" The polite male voice sounded as though the guy was sitting in the backseat. Isis glanced over her shoulder to make sure he wasn't. She had no idea, since the sun shone through the windows, why she felt as though a cloud had just passed overhead. A glance at Thorne showed he was oblivious.

He answered smoothly, "Tell him Professor Magee's daughter, Isis, would like a few moments of his time."

There was an infinitesimal pause before the man responded unctuously. "I will inquire. Please wait."

"Ever heard of him?" he asked quietly.

Isis shook her head. "I did most of my father's paperwork for years. If he was an investor, I'd have heard of him."

Thorne, looking perfectly at ease, rested his elbow on the open window. Isis noticed that he had the gearshift in reverse, ready to back up at the first sign of trouble. She rubbed both damp palms on her thighs and wondered whose life she was suddenly living.

⟨ EIGHT ⟩

Najid kept them waiting for fifteen minutes outside the gates, and another thirty-seven minutes once they were inside his house, which suited Thorne just fine. He used the time to contact his people in London, gathering intel on this clearly well-heeled Najid guy.

He received a response in less than two minutes. Dr. Khalifa Najid was the Minister of Irrigation and Water Resources, had been for thirty-plus years. He was well respected in the community, married young to a wealthy Egyptian heiress, no children. He was positioned to open one of Egypt's largest dam projects since Aswan in a few weeks. Thorne glanced at several photographs of the man and his immediate family, and collected the data, but didn't see any obvious correlation between Najid and Professor Magee.

Didn't see it, but his gut said it was there.

Although he felt naked without his weapon, Thorne had wisely left it secreted in a special compartment in the Jeep.

The metal detectors and body scanner were subtle, but not hidden, as they were led down the long, wide, tiled-floor hallways. Discreet security, dressed in dark suits and looking like American Secret Service agents, were strategically positioned so that they didn't veer off course.

His GPS locating skill had never failed him. The professor had left the basket containing the tassel at the souk for later memory retrieval. The tassel led here. Ergo, Najid and Magee were somehow linked.

"Wow." Isis eyed the opulence of the house as they were led by a white-robed servant through high-ceilinged hallways with niches holding statues and various artifacts tastefully displayed. "Everything here should be in the museum, and before you suggest it, no, I don't think anything we're looking at is a good replica; it's all the real deal," she whispered as their shoes echoed on the tiles.

The doors on either side were numerous, and all closed. The intricate hand-painted amber and lapis blue tiled floors cooled the spaces, while the musical sound of unseen fountains and the fragrance of fresh flowers added to the refined ambience of the place.

Having been raised almong similar wealthy trappings, Thorne was unimpressed. It wasn't a home. The villa was skillfully staged to give the aura of wealth and status, meant not only to showcase the minister's status and wealth, but also to intimidate.

Been there, done that.

They were eventually led through an arch and shown to a vast living room cooled by slowly circulating ceiling fans assisted by an efficient air-conditioning system. Beverages were offered and accepted, and the servant melted away. He returned within minutes bearing a brass tray holding very English-looking china teacups, a teapot and milk jug, and a plate of various small cakes. Very civilized.

Wide-open French doors overlooked what was either a large pond or a lap pool in a shade-dappled courtyard filled with greenery, lush red flowers, and white upholstered lawn furniture. Sunlight beat onto the floor tiles and bounced an amber reflection off white linen sofas and bronze-striped chairs inside the room.

The coffee table was an alabaster sarcophagus, and an enormous limestone fireplace had bas-relief hieroglyphs carved into the surround, drawing the focus to an enormous carved wooden bust of a woman with curly hair, sloe eyes, and no nose. She reminded Thorne in some bizarre way of Michael Jackson, which made his lips twitch. One entire wall was limestone carved to look exactly like a wall in a tomb, with brightly colored glyphs depicting everyday life in ancient Egypt. The execution was remarkable. But he wasn't here to admire the minister's art collection as he prowled the perimeter of the large room, trailing his fingers over priceless antiquities to see if anything popped.

Plenty did. The GPS numbers scrolled in his head like computer code. Nothing jumped out regarding Magee.

Twenty-foot-tall wooden palm trees with black trunks and gilded fronds filled the four corners and led the eye to the intricately painted ceiling overhead. On beauty overload, Thorne half expected Salome to appear and strip off her seven veils. It wasn't difficult to imagine what Isis's pale breasts looked like beneath diaphanous scarves, or how her nipples would peak at the brush of his fingers. Inappropriately aroused, he tamped down the image of Isis in nothing but sheer colored silks, and did another circuit of the room before seating himself in one of the numerous striped chairs. He chose carefully—the bright sunlight behind him, but the chair positioned so his back wasn't toward any doorway. Crossing his legs took care of his semi-erect state, but nothing blotted out the image of Isis spotlit by the sun, wearing nothing but a mist of color.

His leg ached and the back of his neck itched. He ran his palm around his nape so he didn't grip his thigh. Oblivious to his thoughts, Isis, head down, was clearly edgy as a cat on a hot tin roof as she paced along the outer edge of an area rug the size of a rugby field.

"This carpet should also be in a museum," she said sotto voce as she paced. "This was probably woven in the sixteenth century, and yet even muted, look how beautiful the colors are still." She crouched down, disappearing behind the back of a sofa. "Wool. Asymmetrical pile . . ." she murmured to herself. Thorne imagined her stroking the damned carpet and all the hair on his body lifted in response.

"Based on an old Persian design—Egyptian wool, and the workmanship indicates Cairene weavers. They, along with quantities of Egyptian wool, were taken to the court in Istanbul—"

"I don't give a damn how old the carpet is." Thorne sounded more annoyed than he should.

She rose to her feet and waved a vague hand over the floor. "I was looking for—you know."

"We're in the right place," he said without elaboration. Under a long, tall narrow table holding an exquisite bust of Queen Something or other, Thorne had already spotted the place on the carpet where the tassel had been removed.

He was no expert, but he'd bet his next paycheck that the bust, along with the rest of the beautifully curated items in the room, was the real deal, and that Isis was correct. Everything should be in the museum.

"Come, sit down and drink some tea; it'll cool you off." Thorne never trusted that he wasn't being bugged or recorded. He gave her a meaningful look, and she navigated the furniture without further comment.

He felt his phone vibrate once. The research people in London were fast and top-notch. He scanned the closely spaced text, then deleted the information, returning the phone to his front pocket. They had found no connection between Magee and Dr. Khalifa Najid. No meetings were recorded, no clandestine midnight encounters witnessed.

And yet Thorne had the tassel from this very carpet in his pocket.

Isis poured the hot, strong tea. "Milk or lemon?" When he indicated his choice, she added milk and tonged a couple of cubes of sugar into his cup before handing it over to him. The fragrance of her skin, an erotic combination of cinnamon and perspiration, made his mouth water and his pulse kick. Her face and throat had a damp sheen and looked as silky and soft as dewy rose petals. Thorne found he didn't have to have eyes on her to be turned on. Just the humid, spicy, Isis-scented perfume of her turned his dick to stone.

He sipped the tea he didn't want.

Picking up her own filled cup she sat down gingerly on the white sofa nearby, cradling her saucer in both hands, her orange T-shirt loud and cheerful in the muted décor.

Ignoring the tantalizing smell of her, turning a blind eye to the way the light stroked her skin with a pearly sheen, Thorne asked, "What business would the professor have with the Minister of Irrigation and Water Resources, do you suppose?"

"Water resources?" Her eyes widened in surprise before she shrugged and pushed her glasses up her nose. A line of perspiration outlined the leather strap between her breasts, and her hair, absorbing the humidity, had doubled in volume. She looked damp, rumpled, and sexy as hell. "I can't think of a thing. Unless he *was* a sponsor, or had some kind of issue with the dig. My father tended to stay away from anyone official whenever possible." Her tone was dry.

"Mr. Thorne. How may I be of service?"

Thorne had heard the sibilant footsteps and was aware the man stood just outside the door. Thorne waited until their host came fully into the room before he placed his cup on a nearby table and rose to his feet.

Even if he didn't recognize Najid from the small photograph he'd just seen on his iPhone, he'd have known this man was not only wealthy, but incredibly powerful just by his bearing, which was very similar to that of the Earl. His charcoal suit was Savile Row, his highly polished dress shoes Tanino Crisci, his watch Chopard. His black beard was neatly trimmed and his dark eyes too black to read.

"Thank you for meeting with us at such short notice, Minister," Thorne said easily, his limp intentionally more pronounced as he walked forward, hand extended to greet their host.

Najid's handshake was firm and quick. "Unfortunately, I do not have the luxury of much time to converse. I must return to my office for a meeting. How may I be of service?"

Thorne extended his arm to include Isis in the conversation. Najid had not so much as flickered an eyelash in her direction. She might as well be invisible. "This is Isis Magee, Professor Magee's daughter. She's tracing her father's footsteps in his search for Cleopatra's tomb and thought you might be able to assist her with any information you may have."

"I have heard of Professor Magee, of course. But there has been no discovery of Queen Cleopatra's tomb by him or anyone else, to my knowledge."

"Was the discovery of the tomb something you discussed with my father when he visited you in the spring?" Isis asked tightly. Thorne curled his fingers around her shoulder in warning.

Najid gave her a black-eyed glance down his hawk

of a nose. "I have never had the honor of meeting your father, Miss Magee." He shot his cuff to glance at his watch. "I'm afraid that is all the time I can afford you. I'll have Jafari show you out."

Isis took a step forward. "Are you saying my father never visited you here?"

"As I stated quite plainly, I have never met Professor Magee. I'm sorry I couldn't provide the information you wanted. Good day, Mr. Thorne. Miss Magee."

"He's lying!" Isis said under her breath as they watched him leave the room.

"No shit. Now to find out *why*. Come on."

The eyes of dozens of surveillance cameras followed them through the house and outside to their vehicle.

"WHY WOULD HE LIE?" Isis demanded like a dog with a bone. She was turned sideways in her seat as he drove over July 26 Bridge back into the city, the late-afternoon sunlight making a glowing nimbus of her dark hair. She hadn't even blinked when he retrieved his weapon from the hidden compartment under the floor mat on the driver's side, where he'd stashed it, and laid it on the seat between them.

She pulled her camera case into her lap and dug in it for her phone. "I'm calling my father. Let's see what he has to say." She hit speed dial and put it on speaker so he could hear the ringing on the other end.

"Darling girl."

"Daddy, how are you?"

"I found her, Isis. I found her!" The professor's voice rose with excitement.

The her, Thorne presumed, was Cleopatra. The professor's voice sounded eager and robust. But from reports, he was a pain in the ass and a demanding patient at Cresthaven, an Alzheimer facility just outside Seattle. Given that the place cost Isis more than she could afford made Thorne want to tell him to shut up and not add more burden to his daughter. But he knew she wouldn't thank him for it. What did the professor want, an eighteen-hole golf course and a fishing lake?

"Found who, Daddy?"

"Cl—you know who," he stage whispered. "I'm meeting my team after breakfast. I tell you, baby, this time the entire world will sit up and take notice! Tell your mother I won't be home for several months. Perhaps you girls can come and visit me here in the summer. Would you like that, honey?"

"That will be great, Dad." Isis kept her voice steady, but Thorne could feel her tight shoulders, and her set expression spoke volumes. "I just wanted to check to see how you're doing."

"We're in a hotel right now. The food's not bad, and the beds are clean. We head out to the site at first light."

"Where is the site, Dad?"

There was a long pause before he said hesitantly. "I can't tell you that, honey. You know even the walls have ears. I don't want this to leak until I've found definitive proof my find is genuine."

Isis squeezed her eyes shut. "Do you remember leaving a small basket containing a carpet tassel at Beniti's?"

"Why would I do that? A carpet tassel from where?"

Isis met Thorne's eyes and pulled an expressive face. Her father believed he was in Egypt and about to start the dig. He still had no memory of the events leading up to his supposed discovery of the tomb. So if he'd met Dr. Najid, it must've been very close to the time of his attack. All his memories stopped and started around the time he'd come to Cairo on his last dig. The most crucial month was gone.

Thorne avoided hitting a gang of street urchins running between heavy traffic. Horns blared, but nobody slowed down. A glance in the rearview mirror showed a blue Mercedes E Class on his right, about ten cars back, and an ancient-looking tan Audi directly behind him, weaving between the other vehicles.

He pressed the gas, listening to the disjointed conversation with only one ear as he navigated the congested road and watched the tails.

"The tassel led us to the Minister of Water and Irrigation, Dr. Khalifa Najid," Isis pushed, determined to get something out of the old man. Thorne wanted to tell her she was wasting her time. "Does his name ring any bells?"

"None. I don't like it here, Isis," he said petulantly. "When can I leave?"

"Aren't you about to go on a dig?" Isis asked tentatively.

"I—I am? No, honey, I think we're at Connie and Al's

place . . . Or maybe this is the Mihms' house? Let me ask your mother."

"I'll tell her you're looking for her." Her voice broke, and Thorne watched her straighten her spine as she told her father bracingly, "Why don't you wait for her on the bench by the front door where it's nice and sunny?"

"It's raining! I'm bored. I should be with you looking for her. Why don't I come out for a bit and help you?"

Isis curled her fingers into her palms. Thorne laid his hand over hers, and she shot him a grateful look. "Daddy, you're in Seattle, and you were hurt the last time you were in Cairo. You're in a place I know you'll be safe. Please be patient. I'm here in Cairo, and we're looking for her. I'll find her for you, I promise."

Several moments of silence went by while the professor seemed to be trying to process the information. Isis had a shitload more patience than Thorne would've had in a similar position.

"You're a good girl, honey. Call us and let us know how you're doing. Your mother sends her love."

"I will, and you call me if you remember anything. Even the smallest thing might help us. I love you, Daddy. Be good."

"Find her for me, Isis. Just find her. I don't know why, honey, but she's in *grave* danger."

She put up a hand even though Thorne wasn't about to say anything. "Give me a minute, okay?" She put her phone back in her camera bag and sighed. "My mother died fifteen years ago. And Cleo in grave danger? She's been in the same resting place since thirty BCE!"

Thorne took his hand off hers to rest on the gun lying beside his hip. He wasn't sure if sympathy was what she needed right now. Hell, if it was, he wasn't the man for the job. Her sadness was palpable, but she didn't cry as he suspected she wanted to do. She held on to her emotions by a tenuous thread.

"It's so unfair. As wacky as he can be, my father has a brilliant mind and a talent for archaeology. At one time he was *the* top Egyptologist in the *world*. It's so damned unfair."

"He's being well taken care of."

"Right," Isis said briskly. "And we have a puzzle to solve. Clearly *something* is going on. Najid doesn't know we can't confirm him ever meeting with my father, so a lie was pretty risky—if that's what it was."

And maybe he *did* know the good professor was incapable of remembering, so he felt he could lie with impunity. "We don't know that what he said isn't the truth. But you know that people lie for any number of reasons. Deceptive gain, or to escape punishment—number-one reason: to cover their arses," he said dryly. "How about we pay a visit to your father's friend in the hospital and see if he can shed any light on a possible connection between your father and Najid?"

"Sure," she said, biting her lip, something Thorne wanted desperately to do himself. "Keep heading this way; you'll see the hospital off to the right. I hate to say it, but I'm not sure what to do next. I have no idea where my father might have hidden more clues, which means we're at a dead end, right?"

"Not necessarily." Thorne kept an eye on the two vehicles tailing them. An innocent man didn't follow the daughter of a man he claimed not to know. "Beniti al-Atrash might have more insight than his son."

Thorne changed lanes, speeding up. The Jeep might look like half the other vehicles on the road, but the engine was souped up and could outrun anything chasing them. Thorne didn't want to put that to the test. He hoped the men following them were there merely for surveillance. He didn't want a shoot-out with Isis in the car.

The vehicles kept pace. Local plates, tinted windows. He punched in the license plates one-fingered on his phone, then added a question mark. Let London ID them.

"Fingers crossed."

Thorne didn't believe in crossed fingers or lucky rabbits' feet. His good-luck charm was an automatic weapon. His Glock tended to even the playing field.

It didn't take long to reach the hospital on El Kasr El Aini Street in Garden City, and they found al-Atrash's room on the second floor without incident.

Christ. He hated hospitals. The smell of antiseptic curled through Thorne's nervous system and settled like an oil slick in his gut. The sight of a wheelchair, shoved against the wall, made him remember . . .

"Are you all right?" Isis asked, laying her hand lightly on his arm. He felt a sizzling arc of electricity resonate through his bones. Static electricity, nothing more.

"Why wouldn't I be?" His voice was curt. He hadn't set foot in a hospital in months, but his body reacted to the stimuli as if he were once again in a hospital bed, where even a morphine drip hadn't been enough to mask the pain.

"Because you're limping more, and gritting your teeth. Your leg hurts from all that damned running around, doesn't it? Maybe we should have it looked at while we're here?"

"I'm fine." He'd had enough fucking doctors poking and prodding him for a lifetime. "This is the room."

"Let me go in and see if he's up to visitors first."

Thorne motioned for her to go ahead. He leaned against the wall outside the door and surveyed the people milling about. Doctors, orderlies, a couple of women sitting outside a room wringing their hands and talking quietly. Normal hospital activity. His mother had visited him. Once. She couldn't handle his "infirmity." Better that way. In those months it had taken everything in him not to chuck it all in and wave the white flag for Boris Yermalof to fucking come and finish him off. It had taken a little too fucking long for the anger to become stronger than the pain. Once that happened, he did everything in his power to get the hell out of there and start living.

He still had an itch on the back of his neck. One of the cars following them had turned off with him, parking seven cars over in the lot. Thorne went over to the window and looked down. Two shadowy figures were all he made out through the tinted windows. Thorne figured he had multiple choices of just who'd sent them.

At any other time, Yermalof would've been at the top of his hit parade. God only knew, the son of a bitch was mean enough, angry enough, determined enough to track him down to the ends of the earth in retaliation for what Thorne had done to him.

The losers who'd attacked him in the underpass, the guys who'd chased them earlier that day, Dr. Khalifa Najid . . . hell, he'd even add Husani the Kiss Whisperer, and Dylan Brengard, the casual ex-boyfriend.

The list was growing, and they'd barely been in Cairo forty-eight hours.

The door opened and Isis popped her head out. "He's doing much better. Come in. I told him you were my boyfriend to keep things simple."

Whatever Thorne was feeling right then, *simple* it was not. This wasn't a mere case of finding a long-lost tomb and restoring Magee's dubious reputation. The professor had enemies. More than one if Thorne was the judge of the situation. And the man's daughter tied him in knots.

He followed her inside.

The second bed was empty, the curtain pulled back. Just the three of them in the room with the door closed. Beniti al-Atrash was in his late sixties. He looked like he'd done a couple of rounds with middleweight champion Carl "the Cobra" Froch. His arm was in a cast, supported by a sling; one eye was swollen shut; the four-inch gash to his cheek was black and blue and stitched like Frankenstein's monster. That must've hurt like a son of a bitch. Thorne approached the bed as Isis introduced them.

"Isis has explained some of the circumstances surrounding August's discovery of the tomb of Cleopatra."

Al-Atrash cut to the chase as he tried to straighten against the pillows Isis was mounding behind him. When she was done fussing, he brought his palm to her cheek and smiled at her before addressing Thorne.

"Do you concur with little bird's theory that my attacker, and the two attempts on your lives, are a direct result of whatever it was my friend unearthed when he was here three months ago?"

Thorne sat on the empty bed, and after a moment Isis came and sat beside him. She slipped her much smaller hand into his, clasping his fingers where his hand rested on his knee. "It's very likely, sir. This many violent confrontations in such a short space of time after our arrival, coupled with the unprecedented visits to your shop and stall, would indicate that everything is tied in to Professor Magee's find. Can you tell me anything about your attackers?"

"I had closed the stall first, then gone through to close the shop. The three men were inside when I came through the back. One man demanded, 'Where is it?' Since I had no frame of reference, I presumed he wanted the cash box, which I gave him with all haste. He took the money, stuffed it into his pockets, and swore at me, then asked again.

"I asked what the 'it' was he referred to. One of the other men hit me with his gun." The older man touched his left eye with his fingertips. His hand shook. Isis tightened her fingers between Thorne's and he squeezed back.

"The third punched me in the stomach. I don't

remember much after that. Husani found me when he brought the goods inside from the street."

"Did any of them mention my father by name, or *say* Cleopatra?" Isis asked.

"Not that I recall, little bird. I am deeply sorry."

"God!" she said achingly, as her eyes filled with tears. "*I'm* sorry this happened to you." She turned to Thorne. "Is there even a remote chance that this has nothing to do with my father?"

"I don't believe so. This is all too premeditated to be unrelated. And the only thing everyone seems to have in common *is* your father." The only person who didn't fit was the Russian, although Thorne didn't rule him out entirely.

"You were with him just before he flew home in April," he said to al-Atrash. "Do *you* believe he really did find Cleopatra's tomb at last?"

For several minutes Thorne thought the man had fallen asleep. But eventually he opened his eyes. "They called me from this very hospital to say he'd been found by a group of tourists out on the sand. He was disoriented. Extremely confused. I wanted to believe him, but to be frank? I don't know if he found the tomb and was moved away to deflect curiosity while someone else plundered it, or if he became confused and was set upon by bandits."

"But all his companions were killed."

"Seven men who had been on various digs with him before, yes."

"The police considered it a gang-related crime," Thorne

mused. "All the valuables were stripped from the men, and anything of value was removed from their camp." He rubbed his thigh absently, then abruptly stopped when Isis gave him a sympathetic and worried look. "Is there anything else you remember between the time you came here to see the professor and when you put him on the plane back to Seattle?"

"August searched for Cleopatra's tomb for almost twenty-five years. Do I think he was desperate enough to prevaricate one last time? Perhaps. But the day after he was brought to the hospital he seemed quite lucid, and he assured me that he had indeed found it."

"That's when he called me and told me to arrange a press conference," Isis said quietly. "After the last time, I refused. Unless he could show me irrefutable proof. He claimed he had it and he'd show me when he got home. But by the time I picked him up at Sea-Tac the following day, he didn't even remember that he'd returned to Egypt, let alone that he'd found the tomb." She rubbed a hand over her eyes.

"I don't know what to believe anymore. Did he leave anything else with you for safekeeping? You know how he loved to leave himself clues to jog his memory at times."

"No. Nothing. I believe he donated all his notes and artifacts from his digs to the London Natural History Museum to preserve his legacy before he came here last."

"He did, and we came from there after going through as much of his work as possible. They're in the process of mounting his exhibit now. It'll be open next month. I'm hoping he's well enough to attend."

"Insha Allah."

"Na'am," Isis said softly. "God willing. Have you noticed any unusual antiquity activity in the last few months?"

"No more than usual. I have procured some *very* good pieces that are genuine, and many more that are not. Are these pieces from the tomb of Cleopatra? I can't say. There was nothing that I saw that would identify them as such."

"So we're back to square one. Do you still have any of these pieces?"

"We still have three coins and a necklace with exquisite workmanship indicating royalty. See Husani; he will show you. They might give you the clue you seek. Are you an antiquities dealer, Mr. Thorne?"

"No, I'm a banker. I'm merely here to lend support to Isis while she's here. What can you tell us about Dr. Khalifa Najid?" Thorne changed the subject to safer ground.

"The Minister of Water Resources and Irrigation?" Al-Atrash glanced from Thorne to Isis and back again with a puzzled frown. "I don't understand. Surely you are not suggesting that *he* has anything to do with these attacks?"

"We believe my father visited him around the time he found the tomb. The basket you were keeping for Dad contained the tassel from a carpet. Dr. Najid's carpet. We think my father left it as a clue for himself, but we can't figure out what their connection was. As for the broken stick—" She shrugged. "Do *you* have any idea why he'd want that? The minister denies knowing or ever meeting my father."

"There would be no reason for their paths to ever cross. Dr. Najid has held that prestigious position for more than three decades. He is considered a big hero for bringing water to the desert with the new dam in the Valley of the Scorpions. He's well liked and well respected in the community. He's known as a connoisseur of Egyptian artifacts, and has a well-documented and well-publicized collection. But as far as I know he doesn't sponsor digs, at least not that I've ever heard."

Isis's palm was damp, but Thorne kept his fingers twined with hers. He didn't remember when he'd ever done something as simple as hold a woman's hand. It felt oddly . . . right. "Would their paths have crossed socially?"

The older man smiled. "Socializing in that rarefied environment would make August supremely uncomfortable. And while I consider him my brother, and mean no disrespect, he does not enjoy feeling inferior socially. His milieu is the area in or around his precious tombs. That was where he always took prospective sponsors. Out to whatever dig he was showcasing, where he was in control and, how do you say it—the star of the show. Not to detract from my old friend, but he was a showman. And he knew what pleased the moneymen."

He shook his head. "No. I cannot see August attending afternoon tea, or a soirée in Dr. Najid's social circles. This would be highly unlikely."

Thorne saw that the older man was tiring, and got to his feet, tugging Isis with him.

"We'll go now," Isis said, then walked over to wrap her arms gently around the older man's shoulders. She rested her check against his for a few moments, then kissed him and stepped back. She slid her hand back into Thorne's. "If you need anything, Husani will contact us."

✐ NINE ✐

They got back in the car. Isis didn't ask where they were going. Right then she didn't give a damn. She was hot and sweaty and scared. Turning up the AC to high, she directed the vent on her chest.

"I'd rather these people get what they so desperately want," she said bitterly as cold air hit her damp shirt. "What's their agenda? They left my father for dead; they almost killed Beniti. God—they almost killed *you*."

"What are you saying?" Thorne asked, starting the Jeep and pulling into the street. He seemed distracted, and even more curt than usual, his eyes flicking to the rearview mirrors now and then. Isis knew a car was following them. She'd seen it in her side mirror as they crossed the bridge. She knew he knew it was there. There didn't seem to be any point discussing it. His gun had been in the seat between them the whole time.

The knots in her shoulders had knots.

He cut in front of a flatbed truck carrying metal pipes, then wove between five cars in quick succession. She liked the look of his large hand on the steering wheel; it looked competent and strong. Neither of which she felt right then. The bright sunlight accented the thin, shiny white scars across his fingers.

"You want to find Cleopatra and hand her over to thieves and murderers?"

"Yes. No." She took off her glasses to rub her eyes. "Of course not." She put her glasses back on. "But if doing so will stop this insane cat-and-mouse chase, then maybe that would be the wisest course of action." It would literally kill her father to know someone else would get credit for the discovery of the century.

But they'd all be *alive*, and he could spend the rest of his life whining about it. Her shoulders slumped. "I want to find Cleo, and I want the bad guys to leave us alone." She knew she sounded petulant, but it was the truth.

"It's good to want things. One's not going to happen if we continue along the path that's already set. It's obvious they—whoever the hell they are—believe you know where the tomb is. Whether they know your father doesn't remember, or whether they don't give a flying fuck what he remembers or doesn't remember, you're the one in Cairo asking questions. It's just not clear to me whether they're trying to kill you, or prevent you from reaching that tomb."

"Now you believe there *is* a tomb?"

"I believe that whoever these arseholes are, *they* believe it's real. That's good enough for me."

"You were the one they attacked in the underpass."

"And I suspect that once they killed me they'd help themselves to you, and force you to take them to the tomb."

"But I don't— *Kidnap* me, you mean?"

"It's what I'd do."

"And then kill me when I couldn't do as they wanted."

"What I'd do," he repeated. "We're going to ditch this vehicle in two-point-seven miles and find something else. Gather your stuff and be prepared to move fast."

"All I have to my name is what I'm wearing and my camera."

"Then keep your clothes on and your eyes sharp." His voice was neutral, his fingers on the wheel relaxed. Only his eyes showed heightened awareness, like a circling hawk. Isis rubbed her arms.

When her phone rang she jumped as if someone had poked her.

"Are you going to answer that?"

She shook her head. "After all this? Are you kidding me?"

"It might be your father calling back because he remembered something."

"God—of course." She scrabbled in her bag for the phone. "Daddy?"

"Isis, this is Acadia. We have Uncle August, and he's fine. Is Thorne with you?"

Isis's heart went manic at her cousin's words. "Yes. Let me put you on speaker." Her fingers were clumsy as she searched for the right button. "What happened?"

"Cresthaven called us about half an ago when you didn't answer your phone. An orderly discovered two men in your father's room. The police have them in custody. Hang on, let the guys talk. Honey—"

"No! He's my father." Fear and anger tangled up

inside her, causing Isis's heart to race and her palms to sweat. "Talk to *me!*"

"Two Egyptian nationals broke into the professor's room," Zak Stark told them evenly. "Their attempt to inject him was foiled by the armed security man I had stationed outside his door, and a sharp-eyed orderly. August was scared, but unharmed."

Isis had dozens of questions, but they raced around in her head like rats in a maze.

"I thought you were in South America?" Thorne said evenly.

"We're en route back to Seattle as we speak. My security people have August at our home in Queen Anne Hill; security has been amped up. No one can access him there."

"Why didn't I know you'd posted people to protect him?" Isis demanded. "Not that I'm not grateful, but how did you know to do that?"

"Honey," Zak said gently, "your father was attacked after he made a major discovery. I just thought it prudent to watch his back until Thorne could ascertain the facts."

Knowing her father was safe was her top priority, but it had stupidly never occurred to Isis that the people who'd left him for dead in Egypt would travel halfway around the world to finish the job. Bile rose in her throat, and she pressed her palm to her chest. It was hard to draw breath as fear and guilt ate at her. "Thank you. God, Zak, thank you. He's all I have. If anything—" Her voice broke. "Thank you. I'll come home, and—"

"Wise idea. Yes." Thorne inserted his voice hard and no-nonsense. "I'm taking her back to Cairo as we speak, and will put her on a plane bound stateside. I'll continue on here as planned."

"Excellent idea," Zak said firmly, the drone of the plane's engines faint in the background. "Let Thorne deal with the situation, Isis. Your father will be happy to have you with him."

"He would," Isis agreed, torn. "But he'd rather I was here finding Cleo than sitting around holding his hand in Seattle."

"We've had some activity of our own over here," Thorne said dryly. "I'll have London read you in, so you know what's going on on our end. Right now we have a situation to deal with."

"What can I do to help?"

"Watch your six, and protect the professor. These people aren't playing nice, and they're determined."

"Yeah. Got that," Zak said, his tone grim. "I'll expect that intel in the next fifteen minutes."

"I'll take care of it."

Curling her numb fingers around the small phone, Isis listened to dead air for a full minute before she disconnected on her end. "I should've thought they'd try to get to him. Why didn't I—"

"Because you were already running on empty," he told her, fingers flashing on his own phone as he drove, texted, and talked. Thorne took multitasking to another level. Somehow he even managed to keep an eye on the rearview mirror. Isis was too numb to worry about barely missed bumpers and madly honking horns as he slalomed the Jeep through heavy traffic.

She automatically turned to look back as well. The blue car was weaving and dodging through traffic, and now only three car lengths behind them.

"Don't beat up on yourself. The situation was averted, and the professor is as safe at Stark's place as he would be in Fort Knox." He stuck the phone in his pocket, picked up the gun on the seat beside him, and tightened his fingers on the wheel.

"Brace yourself; it's going to be a bumpy ride." He floored the engine and the Jeep leapt forward like a racehorse from the starting gate.

THORNE FIGURED THAT EVERY damned one of the twenty million people living in Cairo was driving on the main road toward the city. He briefly checked the rearview and saw his tail intact. Returning his attention to the congested highway, he cursed. Every sodding one of them was in his way.

"For Christ's sake." A dark-haired man cruising at about seventy with a car full of unseat-belted children swerved in front of him. No blinker. Thorne eased into the next lane, avoiding the man's fender by an inch. His military training allowed him to keep a cool head. High speeds and heavy traffic, combined with the sheer ineptitude of the majority of drivers, upped the ante of the harrowing chase.

He heard Isis's quick, shallow breaths. At least she was breathing—and it was his job to keep it that way.

Locals refused to wear down their car batteries by using headlights against the settling dusky skies. Thorne flipped his on, gaining an immediate advantage. He could see who he was about to hit. People wove through the three lanes as if there were no rules. Vehicles competed with street dogs, animals, carts, and pedestrians. Everyone ignored traffic lights as if they weren't there. People on foot played chicken to cross the road. He who was bigger, or had his nose out front, had the right of way.

Thorne laid his hand on the horn and kept it there. There were no rules.

Drivers here broke the law of physics, since it seemed they wanted to occupy the same space at the same time. Thorne crossed three lanes of traffic at right angles and got nothing more than a few honking horns for his trouble. He narrowly missed a donkey cart piled high with cauliflowers, only to clip the edge of the bumper in front of him. The driver yelled obscenities out his open window.

A glance in the rearview mirror showed the blue Mercedes hard on his heels. Isis braced her white-knuckled hands on the dashboard, her feet applying invisible brakes on the passenger floorboard. "Breathe before you hyperventilate. We have no time to haul your ass back to the hospital. In. Out through your nose. Good girl. Now get out the map."

Isis dragged in a shuddering breath, then popped the

glove compartment. "For someone who doesn't have a clue where he is," she said, straightening her smudged glasses with a huff, "you seem to have the city memorized."

"I don't." The setting sun in his eyes made the mad race that much more dangerous. "Tell m——" A bullet hit the rear window, shattering it. The safety glass didn't break, but the mass of small opaque bits of glass became impossible to see through.

"Fuck. Get down!" She didn't move fast enough. Life or death. Thorne used his gun hand to press down on the crown of her head until she was below the protective seat back.

Horns blared as the Mercedes slammed into the rear bumper of the Jeep with a teeth-jarring jolt and the crunch of metal. Theirs. The Jeep was of reinforced steel and built like a tank, and while Doug Heustis had assured him the windows were bulletproof, Thorne wasn't prepared to stop and test the validity of the Mossad operative's claim.

Another bullet slammed into the window frame inches from his head. Opening the window to shoot back was a stupid move, so Thorne pressed down on the accelerator, giving the engine the last bit of juice. "Isis! Give me directions to——fuck, *anywhere!*"

He twisted the steering wheel hard left, slamming the front wheel into the Mercedes, bulldozing it aside. "In three or four exits." Keeping up this cat-and-mouse bullshit was dangerous to innocent bystanders. And he didn't like the way Isis's cheeks paled. "We have to regroup. Come up with a plan. Having the advantage puts me in control. Us. *We* get control. Come on, darling, find us an exit."

Isis peered over the dash to ascertain where they were, then returned to her safe slouch, using a finger to trace the route despite the speed they were going. "Head toward May 15 Bridge. Keep right at the fork."

"I'm going to change lanes at the last possible second to take that exit, so hang on."

"When am I *not* freaking hanging on?" she asked rhetorically, bracing her hands and feet. The dented Mercedes came alongside, the car obviously built with a few extras, just like the Jeep. Thorne's window spiderwebbed with a dull thud and crack. Isis let out a shocked shriek as she saw the bullet, clearly visible, embedded inches from his head.

"Bulletproof glass, relax."

"This is relaxed," she muttered dryly, flinching every time they were slammed by the other vehicle.

Thorne yanked the steering wheel hard left. He grinned with satisfaction, hearing the Mercedes's fender crumple. He could barely see a thing though the shattered glass, but he managed to use the Jeep like a plow and shove the Mercedes onto the center divide and oncoming traffic. "Where to?"

IT WAS EXTREMELY DIFFICULT to read in a vehicle moving ninety miles an hour. Isis glanced—once—at the speedometer and didn't look again. In fact, despite the bumping and high speed, she'd rather be trying to read the small print on the map than watching the means of her imminent death.

The Nile ran on their right. "Stay on Kornish El Nile." There was a *bullet* embedded in his side window. Isis inched lower in her seat until she was practically sitting in the small space on the floor. Dear God, this was crazy. Stuff like this didn't *happen* to people like her.

She considered getting out her camera to take a picture of the bullet lodged so close to Thorne's head, for proof or something, but opted to hang on for dear life instead.

The Jeep made a right-angle turn. Even though she couldn't see the cars Thorne cut off, she heard the strident, annoyed horns, the screeching brakes, and imagined she smelled the burning rubber of skidding tires. Bowing her head, she promising herself that she couldn't die until she'd ticked a few more things off her bucket list.

"In three blocks, turn left onto the Kornish El Nile— *no*. Sorry! I mean left on—" She covered the bloodcurdling scream induced by a jarring slam to her side of the car with a hard palm across her mouth. Freaking out wasn't going to help Connor elude these people.

"Left on Manzal Kobri," she managed to say, sweat trickling down her temples and between her breasts.

"Grab the steering wheel."

Her stomach knotted with apprehension. "What? *No*, I don't think s—"

"Get over here and take the wheel. Damn it, *move. Now!*"

At his commanding voice, she lunged across the seat until her face was buried in his lap, then curled her fingers around the bottom of the wheel. Her glasses bit into the bridge of her nose.

"Somehow," Thorne said dryly, his hard thigh muscles flexing under her cheek, "this isn't what I pictured for our first time."

"Cut the jokes." Her voice was muffled. "Now not only can't I *see*, I can't *breathe!* What are you doing?"

He wrapped his fingers around hers to keep the wheel steady. "Just like that. We're not *likely* to end up in the river . . ."

Funny man popped open his door. The wind whipped her hair around her head and his hips. The sound of tires against pavement mere feet away terrified her. "Oh, my God, Thorne, what the hell are you—"

He leaned out, way out—until her nose was smashed against his hip bone. He fired a barrage of shots. Each blast made her flinch and squeeze her eyes more tightly shut.

He reached back to adjust her stiff fingers. God. *He* wasn't holding on to anything!

"Damn it, Isis! Keep it steady!" His thigh muscle flexed under her cheek as he manipulated the accelerator. Not easing up, but pressing his foot flat to the floor.

The stink of car exhaust and gas fumes, and the thrum of the tires speeding on the road surrounding them, were nothing compared to the terror she felt holding that steering wheel in a death grip as they raced along blindly.

For God's sake. *Neither* of them was looking at the road!

He was hanging out of the open door, firing, his head almost on the road racing by beneath them. Protected, she hoped, by the door panel. But she doubted his view of the other car was any better than her view of the road. In other words: nonexistent.

Metal pinged against metal as his shots were returned.

She *expected* the sound of cars crashing behind them, but Isis still flinched and bit her lip at the voracious crash and crunch of the cars smashing into one another a few seconds later. The blast of an explosion rocked their car. The furnace heat of an exploding gas tank warmed the crown of her head and shoulders as a ball of fire exploded far too close by. Red bloomed behind her tightly closed eyes.

"Slide over," Thorne said grimly, giving her a little shove. Numbly, Isis slid back across the seat, eyes still squeezed shut. Shaking, she huddled, half on the seat, half in the footwell as his door slammed, shutting out the majority of the cacophony outside, so that the sound of her rapid heartbeat in her ears was deafening.

The Jeep didn't stop, or slow down.

After a few moments, Isis opened her burning eyes and swallowed dryly. "They stopped following us." That was the best she could manage. Whoever had been in that car, or God help them—those *cars*—was very dead. No one could have survived that conflagration.

"No. *One* car stopped following us. The Audi is clos- ing in, and fast. What's the next turn?"

She was half sitting on the open map, and lifted her hip to free it. She straightened her glasses and found her place with a shaking finger. "Turn right onto Abd El Khalik Tharwat." Calm descended. Probably shock, but she would take it.

He veered sharply from the left lane across traffic to take the right-hand exit. Isis didn't even flinch when cars blared their horns and tires screeched to avoid them. Same old, same old.

She struggled half up onto the seat so she could see where they were. Streetlights flickered on, shop win- dows brightly lit against the evening shadows. Lots of foot traffic now that they were off the main arteries. She recognized the area. "Continue on to Gohar al-Kaed for about a mile and a half."

"Do you have a destination in mind, or are we just driving?" He almost mowed down a donkey cart filled with tomatoes and giggling children, and had to go up on the curb to avoid two old men shuffling across the street in the semidarkness.

"We're heading toward Insaid al-Azhar Gardens. Lots of tourists, but better still, only a few blocks from Husani's apartment. I know the park quite well; we played there as children."

He checked the review mirror. "Good enough."

"I don't want these clowns to follow us to Husani's place, Thorne!"

"We'll shake them. Where next?"

"Sharp left. Stay on Passages Insaid al-Azhar Garden, then keep left at the fork. We're almost there."

IT WAS A WARM evening, with just a hint of a breeze scented with fresh-mown grass and night-blooming flowers. Thorne abandoned the Jeep in a gully running alongside the full parking lot and grabbed Isis's hand. She pulled him into the green park, beyond which he could see the glow of Cairo's lights reflecting off a scudding cloud cover.

A concert in the amphitheater was drawing a large crowd of cheerful, jostling teenagers who inhabited the hilly lawns and winding paths of park like ants at a picnic before the music started.

"This way," she said, tugging his hand. "I know a shortcut. I spent several months each year in school near here, and learned all about it. They spent thirty million dollars building this oasis in the middle of the city. It was a garbage dump for five hundred years! Can you imagine that?"

Thorne didn't give a flying fuck but let her rattle on about hidden walls and something about the park being expensive as they walked at a fast clip. Hedge-lined plazas, rolling lawns, flowering plants, and tall palms framed spectacular city views. Of greater interest was who, if anyone, might be following them. He kept a sharp eye out as they walked. He wouldn't bring danger to Husani's home and was prepared to run like hell if necessary.

Water features misted the air with their cooling spray

as Isis and Thorne mingled with the crowds, blending in as people streamed to the amphitheater. "Keep going; I'll catch up with you," he said in a low voice.

"*No.*" Her fingers tightened in his. "I don't want you going off alone."

That elicited a short bark of laughter. He'd been shot, stabbed, and almost gutted over the years as an MI5 operative, but no one had ever given a damn. "It's not my first day at kindergarten, darling. I'm going to double back to see if we're being followed."

"Then we go together." She met his gaze, his eyes shadowed by her glasses. Chewing her lower lip, Isis admitted, "Frankly, I don't want *me* to be alone, either."

He should've considered that, especially after what she'd been through in the past few days. He rarely worked with a partner, so being autonomous was par for the course. And the last time he'd partnered up—

Goddamn it, he didn't *want* to be responsible for anyone else's safety. Clearly he was shit at the job. Ask Lynn Maciej and Troy Ayers. "We'll double back to that fountain where the kids are playing. We can remain concealed by the hedges along the way."

She smiled her thanks. They went back, then casually drifted into a rowdy group of teenagers and adults. No one looked as though they were skulking, but then, professionals wouldn't. They, like himself, would blend undetected.

It was an exercise in futility. Too many people about, and he had no way to ID the men in the tan car. Unless they happened to be *in* said car. "I don't see anything. Let's head to Husani's and regroup."

HUSANI'S WIFE, RABIAH, WAS preparing dinner when they arrived. The small, crowded apartment smelled deliciously of roasting meat and spices. Isis's mouth watered as she was urged to the table. While they ate, Thorne pretty much interrogated her friend.

Husani and Rabiah had been surprised, but instantly welcoming when they showed up unannounced. "I'm sorry, Thorne doesn't mean——"

"Thorne *does* mean," he corrected as he rested his hand on her wrist. "Someone is trying their damnedest to kill us. I want to know who, and how they know we're even here. Are they after you or are they trying to kill me?"

That was pretty plain and out there. "I've been thinking about this in my copious spare time," Isis said facetiously.

"Maybe someone thinks you know something?" Rabiah suggested, spooning another slice of fiteer onto Isis's plate.

The light, flaky pastry stuffed with lamb and white cheese was mouthwateringly delicious, and even though Isis was full, she took another delectable, gooey bite. "Then they should politely stop me and ask a freaking question."

"You were followed from the minister's house, *aiwa*?" Husani gave her a worried look. "These men must've followed you from there." Thorne cocked his head in response. "Or from the market."

Thorne looked grim, his mouth tight. "Either. Both. I'm here to assist Isis in finding this tomb her father claims to have found and lost. But it's very possible someone from my past has caught up with me. I'm a British intelligence officer on inactive status. This man could be—probably *is*—behind these attempts. Both MI5 and the Mossad—"

"You are working with al-Mosad lil-Istikhbarat wal-Mahamm al-Khassah?" Husani asked, clearly impressed.

"Yes. Israel's Institute for Intelligence and Special Operations is vested in helping me find a man or syndicate who has been stealing and selling the Middle East's most priceless antiquities on the black market for years."

"And you believe that this man has heard of the professor's claim of finding Queen Cleopatra's tomb, and wants it at all costs?"

"That's where I'm heading. But as yet there's nothing concrete to tie Professor Magee to Boris Yermalof."

"Other than a frigging queen's ransom in priceless artifacts, you mean?" Isis said flatly, leaning forward, her arms on the table.

"Yeah, I must admit, it's the only thing that makes sense."

"It would've been nice of you to share your thoughts along the way," she told him.

"My contacts have drawn off the men chasing us this evening. I also have two men posted at the hospital in case your father's attackers decide to go back. He's secured, and no one followed us here. But Isis must be returned home, where she can be kept safe while I resolve this."

"I concur." Husani cradled his coffee cup, a deep frown creasing his brow.

"May *I* be allowed to insert a word in edgewise?" Isis straightened from the table. "*My* father was attacked only a few hours ago in Seattle. I won't be much safer *there* than I am *here*."

"*There* you'll be under the protection of Zakary Stark and a full security team."

Isis slumped back in her chair. "Excellent point."

"What do you need from us?" Rabiah asked quietly as she sat down beside Isis, who'd left a small amount of food on her plate as was the custom, so her hostess wouldn't keep refilling her plate.

"You've been more than gracious serving us this delicious meal, and giving us respite from the men following us." Thorne smiled at their hostess. He had a sexy smile when he bothered, and seeing it now made Isis's heart skip a beat.

She picked up her glass of orange Fanta, sipping the sweet soda to prevent herself from lunging across the table to kiss him. Despite, or because of the danger, and the crazy rush of endorphins, pheromones, and whatever else, Isis wanted her hands on him in the worst possible way.

"We'll find a hotel off the beaten path," he told their hosts, apparently oblivious to the neon sign over her head blinking out TAKE ME. "I'll call in some favors. See if anyone on the street knows anything about these dangerous men. See if I can charter a private plane to get Isis out of the country as soon as possible."

"We own an empty rental apartment one floor below," Husani offered after a silent communication with his wife got a nod. "It's furnished. You can stay there as long as you like. I'll lend you my computer should you need it."

❧ TEN ❧

Claiming that the tiny room was an *apartment* was a stretch. Barely five hundred square feet, it held an aging sofa bed, an armchair, a hot plate, and a minibar-sized refrigerator. It smelled strongly of insect repellent and cleaning products.

Isis placed her camera bag on the table beside an antiquated boxy nineteen-inch TV as she looked around. "At least it's clean and varmint free—"

Thorne grabbed her upper arm, spinning her around and into his arms. Off balance, she fell neatly against his chest, her hands coming to rest over his heart. Her eyes widened as he slid off her glasses and stuck them in his back pocket. He took her mouth. She tasted of orange Fanta and hot silky female. A lethal combo Thorne didn't waste time resisting.

It had been a long fucking day, and adrenaline still surged through his body despite several hours spent relaxing with her friends. The longer he'd sat there, trying to appear engaged, the longer he'd observed the sweet curve of her mouth as she talked, and the soft, plump outline of her breasts shifting under her thin cotton T-shirt as she breathed.

Thorne was done observing.

Her eager response made him crazy as she feasted on him, her lush mouth eager and active, her tongue dancing and playing against his. The taste of her went to his head like fine, aged brandy. So good in fact that the kiss almost blew the top of his head off. He forgot to breathe as he gathered her supple body against him, and ignored the surge of numbers tumbling through his brain like jumping beans before they streamlined into a long, endless parade of numbers superimposed behind his closed lids.

28332903283332903283332903283332903283332903 28332903.

Bloody hell. Not *now.*

Sliding both hands down her slender back, he cupped her shapely arse through the thin cotton of her pants. She arched against him, pressing her pelvis against his erection as her nimble fingers skimmed under his shirt and up his back, her short nails scoring his skin. His dick jumped in response. Without opening his eyes, he walked her backward toward a horizontal surface—the swaybacked sofa a few short steps across the threadbare carpet.

Barely separating their mouths, he yanked her neon orange T-shirt over her head. Her moan of pleasure vibrated against his chest as he glided a hand up her side, then slipped his fingers inside the cotton cup of her bra to fill his palm with the sweet, silky weight of her breast.

Her skin felt impossibly soft, slightly damp, her nipple puckered and hard against his palm.

Oh, for God's sa— *28332903282832903328332903.*

Skimming his hand up her back, Thorne unclasped the thin wisp of her bra as they came to a halt against the edge of the sofa. Isis's fingers latched onto his belt buckle . . .

28332903. He blew out a frustrated breath. Lifting his mouth a breath away from hers, he muttered thickly, "Where is it?"

"Hmm?" She opened slightly dazed eyes. "Where is—what?"

"You have an article on you that you weren't wearing before. Hand it over."

He observed the glaze of passion clear a little. "Wow, you *are* good." She pulled an inch-square chamois leather pouch out of her back pocket. "But can't we finish the kiss first?"

Thorne tilted her face up and raked his teeth on her bottom lip. "That and more," he promised, voice thick as he shifted to put some space between them.

Reaching back, she frowned and refastened her bra. "What we were just doing is more important than a cheap reproduction necklace."

Wasn't it, though. The numbers, however, weren't going to stop because they were randy. Loosening the cord, Thorne tipped the pouch over his open hand. A delicate gold chain slithered onto his palm, followed by what looked like a small oval amulet. The goddess Isis, her wings spread. He'd seen this image everywhere at the souk and even on posters at the London Natural History Museum. "Where'd you get this?"

Her hair curled wildly over her bare shoulders, and Isis pushed it out of her face impatiently. He could see the dark areolas through the delicate beige satin of her bra, still-hard peaks begging for his touch. The dim lamplight shone on her skin, made it appear milky pale. He wanted to taste it, damn it.

28332903.

"My father gave it to me years ago—the amulet, not the chain. It's my lucky amulet, but the chain is so delicate I don't wear it very often. With all this crazy running around, I took it out of my camera bag and stuck it in my— You're being very mysterious." Isis bent to pick up her T-shirt from the floor. When she pulled it over her head it was inside out. Not a problem, since Thorne had every intention of stripping it off her again in a few moments.

"Even though it holds great sentimental value," she told him, squinting to apparently bring him into focus as she pulled the shirt over her hips, "it has no *monetary* value, you know."

*28332903283332903283332903283332903283332903
28332903.* "I'm getting a GPS reading from it."

Her eyebrow rose into her bangs. "For Khan el-Khalili bazaar? Because that's where he told me he bought it—"

"Hold that thought." Thorne pulled his comm out of his back pocket, handed her back her glasses, then punched in the longitude and latitude running through his mind like a ticker tape. "Valley of the Scorpions."

"Really? That can't be right. He never found anything there."

"But that's where he told you he was when he called you that night, right? Maybe he didn't get this there three months ago. But this is the location I'm seeing."

"What? Are you telling me this is from Cleo's tomb?"

"I have no idea whose tomb it comes from, but it *didn't* come from the bazaar."

"Are you positive?"

"Unequivocally."

She drooped down to the sagging cushions of the sofa. "Are you saying he did find her tomb in the Valley of the Scorpions? For real? The same valley that's below the dam and about to become a giant freaking *lake* for water-skiers and fishermen?"

He sat beside her. The ancient cushions obligingly threw her against him. He wrapped an arm around her shoulders to steady her. "That would be the one."

"It's being flooded next week; you remember that small detail, right?"

"Take a breath, you're hyperventilating. We need to get out there and see if this is even a possibility."

"They can't be allowed to flood the valley if there's even a small chance that Queen Cleopatra's tomb is right there!" She pushed out of his hold and maneuvered herself off the lumpy cushions to stand up. "They *can't*. Who do we talk to first? Minister of Water? Or Minister of Antiquities? This is *the* find of a lifetime. My God, my father was there—"

"We don't know that for sure."

"*I* know for sure! Thorne, he was digging in that valley a year ago. And now—now I *bet* that was where he was digging three months ago when he was attacked."

"He was discovered two hundred miles away from the valley, Isis. Two *hundred* miles. Possibly he found this little amulet a year ago and gave it to you as a memento. Do you have any proof that it was found in Cleopatra's tomb? No."

"I just *know* it was," she said stubbornly, folding it gently in her palm, then resting her fist over her breast. "It doesn't have to be based on anything but faith. I've never doubted my father. He might be confused, he might be a lot of things, but he found her, I know he did.

"Cleopatra was obsessed with Isis, and they say paintings and statues were all over her homes. If you're sure this wasn't purchased in the bazaar, as my father claimed, then it has significant value. And knowing him, if he lied about where he found it—even to me—then I know this came from her tomb. Just as much as I know that my father found the tomb, and was robbed of his discovery! And that tomb is about to be destroyed if we don't put a stop to the opening of that dam. They moved Abu Simbel when they built Aswan; they can move the contents of Cleo's tomb before they flood the Valley of the Scorpions!"

"In less than a week?" he pointed out reasonably.

Her cheeks were flushed, her nose pink, and her eyes looked enormous magnified by tears behind her glasses. "Yes. *Whatever* it takes."

Thorne leaned back, crossing one leg over his knee

and stretching his arms out along the seat back. Bloody hell. This was already a clusterfuck without her trying to stop a massive decade-long project. "That takes *years* of planning. Particularly if this really is her tomb. The national spotlight will be glaring. Thousands of lives and billions of dollars are at stake. No one is going to be willing to risk so much on so little."

"Are you kidding me? The discovery of this tomb will be *monumental*. Bigger than the discovery of King Tut-ankhamen! We have to stop them from flooding the valley. That's all we have to do. Stop the flooding. *Look*. Find if it really *is* her. We can go from there, right?"

Thorne reached out to snag her wrist, tugging her back to sit beside him. In a well-orchestrated move he stripped her T-shirt over her head and crowded her down against the pillows. "We can't do anything until morning." He breathed in the scent of her skin as he kissed his way down her throat. Her pulse was rapid because of her agitation, but he was about to change that to a different kind of stimulation. "We have hours to kill before then."

"Hmm," she murmured indistinctly, lifting her mouth for his kiss. "And you weren't planning on sleeping much, were you?"

"How about not sleeping at all?"

LACING HIS FINGERS WITH hers, Thorne held them above her head so they were palm to palm, his hard chest pressed against her breasts. "You drive me mad, woman." His breath fanned her face.

"It's purely intentional." Isis bit his lower lip and felt

a curl of satisfaction as he growled low in his throat and his mouth crushed hers.

Lifting his head, he stared into her eyes as if he was reading her mind. The naked hunger on his face stole her breath and made her heart beat even faster. "Are you absolutely, positively *sure*? Because this time I'm not backing up."

Isis met his intense gaze inches from her own. Heart hammering hard against her rib cage, she combed her fingers through the short, velvety-soft pelt of his hair above his ears. "Absolutely, positively."

He reached out and plucked off her glasses, setting them somewhere behind him. A prickle of anticipation mixed with hot need as his head lowered the last few inches. His sensual mouth didn't need to coax hers open; she wanted him inside. She met his bold, eager tongue with her own, craving more, wanting to crawl inside his skin.

The hot, devouring kiss was unlike any she'd known or even imagined. She loved kissing, but this—locking lips with Thorne was more than she could've fantasized. She fell into it headlong, intoxicated by his heat and the rich, heady taste of the strong coffee he'd been drinking at dinner.

Isis glided her fingers up his sides but kept getting distracted by hot satin skin and the kiss that was soul-eating and delicious.

Tangling his fingers in her hair, he used one large hand to hold her head exactly where he wanted it, and the other to skim under her T-shirt and glide up her body. His fingers were hot, slightly rough, and in a hurry.

He smelled so good—soap and starch, and man. And his own unique dizzying smell that was part all of those, and part the natural musk of his skin.

He rolled off her without warning, leaving Isis blinking and bewildered as he toed off his shoes. Maintaining eye contact, he yanked his T-shirt over his head, tossing it on the floor. She'd wondered forever what his body would look like, and here he was, in living, spectacular 3-D. Tall, lean, muscular, and a hard ass, he was her every fantasy rolled into one delicious package.

She drank him in. Tough guy. The dark stubble on his stubborn jaw made him look like a pirate. How was it possible for a mouth to be so serious, and yet so sensual? Isis wanted to stroke his face, to explore every masculine dip and curve. Satin skin stretched tightly over clearly defined muscles. His broad shoulders blocked out the lamplight behind him, and Isis imagined she could feel the glide of his shadow against her skin as he undressed.

She admired the crisp dark hair disappearing into the waistband of his jeans as his hands went to his belt buckle. Her tongue stuck to the roof of her mouth and her heart beat loud and fast as she saw a wedge of dark hair behind his fingers.

Heart thudding, Isis looked her fill. "You're beautiful."

His cheeks darkened and his lips tightened. "Different reaction in a second; brace yourself."

She sat up on her elbows, barely registering his words, fascinated by the striptease just a few feet away. She'd never seen anything as sexy as Thorne's slow reveal of his rock-hard body. The wedge between the teeth of the zipper widened to frame the long curve of his erect penis, which brushed the taut muscles of his belly.

Already unbearably turned on, Isis's breath caught as her body pulsed and moistened in response to the visual stimuli. Her hands might not be as steady as Thorne's, but she too scrambled to get naked. Reaching behind her back to unclasp her bra, she watched Thorne's jeans inch down a little more, showing a lot more. Dear God. The man was built . . . *large*, she saw, fascinated as he exposed the rest of himself to her hungry gaze.

Feeling as sensual and sexy as his eyes telegraphed, she tossed her bra over her head to land somewhere on the floor behind the sofa. Feeling buoyant and heavy, giddy and unbearably focused, Isis slid both hands down her belly, feeling the softness of her own skin, and the warmth as her skin heated. A hard, unsteady pulse throbbed in her breasts and between her legs.

She might explode from longing, and he'd yet to touch her. Anticipation made her almost delirious, and the brush of her own fingers as she slowly slid the pants down her hips was almost unbearable. The cotton pants had an elastic waistband. Handy. And *quick*. Lifting her butt without taking her eyes off him, Isis slid the pants and her panties down her legs.

Not knowing where to look first, wanting to run her hands all over him, her gaze tracked up his belly, over his deeply muscled chest, up the strong column of his throat to his tense expression. But his penis drew her gaze like metal to a magnet.

Deep inside, her muscles pulsed in time with her heartbeat. Shifting on the sofa, she held out her arms to him.

His desire for her was evident. Boy howdy was it evident. Her fingers flexed on the sofa cushions. "I want you, Connor James Thorne." Her voice was unrecognizable, it was so husky and thick with longing. She felt hot, then shivery cold, aware of the rough texture of the cushions beneath her, and the almost imperceptible drift of cool air on her naked body.

His eyes burned like twin green flames as he ran his gaze from her face, over her bare breasts and down her legs. She felt the *heat* of that look like a physical caress.

The distended cords in his neck visibly throbbed, and a light film of sweat turned his skin to metallic bronze. He looked more powerful than any Egyptian god, sexier than a mortal male had a right to look.

She wanted to feel his heavy body push her deep into the pillows; she needed him to spread her legs and wedge his narrow hips between them. She had to feel his thick shaft deep inside her, and God help her, she couldn't wait much longer. The suspense was killing her.

"In every way there is," she admitted softly, "I want you."

"Yeah, well—" His voice was suddenly tightly neutral. His broad chest rose and fell as he dropped his jeans and any underwear he might've been wearing to the floor, kicking them aside. Then he just stood there.

Isis froze, sucking in a horrified breath as she stared, appalled. Her tongue stuck to the roof of her mouth, and her lips felt numb. "Dear God—"

Her vision blurred, and she had to blink furiously to

see him clearly. No wonder he was in pain all the time. Of *course* he limped. His leg was a mangled mess. The skin angry red, puckered and stitched like a patchwork quilt. There were pins holding his leg together, metal that would set off airport detectors, metal that fought against his body even while it healed.

There was a heart-wrenching disconnect between his wounds and his strong, stunningly healthy body. A contradiction between vulnerability and strength. And she wanted to weep.

Trying to breathe through the tight ache in her chest, Isis swung her legs off the sofa, then sank to her knees in front of him. Curving both hands gently around the back of his thigh, she laid her cheek against the ravaged scars. "That sick son of a bitch almost killed you!"

For a few heavy beats of her heart, he didn't say anything, then murmured thickly, "You unman me." His fingers tangled gently in her hair as she pressed her hot cheek to his leg where shiny surgical scars felt cool, and healthy skin burned to the touch. "I thought you'd pass out when you saw this mess."

"Then you don't know me at *all*." This time the tears of fury threatened to spill. She gritted her teeth and forced them away. "I want to find this guy and do unmentionable things to hi—"

Thorne's laugh sounded rusty as he combed his fingers tenderly through her hair. "Do them to me instead."

"Can't I just have a moment to fantasize about causing him excruciating pain?"

"How about giving *us* excruciating pleasure instead?"

Brushing another kiss to the indentation of a once well-developed thigh muscle, Isis skimmed her hand across the delicate skin above the hideous wound, where his flesh was still smooth. His body tightened. "Sensitive?"

"You're damned close to where I want you to be." His voice was thick.

His golden body was lightly furred with silky dark hair as Isis glided her mouth after her hand. Velvety skin to rough hair. She pressed her face to him there, where smooth met coarse, and inhaled his heat. His body humbled her. His strength and vulnerability. Trailing her lips upward, she let her hands lead the way to the thick curve of his penis.

Curling her fingers around the velvety length, Isis brought her mouth over him, licking the satiny vein pulsing beneath her tongue, then taking him in her mouth, making him shudder and tighten his fingers in her hair. "You don't—" His fingers tightened in her hair.

Ignoring his halfhearted protest, she loved him with her mouth, her teeth, her tongue. Sucking him deep, savoring the musky male smell of him, his hot salty taste made her impossibly hotter. She wanted to give him exquisite pleasure to at least momentarily blot away the pain. His heavy, rapid heartbeats pulsed against the inside of her cheek. She scraped her teeth delicately over the entire length, and reveled in the hard shudder that racked his body. Isis slid her other hand around to caress the taut cheek of his butt as it flexed beneath her exploring fingers.

Suckling harder, she pulled him deeper, until his hips arched against her and he made a rough sound, fisting his hands in her hair. Milking him with her hand, Isis swirled her tongue, caressing his length, reveling in her power to make him this helpless. She felt the unbearable tension stiffen his body. "You don't have to—God—"

She *wanted* to. Holding him tightly she rode his wave, her nails digging into his butt cheek, her fingers tightened around him to hold him there as he came.

His large hand pressed her face against him as his hips bucked. After several moments he let go of her and pulled her to her feet. Closing his arms around her, Thorne pulled her hard against his sweat-dampened chest, his breath ragged, his heartbeat manic. They were both shaking as she wiped her mouth on his shoulder, and he stroked her back.

"The tongue is mightier than the sword," she teased, her own need a powerful driving force that made her knees wobble and her hands shake. The brush of the crisp hair on his chest against her tender breasts made her crazy with need.

Thorne laughed as he backed her the few feet to the sofa. "Let's see how you like the tables turned, darling."

Isis liked it just fine.

She went from standing to prone before she knew it.

His breath was as rapid as her own as he supported his weight on his elbows and slid over her. "Yes!"

Still semi-erect, he slid into the delta of her thighs, making her pant lightly. She wiggled to give him more room, and herself more air. She felt crazed, balanced precariously on a knife's edge of lust and longing. "I'm not sure I'm going to make it through too much foreplay," she warned as he cupped her breasts.

"Define 'too much.'" He didn't give her time or breath to answer as he slanted his mouth over hers in a fierce, primal kiss that curled her toes and made her moan.

When he lifted his head her lips felt bee-stung and hot. "M-more than two minutes before you're in-inside me?"

"Shall we see?"

"No, I—"

Thorne slid down her body, his breath scalding her breasts. Taking a hard nipple deep in his mouth he sucked and swirled his tongue around the bud until Isis lifted her lips off the couch to achieve contact. "Don't torture me, when I gave you—"

"Unspeakable pleasure," he finished, his moist breath trailing down her belly.

She wanted him so badly her head thrashed against the cushions. "Thorne." His hair was too short to grab, so she took hold of his ear instead. "I'm too sensitive for this right now. Another ti—"

"I feel your heat." Easing her legs apart with his callused, roughened palm, he slid his hand higher, fingertips brushing maddeningly across the sensitive skin of her inner thigh. The path of his clever fingers produced intense heat and a pulse of longing deep inside.

"Well then, you—you know I'm going to c-come just by you looking at me."

His shoulders pushed her knees wide, so that she was exposed and vulnerable. She squirmed against the too-intense sensation, poised on a peak of jagged, feverish need. Her fingers dug into his shoulders as his hands cupped her butt cheeks. She wasn't sure who trembled more. "I'll get you back for this, you sadistic bastard."

His hot breath fanned her moist heat and she shuddered before he laid his mouth on her. "Fair enough." Pressed his mouth to her mound. "Name the time and place. I'll be ready."

She loved the hardness of his broad shoulder under her tightly clenched fingers. "I might t-tie you down and have my wicked way with you while *you* th-thrash and beg."

"I'll bring the restraints."

Weakly she sat up on one elbow. It was shocking how turned on she was seeing his head between her legs. *"Seriously?"*

"Oh, yeah. Seriously."

"I don't think I'd enjoy being restrained."

"Oh, I think you'd enjoy the hell out of it."

"I hate feeling helpless."

"There are times when helpless feels good."

She gave a strangled laugh. "You've never been helpless a day in your life."

"There's a time and place—"

She felt his hot, moist breath inches from the soft curls at the apex of her thighs. "Oh, God," she said in a harsh, muffled voice, flinging an arm across her eyes and biting her lip as his arm tightened around her hips and the spear of his tongue parted her slick folds. *"Connor . . ."*

"Hmm?"

Her entire body trembled as he slid his tongue into her wet folds. He tasted her, hummed his appreciation low so that his hot breath and the vibration shot through her and her body responded like a tuning fork. "Maybe we— God, Connor— Wait! I'm— Give me a minute. I *need* full body contact—" Her back arched as he set his mouth on her, and she came so hard she almost bit off her tongue.

Hot sunbursts spiraling from her core made her gasp and shudder in his arms. He held her, his face pressed to her belly, as the shudders rippled in widening circles and she could drag in ragged breaths. "Incredible. I can't move. Let yourself out."

He chuckled, stroking his palm on her belly, which was in no way calming. "Not going anywhere."

"I need a nap."

He slid his way up her body, supporting his weight on his arms. "A full eight-hour nap. After."

She punched her fist against his shoulder. It was a pretty weak blow since she didn't have an ounce of energy in her. "Get off me; you can sleep on the floor."

He cupped her face in his large palm, his eyes hot as he looked down at her. "Not kind under the circumstances."

Isis slipped her hand around the back of his neck and gave a little tug. "Tit for tat."

He cupped her breast, strumming his thumb across the sensitive tip. "And these are perfection."

Isis smiled even as she shuddered from the contact.

His head swooped down and he gave her a fierce, ravenous kiss that tasted of the ocean, tasted of her. While her body was racked with hard, deep shudders he surged up, then plunged inside her, his hips immediately pumping hard against her.

He shook as hard as she did, muscles rigid, skin burning hot.

His grip was hard, instant, right on the edge of painful, but it was a good pain that only he could assuage, and she moved her hips in counterpoint. He was long and thick, and her body welcomed the invasion. Isis pressed her damp face into his neck as her internal muscles pulsed and clenched around him.

They came together in a spectacular light show that left them both limp and panting.

"Christ. I think I just flew into the sun," Thorne said against her sweaty throat. He was heavy, and their skin was glued together. "Am I squashing you?"

"Yes." Isis held him in place with a weak grip on his buns. "But don't move. I can't take the excitement."

Thorne smiled against her throat, then flexed his hips.

⫷ ELEVEN ⫸

I will procure two men to go with y—" Husani's gaze flickered over Isis's shoulder. His face hardened. "Brengard approaches on your right. He is already schooling his features as if surprised to encounter you."

They'd accompanied her friend to the souk the next morning so they could pick up a new car. Isis half turned, moving closer to Thorne. She saw herself reflected in his sunglasses. Once again the humidity had turned her hair into a dark cloud of out-of-control curls around her shoulders. Husani plopped a wide-brimmed straw hat on her head, and she twisted the unruly mass into a knot, stuffing it beneath the crown to bare her neck to any stray breeze. There wasn't one, but she lived in hope.

Even the hours of delicious lovemaking the night before couldn't compensate for her lack of sleep. She felt sweaty and disheveled and decidedly grumpy. Thorne looked cool, calm, and annoyingly affable.

They'd stopped only long enough to buy more new clothes—something *not* in Isis's budget. At least Thorne was a cheap date. Thank God he was happy in jeans and a navy blue T-shirt, which did lovely things stretched over his broad chest. She grabbed jeans and a purple T-shirt with her namesake Isis, wings spread across her boobs.

Everything she owned in the world was slung across her chest in her camera bag.

"Do you believe in coincidences?" Through her darkened glasses she watched Dylan's approach. Thorne, too, tracked him as he wove his way through the throng of people, heading directly for Husani's shop.

"Never."

She looked up at Thorne. His features had turned grim, dark, and immovable. A different man than the tender lover she'd discovered the night before. "Neither do—"

"Isis? My God. Is that you?"

She turned to face her father's protégé. "Dylan. What a . . . surprise." Just seeing him pissed her off, and she deliberately kept her tone borderline rude. He was no more surprised to see her than she was to see him, and she hated that they were playing this fake social game. *Was* he the moron who'd shot at them last night and tried to run them off the road?

"It's great to see you!" When he looked as though he was going to pull her in for a hug, Thorne blocked him, taking Isis's hand and tugging her against him. She liked feeling his hard body against hers, even if they were in the middle of the souk with Dylan blocking the way. Husani came to stand on her other side. It was sweet of the two men to want to protect her, but Dylan wasn't likely to do anything in a public market. Thorne gave the other man a cool nod. "Thorne, Isis's fiancé. You must be Brengard."

Dylan's gaze flickered from him back to Isis. "This *is* a surprise. This is the last place I'd expect to see you, what with your father . . ."

Isis liked that Thorne didn't pretend he didn't know who Dylan was, or mangle the other man's name just to prove a point. She, however, wasn't quite as evolved. She pushed her glasses up her nose with her giving-the-bird finger. "He's doing much better, thanks for asking."

Dylan flinched at her sarcasm. "If you'd give me a minute, I was just about to. How is the professor?"

"Fighting fit, and in top form," Thorne inserted smoothly.

Dylan looked momentarily nonplussed, but regrouped quickly. He was like a damned cat, always landing on his feet. Isis had known he was a little too smooth, but she hadn't realized until this very second that he wasn't smooth, he was *slick*.

"That's . . . That's good to know. Is he here with you?" He glanced around somewhat nervously, as if expecting her father to jump out of one of the nearby baskets.

"No, he's getting ready to go to London for his exhibit." He would be, if he remembered the event was about to take place. Which he didn't, having freaking *Alzheimer's*. Of course Dylan would know that if he'd really paid any attention to her father or cared about him. Isis's entire body bristled with resentment. Directed at whom, she wasn't quite sure, but since Dylan was standing in front of her, he'd do.

Dylan frowned. "Ah." He glanced from Thorne to Isis. "Fiancé?"

"It's very recent," she said dryly. Like a nanosecond ago. "You look well." He did, annoyingly. Tanned, fit, and ridiculously handsome. A Ken doll, dressed in ironed khakis and his usual affectation: a brown felt Indiana Jones fedora. Indiana Jones could cream his ass with his whip hand tied behind his back. Thorne could do it with *both* hands tied behind his back and his eyes closed. Isis would buy tickets for *that* match.

"Seriously, how's the professor after that incident?" He fingered a length of purple silk piled haphazardly on the table. To avoid eye contact? Oh, yeah. He quickly dug into his breast pocket, took out mirrored aviator shades, and slid them on, effectively blocking where he was looking and the expression in his eyes.

Ass. "Curious as to why you haven't inquired after his health in all this time," Isis told him coolly.

Dylan's face darkened. "I was quite ill, and then he returned to Seattle . . ."

"That's right, you weren't able to go with him on that last dig. What was it? Food poisoning?" Her face, reflected clearly in his glasses, showed her disbelief. She'd never been good at poker. What she thought came through loud and clear in her expressions. Fortunately she didn't care if Dylan saw them or not.

"Right, bad fish. Awful."

Thorne glanced down at her with a small frown, then directed his X-ray eyes at Dylan, like a death ray right through his sunglasses. "I heard it was the flu." His tone was cool and clipped.

"Right, right. Both, actually. It was touch and go."

"One has to be careful what one eats here, that's for sure. Are you here on a dig?" Thorne asked conversationally.

Dylan moved into the shade of the awning, out of the hot sun. "I am. I came to hire a few more men . . ." He glanced over at Husani, who gave him a stony look in return. There'd never been any love lost between them. Husani had a keen nose for bullshit. Now that she'd gotten a whiff of it off Dylan, it was easy to sense. What exactly had she seen in him beyond his Ken doll looks?

"Oh?" Isis said curiously. If the son of a bitch was anywhere near her father's site she'd—she'd sic Thorne on him. "Must be something important to work here at this time of the year. Who's lead on the dig?"

"I am."

"Really?" She made sure her contempt of that notion came across loud and clear. "And where is it?"

"Abusir," he answered smoothly, trying to brush a fly off his cheek. Unintimidated, it stayed put, as flies here had a tendency to do. Apparently the fly knew bullshit when he smelled it.

She narrowed her eyes, jaw tight. *"Abusir?"*

Thorne squeezed her hand when her entire body jerked in reaction. "And what's there?" he asked her calmly.

"A two-thousand-year-old temple to the god Osiris," she said through gritted teeth, giving Dylan a death stare.

"It's an ancient site at the third-century BCE Taposiris Magna temple.

"My father dug there a year ago and found nothing of note," she continued. "What a strange coincidence that you're back in the exact same place without him, especially since I believe you were the one who said it was a 'colossal' waste of time."

"We were off by half a mile," Dylan said with a defensive shrug. "And even if he *had* found this particular tomb, he never went deep enough. Besides, he dug elsewhere that year, remember? He had several digs going at the same time. I told him then, and I'm telling you now. He spread himself too thin, spread our *resources* too thin . . . You must admit patience was never the professor's strong suit."

"Here's a good idea," she snapped. "You don't talk about my father, and I don't punch you in the nose for stealing his find."

Dylan rotated his shoulders, a sign he was uncomfortable. "You were never prone to violence, babe. What's wrong with you? You know how this business works." He leaned against the heavy metal pole supporting the awning, the picture of nonchalance and innocence as he tucked his fingers in the front pockets of his loose khaki pants. "The professor had thirty years to find the tomb. Now it's my turn."

"Using everything he taught you, and stealing his claims and maps?"

Dylan picked the fly off his sweaty chin, dropping it to the ground, then stepped on it. "How— Don't start accusing me just because your father is washed-up. It's early days, yet, but I believe *I've* found Queen Cleopatra's tomb. I'm sorry, Isis. I was going to call and let you know as a courtesy to your father."

"Were you?" Her fingers ached, and she realized she was holding so tightly to Thorne's hand that her fingers had gone bloodless and numb. She loosened her grip a little. "What made you decide to revisit the site?" He was a moron. There was absolutely nothing in those tombs. She'd been with her father when he and Dylan had discovered them. Empty, nada. Not a scarab.

The fact that Dylan was back in *that* location was odd. He was an opportunist, not a fool. Digs were expensive, the red tape extensive. If he was there it was because he believed he would discover something of value—which meant that when he'd worked for her father, he'd discovered something and not passed on the knowledge.

"Radar survey identified three underground sites, not just the one. The area was untouched, ripe for excavation."

Ripe to rape and pillage, he meant. "And what? You hit the jackpot? Did you *find* her actual tomb?" Anger clarified her senses, heightened her need to protect her father. Get rid of the skunk bastard they'd trusted. Thorne could help her hide Dylan's body.

"We found *ten* nobles' tombs nearby—"

"Interesting, but not Cleo." Would he tell her if he had? The answer to that was yes. *If* he'd excavated and pulled out all the artifacts and documented them. The answer was no if he'd barely started and didn't want her poking a stick into the wheels of his dig. She could go back to the ministry and reopen her father's claim.

"Twenty-some coins with *her* face and name inscribed on them. I also discovered a ceramic fragment of a mask I believe was of Mark Antony."

"You found Mark Antony's death mask?" If this was true, Dylan had made the discovery of the century. Her *father's* discovery. Her stomach knotted.

Dylan shrugged. "It has the cleft chin of the Roman general—"

She made a rude noise. "Maybe it was a prop for Richard Burton's role as Antony in the movie," she suggested, trying to unclamp her tight jaw.

"Denial is a waste of time. Your father had his day in the sun; now I'm having mine. And if you think for a moment that I didn't cover all my bases with the MSA, you're mistaken. The professor's rights to those sites ran out weeks ago." The Ministry of State for Antiquities was responsible for regulating, conserving, and protecting all antiquities and archaeological excavations in Egypt. Dylan had always had an excellent rapport with the members of the Administrative Council. Her father had not. "Where's the money coming from, Dylan? Who's bankrolling you?"

"I have several sponsors. Just as the professor had." He pushed away from the pole, making the tassels lining the top edge of the awning dance in the harsh sunlight.

"I'm trying to figure out," Thorne inserted, voice deceptively quiet, "what the fuck your angle is, Brengard. One minute you're sucking up to an old flame, next you're doing everything in your piss-poor arsenal to tick her off. Not smart." He deliberately moved into Dylan's space. "Piss her off, and you piss me off. We've been here less than forty-eight hours, and we've been chased, shot at, and run off the road. What do you have to do with that?"

Dylan's mouth tightened and he took a step back. "Absolutely *nothing*. I didn't even know Isis was here until a second ago, and I resent your insinuation that I——"

Isis sensed Thorne's simmering anger, and was rather sorry that he remained rooted in place. His animosity was—to her, anyway—crystal clear. "If I discover you had anything to do with putting Isis in any danger, I'll rip your balls off and stuff them down your throat."

Stunned at how something said in such a calm voice could make every hair on her body quiver, Isis demanded of Dylan, "*Have* you been following us?"

"What on earth would I follow you *for*? I've found Cleopatra's tomb, Isis. You have nothing I want."

"Fortunate." Thorne lifted their clasped hands to his mouth to kiss her knuckles. "Because Isis has everything *I* want, and I don't share."

"THAT WAS SCARILY IMPRESSIVE." Isis's cheery tones followed him as they got into another Mossad-supplied vehicle parked in the garage near the mosque. She took off the straw hat, tossed it in the backseat, then ran her fingers through her hair as he got in on the driver's side. The last thing she acted like was scared. His ego warmed as he acknowledged that she sounded, if anything, impressed.

"I did my job." His job as an MI5 operative, not a Lodestone agent. He buckled up and indicated she do the same.

"You threatened him *and* staked a claim in two seconds flat." She fastened her seat belt while he went through the compartment under his floor mat. A second Glock. Couple of clips. Knife. Thorne left everything, but shoved the clips in his pockets.

"About that," he said flatly. "I'm sure it doesn't need pointing out, but I come from a long line of cold bastards. I don't do warm and fuzzy."

She turned big brown eyes on him. "And you're telling me this non–news flash—why?"

"I don't want you getting the wrong idea." He didn't want to give *himself* the wrong idea, either. Her future happiness had nothing to do with him. Couldn't have anything to do with him. He was all about his job. Without MI5 he didn't know what the fuck to do with himself, and he couldn't do Isis Magee as a temporary filler until he was back at the agency. There were rules. And he'd abide by them. Even if they were of his own making.

She gave him a narrow-eyed glance. "What kind of wrong idea? That you were serious back there? Trust me, I didn't—don't."

Bugger it. She was hurt, and why the fuck wouldn't she be? A woman like Isis Magee only saw the good in people. He'd lost his halo a long time ago—with no apology. But she deserved the white-picket-fence fantasy she'd planned, so long as she didn't picture him at her outdoor BBQ wearing a checked apron and holding hamburger tongs. His gut clenched at the image.

Better to get any illusions settled, bruised feelings or not. "Glad we are on the same page." Gazing ahead, he heard her shift on the seat. "As much as I enjoy the sex, when this is over, I'm going back to my job at MI5." Sure, he felt like a shit for being so blunt, but the cards had to be on the table before she started embroidering him into her rosy, happily-ever-after needlepoint. This was not a conversation he'd ever had with any other woman he'd been intimate with. They all knew the score and didn't need it spelled out for them. Isis was different. "Operatives must remain unencumbered for obvious reasons."

Isis flushed, her skin moist from the heat. Pushing her glasses up the bridge of her nose, she turned to face him. Without blinking an eye, she lobbed his plain speaking right back. "I enjoy the sex, too. No worries— I have zero expectations. You're a warrior, not a hunter-gatherer." Her lips tilted but the smile didn't reach her eyes. "Your bachelorhood is safe with me. I promise, I won't drag you kicking and screaming to the altar."

Uncomfortable at the picture she presented, he spoke somewhat defensively. "Marriage isn't in the cards for me. Never has been."

"You've made your point, Thorne." There was a bite to her voice now as she adjusted the air vent. "With a sledgehammer. I get it. There's no need to flog a dead horse."

Isis's annoyance angered him, creating a desire for her

to understand. And what? Give her fucking blessing for him being an ass?

Last night Isis had taken Thorne to another level of sexual awareness, her damn touch imprinting itself on his skin. He shivered in memory. Mentally, physically, she'd forged a connection he'd never experienced before. Her caress, her openness, her willingness to be a partner as they'd joined in the best sex of his life.

Still. He wasn't marrying her. Coldhearted now, he imagined by looking at his father that he'd only get chillier with age. Then Isis would be miserable, they'd divorce, and she'd be left with shattered dreams. Better to keep away from the get-go. As soon as his doctors signed off on him, he'd be back in the thick of things.

"I don't think anyone has *ever* threatened Dylan that way. I must admit, I enjoyed seeing him squirm." She neatly changed the subject, cutting him loose.

Thorne didn't like feeling like a right bastard for stating the simple truth, but he didn't want to hurt her. He couldn't let it go. "I like you. The time we've spent together."

"No happy ending, Thorne." Her voice, matter-of-fact, challenged him.

"Right, then." He turned on the engine, cranking up the air, then gestured for her to hand over her glasses. She did, and he cleaned the lenses with the bottom of his shirt. "I never say anything I don't mean, and never make threats I don't intend to follow through." He handed her back her glasses.

"Thanks. I think you may be the one flogging that dead horse. Things over here are crystal clear."

No crying, no pouting. Digging in his pocket he took out a fifty-piastre coin. "Call where you want to go."

"What are my choices?" Her brow arched. "Back to bed?"

Expecting a small debate on the virtues of marriage, he was pleased to find her reacting sensibly instead of emotionally. And hell, if sex was still an option, she probably wasn't too pissed about the matrimony thing.

His views left no room for argument.

Isis enjoyed taking charge of things, so maybe she appreciated having the situation spelled out, with no room for misinterpretation.

"Unfortunately," he said in a dry tone, "*that* wasn't one of the choices. Heads, Valley of the Scorpions. Tails, Abusir to see what Dickhead has really found."

"Heads."

Thorne flipped the coin, then slapped it on the back of his hand. "Tails."

She shrugged. "It doesn't matter. I still believe Cleo's resting in the Valley. There first, then when I see Dylan again, if I'm incarcerated for his murder, I'll know where she is one way or the other."

"Valley it is then." The air-conditioning kicked in, blasting like a furnace inside the already broiling vehicle. "If Brengard's responsible for all that crap yesterday?" he continued as if they hadn't paused to make choices. "Bloody right I'll hurt him." Just because he wasn't offering marriage didn't mean he had no feelings for Isis. And when it came to her protection, he fought to win. "Are you all right, after seeing him?"

"I'm fine . . ."

He gave her an incredulous look.

"Honestly? Not really." Isis wriggled in her seat to get more comfortable, her back against her door, her knee curled on the seat. "That encounter left me shaking. Look." She held out a flat hand, not a shake in sight, but her voice was tight, and after dropping her hand into her lap, she curled her fingers into a fist.

"I'm annoyed. Scared. Incensed. He *knew* I was here. I *know* he did. And if so, *how*? People leave at this time of year. Go where it's cooler. This is *the* worst season to dig. I'm suspicious times two."

"He needs something from you."

"What? *I* don't *have* anything. If I did, I'd be the one financing a dig. Okay, I wouldn't be able to do that, but in theory. I'd be the one digging. With my bare hands if I had to."

So far her father's "clues" had given then bugger-all. Thorne doubted even the professor's mind could be jogged with the random items he'd left. A tassel from a minister's carpet. A broken stick . . . Not a shitload to go on.

"He claims to have a crew and sponsors," Isis continued, incensed. "He didn't put that together yesterday! That takes *months* to set up. Which means the slimy bastard was working this site while my father was working somewhere else. Thorne, this *has* to be my father's find. Dylan wouldn't have had time to verify a potential dig *and* get the backing that quickly all on his own."

The air pouring out of the vents grew cooler. The Range Rover was another souped-up vehicle with bulletproof everything. Fucking annoying as hell that it was a necessity at all, but obliging of the Israelis to be so accommodating, considering his vehicular track record on this trip.

"*Has* he really found Cleo?" Isis shrugged. "Who knows? I can contact the director of MSA, see where Dylan's excavating—*if* he'll tell me. He and my father never exactly saw eye to eye." Her voice was dry. "But he might tell me if indeed my father's permissions were revoked and why . . ."

"You sure Brengard isn't just flat-out lying?"

"I believe Dylan—he's working *a* site. He probably does have a legitimate claim to excavate wherever the hell he is. Husani and his father are our friends. If Dylan went to them to hire on more men, he'd know they'd check on my father's behalf to make sure he was on the up-and-up. They worked with him when my father was around, and while they didn't actually come right out and *say* so, I know they never liked Dylan."

"Good instincts."

She frowned, apparently at her own lack of instinct about the man. "Apparently."

"We'll call the minister and confirm that. Also confirm exactly what Brengard's location is. Either he's located

Cleo's tomb at the Abusir site, or he hasn't. Your amulet tells me it was found near the dam. Perhaps your father told you he purchased it so that if anyone asked you about it, that's exactly what you'd tell them. All I know was where it was found. I have no idea what archaeological significance it might have. A hundred miles separate the two locations. One thing we know for sure: Cleopatra wasn't buried in two places at once."

She leveled her gaze at him, the knots of her fists turning whiter. "Do you think he suspected I'd come back to see what my father found the last time? Maybe he had someone watching for me at the airport?"

"Maybe." Thorne pulled out of a side street and merged into the free-for-all that was normal traffic. Lifting his hip, he took out his phone and handed it to her. "Call the ministry and get that ball rolling, unless you want to stop by their offices?"

"No, a call should do it." Isis took the phone and keyed in the number, clearly from memory. "It'll take— what? A couple of hours to get out to the dam? Half the day will be gone by the time we get there."

He'd give her this, an afternoon to at least see where her amulet had been found. Then he was putting her on a plane back to Seattle, if he had to hogtie her to do it. He'd hire Doug Heustis to accompany her, instruct him to sit on her if necessary.

His preference was to make a U-turn and take her to the airport right now. But he knew Isis-bullheaded-Magee well enough now to know she'd refuse to go.

No. He had to show her what she needed to see, *then* he'd use all his negotiating skills to make her see things his way. The trip there and back would take the better part of the day. But he'd still have time to get her on an evening flight.

Thorne headed west as Isis talked to someone at the MSA, then handed him his phone. Since he'd overheard the conversation there was no need to recap. Brengard had all the correct permissions filed.

"If he really *has* found Cleo," Isis said tightly, "I'm going to have to do him serious bodily harm. Son of a bitch *did* steal my father's maps. And I wouldn't be surprised if he was involved in the attack—our attacks, plural—and also responsible for putting Beniti al-Atrash in the hospital. And if he's glomming on to my father's dig with an Egyptian fly's tenacity, then perhaps he had a part in my father's attack three months ago as well."

Oh, Thorne didn't doubt that one for a minute.

She massaged her forehead, then took off her glasses to rub her eyes. "It seems surreal, but *someone's* responsible for everything that's happened, and he sure fits the bill."

He kept a firm grip on the steering wheel, weaving in and out of traffic. There was less time than she thought. "We know where he *wasn't* during those few days—in any hospital. So his whereabouts are unaccounted for. So, yes, I'd put my money on him being neck deep in all this."

A mixture of betrayal and fierce anger flitted across her features. "My father trusted him. Hell, *I* trusted him. Dad shared *everything* with Dylan, past, present, and future—"

"He didn't tell him about the carpet tassel clue."

She leaned her elbow on the window and cupped her forehead in her hand. "You know that sounds ridiculous, right?" she said with a return to her pithy self. "That we know of," she answered his rhetorical question.

"Do you still feel as strongly that her tomb is about to reside at the bottom of a lake, and *not* thirty miles from Alexandria as Brengard claims?"

"That's what my gut feeling is. But honestly? That's not based on anything tangible."

"My reading on your amulet is about the only solid clue we have, and *that* says, unequivocally, that it was found in the Valley of the Scorpions."

She patted her back pocket. "Yes, but it doesn't say *Queen Cleopatra's* tomb." She curled her leg beneath her and faced him with a heavy sigh. "Dylan is a braggart and an opportunist. But if he's lying, he'll soon be found out. He won't be able to keep a find like this quiet for long. Even with everything that's been going on with my father these last few months, I would've heard something from *someone*.

"Everyone in the universe knows how badly my father wanted to find Cleo's last resting place. Someone would've taken great pleasure in rubbing his nose in the fact that somebody else did what he's spent a lifetime trying to do. But I haven't heard a scintilla of a hint of a whisper. All of which means that somehow, some way,

Dylan has greased palms or kissed butts. He would have had to name the find in his paperwork—and considering he was connected to my father and the number of times he claimed to have found Cleopatra's tomb, the news would have spread faster through the archaeological community than fleas on market rats."

Thorne frowned. He needed specifics if he was going to plan out their next move. "How long before he makes a public announcement?"

"Excavating a tomb won't be quick. Even he's not stupid enough to make a false claim until he's absolutely sure of what he's found. It would have to be something big and definitive—her sarcophagus would do it. We can go there tomorrow, see what he's doing—"

"What we don't have time for is to wait to see what's on the valley floor before it becomes a lake next week."

"But if there's a chance, even a small chance, that my father was in the Valley of the Scorpions three months ago, or a year ago, and this amulet was taken from there . . . then the lake project will be forced to wait. Right?"

He shrugged. "It took four years to move the Temple of Abu Simbel to higher ground."

"But it *was* moved."

He suspected that if necessary, Isis would supervise the move personally if the tomb were found. But he also suspected that in six days the valley would be a pleasant recreational lake beneath the cofferdam, and all this supposition would be moot. "Do you want to visit Dr. Najid at his office?"

She shook her head. "I'd like to go out to the site first. Just to . . . *see*."

"Then that's what we'll do."

"GOD. WE WON'T BE able to stop this, will we?" Despite her dark glasses, Isis shaded her eyes against the intensely bright sunlight reflecting off the pale sand. The heat seeped through her shoes and burned her legs beneath thin cotton pants. Very few people were stupid enough to be outside when it was this hot, and the shiny new settlement was a ghost town of pristine, empty buildings and emptier streets.

Perspiration and the humidity caused her hair to puff up and curl around her neck and shoulders. She scooped the mass up in one hand to shove under her hat.

Thorne, too, shaded his eyes as he looked across to the other side of the deep valley, where mirror images of the buildings and green strips of grass and trees waited for tourists and locals alike to enjoy. Docks strategically placed along the edge of the ravine looked oddly surreal jutting several hundred feet over sand, marking where the level of the lake would reach in a week. "It won't be easy," he admitted.

He'd pointed out where he "saw" the GPS location of her amulet's original resting place: across the deep valley and snugged into the hillside, in a skinny ridge that snaked along the eastern wall and looked from here like piles of rocks. To see anything she'd need powerful binoculars. Everything was the same sand-colored *sand*.

There was no frantic activity with large machinery, or

the thousands of people who'd been involved with the preparation for the flooding of the valley. Their work was done. On the hilly rim circling the mile-long Valley of the Scorpions were the new hotels, restaurants, and shops, the paved streets, parks, the recreational buildings for boat rentals and ski equipment—empty now, but all with a future ringside seat to the second-largest man-made lake in Egypt.

They'd passed the hydroelectric plant several miles back, and the faint throb could be heard even here. The graceful, multiple arches of the cement buttress coffer-dam wall held the water in the upper dam. Leaking moisture quickly evaporated in the stifling heat, leaving a sweat stain on the gray surface.

Behind them the blank eyes of hotel and shop windows looked out over the valley of sand and rock, but in a week a hundred million acre-feet of sparkling blue water would fill the valley. Feluccas would unfurl white sails, speedboats and skiers would cut through the water, and swimmers would lounge on the man-made beaches, already curved, groomed, and ready, hundreds of feet above the floor of the valley.

Isis put a hand on his arm. "Let's go back to Husani and get the men and supplies and come back first thing in the morning when it's cooler. We'll go down to recon-noiter, see what we can see, and go from there." She bit her lip when Thorne made no comment. "You're right. We should stop by and see Dr. Najid first. At least we can get the stopping process in motion."

"He won't be predisposed to stop a multibillion-dollar

project without concrete *proof*. I suggest we take a breath and regroup. If you're up to it, we'll go down since I know exactly where we need to be. We can drive most of the way, I don't think it would be much of a walk to reach the place. You take plenty of pictures, and *then* we'll go and see him. Good enough?"

Isis took off her hat to swipe at the sweat running down her temple, using the large red and blue cotton scarf tucked in her belt. "Good idea. She's down there. Waiting." Plopping the hat back on her head, she squeezed his muscled forearm and grinned up at him. "I can feel it."

⤾ TWELVE ⤿

I f the lakeside businesses had been open, Thorne would've checked into one of the hotels, grabbed a cold shower, and fallen into bed wrapped around a hot Isis. After the heavy workout the day before, his leg was stiffening up. All the hours behind the wheel today had made it throb like a son of a bitch. He should probably get in some of the exercises prescribed by his London physiotherapist. Running through the streets and hand-to-hand altercations weren't part of her suggested therapies. Neither was a marathon bout of sex. On a sagging sofa, on the floor, against the wall, and finally in the shower . . . no, once more on the sagging furniture before they succumbed to exhaustion.

In fact, if he bothered to recall several conversations between himself, the therapist, and his surgeon, running and getting shot at were right there at the top of the Do Not Do list if he wanted to fully recover the use of his leg. They'd made no mention of sex.

He didn't relish clambering around the rocks and sand in the valley searching for a tomb he didn't give a rat's ass about. But since it needed to be done, he wanted an early start, Husani's well-armed, able-bodied men, and the correct supplies and equipment.

Tomorrow.

For today he'd take Isis where she wanted to go. Show her whatever, then get her on that plane.

The intense heat made a mirage shimmer on the road ahead, and he cranked up the air to blast musty-smelling, relatively cooler air into the interior of the vehicle. He smelled Isis: a turn-on combo of clean perspiration and sexy cinnamon.

The road from the dam project back into Cairo was deserted. A couple of vehicles—an electrician's van, a flatbed truck with plastic irrigation piping, and several black, tinted-window sedans—had passed them, heading the way they'd come. But those had passed half an hour before. No one behind them. Thorne was driving an easy hundred miles per hour, which out here on the vast, undulating sands of desert felt like standing still. Nothing but dunes as far as the eye could see. Sand, pale sky, black-tarred road. Midafternoon and the dunes on either side of the road were bleached blindingly white by the sun glaring from the pale blue bowl of the sky. The air shimmered in undulating waves with both heat and moisture.

Isis rubbed her plastic bottle across her flushed cheek before chugging down the rest of the water. "Is there anything I can do for your leg?"

Thorne realized his fingers were clamped tightly around his upper thigh, and he withdrew his hand from the daggerlike pain. "I'm fine."

"Then why are you massaging it? I can do that——"

He grabbed her wrist as she reached out to touch him. "I just need to stretch. We'll be in the city in a couple of hours; it can wait." She settled back in her seat.

"We passed a small village," she said after a brief silence. "We can stop there. I'd be happy to walk around a bit, too. This heat is making me a little sick to my stomach. I'll grab some cold water at the same time if they have it, and see if perhaps they have a cane or close facsimile."

He didn't like using a cane, he wasn't incapacitated by the injury and didn't want a bloody crutch, but he didn't argue.

Although the oasis and small village were about ten miles ahead, near their turnoff to descend to the valley floor, he had no intention of stopping. The area was too isolated and he had an itch on the back of his neck. He scanned the surroundings. Sand. Road. Sun.

Several miles went by in silence. But Thorne bet Isis wouldn't maintain the blessed quiet for long—the very air seemed to vibrate with her thoughts. He could feel the questions coming. Things he didn't want to remember, let alone discuss.

"Will you tell me now what happened?"

"I fell down the stairs."

She made a rude noise of disbelief. "No, you didn't. If you tell me, will you have to kill me or something?"

He slid her a suggestive glance. "Or something."

She smiled, shoving her glasses on top of her head and curling her legs under her, clearly settling in for a heart-to-heart. "No, really, what happened?"

Damn. She was more tenacious than he'd anticipated. But then, it was something that, under normal circumstances, he appreciated in her. She kept going no matter what the obstacles. And for that she deserved the truth. At least a sanitized version of it.

"A year ago, a very unpleasant man killed my two partners and had a crack at me." Blood splatter, bits of body parts, and agonized screams superimposed themselves on the view of the road and the sound of the tires on the gritty pavement. "I'm in the extremely auspicious position of having rods and pins in my leg. My partners weren't as fortunate."

"It's not fortunate that you got shot." Isis's clear brown eyes narrowed. Her skin looked silky soft and fine-grained in the sunlight streaming in the window, dewy with perspiration. Her soft mouth looked lush and inviting, and he wanted to pull over and kiss her into stopping the questions he not only didn't want to answer, but didn't want to think about, either.

Cradling the empty bottle in her lap, she twisted even more in her seat, so that her back was to the passenger door. He glanced over at the door locks to make sure they were engaged.

"What's the prognosis, and what are your limitations?"

Pissed that she even had to ask if he *had* any bloody limitations, he cast a mocking glance her way. "Do you have a medical degree now, Dr. Magee?"

"No, Thorne," she said with some asperity. "I don't. However, someone is doing their damnedest to kill us, stop us, or . . . *whatever* us. We don't know who, and we don't know why. I can shoot them with my camera, but *you* are the man with the big gun and the bullets. You can shoot them more efficiently. And, as said gunman, *you* are all that stands between me and them. I need to know what your constraints are, realistically, without you minimizing them, so that I can make informed choices as we go on." She paused. "You have no constraints in the lovemaking department, in case you're asking."

Foiled by logic. Damn. "I've kept you safe." He glanced automatically in the rearview mirror. There was a vehicle of some sort in the distance behind them, but the shimmer on the road made identification impossible. He monitored the other car's progress.

"For which I'm grateful. Spill."

"The name of the man who captured and killed the members of my team was Boris Yermalof."

"And what's his claim to fame?"

"He shot me," he said wryly. The surgery had taken eighteen hours, and he'd died on the table. There'd been shitloads of pain afterward, and they'd told him he'd probably never walk again, and just to be thankful he was alive. What they hadn't told him was that numbers would be scrolling through his head. At first he'd thought he was hallucinating from the pain meds they dripped into his veins. But then Stark had told him about his own strange ability, and when they'd let him go from the hospital, he'd been drafted into service for Lodestone. What he felt now was a reminder that he'd almost died twice, and he was lucky to be alive. He had no bloody complaints.

"I have a rod in my leg that will set off airport metal detectors for the rest of my life, and assorted other hardware that enables me to do everything I always did. Like last night, for instance."

"Yes, last night was amazing," she told him, then without skipping a beat or changing inflection, pointed out, "You were limping more this morning than you were yesterday. Is the pain debilitating and you're just being manly, or is it something an ice pack and some muscle relaxants will help?"

"I won't take drugs, and an ice pack would probably help," he said honestly. "But since we're in the middle of the desert, both will have to wait."

"Who's this Boris guy? Why did he shoot you and your people?"

About to say it was on a need-to-know basis, Thorne then continued *that* mental conversation and decided he might as well cut to the chase, because since she'd been shot at, possibly by Boris or his men, because of him, she had a right to know. "We were tracking a man we knew was trafficking black market artifacts from the Middle East and North Africa."

Her eyes widened. *"Black market artifacts?"* she demanded, pushing away from the door. "As in *Egyptian* black market artifacts?"

He nodded. "Many of them, yes."

"And you didn't think this was relevant? My God, Connor. Clearly it is relevant! Those men shooting at us are after *you!*"

"It's possible, but not likely. Very few people know I'm back." He flicked his gaze to the rearview mirror just to make sure that was true. No traffic had passed them in the last hour but back on the horizon there was still a smudge of dark keeping its distance. Was it a vehicle or merely the sand blowing across the road?

Isis's fingers rubbed her temple in slow circles and her chest rose and fell as she took shallow, annoyed breaths. "Are you freaking *insane*? How many people know you're *back*? Half a dozen at least! Maybe more."

He kept his tone level. "None of them are involved or even know about Yermalof."

She swallowed several times, and he wondered if she was going to be sick. He handed her his bottle with an inch of water left in it.

Unscrewing the top, Isis demanded, "Were you here? In *Egypt* with this man?" She drank the water and pulled a face because it was warm.

A long pause stretched out before them. The invisible weight on his shoulders increased as the truth pressed in. "We followed him into Israel."

"Oh, my God, Connor! That's a hop, skip, and a damned jump away from where we are right now!"

No shit. "We worked closely with the Israeli Mossad. They're the ones who supplied us with this vehicle, as well as the one we banged up yesterday. He'd stolen arti-facts there as well. He had the world hot on his arse."

"Lovely." She twisted her unruly, sexy-as-hell hair up off her neck and held it on top of her head as she adjusted the air vents to her new position and fanned herself with her other hand. "Are they just lending us cars, or are they looking for your friend Boris?"

"As far as I know, just doing me a favor." In the spy business it was good to dispense and accept favors. The Jerusalem op had turned to shit, but it was Mossad agents who'd hauled his bleeding butt out of the barn where Yermalof and his men had introduced them to Hell. Only the fact that he was bleeding out and unconscious had gotten him out of there without trying to save Maciej and Ayers.

"Well, I think we need to pause and rewind and see what they know that they haven't told us. Because we should at least know who it is that's after us, don't you think?"

"This whole trip has been a cock-up." Thorne hadn't realized how pissed off he was until he heard the anger in his own voice. Most of that anger was directed at himself. "It's high time I took you to the airport and put you on a plane back to Seattle."

"You should have thought of that yesterday when those men tried to shoot our car!"

No shit. It might be late in the game, but he prayed it wasn't too late in the game to get her gone. "You're right. I should have. You'll be wheels up in three hours."

"And you think I'll leave and let Dylan stake a claim to Cleopatra? After all *this*?" she scoffed. "Think again."

"I have a gimp leg. I'm a piss-poor bodyguard for you. Whoever's gunning for us is going to pick us off like fish in a barrel."

"You're an excellent bodyguard. But just out of curiosity, if I went home, where would you be?"

"Here. Getting to the bottom of things. When the dust settles I'll bring you back. Bring your father. Have a fucking party." His palms tightened around the steering wheel and his damn leg ached like fucking hell, making it hard to keep a steady pressure on the gas pedal.

A glance at Isis showed she was pale despite the bright heat splotches on her cheeks. He wasn't feeling so hot, either, now that he thought about it. It wasn't uncommon for local shops to sell tap water in commercial water bottles. All he needed right now was Montezuma's revenge from the drinking water. Bloody hell.

"No one shot at us, or even tried to run us off the road today. Maybe they lost interest."

Big fucking deal. "The day is young yet. And I doubt if these people have 'lost interest.' More likely they're scouring the streets looking for us."

Isis's eyes narrowed. "How will they find us? We have a different car today, and you said no one saw us leave the bazaar. You said the Israelis were helping us out."

"Let me put it this way," Thorne observed dryly. "What we don't know can, and probably *will*, hurt us. If these people are determined, they'll eventually be hot on our tails again. When that happens I'd like there not to be an *us*. There will only be me. This isn't personal. Got it?"

Turning to look straight ahead at the long ribbon of road where the first car they'd seen in forty miles approached at breakneck speed, Thorne edged the car over. Isis chewed her lip. "I don't want to leave. Finding Cleo is *so* close, I can feel it . . ."

"Are you willing to die for someone else's dream? Certainly he's your father. But the reality is, *he* doesn't care anymore because *he* doesn't remember."

She glared at him. "That's a lousy thing to say."

God, he didn't want to do this. But he had to. The sooner he got her out of here, the less danger she'd be in. He should have manned up from the beginning and told Stark to go to hell. He wasn't taking any woman on any op anywhere at any time, no matter what Lodestone paid. He drew a breath in through his nose, laced with the scent of her, and pushed the words out, making them as cold and brutal as he could. "It's the truth, though, isn't it? You'd die here, and he won't even remember he had a daughter."

The air stilled. A sheen of unshed tears glistened in her eyes. Isis turned away from him and faced out toward the road in front. "You really are a bastard, aren't you?" Her voice was thick with emotion.

"Unfortunately for me, my parental units claim otherwise." He should have packed her off yesterday, and he cursed himself for being a sentimental fool. "We don't know how far these people will go. If they're Cleopatra people who don't want you back because they think you might know something they don't—will they kill you for information? Are they trying to scare you off? We have no idea what the answer is, do we? How far are you willing to go to prove your father's point? With bugger-all to go on but a tassel from a carpet and a gold amulet?"

She fisted her hands in her lap. "You said the amulet was from the Valley of the Scorpions—"

"Yes. But that doesn't mean it had anything to do with *Cleopatra*. It could've been from one of the gift shops nearby. All I get is the location, love, not the provenance." It wasn't from any of the gift shops. His sixth sense, as odd as it was, was pinpoint accurate to the last foot. The amulet had once been deep inside the valley. Sure, someone could've been at the location and dropped it there, but his gut said that wasn't the case. No coincidences in his line of work.

Thorne knew exactly where he was going to look. As soon as he escorted her to her gate and watched her plane take off.

He shot a look at her. Her jaw was tight, her hands fisted in her lap. She had the look of a woman about to argue. She wasn't staying and he wasn't willing or interested in hearing her rebuttals. It wasn't safe here, and until he made sure that some arsehole wasn't trying to kill her, she'd be safer in Seattle, where he'd have his people meet her plane and sit on her until they got word from him.

"Go home, Isis. We'll go down so you can have a look. But if Dylan has found Cleopatra's tomb there's nothing you can do about it. If the tomb is in the Valley of the Scorpions as I suspect, I'll do everything in my power— pull what strings I can—to have them hold off on filling the lake until the tomb can be authenticated and the authorities decide what has to be done to preserve it."

"By yourself? In a week?"

He shrugged. "I can only promise I'll do my best. I still have resources——"

She shook her head. "I think I'll——"

"Look, I don't want to scare you any more than any sensible woman would be scared right now. But Yermalof didn't want to be found, and he didn't like us nosing into his business. He kidnapped an experienced MI5 agent from her hotel room, took her without anyone seeing him, cut off her"—*tongue?*—"*finger,* and had the package delivered to us with our breakfast the next morning."

"Is that true?"

"True and whitewashed. He was willing to trade Maciej for Ayers and myself. We knew it was a trap and went anyway. He killed them both. They died hard and they died bloody, and, Isis, they died *slowly.* If there's even a minus one percent chance that any of this is tied into anything Yermalof, I don't want you on the same continent."

"Okay."

He narrowed his eyes. "Okay?"

"Okay, I'll go home." Her voice slowed and became thick. "And . . . trust . . . you'll call m——"

His gut curled uncomfortably. He wanted to believe her. Wanted to think she could be persuaded by logic, and could be kept safe, but somehow his gut told him this was far from over. He waited for her to finish what she was saying, and glanced over to find her slumped in her seat, her head on her chest, out cold.

Thorne smiled.

She looked cute sprawled out across the seat, cute but damn uncomfortable. He considered straightening her body out so she could sleep, then decided to leave her so as not to wake her. They'd be in the valley in about twenty minutes, Cairo in less than an hour after that; she could sleep all she wanted on the flight back to Seattle. He was still a little shocked she'd agreed to go home.

He felt lethargic from the heat himself and looked forward to finding an out-of-the-way hotel . . . But a few minutes later his lids felt weighted, and the lethargy was interfering with his concentration. What the hell? He'd gone seventy-two hours or more without a break on ops, and he'd never fallen asleep on the job.

He pressed the button for the tinted side window and it slid down. Gritty, furnace-hot wind blew into his face, stinging his cheeks. The heavy car slewed as his fingers went numb and he lost his grip on the steering wheel. His foot, leaden and uncooperative, dropped off the gas pedal. The car veered onto the sand alongside the tarred road, and slowed as the tires sank. Darkness closed like a camera aperture, leaving the sunlight a bright pinpoint in his vision. His body, limp and unresponsive, slid sideways down the seat back until his head fell on Isis's hip.

Thorne fought the darkness and the lassitude with everything in him. But they sucked him under like black quicksand.

ISIS WOKE TO PITCH darkness and lay still, trying to figure out where she was. Something hard dug into her side, and she felt around until her fingers encountered the familiar size and shape of her camera bag, still slung across her body. She shifted it aside.

Typical, Thorne hauling her all over God's creation and then leaving her who knows where. She certainly wasn't on a plane, so he hadn't tossed her on board and left her there. She presumed she'd fallen asleep as they were driving. Not that she remembered one way or the other, but she didn't feel rested. The darkness was disorienting, and not having any idea where she was or how she'd gotten there was also discombobulating.

Sitting up, she felt around, trying to figure out what she was lying on. Something firm . . . sand? A sleeping bag? She still wore the cotton pants and T-shirt she'd had on this morning.

"Thorne?" she called softly. It was odd that there wasn't a scrap of light. "Connor?" Isis called more loudly, starting to feel a heavy sense of foreboding when she didn't hear anything.

She stuck her arms straight out in front of her and started feeling around. Canvas? What the hell? Had Thorne decided to set up camp in the desert and wait for morning to take her to the tomb? She was definitely in a tent. Rolling onto her knees she felt for the opening, and after fumbling around, found a heavy zipper and pulled it up.

Not pitch darkness after all, she saw as she crawled outside into the balmy night air. The temperatures had dropped dramatically, but it certainly wasn't cold, probably in the low seventies. The sky was black but filled with millions of pinpricks of white light. No moon. The stars showed a black and white desert landscape of nothing but rippled sand and mountainous dunes.

The tent was a good size, and would sleep two. A camp was set up, with assorted supplies piled haphazardly nearby. "Thorne?!"

No response. The only sound was the susurrus of grains of sand drifting in the breeze. "Pretty damned odd, if you ask me."

Before she looked at any supplies, she wanted to check her precious Canon. Dropping to her knees in the sand, she snapped open the bag. Everything was there. Carefully she removed the camera, holding it this way and that to inspect it in the starlight. It looked okay. Thank God. Removing the lens cap, she took a few shots of the tent.

A quick look showed her it was working like normal. Returning the lens cap, she stuck it back in the bag and hooked the strap over her shoulder again. Even out here she didn't trust that she wouldn't be parted from it. And since it now appeared to be the only thing she owned, she was hanging on to it.

"Hey, Thorne? Where are you?" Isis raised her voice as she walked over to see what the supplies consisted of so she could gauge just how long he expected them to be out there—wherever "there" was. She was parched and rummaged in a pack to find a bottle of water. "Eureka!" Opening it, she chugged it as she looked around.

A crude-looking campfire had been built in a scooped-out depression in the sand, but it hadn't been lit. Beyond the cold fire was a long lump—probably a duffel bag, or more supplies. Isis wandered over to inspect it, hoping she'd find something interesting to eat; her stomach was growling.

Nothing to eat, and not a duffel. *Connor Thorne*, fast asleep, curled on his side, half his face smooshed in the sand as if it were a feather pillow. Isis plopped herself down in the still-hot sand beside him. "You'd've been more comfortable in the tent with me, Double-O Seven." She rubbed her bare arms as the breeze chilled her skin and made small whirlwinds of sand particles.

"Why are *you* sleeping outside, and I was in the tent? And why we're the middle of apparently *nowhere* is a mystery. Do you hear me?" She looked around, starting to feel uneasy in the vast silence. "Where's the car anyway? Wake up and give me a clue, Thorne. Where did the tent and supplies come from? Was all this camping gear in the car your buddies lent you?"

None of this made any sense at all, and the fact that he slept through her monologue was disturbing as well. He never slept this deeply—at least from what she'd observed. "Why am I here with you, when this afternoon you were determined to send me packing?"

She sipped the water, watching his chest rise and fall with the regular slow rhythm of deep sleep. He looked much younger asleep than he did awake with all his shields up. His sleeping this deeply felt . . . wrong. He was a soldier. He'd told her he was a light sleeper, but right now he slept like the dead. And if she hadn't watched his chest moving, she'd think maybe that was the case.

With a frown, getting more scared by the minute, she reached out to brush the sand off his face, wishing he'd wake up and tell her why the hell he'd brought her way out here.

Isis barely touched his cheek and he erupted into action, throwing her on her back, his forearm a steel band across her throat, his fist raised to strike. "Connor!" she yelled at the top of her lungs, grabbing his arm to keep him from choking her. "Stop, it's me, Isis!"

His fist dropped out of sight and he eased his arm from her throat. Dropping his forehead to hers, he rasped, "Bloody hell."

"It's okay." She slid her fingers into the soft pelt of his hair, holding his head against hers as they both fought for breath. Her heartbeat sounded like a rock band in her ears. "I'm sorry I startled you."

Thorne lifted his head, eyes glittering in the meager light. "It's not all right. I almost killed you."

"Well, fortunately you didn't. Would you mind letting go? I'm getting sand in my hair."

Still crouched over her, he kissed her gently, then helped her up, brushing the sand off her back and shoulders. "Sure I didn't hurt you?"

"Positive."

He looked around. "Are we alone?"

"Why? Were you expecting dinner guests?"

"How long have you been awake?"

"A few minutes. Thorne, you're scaring me. Why are we out here? I thought you——" He put his finger over her mouth and uncoiled to get to his feet, then staggered in the sand before catching his footing. He held up a hand, cautioning her to stay where she was.

For such a large man, and with an injured leg, he moved with surprising speed once he got going. Isis watched as he searched around the tent, then looked inside. He motioned her to remain still, and made his way up the dune nearby. His cautious, careful movements ratcheted up her fear, and by the time he came back to her, she was on her feet, heart pounding painfully.

The breeze brushed chilly fingers over the film of nervous perspiration on her skin. She put a hand on his forearm. "What's going on?"

"We were drugged in the car. Isoflurane or some other inhalation anesthetic. I smelled a musty odor, but attributed it to the air-conditioning. *Fuck it.*"

Isis frowned. What he was saying made no sense at all. "Someone put an anesthetic in the car?" Repeating the words didn't compute, either. Who did something like that outside of a movie?

"It caused profound respiratory depression, and decreased our blood pressure. They put us to sleep. Fuck," he said again.

"And then built us a *campsite*?" Isis asked incredulously. "Why? So we'd be comfortable until they come back to kill us?"

"I suspect we're miles from civilization." His voice was grim. "I don't believe they have any plans to return for us."

"Okay . . . Why then?"

"I think the idea is to make this look as though we came on a dig looking for your Cleo's tomb—there's a rough stone entrance on the other side of this dune—and succumbed to the heat, or ran out of supplies, or our vehicle was stolen. Or all of the above. Whatever the plan is, it's a good one. Because we clearly *are* miles from anywhere. If those duffels are any indication, they're filled with empty cans and wrappers so it looks like we ate and drank the contents. Check out the tire tracks—one car in, one car out. I'd bet our vehicle will be presumed stolen while we slept."

"So they want us to die."

His eyes were hard and cold. "They want it to look like we fucked up and died of stupidity. I don't know about you, but that doesn't sit well with me."

A flush of heat washed over her skin. There was no way in hell she was letting Dylan make her death look like a stupid accident any college freshman on a dig would have had the sense to avoid. "So how do we beat them?"

"Instead of conveniently dying, we find what we came here to find."

✇ THIRTEEN ✇

Let's see if they left us anything useful," Isis suggested, prosaically, sounding a hell of a lot braver than she felt. The starlight made deep pockets of black shadow in the dips and valleys of the surrounding sand dunes, and the scrape of sand blowing across the nylon fabric of the tent was like sandpaper on her nerves.

Still, if she had to be stranded in the middle of nowhere, she was grateful it was with Connor Thorne. He looked large and formidable with his face in shadow and his broad shoulders blocking the endless, shifting, barren hills behind him.

"If your hypothesis is true"—her voice seemed loud in the quiet so she lowered it—"we're miles from civilization, right? It could be years before anyone came across us. So with that in mind, I say we rescue ourselves."

His teeth flashed white in the ambient light. "You're something else, you know that, Isis Magee?" he murmured, using a finger to tilt her face up so that her mouth was right where he wanted it. He combed his fingers through her hair to bracket her head between his large hands, holding her a willing captive.

Isis closed her eyes as he slanted his mouth over hers in a leisurely kiss that was completely at odds with their circumstances. He deepened the kiss, his tongue teasing hers in a game that made her pulse race, crowding fear from her mind and replacing it with heat and need. The kiss became hard, filled with longing. She hoped from both sides, because her heart pounded erratically against her rib cage, and she was vaguely aware it was more from passion than fear.

Sand shifted beneath her feet and blew against the back of her legs as he drew her more tightly against him. The heat from his body warmed her everywhere they touched. Waves of pleasure rose like a tide inside her, the swells getting incrementally bigger as the kiss deepened.

The kiss, the embrace, was an affirmation of life in this desolate place and Isis soaked it up like rain on the parched desert sands. She needed this right now. Needed him.

She sighed, slipping her hand around his neck, and up into the short strands of his hair at his nape. She used her other hand to cup his firm butt, which flexed as her fingers tightened. She felt the small twitch of his lips at the contact.

God, he smelled so—male. The smell of his sweat, the scent of cold desert air on his skin, and the welcome heat of his hard body pressed tightly against hers turned her on like nothing else.

She knew what it felt like to have him buried deep inside her, knew the pull and pulse of her internal muscles in response to his every thrust and parry. She knew the sounds he made, and the feel of his hair-roughed chest against her sensitive breasts. She knew the sounds he made when he climaxed, and the weight of his body when he was replete.

And she wanted to feel all those things *now*. It was only when he brushed his fingers over her cheeks that she realized how cold she was everywhere they weren't touching. He disengaged slowly, leaving her lips damp and chilled. "Fortunately," he told her, his broad hands sliding down to cup her upper arms to hold her steady as she swayed unsteadily, "we have a lodestone that will take us straight back to your Valley of the Scorpions."

"We do?" She blinked back her good sense. "Oh! We do!" She dug it out of her back pocket and handed him the little chamois pouch.

He took it and stuck it in his front pocket, then stepped back, scanning the area. "Unless they left us with my GPS or watch, which I doubt, it'll be a little harder to pinpoint the location, but I know when I'm heading in the right direction."

"You're right, let's gather everything we can use, then get a good night's sleep. We can set out at first light."

"Sorry." Thorne cupped her cool cheek. "No good night's sleep for us tonight. We don't know if or when they might come back. We'll do better walking while it's cool. Hopefully we'll reach civilization at sunup."

Briskly she rubbed the goose bumps on her bare arms, the cold invading more than just the surface of her skin. She'd had other plans in mind that had nothing to do with sleep or walking through the wilderness. "Seriously?

Wasn't it enough to dump us out here? Now you think they're coming back to finish the job." Wrapping her arms around her body, she shivered. "I wouldn't be able to sleep anyway."

"Tuck your pants into your socks to discourage wild-life, then grab that bag over there, and let's see what they've given us to work with."

"I still have my camera bag. There's a little money if we need to pay someone for transportation or food." That was, if they didn't end up walking in circles until the vultures or heatstroke got them.

"Water's our priority. Okay, let's see what we have to work with."

Glad to have something constructive to do, Isis stuffed her pant legs into her socks, then hauled the light duffel bag over to where Thorne was dumping the other two. Heavy boots would better serve them out in the desert than running shoes, but at least they hadn't been wearing sandals when they'd been taken. She was grateful for small mercies.

Unzipping the bags, they tossed the contents onto the sleeping bag. Some clothing, his and hers. Isis held up a familiar T-shirt. "Isn't this the shirt you wore in London? It is! And here's my bra! This is the stuff from our suit-cases that we left in the cab from the airport."

"I suspected it might be. They'd want it to look as though we came prepared to stay for several days."

Isis shuddered. "Dear God. They've set up a perfect crime scene."

"Yes, well, the only thing missing will be the bodies." He handed her a wad of fabric. "Layer. Put on what you can."

"These bastards have been tracking us for *days*." Her voice rose as she pulled a long-sleeved T-shirt over the short-sleeved one she was wearing. She wasn't just surprised at the bad guys' forethought. She was furious. Each incident had blended with the fright of the one before it, but now, in the quiet and darkness of the barren desert, the realization of the machinations that swirled around them put the fear of God in her. They hadn't just been followed. They'd been relentlessly *hunted*.

"That certainly appears to be the case." Thorne sounded calm, his voice strong and even.

She shot him an annoyed glance from where she knelt beside the bag of clothes. "I guess you're *used* to people trying to kill you."

"It never gets old." His attempt at levity was replaced with concern. He crouched beside her, taking her in his arms. "Hey, you remember I'm a professional, right? We'll figure this out *and* live to see another day."

"It's a good thing you're a man of your word."

"Depend on it. Isis, I——"

He was so close, his face etched in black-and-white. Starlight glinted in his eyes and cast a silver sheen on the stubble on his chin. Her heart clutched because Isis saw him in fifty years, and she wanted to be *with* him in that distant future when he was stooped, his hair silver. She brushed his jaw with her fingertip. The hair was springy and tickled her hand. "What is it?"

"I've had extensive wilderness training. I won't let anything happen to you, I promise."

She was pretty sure that hadn't been what he'd been

about to say. But whatever it was, it could wait. Extensive wilderness training right this second was probably more important. When he started to rise, she placed her hand on his wrist. "I promise I won't let anything happen to you, either."

He smiled, then pushed to his feet stiffly. The man's leg was mangled. It must be painful to walk on the uneven, shifting sand, but he didn't show it. How the hell did he think he could walk them out of the desert?

Upending a heavy bag, he said briskly, "Nice of them to give us a frying pan. Too bad they didn't include anything we could cook in it."

"Three bottles of water," Isis said, relieved. Three bottles wasn't enough, but it might mean the difference between life and death. Food they could do without, but not water. As soon as the sun came up and started baking the sand, dehydration would kill them. She'd heard of an archaeologist who'd been so excited by his find he'd forgotten to drink. He'd been dead within hours.

Three bottles of water was good.

"I found this." He turned on a small flashlight, and a thin stream of yellow light illuminated the dancing sand blowing around them. He turned it off. "Anything in any of those packages?" Thorne asked, as Isis picked up a handful of candy and food wrappers.

"No, but people will wonder that we didn't die of diabetic shock considering how much crap we're supposed to have eaten. This is a pretty damned elaborate plan to kill us. They thought of everything."

"It took a lot of planning and forethought, yeah." He

jerked his head, indicating the contents in her hand. "Put that pencil aside," he said absently. "We can use it as a weapon."

"To do what? Write a rude note? If someone is close enough to me that I could use a freaking pencil as a weapon, I'll be in big trouble."

He grinned. It was a confident, boyish grin that made heat reignite in her belly. If nothing else, he could take her mind off dying when they ran out of water by charming her to death. "Haven't you heard? The pen is mightier than the sword."

"Cute. We have a pencil and a small frying pan. What we need is an Uzi and a helicopter." She glanced up. "At least it seems to be getting warmer, but the wind is picking up as well, which isn't a good thing."

"Too late in the year for khamsin."

"God, I hope so." The hot, dusty southwesterly winds could blow fiercely for weeks on end, obliterating landmarks, eroding the paint off vehicles and the skin off people. The punishing winds made travel impossible and kept people indoors until it passed. Out here, it would kill them without protection.

"I experienced my first khamsin with my father when I was about thirteen." She pulled another T-shirt over the first two, then shook out her hair and rewrapped the long scarf around her neck a couple of times. "That terrifying dark wall of dust and sand coming at us in a suffocating blanket totally freaked me out. Have you seen it?"

She needed to get a grip here. This wasn't khamsin, but merely a bit of wind kicking up sand particles. It was the wrong time of year for the devil winds. High winds weren't uncommon out here in the desert, though, and even a mild windstorm would make finding their way to civilization tricky, if not downright impossible. She looked across the sea of sand as particles danced and swirled on the surface.

"A couple of times. A sandstorm is kicking up, but it won't be of that magnitude. Keep that scarf handy, and cover your face. If this wind gets any worse, we won't be able to walk in it, and we'll need better shelter than the tent. Let's get the lead out. Finish going through our supplies; I want to go up on that tall dune to look around before we wander off. Hopefully I can see signs of life from a higher elevation and we can start walking. If not we'll hunker down and wait it out."

"Good idea." She stood with him, winding his long blue and white scarf loosely around his throat a couple of times the way Beniti al-Atrash had taught her when she was a little girl. A protection against the sun, flies, and sand. "How long will you be gone?" She sounded like a worried wife.

"Twenty, thirty minutes. You can watch me all the way up that dune."

She patted his chest and rearranged the scarf. Needing to touch him. "Good, I like watching you. You have a very nice butt."

He bent to brush her lips with his. "I'm extremely partial to all your parts as well."

"They'll be waiting for you to hurry back. Be careful walking in the sand; it can be—"

"Twenty minutes."

She dug through several layers to find her front pockets, and shoved her hands into them to prevent herself from grabbing on to him like a baby monkey on its mother's back. "I'll be right here."

Isis didn't relish being apart from him, even if he wouldn't be gone long. She felt as though she had a target painted on her back. But separating so he could see where they were was expedient.

Gait slightly uneven but unhesitant, Thorne strode off across the sand, lifting a hand in farewell without turning around. Isis watched him for several minutes, then went back to rifle through their supplies, setting aside anything she thought could be useful. It was a dangerously small pile. Clearly whoever had left them there wanted them to die sooner rather than later.

Shivering in earnest, Isis retrieved the brand-new sleeping bag and, taking the frying pan with her as a makeshift weapon, settled in the sand with the down bag around her shoulders to wait for Thorne. She ignored the rumble of her stomach. Being hungry was the least of her problems. In the vast open space, hearing the rough sigh of the wind, and with the dusty smell of the breeze swirling around her, Isis had never felt so alone in her life.

The black bowl of the sky, studded with millions of crisp white stars, seemed close enough to touch, but its vastness made her feel very, very small. If she died out here, her father wouldn't even know she was gone. It was a terrifying realization that her death wouldn't have an impact on *anyone*. She'd traveled so much growing up that she hadn't formed lasting friendships, and the friends she'd made as an adult would wonder what wild adventure she was on—maybe even miss her—but would eventually get on with their busy lives. Perhaps the only person who might miss her return would be Zak, and that would be because she still owed him the other half she'd agreed upon for Thorne's services.

No, that depressing thought was unfair and untrue. Her cousin Acadia wouldn't rest until she was found, and she had friends who would ask questions relentlessly. That was a small comfort.

With the frying pan clutched in one hand, she folded her arms on her updrawn knees. Putting her head down on her arms, she squeezed her eyes shut, glad Thorne wasn't there to witness her pity party in all its glory. She gave herself five minutes to wallow, then she'd get up and pull on a few more T-shirts and pants to ward off the chill. He could warm her when he got back.

She refused to even consider that he might not come back at all. That whoever had abandoned them there was lying in wait for him over that dune. That they'd finished him off, and were coming to do the same to her. But her fingers tightened around her weapon.

THIRTY-SEVEN MINUTES LATER, THORNE returned to camp to find Isis huddled inside the downy folds of a sleeping bag. She got to her feet when she saw him, her camera bag slung across her body, a frying pan in one hand, her feet spread. Ready for battle.

"I found a cave or partial excavation in the hillside about ten minutes away," he told her, picking up the down bag from the sand and wrapping it around her shoulders like a cape. "The wind's picking up. We need to get out of it before it gets worse and visibility is shot. Ready?"

Strands of her hair lifted on the fingers of the wind, then danced around her head. In the starlight she looked like a pagan goddess. Snugging the bag around her throat, she gave him a small smile. "I was worried."

"You didn't think I'd wander away and leave you out here, did you?"

"I was worried about *you*, not myself," she told him, wrapping her long scarf around her head and face so just her eyes, protected some by her glasses, showed. "You didn't take any water. That's dangerous.

"Here." She handed him a full bottle. "Wet your scarf before you tie it over your face; it'll help from inhaling particles, then drink the rest. I've done the same."

"Okay."

Her eyes were hidden behind the reflection of the starlight on her glasses, but he felt her watching him chug down the better part of the warm water before using the rest to dampen a portion of the scarf, then lifted it to cover his mouth and nose and wrapped the rest around his head.

"We have one bottle left. This"—she indicated a duffel at her feet—"is the smallest of the three. I've packed anything useful in it. Which way?"

He loved her take-charge attitude. Bossy? Sure. But he knew it was her way of handling stress. She'd been put through situations no one should have to endure and she'd taken each event, if not in stride, then at least with admirable bravery.

Picking up the heavy bag, Thorne pointed, then fell into step as she immediately started walking the way he'd come. "Isis Magee, you are one hell of a woman." He didn't bother hiding his limp—didn't bother, and couldn't have disguised it even if he tried. Recent activities, coupled with trudging through shifting sand, had done a number on his thigh. The sharp, biting pain held his leg in a searing grip that lay somewhere between an animal trap and a rabid British bulldog.

"We're actually fairly close to the Valley of the Scorpions." He didn't believe in coincidence. Certainly not at this juncture. Was their location intentional, or had their kidnappers merely driven them randomly into the desert and dropped them where they were unlikely to be found?

"That's fantastic!"

"Don't get too excited. I didn't have a visual, nor did I see the dam. My calculation might be off."

"Your calculations are never off. If you say we're near the valley, then we are. We just have to figure out how to get from here to there."

"Pollyanna."

She smiled, unrepentant. "Cynic."

Yeah, he was. But he was also a realist. Thorne hadn't seen the valley from his vantage point, but knowing his present position, and having the mental, running GPS numbers in his mind, indicating the original location of Isis's amulet, he could make an educated guess on the distance between the two. A handful of miles as the crow flew, at the most.

Walkable if necessary. Unfortunately, the wind was steadily increasing, blowing hard against them, pushing them back as they needed to move forward. He was glad for the face covering, and the clothing Isis had insisted they put on before leaving.

"As soon as the wind stops, or it's light, we can follow the heading. Once we're in the valley, we'll be able to hitch a ride into Cairo."

"And go to the police." Her tone was grim. She was panting slightly from the exertion, and the sounds she was making reminded Thorne of the sounds she'd made when they made love.

The sound of her and the smell of her sweat-dampened skin turned him on, even here and now in the middle of nowhere, facing death head-on. It seemed that pain, trying circumstances, and exhaustion couldn't keep a good boner down.

"I'll get in touch with my contacts at MI5," he amended, cursing his body's response to her, which made walking even more of a challenge. One stiff leg was more than enough. Thorne concentrated on not thinking about it as he dug one foot in front of the other while they climbed a steep hill of shifting sand. He hoped he didn't have to climb or descend it again. Up, down, and up again was more than his leg wanted to deal with.

Isis slithered backward on all fours, and he backtracked to grab her arm and help her climb. The wind-driven sand flayed every bit of exposed skin, and he tugged her scarf up as it threatened to blow off her hair. Trudging up a steep dune, Thorne held on to her arm to assist her so she didn't tumble head-over-heels back down the hill again. It was heavy going in the dry, shifting sand and they had to lean into the persistent wind to make progress.

There was no point talking—they didn't even try. Just kept moving, backsliding, grappling to remain upright, and moving again.

He didn't have much, if any, faith in the locals. Kidnapping might not be a cottage industry in Egypt as it was in South America, but the local authorities were more likely to turn a blind eye than investigate. This was above their pay grade. The kidnapping plot was sophisticated and elaborate, well thought out and flawlessly executed. In other words, professional. These were no backwater thieves looking for a quick payout.

Too bad for their kidnappers that it wasn't going to fucking well work. He'd die trying to save Isis, and she was equally determined to live.

It was hard to tell if what he'd found was a cave or a long-forgotten tomb entrance, but it was imperative they find shelter until the storm stopped. The good news was, the bad guys weren't going anywhere in the sandstorm, either.

What looked like a pile of fragmented mud brick blocks, almost completely obscured by piles of sand taller than he was, indicated an opening. "This way."

Isis spread her hand on one of the blocks for balance as the wind picked up velocity, almost strong enough to knock her off her feet. "This looks like the access corridor to a burial chamber." She raised her voice over the rustle of sand blowing against sand. Without further ado, she turned sideways and slipped into the narrow, dark opening.

The woman was fearless. Denizens of the desert would have the same sense of self-preservation, and Thorne expected to encounter snakes and scorpions as well as assorted other critters waiting to welcome them inside. Venturing into a pitch-black, confined space—while unavoidable—could prove as fatal as staying outside in the elements.

Thorne paused to look back the way they'd come. Their footprints had already been wiped away, leaving no sign of their passing. A plus. The speed of the wind pretty much guaranteed that their faux camp was blown away as well.

"Connor?"

He loved hearing his name on her lips. When the hell had anyone last used it? His associates called him Thorne. His parents used his middle name, James, and his lovers called him by endearments. The only person who'd called him Connor had been his twin, Garrett. The ache in his chest had nothing to do with squeezing his too-large body through a too-narrow, unyielding opening.

Bending and contorting, he squeezed in after her. The opening was several inches too low and uncomfortably narrow for the width of his body. Letting out his breath, Thorne forced his torso to follow an arm and a leg. But for a moment he was pinned in place, neither in nor out, the pressure of the unyielding stones surrounding him, squeezing the air from his lungs.

The position painfully reminded Thorne of Yermalof's men pinning him down while the Russian finished torturing Maciej and Ayers. He felt the same pressure to survive now, the same urgency.

"Thorne, is it too tight?" There was a trace of panic in her voice, and a slim beam of light flashed through the opening as she shone the torch through the skinny opening.

Closing his eyes, he imagined himself on the other side and pushed his body through the opening like a ship rope through a sewing needle.

❧ FOURTEEN ❧

I t was almost quiet inside. Isis stood feet from the doorway, the flashlight pointed at the ground. She pushed her scarf off her hair and down off her face. "I was just about to see if I had a shoehorn or some baby oil to slip you in."

Unwinding the scarf from around his head and face as well, Thorne smiled. "Hold the thought on that baby oil." He stood for a moment, letting his eyes adjust, allowing his breathing to even out after the exertion. His night vision was above average, and with the faint glow of the small flashlight he could make out most of the shapes and walls inside the room.

The chamber was small, perhaps twelve feet by twelve. Rough-hewn brick walls, dirt floor. It smelled of dust and charred wood from a long-dead fire, evidenced by a tall black scorch mark up one wall and part of the low ceiling, and a pile of half-burned wood in the far corner.

Isis shone the narrow beam of the little flashlight along the walls. "No limestone revetment with reliefs and paintings." She sounded disappointed. "Probably the necropolis of the workers who built a tomb nearby. Hey! If the Valley of the Scorpions is on the other side of this ridge, maybe they built *Cleopatra's* tomb?" Her voice rose, as the idea clearly appealed to her.

"Wouldn't that be an amazingly cool payoff to all the running-chasing-kidnapping we've been through?" She slowly shone the light around. Every now and then Thorne would guide her hand to direct it at something so he could assess their situation.

"I think the stones and rock out there were originally part of a heavy stone plug, something they'd use to seal the tomb to discourage people from coming in after they left. A robber would have to chip away at it for a long, long time to get in."

She directed the beam across the dirt floor littered with fragments and shards of clay, using the light as a pointer. "That looks like part of a stone sarcophagus, and these are pottery shards. Bones over there. Robbers must've stolen whatever they could carry a long, long time ago. But at least it's relatively warm and out of the wind."

The bones didn't seem to bother her, but perhaps she knew they were animal, not human? Two large winged beetles flew into the stream of light. Isis merely swatted them with the flashlight, without the usual female shrieks of fright. His estimation of her went up another notch.

"This was probably the entrance the workers used," she told him, swatting away the various small bugs that flew around the light. "Hey! Look." The light jerked across the wall to illuminate a half-collapsed square hole in the back wall. "That's a tunnel, probably leading to a corridor. And maybe to a burial chamber—"

He had no intention of wandering around miles of underground tunnels to explore. "We're not tourists," he pointed out. "We don't have enough light to sightsee, and I don't want to use more energy than we need to. We only have half a bottle of water between us. That won't last long if we're walking around when we don't need to. Plus we could get lost. As soon as this wind stops we'll go up on the ridge and see if we can spot some sort of a landmark. But there's no telling how long we'll be away from civilization. Once our eyes adjust we should only use the light when necessary."

"*My* vote is to use it as much as we want, and when it dies, we'll be in Cairo at a nice restaurant eating a candle-light dinner."

Charmed by her, Thorne shook his head. She had a point. "Fair enough. The bugs certainly appreciate it."

She crouched down, using a flat stone to scrape off a clear spot in the sand. "This could be a diorite fragment." She held it up. "Perhaps from a vessel of some kind."

"Unless it's a pillow and a feather tick, I don't give a damn. I need to get off this leg, maybe take a short kip, and get an early start."

"Is a kip something that goes with leather and baby oil?"

He grinned. "A kip is a nap, but yes, it could certainly go with leather and baby oil. One of these days we'll have to combine the three and see.

"Here, give me that. We can do what needs to be done

without it for a while." Taking the flashlight from her, he clicked it off, then stuck it in his back pocket, plunging them into unrelieved darkness.

She grabbed his arm and he pulled her closer. "Afraid of the dark?"

"No. I'm afraid of what's *in* the dark."

"Any snakes will be trying to stay warm and shouldn't bother us."

"From your mouth. Turn the flashlight on," she instructed, her voice a little high. "I don't care if the batteries run down. I want a light on."

Handing her the flashlight, he removed the sleeping bag from the duffel, tossing it on the area she'd cleared. She trained the narrow beam where he needed it, without asking. "I'll make a fire."

"With what?" Isis asked, wrapping a bit of clothing around her hand and efficiently picking up two scorpions at the same time. "Two sticks rubbed together?" She tossed the scorpions outside, then shone the light in a grid pattern, presumably to find and kick out any more roommates.

"A lighter." He took a leather-covered keychain out of his pocket. A creative and indispensable item the kidnappers hadn't thought to take off him. It was a combination lighter and Swiss Army knife and had several other features that had served him well over the years. A gift from Zak Stark engraved, FOR THE MAN WHO HAS EVERY-THING. At the time Zak had given it to him, it seemed like Thorne indeed had everything—at least from the outsider's perspective. A rich, titled family, a body in its prime, and a supermodel for a girlfriend. But if anyone had dug deeper they would have seen the darker, seething mess bubbling just beneath the surface.

His father made sure no one ever knew what happened behind closed doors. All the wealth was a payoff for the abuse he witnessed or experienced himself. The girlfriend liked his wallet better than him. And his body—well, he'd learned the hard way you only got one.

He flicked the lighter out of the device. "See if you can find something to burn. Just don't stick your hand anywhere dangerous."

"I know somewhere dangerous I could stick my hand, and we'd *both* get warm."

Thorne smiled in the darkness. "Why, Miss Magee, that's extremely forward of you."

"Here." She shoved a handful of food wrappers at him. "That wood in the corner is probably three centuries old, but I say we use it."

"I'll get it." Rummaging in the duffel, he took out his custom Fioravanti suit jacket. "All I need is for you to get bitten by any of a number of poisonous insects."

"Why is it okay for *you* to get bitten?"

"Let's neither of us get bitten, okay?" Thorne used the toe of his boot to break up the clump of logs and small sticks. A few scorpions scurried away into the darkness. Crouching down, he wrapped the jacket around the wood and carried the bundle across the small chamber, tossing it down near the sleeping bag.

"You don't carry around any perfume with you in your bag, do you?"

"Oh, God—I stink, don't I?"

"You smell incredible." And when she scowled at him, he rephrased: "You smell hot and sexy, and I want you like mad. No, I need an accelerant. Perfume would work."

"How about hand sanitizer?" She opened her camera bag and started taking things out. The little bottle was of course right at the bottom. She fished it out and handed it to him.

"Hand sanitizer is perfect."

It took only a few moments to get a spark from the hand cleaner and candy wrappers, and a minute or two to get a decent blaze going. Orange light flickered on the walls.

THORNE TOOK THE DUFFEL and a handful of shirts and pants and stuffed them in the narrow doorway opening, to keep out the sand, but also so their campfire didn't attract any attention. Satisfied that the glow, small as it was, couldn't be seen from outside, he turned to find Isis standing in the middle of the space, watching him.

He took her hand and led her to the sleeping bag. Sitting at last, he tugged her down beside him and lay back. Thorne suppressed a groan of appreciation for the relief of his pained leg.

Isis came willingly, lying down when he did, her body half over his. Wrapping an arm across his chest, she curled a knee over his hips, then sighed as she snuggled her head into the curve of his shoulder. Soft, cinnamon-scented hair brushed his chin.

A shudder ran through her body and he smoothed his

palm up and down her slender back, pulling her against his side with one hand and tugging the edge of the down sleeping bag over her—or part of her. The back of her T-shirt was damp, her skin cold even though it must be in the low seventies. It pissed him off that she was anything but comfortable.

"I like that," she murmured, her breath warm and moist against his throat.

"What? This?" He trailed his fingers up her back and her arm tightened around his chest

"My father loves me, but he's not touchy-feely. My mom was. It's strange how one can miss something as simple as a loving touch in comfort, not sex." She tilted her head to look at him. "Not that I don't enjoy the hell out of touches prior, during, and after great sex, mind you."

He smiled against her hair. "What happened to her?"

"She had a heart attack. A congenital heart defect no one knew about. She died in her sleep on my twelfth birthday."

"So young?"

"Barely forty. It devastated my dad. My parents had a great marriage, even if he spent most of the time here and not with us in Seattle. Mom anchored him to the real world." She smiled at a memory. "She came on a couple of digs. Disastrous," she chuckled. "God, she *hated* everything about it."

"It isn't for everybody." Scorpions, flies, unrelenting heat. Disappointment.

"She let me come. Sometimes for a few weeks, and

several times she let me attend school here so I could be with my father when he made some spectacular discovery and he refused to leave. Her death was . . . difficult for him. He didn't know what to do without her."

"But he was apart from her most of the time," Thorne pointed out gently. Her rose-colored glasses rationalized everyone's actions for the better, without leaving room for her own feelings. "Worse for a young girl losing her mother. Especially at that age, I imagine."

"It wasn't easy," Isis admitted. "I went to live with my aunt. Acadia and I became like sisters. I miss Mom, but Dad's disease is ten times worse. He doesn't know me anymore, and it breaks my heart." Her body tensed a fraction against his. "I have to find Cleo's tomb for him, Connor. I have to prove that all the years he spent away from us were worth it. Can you understand that?"

"Yeah." He brushed his lips across her cheek. "I can."

"Tell me about Garrett. Were you identical?"

"Mirror images. People frequently confused us. It was great fun in school." And hell at home. "He was a great brother and a good friend. And I miss him every day."

"What made you different?"

"Everything other than our looks. Garrett was the better man in every way. He was everything my parents trained him to be from birth. No rebelling for him. He was the brain, I the brawn. But Garrett didn't have the freedoms I enjoyed.

"I played hard, and he studied hard. He'd been moody and quiet for months. The pressure of reaching his majority, and dealing with everything His Lordship was throwing at him, plus that law degree our father so prized. There was a ridiculous amount of pressure put on his shoulders, and he never seemed to take time for fun unless I coerced him into playing truant now and then. He loved reading, would camp out in the library at the house or up in his rooms all day if I didn't drag him out to the pub or a rugby game. I was the one who insisted on going sailing that day, despite the weather warnings.

"We'd just turned twenty-one, and I was full of piss and vinegar and feeling invincible." Thorne dragged in a harsh breath. "I dragged him with me because I wanted his company and thought he'd enjoy a day out on the water.

"We'd been fighting the high winds and currents for an hour, trying to head back to port. I loved it, but Garrett was pissed at me. He wasn't fond of sailing, and was afraid as the boat tossed and turned. I made sure—for about the seventh time—that his safety harness was clipped to the jackline, and his life vest secure, then sent him to secure a line. I don't know why the hell he unclipped his safety line—stubborn bastard, had to do it his own way, by damn. A wave broke over the stern, and he was just . . . gone."

Isis's arm tightened around his chest. "I'm so sorry. It must've been hideous at the time, and unbearable to have to go home and tell your parents."

Hideous was an understatement. "They never forgave me. And I don't blame them."

She didn't say, as some of his peers had done, that it hadn't been his fault. He hadn't forced his brother to go out with him. He'd attempted, numerous times, to tether him securely. It didn't matter what the hell he'd done to ensure his brother's safety. He'd failed. And failed monumentally.

"Why would anyone in their right mind keep taking off a safety harness?" she asked softly, bringing her fingers up to touch his face.

"Who knows?" Thorne shrugged, chest tight.

"You know," Isis whispered in an achingly soft voice, her breath warm on his throat. "Did your parents?"

She'd gotten it after one conversation when others, who'd known them well, had seen no further than the nose on their faces. "No. Only me."

He felt her tears against his skin. "Oh, Connor . . ."

Pressing his lips to her forehead, Thorne's fingers tightened in her silky hair as his heart swelled with an unnamed emotion. "Thank you." It took him several seconds before he could speak normally. "Now close your eyes. The wind doesn't appear to be stopping. Sleep for a couple of hours."

"I can't sleep," she whispered, shifting restlessly against his side. "It's been an insane day." She slid her hand from his chest. Thorne's belly contracted as she glided her hand beneath his belt and found his hard length unerringly. Cool fingers curled around his dick.

Lifting her mouth to meet his she murmured, "Make love to me, Connor."

THORNE LIFTED UP ON his elbow. God, she was pretty. Without her glasses on she looked younger, innocent, and achingly sweet. Not his type. Not his type by a long shot. But feeling the brush of her fingers on his chest, having those heated Bambi eyes directed at him, almost made him a believer.

Or maybe having someone else share his secret burden made him feel—lighter.

Primitive firelight danced on the walls, bathing her skin, turning her creamy complexion to a warm caramel and her dark hair to flame. With a little hum of appreciation that vibrated in his groin, she slid her palm up his chest, then curled her hand around his neck, her fingers cool and smooth as she tugged his mouth down to hers.

"One day," she said wistfully, "I'd like to make love in a big bed with crisp sheets, and while we're at it, twenty-four-hour room service."

"I'll book us into the presidential suite the minute we get out of here."

"Promise?"

Thorne stroked his thumb over her plump lower lip. "Jacuzzi, hot shower, big bed. Champagne." *Baby oil.*

"I'll hold you to that."

He kissed the smile curving her mouth. A promise, not so much to find that hotel, but to get her out of there, safe and sound. A promise he refused to even contemplate breaking.

"You're like catnip to me." Devilish humor danced in her eyes. "I can't get enough of you." Snaking her other arm from his back, she started to tug at his belt buckle with impatient fingers. "A little assistance, please?"

"Getting naked, here and now, is the height of folly,"

he murmured, pushing her hand away so he could glide all the T-shirts she was layered in up over her breasts. He was a man who appreciated sexy underwear. Lace and silk. Satin was one of his favorite fabrics to see hugging a woman's assets. But Isis's unadorned nude cotton bra was the sexiest thing he'd ever seen. Her nipples, poking beneath the thin fabric, begged to be tasted. He lowered his head, brushing his lips down the plump valley between her breasts. The familiar scent of her skin, a bite of cinnamon, a touch of salt, the heated spice of her arousal, made him so hard he could use his dick to break out of there.

Isis combed her fingers up his nape, then cupped the back of his head in her palm as he suckled one hard tip into his mouth. Her back arched and she made a low hum in the back of her throat.

"So sensitive."

"Skip the chitchat, Thorne." She pressed his head more firmly against her breast. "That's too gentle. Harder."

He bit down lightly through the material, then sucked deeply, pulling the extended tip deep into his mouth as his lips curved in a wry smile. Even here, she wanted to be boss.

Lifting his head from her breast, he nibbled at her chin, teasing her until he took her mouth in a breathless kiss that fired all his cylinders. Still kissing her, Thorne ran his hand down her hip, then undid the button on her jeans and tugged down the zipper. He lingered for a moment on the indentation of her navel, stroking a single circle before slipping his palm down the satin of her belly beneath her panties. He enjoyed the flutter as her muscles contracted at the brush of his fingers along her hairline, and felt her humid heat at his fingertips.

Her fingers tightened in his hair as she lifted her hips off the sleeping bag. "Hurry!"

He dared not fully undress her. But he pushed her jeans and sensible cotton panties down to her knees, inhaling the spicy mélange of cinnamon and the hot heady scent of her sex.

Kissing her while one-handedly undoing his own clothes was a gymnastic feat. Even his own touch threatened to blow the top of his head off.

Having exposed only what was necessary, he slid two fingers into her slick channel. "If I tasted you here right now you'd taste salty sweet and luscious."

"B-be my guest."

Thorne smiled. She looked and sounded so earnest, clearly so engrossed she'd forgotten where they were. Even as he stroked her supple body and made love to her, he was aware of everything around them. Alert to danger. The firelight made deep pockets of shadow where any manner of unpleasant things could hide. "Pretend we're in the back of my car at the drive-in movies. By necessity we need to do what we want to do discreetly and with some speed."

She huffed out a laugh. "I've never made out in the backseat of a car before."

"Let me show you the general principle, then. You get to be on top for this one." He half tugged, half lifted her on top of him and was rewarded with a big smile of appreciation. "Yes, I can see you'll take to this position like a duck to water. Spread your legs," he instructed. She bracketed his hips with her knees, her body open and fragrant as she poised above his eager penis. Her T-shirts were still rucked up around her neck, the fabric of her bra wet around her nipples. Thorne reached up to stroke the buds so they tightened to sweet little points. "You're in charge."

Hands braced on his chest, Isis slid down on the spear of his dick, her body clenching and pulsing around him. For a moment she was unmoving, head flung back, eyes closed. "I could die just like this and be happy."

"No one is dying, and you'll be a lot happier doing this in that big bed I promised you." He ran both hands up the baby-soft skin of her exposed midriff, then cupped her breasts. She sucked in a wobbly breath as he rolled the erect nipples between his fingertips. "If you're in the driver's seat"—he tweaked harder and her back arched in response—"*drive*, Miss Magee."

She started to move, slowly at first, and then picked up speed. The sensation of her grinding down on him almost pushed Thorne over the brink. The sensation was too sharp, too fucking perfect to last. He grabbed her hips to slow her down, but it was too late as the avalanche of his climax hit him full force.

Her body bucked and tightened, and she let out a strangled scream as she came. Then collapsed on his chest.

He pressed his face into her damp throat as he fought for control of his body and his emotions. Her fragrant hair tickled his nose; her body was limp. They were still joined. He was still semi-erect. The rhythm of their elevated heartbeats was syncopated, a mirrored throbbing that he felt in every pulse point throughout his body.

Her fingers explored the bones of his jaw with delicate strokes, much the way she'd stroked his injured leg at her friend's apartment what felt like a lifetime ago. Her touch was healing, as if she possessed some form of magic that would take away the pain.

She settled more comfortably on top of him, the weight of her slender body like a benediction as she lazily ran her fingertips over him wherever she could reach. "I like being the boss of you."

"I bet you do," he murmured wryly as he, too, let his hands wander over her back and arms, learning the dips and valleys and imagining how she'd feel right then if she were naked.

Thorne laughed, a rusty sound that filled the small room and sounded alien to his own ears. He didn't remember when he'd ever laughed before meeting Isis. It was a strange and uncomfortable realization having no recollection of being . . . *happy*. Christ.

THE DEEP RHYTHMIC *WHOP-WHOP-WHOP* was so faint that at first, Thorne attributed it to their syncopated heartbeats. She'd rolled off him ten minutes before. He'd helped her pull up her clothing, and she'd helped him with his. Which had involved a lot more touching and kissing, but eventually they'd both fallen silent, and she was in a postcoital doze, if her steady breathing was any indication.

Whop-whop-whop.

Disengaging her arm from across his chest, Thorne jerked upright, senses tuned to the sound. "Incoming."

He jumped to his feet, his hand going automatically to his hip where his weapon should be. He pulled up his jeans and yanked up the zipper even as he strode to the clothing-stuffed entrance.

Bloody hell. He should've known their kidnappers wouldn't leave well enough alone.

"Who's coming?" Isis sounded sleepy and bewildered. Sitting up, she tugged her T-shirts down over her pretty breasts. "The bad guys?"

"Douse the fire."

Thorne fingered aside a sliver so he could see out and searched the black skies. The narrow entrance was easily defensible, but they were trapped like rats in a hole. He pulled out the clothing he had stuffed in the opening. It was still dark out, the stars fading; dawn had yet to break. The air was cooler, and now dead calm. Not a breath of wind moved the sand particles.

"Chopper from the north." Coming in low and dark, a black blot in the star-studded sky. Narrow-eyed, Thorne watched it swoop low over the rise and disappear. Presumably to fly over their campsite.

Heat-imaging sensors would alert whoever was on board that the tent and surrounding area were abandoned. Did they know about this tomb? Yeah, he bet they did. Everything else had been so well scripted they wouldn't forget the smallest detail.

The *whop-whop-whop* grew louder before the black ghost of the chopper rose high enough to clear the ridge.

He knew what he would do if he were them. "Go back as far as you can. *Move!*" Racing back to where Isis stood motionless in the middle of the chamber, he grabbed her around the waist, shoving her ahead of him as he ran back into the chamber.

She gave a muffled shriek as he flattened his body over hers, tugging the scarf that was still wound around her neck, up over her head. He covered her face, then pressed her head against his chest. He used the trailing end of her scarf to cover his own nose and mouth.

A nanosecond later, the sandstone bricks in the entrance exploded in a shower of dust, sand, and sharp shards.

"Who *are* these crazy freaking people?" Isis yelled, her voice muffled against his chest.

"It'll stop in a minute . . ."

"How do you—"

The grating sound of the rocks and sandstone bricks tumbling and crashing obliterated her words.

Thorne pressed Isis's face harder against his chest, holding his breath as the small room filled with thick clouds of dust and sand. Rocks and bricks tumbled and bounced. Something hard slammed painfully into his shoulder. The cacophony of falling stones continued for interminable minutes as the surrounding hillside crashed down outside and sealed them in the chamber.

❧ FIFTEEN ❧

Shell-shocked, Isis took in the devastation as she wiggled out of Thorne's steely grip. Yanking the flashlight out of his pocket, he flicked it on, shining a thin beam of illumination around the dust-filled chamber. Half the room was filled with rubble. The opening was sealed behind who knew how much fallen stone, broken bricks, and debris. She coughed as the thick, swirling dust lodged in her throat.

Eyes stinging, Isis felt the unsteady gallop of her heart and wiped perspiration from her upper lip with a dirty fingertip. "What in God's name was *that* about?" She was annoyed at how her fingers shook as she fastened her jeans.

Thorne shone the light on the pile of rubble blocking their exit. "They wanted to ensure their plan worked. Are you hurt?"

"Thanks to fast thinking, and you being a human shield, I'm okay. The question is, are you?" She ran her hands over his chest, then walked around behind him. "Hold the light over your shoul—"

He moved out of the way, taking the light with him. "I'm fine."

Isis didn't blame him for being cranky. She was feeling decidedly pissed off herself. "Me, too. Getting madder by the minute, but physically fine and dandy." She coughed violently again. "How can causing a rockslide look like an accident? It will, won't it?"

"Yeah. I suspect this was the plan all along. It'll look like we came in here to explore, the hillside was unstable . . ." He used the light as a pointer. "Let's get cracking."

Even though the narrow opening had only just been sealed shut, Isis was already feeling short of breath. She told herself firmly to get a grip. It was simply psychological. There was still plenty of air inside, despite the dust particles floating about. But it wouldn't last long. "Let's try the tunnel."

Thorne shook his head, his dark hair now sand colored and covered with dust, as was every bit of exposed skin. Isis knew she looked just as bad. "They would've considered that as a way out. Don't waste your time; it won't go anywhere." He strode over and started tossing chunks of rock aside.

The flashlight winked out. Isis wanted to scream, nooooo! "Is that it? Are the batteries shot?"

He opened the back, did a guy thing with the battery, then shook his head. "Dead as a doornail. It was nice while it lasted."

The dark was oppressive. The dark and knowing they were sealed in was *beyond* oppressive. "Those despicable bastards." She wet her dry lips. "They're gone, right?

"I heard the chopper in the distance. I doubt they'll

come back to see if their work is done. Not till morning, anyway. See if you can coax that fire a bit."

"Is that a good idea if we're worried about our oxygen supply?"

"I don't want flames, I just want the embers hot."

Isis kicked aside a rock that she'd used to put the fire out moments before, then picked up several wrist-sized logs that had scattered on impact. Laying them across the coals, she bent down to blow on it a few times.

Crouching beside the feeble flames, she dragged her camera bag closer, then hooked the strap over her head before rummaging inside. She found the small plastic bottle of hand sanitizer and gave the fire a good squirt. The alcohol took immediately and the fire leapt to life.

"It could be a corridor into the tomb proper, and give us a better way out." She gave the little flame another breath of air and watched it leap and glow. "The corridor could lead into an antechamber, and those sometimes have another corridor to get to the outside." Using the end of her scarf, she flapped it a couple of times until the flames started taking hold of the half-burnt timbers.

The golden glow of the fire danced against the stone walls as she walked the three steps necessary to stand beside him. "It's worth a try, don't you think?" Before the fire and her panicked breathing ate up all the oxygen.

Dropping the brick in his hands, he straightened to look at her. "How far do you need to go before you realize that way's blocked, too?"

"How many stones do you need to throw aside before

you realize that if you move all those in here, there'll be no room for us?" Isis countered, wiping the dust-encrusted sweat off her forehead with her scarf, her gaze steady. "That's heavy manual labor, and we have about two cups of water left. When the sun's up, and if we *do* manage to get out, we have to walk all day. We'd need approximately four gallons each to survive out there in that heat. We won't make it."

"No," he admitted grimly, dusting off his hands. "We won't."

"All I'm proposing is that we explore deeper into the tunnel rather than working ourselves to certain death."

"Okay. Let's see how far we can get in the tunnel. Drink the water before we go."

Isis retrieved the plastic bottle, twisting off the cap. "Half for me, half for you. Don't argue." Tipping the bottle, she drank just enough to make her realize that she could drink an entire ocean. Two sips. It was warm, had a slight plastic flavor, and might as well have been nectar from the gods. She handed the bottle to him.

"You didn't drink your share."

"You outweigh me, and you'll do more physical labor trying to break us out of here. Drink it and shut up; you're wasting oxygen."

Thorne laughed. "God, you're bossy." He drained the bottle, then hooked his arm around her waist and tugged her in for a kiss, giving her back some of the water he'd just drunk. Lifting his head he touched his fingertips to her cheek. "Swallow."

Isis swallowed, giving him the evil eye, which he

missed as he walked over to their small campsite and started stuffing things in the duffel. "Gather what supplies you can find——" He saw her pick up his dress shirt and held out his hand. "Great, give me that." He took it from her and ripped off several buttons.

"Breathe through your nose; it'll prevent the membranes in your mouth from drying out, and suck on this." Handing her a small button, he popped the other in his mouth. "Scarves pulled up as well; the dust is going to be a problem depending how deep the tunnel goes." Even though he was prepared to go deeper into what Isis was sure was a tomb, he didn't sound that confident that the tunnel would lead them anywhere.

She mentally conjured up some of the drawings of tombs her father had left lying around over the years. While she hadn't formally studied Egyptology, she'd learned a lot from him by osmosis. Or so she hoped. Because right now, their lives might depend on her knowing how to navigate the labyrinth of passages and rooms, if this was indeed part of a tomb.

And at this stage of the game she didn't care whose tomb it was, just that there was an exit of some kind.

And enough air to support them as they searched for it.

THORNE PICKED UP THE sleeping bag, shaking off the rocks and debris. Half a dozen large scorpions dropped, tails curved over their backs as they scurried into the surrounding darkness. Four were the common variety. They'd sting, but the worst result would be a painful red welt. Two, however were the fat-tailed variety, the most dangerous group of scorpion species in the world. Four inches of "man-killer." Powerful neurotoxins in their venom could kill. Being stung by two while they'd been otherwise distracted could've killed them.

"Check your clothes and tuck in what can be tucked," he told her grimly, not wanting to think how close the arthropods had been to their naked body parts. They'd been so consumed with making love, scorpions had been the last thing on their minds.

They both shook out what they were wearing. Nothing dropped out. "I'm okay," Isis told him. "You?"

He thoroughly checked his own clothing, then helped Isis tuck her pants tightly into her socks, then did the same for himself. "Fine. Fire and we're gone."

Picking up a couple of the two-foot-long sticks, which were now red-hot and glowing, he handed her one to carry like a baton. Rolling several large rocks with the side of his foot, he smothered the small fire. "Let's check out your tunnel."

Isis put her hand on his arm to stop him. "Be careful where you walk. Don't put your weight on your front foot until you're sure you're stepping somewhere solid. There could be hidden holes. My father thought they probably hid them under delicately balanced wood manhole covers, so the lightest step would tip the robber into a pit."

"Lovely. An ancient burglar alarm. Except it was death instead of jail. Good to know." He'd never been inside a tomb, but it already seemed like a fucking death trap before they'd even started in. They walked side by side, but he made sure Isis was one step behind him. The smell of burning wood was accompanied by the smell of ancient dust as their feet kicked up little puffs of sand.

"Don't worry about the powder toxins," she said, almost cheerfully. "Those are too old to be effective anymore. You know about the fatal properties of ancient Egyptian medicines, right?"

"Everything I know you just told me," Thorne said dryly. "They no longer work." He walked cautiously and kept his eyes, ears—and now nose—open and looking for danger.

He carried his "torch" high while Isis kept hers low. For now the atmospheric red glow sufficed. The tunnel, running north to south, seemed to be dead straight.

"It's strange that there are no paintings or mosaics in this section." Isis lightly ran her fingers along the rough brick of the wall as she walked. Her soft voice echoed slightly on the hard surfaces. Clearly man-made, the completely bricked corridor was about five feet wide, nine or ten feet high, and disappeared into the darkness in front of them.

Every now and then they came across piles of limestone rubble with a broken potsherd and a few intact painted jars tossed in it like trash. "My father would be in his glory right now."

Her father was probably playing bingo right then, but Thorne didn't say so. "It's an ancient landfill."

"*Here*, but maybe deeper . . . Tomb workers were allowed to build their own 'Houses of Eternity,'" Isis told him, her soft voice filling the space. It was fine if she wanted to play tour guide to dispel the darkness as they walked. Thorne let his mind wander to their determined kidnappers.

"And since they were highly skilled, they usually made their last resting places beautiful, too. It's possible that this was the burial tomb for the workers, although they usually decorated them as well as the royal tomb they were working on. I've been in several, and they're charming and not as formal as the ones they built for their king or queen. But this? Not a pretty thing in sight. Looters could've stripped it of anything valuable. People here have been robbing tombs since the first dynasty."

The piece missing for Thorne was that he knew to what extremes Yermalof would go to stop someone. Thorne had received Lynn Maciej's tongue, then later watched Yermalof flay the skin off her breasts with his small, chillingly effective knife. By then Ayers was dead, and Thorne secured so that he could helplessly watch every cruel, agonizing slice as he was left to bleed out on the floor, just feet away.

"It made sense from a purely economic point of view," Thorne said absently, being damned careful where he walked. "The kings and queens buried in these tombs were interred with all their wealth, effectively keeping all that gold and silver and whatever the most valuable commodity of the time was out of circulation. Tomb robbers put that wealth back into circulation."

"I never thought of it that way." Isis laughed softly. "An ancient savings and loan? It makes a weird kind of sense. Even Husani turns a blind eye now and then when something is brought in by a robber. It's hard to stop." She paused, her steps slowing. "Do you think our kidnapping had something to do with your Russian bad guy?"

The floor started to slope, and he put a hand back to caution her. "If we'd been tortured and left to die slowly, yeah. But this whole thing was set up so that it looked like stupidity. An accident. Yermalof fences extremely high-end antiquities worth multimillions of dollars. Some priceless, which go for a hell of a lot more. *Smells* a little like him but doesn't have the big impact he goes for. If he's involved with the people who are looking for your Cleo, he'd want us alive, not dead. Unless he's setting a trap—"

"He might not have to," she reminded him practically.

"Yeah." Thorne focused on what was ahead in the glow of their fire sticks. "He might not have to."

But what could Yermalof gain by burying them in a hillside? It would get him out of the way for sure. But who, besides him, would benefit from that? For a moment Thorne contemplated his life. Being in the dark end of a tomb did that to a man.

Who else had he crossed, in an effort to win his father's forgiveness over the years, and then for the military, that might want him dead and be willing to work with Yermalof to make it happen?

For several minutes they walked in silence. *Relative* silence. He heard her every breath and listened to her footfall with every step. Close enough to grab her if she fell, near enough to dispel any wildlife that might drop from the ceiling. Or one of the throat-height wires the ancients were so damned fond of for decapitating robbers and felling them in their tracks.

Deep down, Thorne's gut sank further. No matter how sweet Isis's delusions of hope were, there was little chance that this was the way out. He was afraid he wasn't going to be able to keep his promise. They were going to die, buried like so many beneath the sands of this valley.

"IF THE RUSSIAN GUY is behind all this . . ." Isis skirted a pile of chipped and broken stones before squeezing sideways to get through a collapsed doorway. The strong smell of burning wood and dust tickled her nose. It was a good thing she wasn't claustrophobic, because it felt as if the walls were closing in on them in the darkness beyond the red glow of their makeshift torches. "What would his purpose be?"

"Other than having his hands on a wealth of priceless antiquities?"

Every now and then she'd spread her arms wide to ensure that the walls were the same distance apart. "Well, yeah, there is that. No, I mean his purpose in trying to kill us?"

Using his torch, Thorne pulled aside a spiderweb drape at eye level. Isis's meager fiery glow was shrinking, barely giving off any light at all. Hell, she was feeling her way through the tunnel more than seeing where they were going.

"The first thing I'll ask when I catch up with him," Thorne said dryly.

"Seriously. As you said, if your bad guy wanted us dead, we'd *be* dead. Which means he either made a mistake or there's a reason he has us holed up in here. Or it's not *him* at all. We seem to have a smorgasbord of bad guys after us, and we don't have a clue who sent them."

"Yermalof tends not to make mistakes," Thorne told her, his words hardly reassuring. "And he's had time to think this through."

"Again. Not reassuring. This corridor seems to go on forever, so at least we're not going to run out of oxygen anytime soon." Sounding calm and practical was a strain, but panic was going to get them nowhere fast.

They'd been walking steadily downhill. The grade wasn't steep, but *down* didn't feel like *out* to her. This was possibly the worst idea in her life. But then, *down* meant there was more ahead. At least she remembered that much from her father's work.

"And while I know we can go without food for a long time," she continued a little desperately, "we can't go without water." She kept up the conversation because if not, her ears throbbed with the thick silence enveloping them. Talking kept the nerves at bay. "So eventually, if we don't find a well-lit exit sign, we're screwed. Right?"

God, she was babbling now, wasn't she? Why didn't he say something? Anything? She knew he was still ahead of her because of the regular intervals of his breath. Isis wished she'd been more engaged when her father had been on a dig. She'd learned about tombs by osmosis. She'd been far more interested in framing the next shot and in the angles of light and shadow than in Egyptology.

Thorne paused to hold his stick to hers, and the embers threw off pretty sparklers that illuminated the grim set of his mouth. Their shadows danced on the rough-cut walls. "Someone might have a contract out on me." His voice was pretty damned matter-of-fact for the statement. But he'd been pretty matter-of-fact this whole time. At least he'd finally said something, which eased the growing knot between her shoulder blades. Of course, what he'd just said tightened her nerves up again.

"More than just the Russian?" she asked dryly. Very dryly because she was so parched her lips kept sticking together. She shifted the slick little button around in her mouth. It helped, but it wasn't a tall, iced Diet Coke. "I thought you were one of the good guys!"

Thorne shrugged. "Boris Yermalof is one of, if not *the*, top seller of priceless black market antiquities in the world. As elusive as smoke, it took us, MI5, years to track him down and learn his name and then another year to learn his location. His retaliation—and we were expecting it, mind you—was swift and brutal. His buyers think nothing of spending upwards of twenty mil on an original bust of Tutankhamen and hiding it in their basement where no one but themselves will ever see it."

She gave an audible swallow.

"If those same buyers are in the know about a Cleopatra find, they'd draw straws to see who'd pay a hit man to keep everyone off Yermalof's back while he brokered their deal. My returning to London might've been a tipoff that I was back in the game. The Russian couldn't know I was on a medical leave of absence instead of out of the business for good. It's been a while."

"London was my fault—"

"No, it wasn't. I had to go back at some point. I'm not the only MI5 operative looking for him. He killed two of our own; there are many people at Thames House wanting retaliation. They can't go about killing everyone in Her Majesty's Secret Service. If nothing else it would take several lifetimes."

"Funny. Maybe Yermalof has a boss? Someone higher up the food chain whom he reports to?"

"If he does, it's a well-kept secret. We've never heard even a hint that he doesn't work alone."

"Stop!" Isis grabbed his arm as he almost walked into a partially fallen beam as he'd turned his head to talk to her. She held her torch up. The small flame flickered with the movement, casting oddly shaped shadows, but illuminated the stone . . . lintel? "I think this means we're entering a chamber. Maybe it has a back door." They ducked and passed through the V beneath the thick strut where it had wedged against one wall. The room was disappointingly empty. Reliefs had been scribed on the sandstone walls from ceiling to floor, but not painted, and she couldn't see them well enough to try to decipher their meanings even if she knew how to read hieroglyphics. Couldn't begin to know the room's original purpose.

And damn it, she was so thirsty! All she could think

of was a vat of sparkling Diet Coke filled with bobbing ice cubes. She'd swim in it for a week.

They passed through the empty room to another, slightly larger chamber. Here the walls were covered in crude pictures of daily life. She raised her torch as she walked. Even in the dimness, the colors of barges and blue herons, beaked gods, and women washing clothes were still as pure and beautiful as the day they'd been painted.

She automatically reached for her camera case on her hip, then dropped her hand. She could spend all day documenting her find for her father. But now wasn't the time.

"Isis?" Thorne called from the shadowy doorway across the dusty space where he stood waiting for her.

"Coming." She closed the gap between them. "Okay, so our first suspect is Yermalof. Who *else* wants to kill you?"

Thorne smiled. "Surprisingly few people want to off me, actually. Let's look at the professor for a moment."

"You think my *father* wants you dead?" She shot him a teasing glance as they walked into another corridor. Here the floor was marble, smooth under a drift of coarse, gritty sand. Their shoes crunched as they walked.

This corridor was beautifully painted with soldiers going into battle. *Mark Antony?* Her heartbeat sounded loud in her ears. "*He* doesn't know what you've done to his sweet baby girl, so I don't think so. Not yet anyway."

Could she believe what her eyes were trying to tell her, or was she starting to add two and eleven to make ninety-three?

"No, I know your father didn't put out a hit on me. But consider for a moment what would be at stake if he truly *did* find Queen Cleopatra's tomb."

"He'd be vindicated."

"He'd go down in the history books. He'd be feted, asked to travel the world lecturing about his discovery. There'd be endorsements, and sponsorships——"

"Thorne, even if that was all true——my father can't take advantage of or enjoy *any* of that. He has Alzheimer's. If——*when* we find Cleo's tomb, it will give him justification for all his claims." The scenes of war changed to hunting scenes. Pretty brutal, Isis observed absently as the lights passed from one group of images to the next. "But as for him enjoying that vindication——he's not capable of doing so anymore."

"He isn't. But that doesn't mean someone on his team wouldn't be itching to take the glory for themselves at your father's expense."

"Dylan . . ."

"Possibly. He's also got motive. Let's take the bits and pieces you know, and let's say they're gospel. Tell me again what happened."

She exhaled, telling Thorne again what she knew by heart. "He found Cleo's tomb in the late afternoon of May seventeenth. The crew had camped at an oasis about a mile away. While dinner was cooking he went back to the tomb. Knowing my father, he went back to touch the rocks at the entrance. Immerse himself before the dig started. It was a little ritual he had."

One of the images snagged her attention, and her

steps slowed. The green-skinned man, with a pharaoh's beard and partially mummy-wrapped legs, wore the distinctive crown of two long ostrich feathers. Osiris? Isis's heart leapt. Oh, my God. Was it possible . . . ?

Osiris, she knew, was the god of the afterlife and the dead. It made sense that he'd be in every tomb . . .

"All this artwork leaving you a little breathless?"

"I'm fine," she said automatically, her words monotone because her brain was suddenly going a thousand miles an hour. Catching up with Thorne, she blew on the end of her torch to encourage the small red glow so she could look at the eight-foot-tall people depicted along the walls. Before she took a wild leap, she had to be sure . . .

"Isis? Your father's ritual?"

"Sorry. He took a picture of himself at the entrance—the one he sent to me—then was struck on the head," she reminded him, although why he needed reminding she had no idea. He knew the sequence of events as well as she did by now. "He thought he was in the Valley of the Scorpions, but instead he was found at Dafarfa Oasis."

"Concussion. No memory of what had happened."

"Right. Something like us being in a car going one way, and ending up *camping* somewhere miles away in the desert. Put those two events together and there certainly seems to be a similarity, don't you think?"

"I do."

Frustratingly, Isis couldn't identify any of the other ancient Egyptians depicted on the walls. She thought one might be Horus when she passed a bird-headed man wearing a red and white crown. But what did she know? She'd always just admired the style and color of the images, never learned their meanings. *Sorry, Dad.*

"He didn't even remember leaving Seattle to *come* on this dig."

"What if it isn't Alzheimer's? What if the blow to the head caused memory loss, either permanent or temporary?"

"I never considered it wasn't Alzheimer's—nor did the doctors. But of course, given everything we now know, the blow to the head absolutely could've caused his memory loss. And of course people would want to be the first—the first to get the glory and accolades of a monumental discovery, or in the case of your nefarious Yermalof, the first to grave-rob and sell off everything before anyone discovers he's done so."

A woman wearing a headdress shaped like a throne, elegant wings spread wide—

Her namesake. *Isis.* This image she knew. Oh, dear God.

Her brain went blank for a moment as Isis tried, without freaking herself out or misleading Thorne, to assimilate the people painted along the walls.

Isis and Osiris, husband and wife. Even she knew *that* much.

✎ SIXTEEN ✎

If her father were here, he could analyze the archaeological and architectural evidence of the tomb. He'd know when it was built and for whom. He'd understand the significance of the mythology in the painting—Isis had seen him identify iconographical and other evidence based on less.

Did what she was seeing embody the symbolism of divinity and religious ritual of Cleopatra? *Could* this be Cleopatra and Mark Antony's tomb? Maybe? No. Probably not. It seemed too plain to convey Cleopatra's incredible personal legacy. But—damn it. She didn't know. It would help if they had more light—and a detailed guidebook with pictures. Which of course didn't exist, because no one had found the tomb yet.

Back to square one. Isis sighed. "A dig like that would take months and months—hell, years."

"Not if they were doing a smash-and-grab. Taking the most valuable pieces and leaving the rest. And not if they didn't give a shit whether anything left was preserved or documented." Thorne's torch flickered and swayed.

Isis closed the gap between them and curled her fingers in the back of his belt. If that thing went out she wanted to know exactly where he was at all times. "That's terrible. Wait—What? You're saying *Yermalof* was the one who left my father for dead and killed his crew?"

"It's starting to make sense, don't you think?"

It did. But she didn't want it to. "Your Russian guy and my father?" Dear God, had her father brought all this down on his own head when he'd dabbled in the buying and selling of black market antiquities all those years ago? *Stealing* and selling. "You think my father didn't stop selling artifacts on the black market, and got himself in over his head with this guy?"

"Occam's razor."

"What's that?"

"It's the law of succinctness. The principle stating that among competing hypotheses, the one that makes the fewest assumptions should be selected. It has to be considered."

"Well, I don't *want* to consider it," Isis said tightly. But she did. God help her, *this* scenario made sense. She pressed a hand to her roiling stomach. "He promised me that it was a onetime thing, and that he'd stop."

"And then his funding started drying up . . ."

"And then his funding *stopped*." She repeated the truth bleakly. "But he always seemed to have a bit more money to dig."

Thorne stopped and wrapped his arm around her, pulling her close. His chest was broad and solid, and he smelled achingly familiar, his natural musk coupled with the smoky odor of burning wood. Holding her tightly, he brushed his mouth over the crown of her head. "It's just a theory at this point, okay? We don't know anything for sure. Not yet. Let's reserve judgment until we have all the facts." After giving her another one-armed hug, he let her go.

"There's nothing to be gained by you fretting over this here," he told her briskly before turning his back to continue walking.

"I've never fretted in my life," Isis told him pertly.

Thorne laughed, and they continued walking in silence.

Cleopatra had portrayed herself as the human representation of the goddess Isis, wife of Osiris. Isis tried to pull in stray details from memory, bits of conversations, her heart racing. Mark Antony, Cleo's lover, was often considered the human form of the god Osiris.

Isis struggled with her nebulous hypothesis while trying to maintain a logical conversation. She didn't have to consider the possibility of Thorne's theory too hard. Things were falling into place like tumblers in a safe, unlocking current and ancient secrets that had been secreted for centuries.

Her makeshift torch winked out, the crunchy burnt end falling to the floor, dangerously close to her foot. "One down, one to go. I don't want to think about what we'll do when yours goes out, too."

"We've got a bit of time. What do you think about my conjecture?"

Isis could now see only what was directly in front of Thorne's booted feet. The walls were once again dark, hiding their secrets. Their story. "God, it *does* make some convoluted sense." Darkness didn't usually bother her, but this darkness was oppressive and stuffy. She was so thirsty she'd drink . . . *Pepsi*. Her skin itself felt tight and parched, and even her hair crackled dryly around her face. *Water!* she screamed in her head.

There was absolutely no point sharing her desperate thirst with Thorne, who must be even worse off than she was. "But don't you think the coincidence of your bad guy knowing my father is way the hell out of the realm of possibility? Of *credibility*?"

"Granted, I don't believe in coincidences, but they *do* happen. The world of Egyptology isn't that large. It's feasible that the two knew each other, or at least knew *of* each other. It wouldn't have been hard for good old Boris to buy your father a round or two. Here, or in London, or even in Seattle.

"Your father could've bragged about the find of a life-time. Yermalof could retire and not work another day in fifty lifetimes if he fenced Cleopatra's wealth."

"Wouldn't you, in your capacity as an MI5 operative in charge of rooting him out, have heard if the market was flooded with Queen Cleopatra's antiquities?" She was sure Thorne's torch was getting dimmer and dimmer, and she slipped her hand from his belt to lace her fingers with his. The prospect of getting lost in the tomb, and being alone, scared the crap out of her.

Her stomach growled loudly. "Sorry. How long have we been walking, do you think?" *Two, three hours? A month?*

"Half an hour to forty minutes. Are you tired? Want to stop and take a breather?"

"I'd rather take a breather of fresh air while I drink a gallon of iced Coke while sitting in a deep bathtub, thank you."

"The air here smells fresher. I think we're heading in the right direction." He squeezed her hand. "We'll be out of here before you know it."

"From your lips——" The air smelled no different here than it had smelled five hundred miles back. Dust, must, and the sex they'd had earlier. She smelled it on herself, and on Thorne, and just thinking about sex with Thorne made her girl parts throb and she didn't have even a drop of moisture to spare to lubricate something she wasn't going to use for a while.

So no thinking about light, water, fresh air, *or* sex. She was running out of topics.

"Something like what you're talking about would be almost impossible to keep a secret. And Dylan claims he's discovered the tomb as well, *and* he swears to have solid, undeniable proof, and the blessings of the powers that be to dig there."

She thought of the painting of Osiris and Isis in the corridor behind them. Her father had always maintained that Cleopatra and Mark Antony and been buried together.

Two suicides. Antony first, and then his lover . . .

"When we get out of here, let's go find your ex-lover and see what he has to say."

The walls and ceiling were covered with images, too many to even try to guess who or what they represented, And even in the low light, Isis could see the gleam of gold and precious stones. "I told you, I never slept with him." Moving the button around in her mouth didn't produce much moisture, and she licked her parched lips, which just made her thirstier.

"I bet it wasn't for lack of him trying," Thorne's voice echoed. He didn't appear that interested by the seated ten- or twelve-foot-high statues lined up on either side of the corridor now. Isis recognized the ovals depicting names. *Whose,* she had no idea. But they wore the high crown with a snake curved on the front. The crowns might mean royalty, but Isis thought perhaps they also represented Osiris, who was the god of the afterlife.

Or Mark Antony.

"He lied about being in the hospital when your father went out on the dig." Thorne lifted her fingers to kiss her knuckles in a strangely romantic gesture. "Let's see what else he's bullshitting about."

"I know you don't like him." Isis narrowed her eyes to see if that would help her figure out who the people were—royalty? Gods? Several had their arms crossed, holding the traditional crook in one hand and flail in the other. "Frankly I don't like him that much, either," she told Thorne. Squinting didn't allow her to see any better, nor did it help her identify who or what she was looking at.

"But I can't see him masterminding an elaborate kidnapping plot replete with camping equipment, and a helicopter to seal us in here. It just doesn't seem like his style." The doorway up ahead had two giant statues, painted black, with gold headdresses and staffs, standing guard on either side. For such enormous statues the doorway itself was small, the size of a normal door in a house. Not the grand entrance to an important tomb. There was also, oddly, a faint smell of ammonia.

"Maybe not his style, but certainly Yermalof's. And styles change when there are millions if not billions of dollars up for gra— *Bloody hell!*" Thorne stopped dead and Isis bumped into his back.

They passed from the corridor, between the feet of one of the statues, and into a chamber. Thousands of intricate and exquisitely painted images and glyphs decorated the walls. Strange animals, statues standing guard, and gold—everywhere.

In the middle of the chamber, side by side, were two gold shrines.

"Oh. My. God."

"Holy bloody hell!"

The torch went out, plunging them into darkness.

ISIS LET OUT A little shriek the instant it went dark. Her hand in his was clammy and cold. In the few moments he'd had to see where they were, Thorne already knew there were no other openings leading from this chamber; if there had been, none of this wealth would have survived the centuries. This was the end of the line. "Don't panic." He kept his voice low and calm.

"I won't as soon as you tell me why not!"

"This is within yards of where your amulet came from."

"Are you saying my father was right *here*?"

"Close enough." His sixth sense gave him pinpoint accuracy. Professor Magee, or whoever had given Isis her amulet, had found it within a hundred feet of where they were standing.

"Take out your camera. We can use the flash to see if there's another corridor leading away from here."

"God, yes!" Her voice shook slightly as she shifted. "Excellent idea!" Not letting go of his hand, she snapped open the camera bag. "Hold this." She started handing him contents of the case, which he gathered in the crook of his arm since he was still holding the now-dead torch.

He heard her remove the lens cap.

"Point it ahead. Let's see what we have."

A brilliant wash of light illuminated the tomb, and it looked even bigger than it had appeared by the meager, dull light of the sputtering torch. Gold bounced back the light from the flash, reflecting off surfaces so that the whole placed gleamed like a sunbeam breaking through dark clouds.

"I thought I imagined it, I wanted to see it so badly. Mark Antony and Cleo! Oh, my God, Thorne! We found their burial place." She dragged him forward in the darkness. A couple of things fell from his arms, and he paused to dump everything on the floor near his feet in a pile to gather later. If there *was* a later. He didn't want to point out the obvious, that while the find was spectacular—monumental, in fact—it meant they were still at a dead end, literally.

"It doesn't look as though anything in here has been touched in over three thousand years." The flash went off again, giving Thorne a quick impression of the two giant shrines, each measuring at least sixteen or seventeen feet by about twelve feet, and at least nine feet high. They were positioned side by side with just a few feet between them.

"Again," he ordered, reaching out to touch the wall of the one closest to them. Some kind of wood, cedar probably, covered with plaster, gilded and inlaid with precious and semiprecious stones. It looked as though it had just been erected that day. It was mind-boggling to realize it had been placed there three thousand years ago.

The flash went off, showing them the double sloping roofs and some of the hieroglyphics. Another flash. He got an impression of the brilliant blue background, hieroglyphs, and a shitload of gold.

Impressive as hell, undoubtedly the discovery of the twenty-first century.

They'd stumbled across what everyone else was willing to kill for.

"Did you see the double *tyet*-knot amulets? Those are Isis and Osiris." Flash. "And on the end there, the protective *wedjat*-eyes . . . Oh, Connor, I *wish* my father could see this. Look at the details in these." She ran her fingers reverently over a sunken relief of a headless lion.

"Maybe he will one day." Thorne tried to keep each flash image in his head so he could reexamine it in his mind's eye. "Take lots of pictures."

With each burst of light he was more interested in seeing if there was a way out. He wasn't willing to spend a whole hell of a lot more time here. If there was no exit, then they had to negotiate the tunnel back to the original chamber. Isis might've gotten a second burst of energy, but he'd noticed her slowing footsteps and lack of energy fifteen minutes ago. She needed water—hell, they both needed water, to replenish what they were sweating out in the too-warm confines of the tomb.

"Let's walk around to the other side." The stink of ammonia was stronger behind the two shrines. Ammonia usually indicated bats. Tombs were a favorite hangout for them. He didn't hear any squeaking.

"Okay." There was a little bounce in her step as he felt his way along the wall of one of the shrines. "These are like Russian nesting dolls." Flash. "There are usually at least five or six shrines one inside the other before reaching the sarcophagus inside. I would love, love, love to go through each one . . . I'd love getting out of here more, however."

"Working on it." All around the perimeter of the chamber were piles of Coptic jars, statues of all sizes, and piles upon piles of jewelry and ornamentation. What there *wasn't* was a fucking *door*.

"To be the first person to lay eyes on Cleopatra in thousands of years . . ." She laughed as she took another series of shots. "I see now how easy it was for my father to get the bug, and why he never wanted to leave Egypt."

"Flash the ceiling."

She did so. "What are we looking for?"

"Bats."

"Ew. Is that the smell?"

He nodded, which she couldn't see. "I didn't see any,

did you?" Didn't see them, but knew they were some-where close by. "If there are bats around, there's a way in and out of the tomb close by."

"Bats can squeeze into teeny-tiny holes, right? There might be an opening that's only bat—"She stopped his forward motion with a sharp tug of his hand. "Hang on, stand here." She positioned him. "Look straight ahead." Flash.

"Do you see that?" Her voice rose in excitement.

"What am I looking at?" A narrow recessed panel, carved out of limestone, was set in the wall. A couple of statues in rich garb, holding hands, sat in a two-foot-high niche. Like everything else here, it was beautifully executed and covered with gold and stones.

"It's a soul door—a false door." She stepped closer and got off another flash. "The statues are to offer the souls refuge if the body's stolen."

"Lovely," he said with a bit of a bite. "But we're look-ing for a *real* door, reme—" The words cut off abruptly when he heard a faint murmur of voices beyond the wall. He squeezed Isis's fingers, but there was no need. She too had heard the voices, and went dead still.

Suddenly a pinpoint of light shone through the solid stone soul "door" from the other side. "Don't move," Thorne breathed, squeezing her hand.

Moving stealthily, he went to the small hole and peered through it.

At eye level were the bats they smelled. Thousands of them, clinging in a black mass to the ceiling. Clearly not bothered by either the light or activity below them, they clung to the ceiling. About a hundred feet below them was another chamber, brightly lit by massive floodlights. Thorne made out piles of artifacts, carriages, giant statues, shiny trinkets piled in boxes, lids nearby. Furniture, beds, chests, chairs, and tables were piled one on top of the next, and baskets and boxes were everywhere. Some neatly stacked, the rest in untidy piles.

A storeroom of some kind.

A way out.

A robed man circled the room, turning off each light and leaving that area shadowed as he moved to the next. A small group of men, dressed in Western wear, clustered nearby, conversed without fear of being overheard.

Their voices carried fairly well through the soul door. But the susurrus of wings, squeaks of the bats, and distance made it hard to get more than a word here and there. Still, he was pretty sure he could identify the man in charge by his size, and the sound of his voice. Surprising, but not completely unexpected.

Behind him, he heard Isis's slightly unsteady breathing. But she didn't insist on taking a look herself, and she didn't say a word.

The men stayed another ten minutes, walking the area, pointing out objects, which one guy noted on an electronic tablet. A few moments later, the lights and the voices faded away, leaving the stink of ammonia and the rustle of the bats.

"WHAT DID YOU SEE?" Isis asked softly when she heard him move away from the wall. He found her hand unerringly in the dark, and wound his fingers tightly with hers. His touch immediately centered her.

"Looks like they're packing up the artifacts for transportation."

"Who, where, and why?" The indignation in her voice was clear.

"In light of what I just witnessed, I have my suspicions."

"Care to share?"

"The guy in charge appeared to be Dr. Khalifa Najid."

"The Minister of Irrigation and Water Resources? That son of a bitch! He knew the tomb was here all along, and lied to us."

Thorne smiled at her horror. "He's the bad guy. Bad guys have a tendency to prevaricate to cover their nefarious deeds."

If the information wasn't pissing her off, Isis would've smiled at his very British and oh-so-dry delivery. But hearing that the man in charge of the new recreational area, the man who had lied to her face about knowing her father, really set her off and made her want to go and confront him. Preferably with a strong force of police officers beside her. Or just Thorne.

"This is more than a nefarious deed! He *knew* my father found this tomb. Knew, damn him. Worse than lying right to my face, is that he's depriving the world of—" Incensed, the words logjammed. "He's covering up a find with major historical impact! It's a criminal act."

"Well, we can't do anything to remedy that while we're still trapped here. First things first. Did you give me the hand sanitizer a while ago?"

Okay, that wasn't the furious response she was looking for, but she knew him well enough to know he was processing something. She hoped when he was done, he'd fill her in. But she made a mental note that in the future she needed to teach him how to play well with others. Or at least, play well with *her.* "You want to clean your hands?" Of course, that was supposing that there'd *be* a future for them.

He started walking back around the shrine, his limp more pronounced. Isis suspected she was more aware of how badly he was limping due to the stygian darkness. "I want to relight the torch. See how to get down to that level."

"You do realize I have no idea what you're talking about, right? What level?"

"There's a chamber below this one—eight or nine *stories* below this one. The temple must be built on a steep hill. Some chambers on this level, and at least that one on a much lower level. There were men and equipment down there, so that's the way out. All we have to do is find a way down."

He leaned over, and she heard him rummaging through the stuff he'd tossed on the floor. "Give that to me. I'll put it back in my bag. You never know when we'll need a notebook or a pack of tissues."

Thorne squirted sanitizer on his torch, then there was the flare of his lighter.

"Holy cow! I can't believe how much better I feel with that little bit of fire. I'm going to add a lighter to the contents of my camera bag and carry it everywhere I go from now on."

"One would hope you wouldn't be trapped in an Egyptian tomb very often," Thorne said dryly, stalking off to run the torch across the surface of the east wall.

"I'm going to take a bunch more pictures, okay?"

"Go ahead; the flash will help over here."

Isis wasn't any less thirsty or tired, but knowing for sure that there was a way out gave her a new burst of energy. She took shots of the two shrines from every angle. Whether her father had Alzheimer's or memory loss, he'd appreciate the magnificence of Cleo's last resting place.

"There's another soul door over here," Thorne called, his voice carrying across the chamber.

Isis followed the red glow. "You think it's also a real door to the lower level?"

"I'm searching anything that might be feasible. Can you hold this?" He handed her the torch and Isis held it up high as he ran his hands over the surface from the lintel at the top, then down. This door showed an image of what Isis was sure was Cleopatra, sitting in front of an offering table. Scribed into the stone was a reed mat with a loaf of bread on it, as well as bowls of petrified food. She held in her hand a goblet covered with gold.

As Thorne meticulously felt and tapped on every inch, Isis let her artist's eye search, too. Looking for anything out of place, anything that might indicate a latch, or—

Her breath snagged.

All the embellishments surrounding the center panel were in bas-relief with exquisite coloration and intricate detail. The tiles and stone glinting in the flickering light, the gold giving off a rich glow. Except for the small winged god used as decoration on a chalice in Cleopatra's right hand: *Isis*, wings spread, was the only object in *sunk* relief.

"Thorne, give me my amulet!"

"Find something?" He dug in his pocket and handed her the tiny chamois pouch.

For a moment Isis curled her fingers around the bag as she said a little prayer to her patron goddess. Opening her eyes, she carefully pulled the little cord and tipped the bag onto the flat of her hand. "Look," she whispered, her fingers clumsy as she fit her amulet into the image on Cleo's goblet. "A perfect fit—"

As if in a coin slot, the amulet started sliding down, out of sight. Isis lunged to grab on to the fine gold chain as the charm disappeared.

The center panel of the false door screeched open as stone grated across stone.

❧ SEVENTEEN ❧

Thorne judged the narrow opening to be about seventeen inches wide and ten feet high. Beyond it was dense black space. A rush of cool, dry, ancient-dust-smelling air drifted around them.

Isis's fingers tightened on his upper arm. "Am I imagining this?"

"Surreal, isn't it?" Thorne wedged the backpack into the gap, then pushed his arm through the opening, holding the torch aloft. Isis crowded behind him, her hand on his back as she tried to see around him.

She studied the area. "Who used this? An alien?" Her fingers curled into the back of his shirt. "I wish I hadn't said that. People believed aliens *did* help build the pyramids . . ."

"I doubt aliens need stairs," Thorne told her dryly, passing the torch deeper into the void.

"Stairs? Seriously?" Her slender fingers dug into his upper arm, her excitement contagious. "Woo-hoo!"

"Don't get excited. We have no idea where they lead."

"I'm guessing *down*," Isis suggested, resting her head on the back of his shoulder as he assessed the situation.

Thorne loved the feel of her soft breasts pressed against him. He liked the way she held on to him as she peered inside the opening, and the tickle of her soft curls brushing the side of his face. He loved the smell of cinnamon combined with the musk on her skin. And he admired the hell out of a woman who'd been put through some damn terrifying times and still maintained a sense of humor.

"I hate to burst your bubble, darling, but they could just as easily end abruptly midair, with a forty- or fifty-foot drop."

"Buzzkill," she muttered, half teasing, half serious.

Thorne smiled, brushing her nose with his fingertip. "Or they could take us all the way to the lower level and a well-marked exit."

She slid her palm up his back, resting her hand between her shoulder blades. Had anyone else done the same gesture, Thorne would've spun around and taken his opponent out before shoving them unceremoniously down into the darkness. With Isis it was merely an indication that she trusted him, believed in him, was there with him. It was an odd sensation.

"Let's go with that option."

"We'll see . . ." The stairs were carved from solid bedrock. Hazardously steep, the tread, at least from this angle, looked too narrow, the risers perilously high. The stairwell was almost as narrow as the door opening. It would be a restricted, dangerous descent, with no guarantee that there would be a similar door at the bottom. Or if Isis's amulet would open that one as well as this.

Or, Thorne considered, what would happen if the amulet was removed from one door to carry down to a possible second?

The staircase could be just another thing the ancient Egyptian tomb builders had come up with to trap would-be raiders. Both doors could be traps, sealing them inside a tube of solid rock for eternity.

Or they could be what they seemed.

He backed up and so did Isis. "Well?" she asked hopefully.

"I only saw about a dozen feet, but it's hellishly steep. There's no guarantee that after trekking down six or seven flights, there'll be a door at the bottom."

"Let's go down and see." Isis abruptly paused, her eyes narrowing. "No. *You* wait here. *I'll* go. I'm smaller than you are, and my leg isn't killing me."

At her words, Thorne's heart did a double clutch of fear. "No way." Jesus, the woman would be the death of him. "*No.* Absofuckinglutely not."

"If the bad guys show up here," she said in tones of calm reason, "I won't be able to stop them slamming this door closed and trapping you down there. It makes more sense for me to go. I'll be quick."

"Not just no, but *hell no*," he told her flatly, adjusting the weight of the torch as he weighed the pros and cons of taking the risk—something he'd do if he were on his own—or returning to where they'd started and start chucking rocks until they were free. "I don't like it."

Isis ignored him as she fingered the length of delicate chain hanging from the slot. "Let's see if the opening closes if I take . . . thiiiis . . . out." As she eased it out slowly, they held their breath. The portal didn't close.

"Which means I'll probably need it at the bottom. I'll take the torch, okay?" She clasped her fingers below his on the piece of wood. "Connor, don't be macho about this." She gave a little tug when he didn't hand it right over. "Me going down makes the most sense. Admit it. I'll be very careful, and we can talk all the way down. I'll tell you what I see. Please? I'm getting tired, and God knows we're both dying of thirst. Besides, I want to see if that step machine at the gym worked worth a damn."

Every damned thing in him didn't want her going down there. He gave her the torch. "Take your time. Feel every step before you put your weight on it. Use one hand on the wall . . . Jesus, I hate this."

Standing on her toes, she brought her free hand up to cup the back of his head. "I know. You're being very brave."

"Have I told you . . ." He didn't finish the thought, merely slipped her glasses off, holding them in one hand, and used the other to tangle his fingers in her thick hair. Then said, ". . . what a pain in the arse you are?"

"Not out loud." She smiled against his mouth. "Give me a nice kiss to hold me until I get back."

"I'd rather give you a naughty kiss to hold *me*."

"Six of one . . ." She pressed her slightly open mouth to his, slanting her head as she wrapped her hand around the back of his neck. She slipped her tongue into his mouth and Thorne met it with his own. There was precious little lubrication, they were both so goddamned thirsty. But it didn't seem to matter. The more their tongues and teeth mated, the more they kissed, the more moisture they generated. She hummed her appreciation, her fingers gripping his neck more tightly. Without opening his eyes, Thorne used the hand in which he held her glasses to deflect her wrist so the torch she held didn't burn off his eyebrows. Oblivious to where they were, she pressed her breasts against him and parried the thrust of his tongue with her own.

It was Thorne's turn to murmur deep in his throat, and he felt the sweet curve of her lips against his. Slowly he eased back. "We need to get the hell out of here, love. I don't want you to go, but I can't fault your logic."

Her eyes gleamed. "I'll keep that hot shower and big bed in mind. It'll keep me motivated."

Thorne touched her wrist, angling the torch toward the ground, then gave it another squirt of hand cleaner so that it flared. He used the hem of his T-shirt to clean her glasses, then slid the earpieces through her hair and positioned the frame on her nose.

"Okay, Tomb Raider Librarian, don't take any foolish chances, do you hear me?" He spoke against her mouth. "Talk to me every step of the way. I want to hear what you're seeing and what's happening. If anything feels off, you haul your arse back up here."

"Yes, sir. Got it." She started sliding sideways, then came back and gave him a quick, hard kiss. "We'll be out of here just in time for breakfast."

She left, taking the light and her warmth with her.

With a little difficulty, Thorne lowered himself to the

floor, his hips wedged in the narrow opening, his legs inside the stairwell. "See anything interesting?" His voice echoed slightly off the roughly hewn rock. The red glow of the torch danced on the walls, casting macabre shadows as she walked.

"Nope. Just a straight shot so far. But you weren't kidding about it being steep. The actual tread is shorter than my foot, by—I don't know—I think this is only about six-ish inches. What's normal?"

"Ten."

"The riser is way high. Who did they think would be running up and down these stairs, short-toed people with long shinbones? I told you aliens were involved." He smiled, leaning against the wall, his legs stretched out. God, it was good to sit down. His thigh had been begging for mercy for hours. Clamping his fingers around the worst of it, he tried to massage out the vicious knot. Isis had not complained once. Not about any of it.

"I don't think they were thinking of people continually running up and down." He raised his voice so she could hear him. "They were thinking of thieves." Thorne realized he was braced for her scream. For her cry as some fucking ancient booby trap snared her. For her frantic yell for help. What the fuck had he been thinking to allow her to go down there alone? Down there at *all.*

"Make sure you extend the torch so you can see as far ahead of you as possible. And test every step before you put your weight on it." He sounded like—like someone worried for someone else's safety. Other than Garrett,

Thorne hadn't been worried about anyone else to this extent in his life. His heart beat a staccato rhythm as he listened to her footfalls scrape across the stones.

"Anything interesting?" After this he wasn't letting the woman out of his sight. He was not a man to make small talk, or ponder the workings of a woman's mind. He'd never given a flying fuck what made a lover tick, other than in the most basic sense, and yet here he was, listening to every footfall, every harsh breath, eyes straining to see what he knew damned well he couldn't see in the darkness.

"Hmm. No marking on the walls." Her voice echoed up the shaft. "Just rough stone—taking a jog to the right here. Uh-oh, the stairs are narrower on one side than the other . . ."

"It's a winder so they didn't have to carve out a landing."

"Straightening out for a while. Crap. There's a winder going left now."

Thorne didn't like it. He could no longer see even the lightest glow from the torch, and though her voice was clear, it was fainter.

"Talk to me."

"It's kind of hard to be going down three million teeny stairs and chat at the same time, Thorne."

"Humor me."

She continued the running commentary—loudly for a few minutes—and then all he heard was the grit of her rubber-soled shoes on sandy stone resonating up to him. "Isis?"

"Oh, crap. It ends at a wall." Even with the echo, and from this distance, Thorne heard tears in her voice.

He got stiffly to his feet, his leg protesting directly into his cerebral cortex as if someone had taken a sharp knife and sliced him from skull to ankle. Oh, yeah. Someone pretty much had. "Take a breather and come back. We can—"

"Hold your horses . . ."

He wiped damp hands on his jeans and sucked in a breath, holding it so he didn't miss any sounds she might make.

She gave a whoop of excitement. "But no. *Not* a wall. Hang on . . ." He heard a teeth-jarring high-pitched screech bounce off the narrow walls, then Isis shouted up. "Smell that? That, Mr. Thorne, is the stink of a million bats and freedom! I'm coming back up there—"

His shoulder slumped against the opening, and he let out his breath. "No. Stay put. I'll come down."

"I have the torch—"

"I'll find you." Anywhere, anytime. Every time.

He started down the stairs. On the seventh tread, the door above him ground closed, the sound resounding in the stairwell. The darkness was absolute.

"Oh, God. What was that? Are you okay?"

Thorne laughed. "I'm on my way to see these bats for myself."

He followed the stink of bat shit, and the sound of Isis's voice down the stairs.

ISIS COULDN'T SEE MORE than a couple of feet in any direction. She wrapped her long scarf over her head and face, but she could still feel the air move with the beat of the bats' wings overhead.

She winced with each of Thorne's heavy steps as he navigated the stairs. Her leg muscles were quivering with exertion, and she didn't have a sliced-and-diced thigh. "Almost to the bottom!" she yelled. Having no idea how far down he was, just wanting to be his cheering section.

Her head swam and Isis sat down before she fell down. No water, no food, no more adrenaline. The slog down the stairs had taken all her reserves. She plopped her butt down on the sandy marble floor, her back against the threshold to make sure the door stayed open. She peered into the unrelieved darkness, resting her elbow on her undrawn knee and cupping her hand over her nose and mouth.

The room *felt* large, and dear God—the *smell*. Her eyes and nostrils stung, burning from the acrid stench of ammonia.

The space was filled with the cacophony of squeaks, scratching, and wings flapping of assorted rodents occupying the ceiling high above. "Please stay there, and *please* don't crap on me—again."

Pushing to her feet when she heard Thorne's approach, Isis winced. God, it must be so painful coming down all those uneven stairs sideways, the only way his feet would fit on the treads. Wanting to race up to meet him, she stayed where she was, arm extended into the stairwell to light his way. If the upstairs portal had slammed shut without her amulet, she wouldn't budge until Thorne reached her side.

The smell made her eyes water, and she figured if she couldn't see what she'd been sitting on, or walking on, ignorance was bliss. She was already filthy, and in a few minutes Thorne would be just as stinky and dirty as she was. Small comfort after what they'd been through, but, hey, she'd take it.

From a distance she heard a sharp sound of a horn, or car alarm—but when she tried to separate it from the sound of the bats crying and flapping overhead she figured it was just her imagination and wishful thinking telling her they were near civilization.

"When you turn that last left-turn jog, watch the next few steps; they're even narrower and steeper. *There* you are!"

Surprising herself, she burst into tears as soon as she saw him. Dashing the tears from her cheeks, she flung her arms around him and hugged him so tightly he let out a strangled laugh. "Did you think the aliens beamed me up to their spaceship?" he teased, hugging her back. He held her by the shoulders, then used his thumb to wipe away a tear from her chin. "Let's get the hell out of Dodge."

"Under normal circumstances . . ." Isis sniffed, slipping her hand into his because she loved the way he curled his fingers around hers. She handed him the torch, which was now less than two feet long, the tip charred and crunchy, the glow almost out.

"Which," she added, "I'd like to point out, these are

not—having those flying rats swooping overhead and using my head as a toilet would freak me out. However, these are not normal circumstances, and I don't give a damn as long as they stay way up there, and leave us the hell alone. What are you— Oh, God, it was almost better not being able to see this." She squinted into the sudden brightness after what felt like years in the dark.

Somehow Thorne had unerringly found a large spotlight in the darkness and managed to switch it on. He *did* have eyes like a cat.

Self-consciously she put a hand to her head, then dropped it. Her messy hair was the least of her problems. She looked around. "This looks like some kind of antechamber," she said with a frown as she took in the beautiful wood chariot with their elaborate paintings and gold wheels, the twenty-foot-high statues—and the boxes and boxes and boxes of already crated artifacts. Of course. "Looters. Do you think it's safe to have a light on? What if they come back?"

"They were finishing up their haul when we arrived. I suspect they're long gone. But judging by the stuff they've packed up, they'll be back. I suspect with all the activity happening on the rim of the valley that they'll wait for nightfall, and loot under cover of darkness."

"Bastards. We'll call a press conference, let everyone know—"

He tightened his grip on her hand. "Take a breath. There are channels we have to go through, and we're not going off half-cocked. The people have already tried to kill us, and kidnapped us. We still aren't sure who's involved. I'll make some calls. Let's get outside and assess the situation, okay?"

She nodded. "I guess so. I can at least call my father and tell him about this." Would he even understand? She hoped so.

"Take a look back there before we go." Thorne gently took her upper arm, turning her around.

There was no sign of the door they'd come through just moments before. It was now shut, leaving not so much as a sliver indicating it was there at all. But that wasn't what stole Isis's breath as she turned fully to face the way they'd come.

The wall before them—a hundred feet high, by that and more wide—was a solid sheet of gleaming hammered gold. Bas-relief gods and goddesses, birds and soldiers, sparkled with jewels and semiprecious stones. In the very center, about halfway up, a twenty-foot-tall couple stood, hands clasped as they looked over the vast chamber.

The carving was more three-dimensional than everything else on the wall, and so lifelike Isis wouldn't have been surprised if they stepped down off the wall where they had stood joined together for thousands of years. Wearing the royal raiments of Isis and Osiris, they were surrounded by the sun god Ra and the seven venomous scorpions.

Isis brought Thorne's hand, clasped in hers, to her heart, and swallowed a lump in her throat. "Cleo and Mark."

Bittersweet tears welled, making the gold wall shimmer. She wished her father could see this. "I have to take pictures." Unsnapping the catch of her case, Isis took a rapid succession of images, barely taking time to frame her shots.

The perimeter walls had, until recently, been packed with artifacts. And while there were still thousands of things to catch her eye, it was clear that at least half of the items, if not more, had been dragged out. Streaks of dust on the floor where boxes had been pulled, and put onto some sort of wheel cart for transportation out of the tomb, told the story. She got dozens of shots of those, too.

A stack of gilded and bejeweled chariot wheels were braced against the far wall along with ritual couches, beds, chairs, and tables. Isis figured the assorted furniture was worth a queen's ransom, all of it just piled one on top of the other as if this were an ancient Egyptian thrift shop. Intricately carved ivory chests embedded with gemstones awaited pickup by the front entrance.

And a fifty-gallon barrel with a spigot on it. "Dear God. Is that *water*? Thank you, modern times." She tugged at Thorne's hand, hauling him over to the plastic container. "You go first." She expected him to dip his head under the spigot to drink, but he surprised her by cupping his hands.

"Pour," he said, catching the stream until his hands were full. "Drink." Not looking a gift horse in the mouth, Isis drank from his cupped hands, a surprisingly intimate thing to do. Before her thirst was quenched, she lifted her head. "Your turn. There's plenty."

She held the spigot until they each slaked their thirst. "I'll never take water for granted again," she said.

Satisfied, she waited her turn and splashed room-temperature water on her face. Thorne took her elbow as she used her T-shirts to dry off.

"We've got to go. Who knows when they'll be back?"

"They'll know we were here. Does that matter?" She walked beside him, taking pictures as they crossed the space.

"We'll be long gone. It's a good thing you're getting shots of this—no time for cataloging, but it might be the last image anyone will see of this place. So much empty space means they've already taken a lot. The organization for this kind of operation had to take months, if not longer." He waved his hand at what was left. "If this is what they decided to leave for last, imagine what they *did* take."

Her chest ached. Her father had worked his entire life to see this, to prove that this tomb existed. "They'll sell off everything to private collectors, and the public will never know that Cleopatra's tomb was discovered."

Thorne stopped walking, to turn to her. "The items will have no monetary value unless they can be tied unequivocally to Cleopatra's final burial place."

Anger made her heart beat too fast as she said with uncommon bitterness, "Which will be filled with water."

"No. It just came to me, as I saw all of the tags on the items. I think they want to reconstruct the find—what if this site is suddenly 'discovered' a hundred miles away at Abusir by your friend Dylan Brengard?"

"Oh, my God." Her stomach rolled and the water rose up in her throat. "That's—that means that Dr. Najid and Dylan must have been working together all along." She ran to a tag, then another one, realization dawning with acrid horror. "My father came here, found Cleo"— she met Thorne's compassionate gaze—"and of course he would tell Dylan, who planned with Najid to kill my father and take the glory." Her eyes burned and her fist clenched. "There aren't enough curse words to describe them," she said in short syllables, furious beyond anything she'd ever felt before. Heat pulsated behind her eyes and her body shook.

"I'm sorry, Isis." His hand on the small of her back was a comfort, but also a prod to keep moving. "I'd hazard a guess," he said, "that Yermalof is up to his eyeballs in this as well. Once the tomb is found at Abusir, where most Egyptologists have long believed it to be, and there's an official provenance for the items, he'll sell whatever they siphoned off the top. The rest will be artistically placed in the new tomb. No one any the wiser. It's actually quite brilliant, and almost flawlessly executed."

"It seems to me that it was *absolutely* damned flawlessly executed. Dylan will get his amazing discovery in the history books, Dr. Water District will get his beautiful rec area, and your Russian thief will make all three of them a shitload of money. Seems like a win-win-win situation to me. Slime buckets!"

"There are two glitches to their plans," Thorne pointed out dryly. "*Us.* We've seen the evidence, and your photos are proof."

∽ EIGHTEEN ∾

A light wind moved sand and water particles, ruffling Isis's hair around her face as they stepped outside the tomb entrance. The black-streaked sky was a soft, predawn, dove gray, the air cool from the mist coming off the rising waters. Thorne sucked in a deep lungful of fresh, damp air. They'd never get the bat stink out of their clothes, but of prime importance now was seeing the spillway from the higher dam pouring hundreds of thousands of gallons of water in a gleaming ribbon to pound and froth with hellaciously loud sound effects into the valley below. Hence the roar filling the air and the mist. Felt damn good on his skin, but the ramifications of the early water release were huge.

Isis gripped his hand, squeezing as she looked across the valley where a sheet of rippled pewter stretched as far as the eye could see. "Najid opened it a week early!"

It was impossible to tell how long the spillway had been open, or how deep the water in the hundred-mile-long valley was. Suffice it to say the entire length held water, and while its rising was too slow for Thorne to discern, he suspected by the hard rush of water coming from the spillway across the basin that it would fill quickly.

"It'll take days for the water level to reach this high, even longer to reach the actual tomb," he assured her. "We have time." Not plenty of time, but some, if he could move fast and call MI5 into play.

Thorne surveyed their options for getting to the rim. He'd worry about the next step when he got there. The tomb entrance was approximately three thousand feet below the rim of the proposed lake. Half a mile. Above and surrounding the entrance was a vertical ridge of rough rock, loose shale, and sand. Even if he didn't have a bum leg, Isis wouldn't be able to scale that.

A barely perceptible track indicated where the thieves had driven their vehicles close to the tomb entrance. The track led to the tarred road that had, at one time, bisected the valley floor. But that was gone now, part of it already submerged in the deepest part of the valley. There was, of course, no vehicle standing by for them to help themselves to. The road up to the rim was at least a mile away. Not a bad walk all things considered.

"Let's head that way. Once we're up top we'll find a vehicle."

The dirt track—clearly recently in use—was a downhill trek and not too arduous, unless a person had already put in several hours of walking and a torturous stair climb on no food and little water. "Okay?" he asked as Isis trudged silently beside him, her fingers still tight around his. The few rocks were easy to avoid, and the hard-packed sand was a fucking cakewalk compared to the path they'd just traveled.

The paved road, running from north to south through the valley, was submerged, but at the north end it was still viable. A steep uphill grade, but doable.

"Where are we going to find a car?" Isis asked, between fast breaths, as they came to where the dirt met the paved road. The sky had lightened to a dirty gray pink, smudged with thick charcoal clouds. Would people start appearing to go to work? Or to see why the spillway had been opened early? The Minister of Water could easily account for the precipitous opening with any manner of reasons. No one would question him.

"No idea." He walked a little faster, and Isis kept pace, even though her breathing quickened and sweat streaked the dirt on her face. He should be horsewhipped for not getting her on that flight back home before she was thrown into the middle of all this. Thorne, furious with himself for not protecting her properly, said, "We just will."

"Okay. Just don't expect any scintillating conversation, because I'm now officially pooped."

And still no complaints. He lifted their joined hands to brush a kiss across her knuckles. Isis was more priceless than any artifact in that tomb. "Keep that shower and big bed in mind as we go."

He could tell she was on her last legs. The farther they went, the slower her pace became. "You need to rest?"

She lifted her chin, a determined slant to her eyes.

"No. But I want to know, what are we going to do with Dylan when we find him?"

"You mean besides stringing him up by his balls?"

She laughed a little, apparently cheered by the thought. "Well, that might improve his singing voice, but it's not going to make him fess up to what he and Dr. Najid have done. My father is still getting screwed out of his life's work."

"What did you have in mind, then?"

"What if we bury him with the artifacts and come back in twenty years?"

Thorne kissed her forehead, the skin salty but soft to the touch. "And you say I'm harsh. Remind me never to give you a reason to hold a grudge against me, love."

"Seriously, though." She took a breath and tugged at him. "What are we going to do if he's being protected by Yermalof?"

He narrowed his eyes. "Then perhaps we ought to turn them against each other and let them have at it."

She twisted her mouth slightly in a way that begged to be kissed. "Do you really think we could do that?"

He winked, determined to be as upbeat as Isis, though his leg was killing him. "Bait and switch. One of the oldest tricks in the book. And I think Yermalof and Brengard are greedy enough to fall right into it. If they each think Dr. Najid intends to cut the other out by pinning the blame of our deaths on them, it just might work."

"Can we do that?"

He kissed the back of her hand. "Together, my queen, we can do anything."

The thought of besting their enemies brought a little more bounce to her step as she walked beside him, her hand in his. He'd never had anyone look up to him like that. A distinctive ache built in his chest. What would happen to them when this was all over? He shook his head. He couldn't afford to think of tomorrow. All he could do was focus on the road that was growing closer one step at a time.

It took almost an hour to cover the distance, but they were rewarded when the valley road ended in a compound for service vehicles. "Pay dirt." The fenced-off area was full of backhoes, heavy-duty trucks, flatbed vehicles for hauling pipe, and small specialized vehicles used in construction. "Let's take that one." Thorne indicated a dusty, battered-looking pickup truck at the other end of the lot near the gate.

Dog tired, he jimmied the driver's-side door lock with a screwdriver he'd found when they'd passed an unlocked tool chest. He hiked Isis up into the seat. "See if you can find anything useful while I get her started."

"You have the most unusual, yet useful, skill set," she said with an accepting smile.

Getting up into the cab was a feat in itself, but Thorne used his arms and his good leg to get the job done.

Isis knelt on the seat rummaging through a compartment behind it, as Thorne peered under the dashboard and yanked out the wires.

"My namesake is smiling on me right now. I just found a Coke!" Isis said with a tired laugh. "There are a couple of bottles of water, and one PowerBar. A feast. We're all set." At the deep purr of the engine, she plopped her arse down on the bench seat, her treasures in her lap. "Oh, you did that quickly! I'm impressed by your hotwiring prowess, Thorne. If Lodestone or MI5 doesn't pan out for you, you can always take to a life of crime. I'll share my Coke with you . . ."

"I'm impressed that you'd share. Water's good."

Isis twisted the cap off a bottle of water, handing it to him as he headed for the locked gate. She popped the tab on her can and took a long drink. "Ahhh, ambrosia . . . Should I get out to open the gate? *How* will I open it, though?"

"I've got it." Thorne revved up the engine, slammed the gas pedal to the floor, and hit the gate at sixty per, then drove over the metal, smashing it into the dirt. He floored the engine and shot down the road in the semidarkness.

"There is something very satisfying in that."

He smiled, finishing off another bottle of water. Their headlights bounced over the road as he pushed the lumbering vehicle to its maximum speed. Isis laughed. "Dirty Harry has nothing on you, Thorne." She drank half her cola in one long draft, curling her feet up beneath her on the seat. "How are we going to implement Operation Striking Cobra?"

"Striking what?"

She gifted him with a wide smile. "Striking Cobra. Our plan to bring down these thieves and kidnappers needed a name. I thought it had a nice ring to it."

He chuckled. Striking Cobra. The boys back at MI5

would be rolling on the floor with that one. "I don't suppose you found a phone back there, did you?"

"Unfortunately not. Here, honey, I made you dinner." She handed him three-quarters of the protein bar.

He didn't argue, eating it in two bites. He glanced into the mirrors just to be sure Yermalof didn't have eyes on them. "We need to ditch this and find something else in case someone sees us."

"Ew! That was disgusting." Isis pulled a face, hastily washing down the bar with her drink. "I'll make you a real dinner, Thorne, when our lives are back to normal. Something much better than that mummified protein bar."

"I promised you room service, remember?"

"It's all that keeps me going. Oasis in an hour."

"Sooner if we see anything we can help ourselves to."

There was nothing available to steal any sooner than the oasis, and since the truck was gassed up, and they were halfway there, he decided to keep going. They made good time, reaching the center of Cairo right in the middle of the early morning commute.

"Where now?" she asked, using both hands to push her hair off her face. It was a lost cause. The mist and sweat had sprung her hair into wild curls, which Thorne found both charming and sexy.

"We need to ditch the truck and find a phone."

"I didn't see anyone, but is there any chance we were followed?"

"No one was behind us on the road from the hydro-electric plant to here. I kept a close eye out. No one is that good at tailing, especially when we traveled fifty miles with no one in sight either way. I think we escaped undetected. Why?"

"Husani probably hasn't left for the shop yet. And even if he went in early, Rabiah works from home. We'll have the use of a phone, or computer, and a shower."

"Sounds good. We'll head out there."

It took forty minutes to cross town, and another fifteen for Thorne to find a parking garage with a big enough entrance to hide the truck.

BOTH RABIAH AND HUSANI were home when Thorne and Isis arrived at their apartment. The couple looked slightly stunned by their appearance but didn't ask questions. While Rabiah supplied Isis with a change of clothing for both of them, Thorne made a couple of calls to set the ball rolling.

Isis went into the small bathroom to wash before eating. Horrified, she stared at herself in the mirror. "Dear God, seriously?" After all they'd endured it was no wonder she looked as bad as she did, but somehow it was worse seeing herself up close.

Her hair was out of control. Wild and frizzy, and curly around her head and shoulders like the Wild Woman of Borneo. Her pale face wasn't just dirty, it was filthy, the sand and grit smeared around from her hasty attempt at washing while in the tomb. Her sunken eyes looked bruised, her lips dry and cracked. Her clothing was beyond filthy. Hastily yanking off the top two T-shirts, she was marginally cleaner. And while washing her hands and face several times with soap and hot water helped, she was dying for a hot shower and a scrub brush. She left the bathroom and, seeing that Thorne was off the phone, said, "It's all yours."

He passed her in the short hallway and closed the bathroom door behind him. The mouthwatering, stomach-rumbling smell of frying eggs, toast, and coffee lured her to the kitchen.

Rabiah motioned Isis to a seat at the kitchen table, where a glass of Coke on ice waited for her. "I love you, Rabiah! Thank you."

Her hostess smiled. "You look much better."

"Hard to look worse," Husani told her grimly, ducking when Isis threatened to bop him on the head with her glass. "Are you sure you two don't need a doctor? I have a friend I can call to come here——"

"I'm okay, but I'm worried about Thorne's leg. He needs a cane, and since he won't ask, I will. Do you have anything for him to use temporarily?"

"I have some in the storeroom downstairs. Why don't I get him a cane while he's getting cleaned up? I'll be right back."

Husani went off to get the cane.

"Your Thorne is very nice-looking, even when he's scruffy," Rabiah observed as she slid more bread into the toaster.

"He can be very charming when he isn't dragging you from place to place with bullets flying."

Rabiah quirked a brow. "Oh, sexy and dangerous. That's a deadly combination for a woman's heart."

Isis bit into the warm toast, letting the crunchy texture of it roll about in her mouth. Rabiah was right. No matter which way she tried to frame things, she and Thorne had crossed a line somewhere in those tombs. And she ached to think what her life was going to be like without him in it once they tricked the bad guys and saved the tomb.

The last thing she wanted was to bring any danger to her friends, but the excitement of her father being right buzzed in her veins, making her lightheaded. She couldn't wait to tell the world. But Thorne said they needed to wait. Timing was everything when it came to outwitting people like Yermalof, Dylan, and Dr. Najid, and they needed to be precise in their planning.

The bathroom door opened, and a few moments later Thorne limped to the table, his face washed and his hair damp, just as Husani returned. He set a carved cane against the back of Thorne's chair. "Should you have need of it." His nonchalant way of saying it made it easy for Thorne to nod his thanks.

"Appreciate it." Thorne picked up his coffee cup and drank as Rabiah set plates of food in front of them, then joined them at the table.

While they ate the Western-style breakfast, they filled their hosts in on what they knew.

"This was a very involved plan, but the theft of antiquities happens here every day," Husani told Thorne. "For the most part the authorities turn a blind eye."

"It's a disgrace," his wife said, her voice angry. "They are stealing our national sovereignty. There is a new syndicate to stop such things. I hope they punish these men to the full extent of the law."

Husani shrugged. "Like our Minister of Water. It is not uncommon for ministry officials to be involved with antiquity theft. It is hard to police such actions, and even harder to prosecute."

"You don't mind that a discovery like Cleopatra's tomb has been raped and pillaged by these men?" Isis asked, her tone hard on behalf of her father. "That Cleo's wealth is being sold off to the highest bidder and taken out of your country, never to be seen again?"

"I understand your anger, little bird. But such sales and thefts have been happening for thousands of years. It's almost impossible to stop. Too many people benefit by turning a blind eye."

Thorne cradled his cup. "What are the penalties when these men *are* apprehended?" His tone was casual, but Isis suspected that it wasn't an idle question. Besides, she presumed he already knew the answer if he'd been chasing down Yermalof for years.

Her friend shrugged again. "The new law increased prison sentences for smuggling artifacts out of Egypt to fifteen years and a million-pound fine. Double that of ten years ago."

"Clearly this hasn't impacted the sales of antiquities," Thorne pointed out with inflection. If this was the case, what recourse did anyone have against Dylan and the minister? After all this, were they just going to get a slap on the wrist and be let go?

"No, it has not." Husani cast a worried frown at Thorne. "My father——"

"MI5 has had people with him around the clock since this started. He's safe. I don't advise you to open the shop until we know everyone has been rounded up."

"No problem. I can do paperwork from home. Is there anything I can do for you?" He looked from Thorne to Isis, and back again as his wife cleared the table, then poured Thorne another cup of coffee, and brought another Coke to Isis, who drank it down like a crack addict.

"It'll take my people some time to round everyone up. We'll lie low until they do so. I gave them the number here."

"I'll come downstairs to fetch you as soon as they call."

"I GET THE SHOWER first," Isis told him unequivocally the moment the door to the downstairs apartment closed behind them. "I must smell like a thousand-year-old mummy."

With a piratical smile, Thorne turned her around until her back slammed into the door she'd just shut. Without a Mother May I, he started nuzzling her neck with hungry lips. Lacing his fingers with hers, he held them beside her head. "You . . . smell . . ." He punctuated his words with biting kisses up her throat. "Sexy. As. Hell."

Prickly heat swept over her skin, and her breasts instantly tightened with need. Her fingers curled helplessly between his. "You're a crazy man. Let me go, at least until I—" His gaze dropped to her mouth and Isis forgot how to form coherent words as her heart hammered unevenly against her ribs. "You promised me clean sheets and a shower, and then—" There'd been something about leather, and baby oil . . . That thought made her hotter.

Thorne cupped her nape, pulling her so close she felt the hard ridge of his penis through his jeans, right where she needed to feel it, damn him. Sparks of scalding heat traveled from their points of contact to zing through her bloodstream like liquid fire. "I'll deliver—when I'm more rational. Right now I don't give a damn about the trappings. I. Just. Want. You." He kissed her senseless, sucking away her right mind, leaving her panting and lust-crazed.

"Don't talk." Still nuzzling her throat, he turned her around and started down the short hallway with her clasped in his arms. "Don't think," he told her thickly. "Just feel."

"I *feel* filthy," Isis groused, wrapping her arms around his waist as he walked her backward toward the bathroom in what felt like a perfectly choreographed dance.

The all-white tiled bathroom had a blue-and-white-striped plastic shower curtain and a tiny window high on the wall that let in a stream of brilliant white sunshine across the floor.

Thorne laughed. "We'll fix that." Reaching over, he turned on the shower, then backed her against the wall and continued kissing her. His rough jaw abraded her skin as he kissed her forehead, then worked his way across her cheek to her mouth. He tasted of rich, dark coffee and a need too strong to contain.

The bathroom filled with sweet-smelling steam from sandalwood, and he paused kissing her only long enough to add cold water, then tested the temperature on his fingers before returning to crush his mouth down on hers once again.

He skimmed his palm up under several layers of T-shirts to her bare waist. "Your skin is so soft," he said as his damp fingers slid slowly up her sides. "Softer than the most expensive satin."

"Hmm." Isis figured if he was determined to do this, then they should both be naked. Her fingers shook with impatience as she fumbled with the button on his jeans. The ridge of his erection pulsed under her unsteady fingers as she freed him, then she shoved his jeans down as far as she could without being more than an inch from his mouth, which was giving her so much pleasure she vibrated like a tuning fork.

God, she loved kissing him. She loved the smooth texture of his lips, and the way he angled his head to accommodate her. She loved the slick glide of his coffee-flavored tongue mating with hers, and the suck and pull as he played tag inside her mouth. She could kiss him all day and night . . .

"I want to be naked this time," she managed to say, panting slightly because she'd forgotten to breathe through her nose. She used both hands to pull his T-shirt up his body, letting her lips follow the path, up the narrow line of dark hair on his lower belly, up to his rock-hard abs, which vibrated as she kissed a damp trail between his pecs. He helped her pull his shirt over his head.

His skin burned her hands as she ran them over his shoulders. She leaned in to press kisses to the crisp dark hair on his chest, then pressed her mouth there and simply held on as she inhaled deeply. The smell of his skin was like a powerful aphrodisiac. Hot male. Primitive. Primal.

"I assure you"——his voice was tight, his eyes glittering as if he had a high fever——"in less than fifty seconds you'll be in the shower, wet and bare-arsed naked." He pulled the T-shirts over her head before she knew it, and was back nibbling at her bottom lip before she missed him.

"Fifty seconds? You're losing your touch, Thorne."

Picking her up, he tugged her jeans down her legs and tipped her gently onto her feet in the bathtub.

Hot water swirled about her feet and ankles, and she made a grab for the tiled wall with one hand and his shoulder with the other. "I'm wet now." She let go of the wall, because Thorne was all she needed to steady her.

Climbing in with her, he slid his hand between her thighs and gave her a devilish look. "And so you are." For several breathless minutes she could do nothing but dig her nails into his arms and ride his clever fingers. She came twice in quick succession, and could barely gasp out what she'd been trying to say as she pressed her face to his chest, and hung on limply.

She slid her hands down to squeeze the hard flesh and muscle of his taut ass. "This is the order of things, Connor Thorne. You've mixed them up a bit, so here's the *new* order of things."

He cupped her breast, stroking the erect nipple with his thumb as he edged her back under the deliciously hot spray. "Uh-huh."

Isis took a moment to enjoy—enjoy the sensation of hot water sluicing over her parched skin, enjoy Thorne performing amazing sleight of hand between her legs . . . "The order of things is as follows: first, soaping and s-scrubbing. Getting shiny *clean*—"

He pressed his mouth to her neck and took a little nip, making her simultaneously wince and become even more turned on. "Hot, down-and-dirty sex," he murmured at the underside of her jaw.

"Okay. *First.*" Isis ran her palm over his short, wet hair, loving the feel of him, loving to pet him when he made muffled sounds of pleasure low in his throat. "Hot sex where we try very hard not to drown ourselves or each other. *Then* shiny clean. *Then* fall onto that overworked sofa bed and sleep until you're called to duty. How does that sound?"

His arms tightened around her, bringing them both under the hot spray. Reaching out, he grabbed the soap, using her breast and his hand to work up a lather. "You left out the part between fall onto that overworked sofa bed and sleep." He ran his soapy hand over her arm, then under her arm, then around her back.

Soap trickled down her breast onto her belly, tickling its slow path down her body and waking any nerve endings that might still be napping, so her entire body was on red alert. "There *was* nothing between the two."

He soaped her other arm, glided his fingers over her breasts, then curved his hand around her back and all the soapy, slick way down to her bottom. "Make love slowly on a horizontal surface."

"What?" she asked, dazed and hyperaware of what was soaped and what was not. The soap suds felt like an extension of his nimble fingers as they slid slowly down her body. "You're insatiable."

"You talk too much." He kissed her while he made sure all her girl parts were sparkly clean. Then, when she was limp and didn't give a damn what order things happened in, he slid his hand under her knee and guided his hard length into her soapy channel. Isis stifled a scream against his shoulder.

⟪ NINETEEN ⟫

At the sharp rap at the front door, Thorne flung his legs over the mattress, then retrieved a damp towel from the floor to wrap around his waist. Despite the bright sunlight streaming through a chink in the heavy drapes, Isis slept sprawled out on her back with sweet abandon.

They'd made love in the shower. Twice. Washed. Frequently. And managed somehow to open the sofa bed and fall on the clean sheets before going back to devour each other again. Isis had fallen asleep as if she'd run into a wall. Which, God help him, she had. The fact that she'd been able to match him stroke for stroke was, all things considered, nothing short of amazing. Hell, *she* was amazing.

In sleep she'd curled her body against him. A position he had grown to love, one arm and a leg curved around his body. Holding him to her. There was no hold necessary, no hold as strong as his feelings for her.

Thorne hadn't wasted time sleeping. He'd have time for that later. For now, he wanted to absorb her with all his senses.

Whoever was at the door could wait a moment. Thorne stood looking down at her, memorizing the way her waist curved into the sweet round of her hip. The plump weight of her breasts beneath his hand. The soft pink of her nipples. He needed to memorize this moment in case he was never allowed to be this lucky again.

He'd been trained from a young age to keep a stiff upper lip, to show no emotion, to do his duty. Those lessons hadn't taken effect until Garrett killed himself. Then all the fun and fuckup he was, was wiped away. He'd left school, signed up with MI5, and done his best to get killed in every way, shape, and form to make up for his screwed-up youth, without realizing it—until he'd met Isis.

She was everything that was good, while he was— Thorne shoved that realization aside. It was what it was. *He* was what he was.

Once she was imprinted on his brain looking just this way, he tightened the towel and padded to the front door.

Peering through the peephole first, he flung open the door. "Heustis?"

"This was quicker than calling and arranging transport. Here, your pal upstairs said to give you this." He handed Thorne the cane he'd forgotten and tossed him a can of cola. "The spillway has been turned off, at least temporarily, until the authorities decide what to do. We have Brengard and Dr. Najid in custody; they're screaming for their attorneys. Unfortunately, they're not screaming nearly loudly enough for said attorneys to be called in," the Mossad operative said dryly. "The Egyptians have allowed a combined team of your people and my people to ask questions."

A hell of a lot more effective. Thorne cocked a brow. "'Allowed'?"

Heustis grinned. "What do you English say? Finders keepers? We scooped them up. When we're done with them, we'll consider handing them over to the locals." His smile was feral.

"Where they'll be given a slap on the wrist and sent on their way."

The other man shook his head. "I'm sure the Egyptian police appreciate our interrogation techniques, which will have saved them time and effort. So much can happen with a hostage situation—"

The prisoners would be moved to Israel, bypassing the lax Egyptian legal system, Thorne thought with grim satisfaction. "What about Yermalof?"

"In the wind, but we have word he's visiting a lady friend in Alexandria. Your people went to pick him up there. We're holding the other two at a safe house. Want in on the talks?"

"I do. More so when Yermalof shows. Is Najid the mastermind?"

"Seems like." Heustis gave his slipping towel a mild look. "Are you planning to stand there naked all afternoon, or would you like to dress and finish this op off so we can all go home?"

"Give me a minute—"

"Can I come with you?" Isis asked from the bedroom

doorway. She too was wrapped in a towel. It looked a hell of a lot better on her than it did on him.

"Only fair. Get dressed."

She disappeared into the bedroom. "Give us five minutes."

"Car's downstairs. Oh, Thorne?" When Thorne turned back, the other man handed him a polymer-framed, standard Jericho pistol. "Thought you might like the use of my backup."

Magazine loaded, double action, semiauto, short recoil. Thorne hefted the weight. "Thanks, appreciate it."

It took Isis an astoundingly short ten minutes to get dressed and put on makeup she didn't need. "I feel human now."

"You look good enough to eat."

"Thank you, I've been eaten, and have feasted in return, but that's enough sex for you for a while. I want to go and poke a sharp stick at Dylan. Your cane might do the trick."

"Feel free."

"You sit in front. I can stretch out in the back," Isis offered, switching places when Thorne opened the front door of the plain beige sedan for her. He popped the back door and waited until she was inside, then handed her the soda he'd almost forgotten in his pocket.

"How far?" he asked Heustis.

"Twenty minutes, give or take. Can you fill me in on what went down since I saw you last?"

"I'm using Husani's phone to call my father," Isis told him, already punching out the numbers.

Thorne did a quick summary of past events to get the

Mossad operative up to speed, listening to Isis's quiet conversation in the backseat, not with her father, but apparently with her cousin. Her conversation was shorter than his CliffsNotes report to Heustis.

He was just up to the avalanche sealing them inside the upper chamber when Isis chimed in: "Sorry to interrupt for a second——Acadia and Zak are going to bring my father here, probably tomorrow. We decided that it doesn't matter what he remembers or doesn't. He deserves to see Cleo."

"Agreed." Although Isis would be back in Seattle herself by then. "Scorpions and snakes and God only knows what else, but we had——"

Isis's elbow bumped the back of his head as she leaned over the seat. "Acadia asked me about the clues my father left——and I was listing them, when I suddenly realized, we forgot my father's other clue!"

Thorne turned to look at her glowing face and gleaming eyes. His heart double-clutched. God, she was pretty. He smiled at her enthusiasm. "What clue?"

"Seeing the cane Husani gave you reminded me of the broken walking stick my father left with him. It's identical to that one."

"And?" Broken and apparently useless, it had been left at the souk. "Hand it back here. I just had an idea."

Puzzled, Thorne lifted the carved walking stick over the seat back. He caught Heustis's eye and the other man shrugged. "Let me know when you have something to share with the class," Thorne told Isis, turning back to face the front again. "The chopper came over the ridge, and—" He recounted their movements up to their entrance into Cleopatra's tomb.

"Sorry to interrupt your fascinating story again," Isis said excitedly, leaning one elbow over the back of Thorne's seat, "but you might want to take a look at this. But before you do, brace yourself." She handed his cane back across the seat. But this time it was tightly wrapped in a dirty white ribbon.

"Is this the stuff that was wrapped around the basket with the tassel in it?" Thorne took it from her and laid it across his lap. "Where did it come from?"

"I had the ribbon in here." She tapped her camera bag on her hip. "Seeing this cane, I suddenly remembered the ribbon. It had a design on it that I never gave a second thought to. But then I vaguely remembered reading something years ago—and my brain put two and two together and came up with five. Quick! Turn it so it's vertical."

Thorne shifted his feet so he could angle the wrapped stick on the floor. For a moment he simply stared at the writing that spiraled neatly down the stick. The filthy ribbon with the abstract design had become a perfectly legible cypher when wrapped around the article with the exact correct dimensions. The walking stick was the clue. "Bloody hell. This is a *scytale!* Your father left us a usable clue after all."

"We *did* need the cane he left." Isis leaned both elbows over his seat back so that her still-damp, fragrant hair brushed his cheek. "But this is the same, since they're mass-produced. I'm sorry, Connor. Are you shocked?"

"Shocked?" Heustis asked, pulling into an abandoned

parking lot behind a small warehouse and cutting the engine. "What does it tell you?"

No one made any move to exit the vehicle.

"The principal players. From the bottom." Thorne started evenly reading off the names. "Brengard. Boris Yermalof. Dr. Khalifa Najid—and the Earl of Kilgetty."

"Who?" the Mossad operative asked, puzzled.

"The head of the black market ring we've been trying to apprehend for the past five fucking years is my *father*."

THORNE WAS GRIM-FACED AS they entered the warehouse through a side door. Both men were armed. He'd handed Isis his cane when they got out of the car. Even though she was pretty sure he'd done so because he didn't want anyone inside to see he was less than fighting fit, she considered the gesture tacit permission to use it on Dylan should the opportunity present itself.

Never prone to violence, she decided she could make an exception for the slimy-snake-turncoat-turd and was *eager* for that opportunity to present itself.

Thorne had already cautioned her to stay behind them, but he put his arm out, slowing her steps just as a reminder. They passed from blinding sunlight to shadowy interior.

Inside, the huge metal warehouse was as hot and unpleasant as being inside an oven. In the far corner, a bright light was trained on a man tied to a metal chair; the rest of the space was almost midnight-dark. Isis saw that the high windows had all been painted black, blocking natural light once the door was closed behind them.

Her hand rested on her camera bag. The place was atmospheric, threatening, and scary as hell. She could shoot some amazing images here.

Maybe later.

A man cradling an Uzi in his arms like a baby stepped out of the shadows. "Your Lordship," he said with faint British mockery, and with what Isis presumed was a smile curving his lips for a second.

Lordship?

"Cloud," Thorne greeted him briskly as Heustis melted into the darkness. "Who's up first?" He jerked his chin in the general direction of the distant lights.

"Starting on the help and working our way up. The others are being held over there." Cloud used the nose of his big-ass gun to point in the opposite direction, where Isis could just make out small groups of people but couldn't identify who was who.

"We have seven of them here," the other man added, all business. "Just got word a sec ago that Yermalof was caught with his"——the man's eyes flicked to Isis——"in flagrante delicto. He'll be joining us soon."

Thorne's eyes narrowed a fraction. "Who's in charge?"

"Ran Beck. Want to have a word?"

"I do. Let me read him in on a new development first."

"Right. He's over there sitting on Najid."

"Come along," he told her. As if she'd wander off on her own.

"Your Lordship?"

"I don't use my titles."

Isis grabbed his arm to slow him down a little. "Titles, *plural?*"

"This is neither the time nor the place."

"We had this conversation in the right time and place and you told me you——"

"Here's Brengard." They approached the first cluster of four men, who were gathered around Dylan. He was trussed up attractively like a turkey, lying on his side on the floor, legs curled up behind him, ankles tied neatly to his wrists. Even in the dim lighting she saw his face was red with anger. And sweaty, she hoped, with fear.

Thorne clearly knew the men, and after a brief greeting he introduced them to Isis. "She'd like a private word."

"Ten feet do it?" a short, wiry guy asked. Thorne nodded.

Taking her chin in his hand, his face in deep shadow, he looked down at her and said evenly, "Leave enough of him to answer questions when you're done."

Dear God, he trusted her to control her anger around the man who'd tried to kill her father? And steal his legacy? Thorne knew her better than she knew herself, because seeing Dylan made her feel homicidal.

Dylan writhed on the floor. "Wait a damn minute! I demand my rights! I'm an American citizen—you can't——"

For a moment she contemplated kicking him in the balls, but then he wouldn't do much but whimper and groan and that wasn't going to get her any answers. She walked around his thrashing legs to crouch near his head. She planted the heavy cane vertically beside her. "Thorne wouldn't let me bring a gun in here, even though I sort of promised not to shoot you in the balls before I asked questions."

"You crazy bitch!"

Anger vibrated from her head to her toes, and she curled her fingers into tight fists at her side. "Why did you betray my father? No, not why. *Why* was because of the fame and money. Maybe *how* is a better question. You worked for my father for more than five years. Built up a trust. He thought of you as the son he never had."

Dylan made a rude noise that bumped her anger up another notch. "Thorne said leave enough to interrogate. Perhaps you don't need your teeth all that badly."

"The professor is a doddering old fool. He found Cleo's fucking tomb a *year* ago, Isis! Forgot, and came *back!* We'd already packed and shipped half the artifacts for sale, and placed the rest in a warehouse near Abusir so everything could be unpacked and artfully displayed when I found Cleo's tomb in a couple of weeks. We couldn't take the risk he'd suddenly remembered. Yermalof took out the team, moved everyone. Stupid fuck was supposed to die with the others."

Dylan hadn't just wanted her father's fame and fortune. He'd wanted her father *dead*. "Sorry he inconvenienced you. You'll be discredited, of course. Humiliated. Your bank accounts seized—"

Dylan laughed. "Humiliated? Maybe. But I have more money than they'll ever find, and all I'll get here is a slap on the wrist, and I'll give my promise to be a good boy in the future. Whatever way they cut it, I'll be credited with discovery of that tomb, and Professor Magee will still be a laughingstock."

"But you're tied up *here*," Isis reminded him, her fingers tightening on the walking stick. His eyes flickered whitely to her hand, and back to her face. "Anyone know where you are right now, Dylan?" She summoned the coldly cruel delivery of some long-forgotten movie bad guy.

"They can't hold me here forever. Legally, they can't do this."

She laughed, because he was ridiculous lying there, arms behind his back, feet bound together, talking about his legal rights. "Do you know who all these men are?" Channeling the icky tones of a movie villain was very satisfying. Especially since, even in the poor lighting, she saw the sweat begin to trickle down his temples and shine slickly on his upper lip.

She waved her free hand around the warehouse. "British and Israeli intelligence operatives. And you know *why* they're called intelligence? Because they're not stupid enough to hand you over to the Egyptian authorities. You'll be tried and convicted . . ." She waited several ominous seconds before finishing. ". . . elsewhere."

"That's illegal!"

Isis shrugged. "Or questioned and killed here," she added sweetly. "I'm told they're so good, they leave hardly a mark on your body—I have no idea *how* they do that. Special spy skills, I guess." She let her voice trail off admiringly, and heard a snort nearby as one of the men muffled his opinion of her interrogation techniques. Isis got to her feet. Dylan flinched as the movement brought her dangerously close to his private parts. "Goodbye, Dylan. You were a weak coward when I met you, and you're a sniveling creep now. The world will be better off without you." Turning to go, she said to the guy closest to her, "He's all yours now."

"Isis! Wait! *Isis!*"

"DID YOU ENJOY THAT?" Thorne asked, exiting to find Isis leaning against the building, hands on her knees.

She straightened when she heard him. "I did while I was talking to him. Now I feel a little sick."

"He's feeling a lot sicker in anticipation of what's to come, I imagine." Thorne wrapped his arms around her, and she put her head on his chest, sliding her arms tightly around his waist.

Her shaky laugh was muffled against his shirt. "You know what's funny? I was channeling some movie villain when I was talking to Dylan, and feeling quite proud of myself. I only just realized who I was channeling. Cruella de Vil."

He bit back a smile as he stroked her back and buried his face in her fragrant hair. "They're taking all of them to another location."

"Are we going, too?"

His hands tightened around her at the "too." "I'm going to take a later flight and meet them there." He'd take her to her gate and kiss her goodbye. Make promises both knew would never be kept. They'd call her flight, and after she turned to board, he'd stand there waiting until the last possible second to watch her go.

"They have Yermalof in custody, and they should be"—he angled his wrist to check the time, then remembered they'd taken his watch off him when they'd been kidnapped—"arresting the Earl at his London residence within the hour. I imagine it'll be on the six o'clock news."

Isis lifted her head. "How do you feel about him being involved in this?"

Plucking her glasses from her nose, he reconsidered and removed them by the earpiece. "He wasn't merely 'involved'—he started by hiring Yermalof a decade ago," Thorne said coolly, cleaning the lenses on his shirt hem for the last time. He'd miss the silly little ritual. He'd developed a thing for cheeky girls wearing glasses. "Yermalof told him of your father's obsession with Queen Cleopatra, and the Earl cultivated *that* relationship slowly and insidiously over the years. Yermalof put together the Earl and the minister for a trio that was a match made in hell. The minister found Brengard—it'll take a while to get through all the layers. There are a dozen ministers who were involved in small ways, people bribed to look the other way. There's a long food chain."

"I mean do you care *emotionally* that your father will be imprisoned for his part in this? I just care about how it'll impact *you*."

He stroked her cheek with the backs of his fingers. Soft, warm skin, vibrant and alive. His chest ached. "Not at all." His father meant nothing to him. Isis . . . Isis meant everything.

"Then can we go and watch his arrest on TV?" she suggested with relish.

Thorne laughed as he held up the key Heustis had given him on his way out. "Let's. The Four Seasons is only a few minutes away." Another couple of hours with her was a windfall, no, a *reprieve* he wasn't going to pass up.

"DO YOU WANT TO see this?" Isis asked. "They just announced *Scandalous Breaking News!*" She sat cross-legged at the head of a king-sized bed in the Palace Suite at the Four Seasons Hotel, a room service tray in front of her, a glass of soda in one hand and a strawberry in the other. She looked over to where he was standing, using the cell phone lent to him by Husani.

Thorne had booked them in, ordered room service, made arrangements with the boutique for clothing for both of them, hit the jewelry store for a watch, and was currently in contact with his associates to ensure Yermalof was locked and loaded on board a flight to Tel Aviv, and that the prisoners from the warehouse were en route to join him shortly. All in less than thirty minutes. Perhaps if the return to MI5 didn't work out he could be a concierge, he mused, watching Isis nibble on a plump red strawberry.

"Do you want popcorn, too?" he asked, amused as she wiggled her behind to get more comfortable as he sat beside her. It had been *his* nefarious plan to place the tray on the bed. Exactly where he wanted her.

"Are you kid—" She slanted him a glance. "Yes, you are. There's more food here than we can eat in a week."

Not if they holed up in the room for several days, Thorne thought, bringing her hand to his mouth and biting her strawberry in half. She leaned sideways to press her lips to his. "Yum," she murmured, straightening, her eyes glued to the television.

The kiss, so casual, so natural, was so Isis.

"Sound," she directed, hands full. And so was her desire to be the boss.

The remote lay between them. With a small smile Thorne picked it up and turned on the volume as he swung his feet up on the mattress, then stuffed a pillow behind him.

The attractive blond news reader was replaced with live footage of his father standing at the top of the stairs outside the house, flanked by two plainclothes detectives. ". . . Earl of Kilgetty, seen here exiting his London residence moments ago, has just been arrested by police in connection with allegations of trafficking Egyptian antiquities."

"He doesn't seem particularly worried," Isis observed, moving the tray and stretching out her legs beside his, then draping one leg over his good knee as she avidly watched the Earl being escorted down to the street where reporters clustered, shouting questions.

"It's a British thing. Stiff upper lip. Never let them see you sweat."

"He's sweating. Who's that, do you think? His lawyer? Bet he was on speed dial."

Thorne turned around to comb his fingers through the hair at her temples, then took her mouth in a kiss hot enough to melt the mattress. There was only so much a man could take. Instantly her lips softened and her tongue darted out to meet his. She tasted of cola and strawberries and, Thorne knew unequivocally, she tasted of *home*.

Somehow, without taking his hands—or lips—off Isis for a second, he found the control without looking, and turned the TV off.

After several breathless moments, he ripped his mouth from hers. Her lips were swollen and damp, her eyes hazed with desire. Her fingers tightened in his hair to bring his mouth back where she wanted it.

Tracing the sweet curve of her cheek with his finger, Thorne said thickly, "A woman like you should marry a nice guy who's an accountant, or a lawyer. Some well-established, secure man with a comfortable income, who comes home every night. A guy sans bullet holes or debilitating knife wounds. You deserve to have a whole man, not a fucking torn-apart cripple with commitment issues."

Her eyes glittered and she made a small moue as if to say, *I'm not saying anything.*

"You should have that pretty house on a quiet cul-de-sac in suburbia so you can watch your children playing on the front lawn."

"I agree," she whispered. "I should."

Was it possible for a heart to wrench? She was here, but he felt her slipping away. "You deserve that man," he said a little desperately. "You deserve him, but you need *me.*"

"What exactly would you do with the leather and baby oil?"

He paused at the non sequitur.

"You said 'leather and baby oil and a kip.'"

"I don't need to rub you in baby oil to make you hot, do I?"

"No. But I'd like to try it and find out. Order some from room—"

His smile felt a little less strained. "Done."

"The leather, I presume, is to be used as restraints? I must admit, I *would* like to tie you up and have my wicked way with you."

"Would you now? What about if I tied you up instead?"

"Okay." She thought about it for a second. "We'll take turns."

"I love you, Isis Magee."

"I know."

"That's it? You know?"

"I know that I'm absolutely the perfect woman for you. I was just waiting for you to cut to the chase."

He laughed, rolling her on top of him. "You were, were you? And do you know that I love the way you touch me? Or the way you always seem to get fingerprints all over these?" He removed her glasses and placed them on the bedside table.

"Dirty glasses are quite endearing. It was my master plan to snare you."

"It worked.

"We'll balance each other out," she told him softly. "We'll love each other till we're old and gray and sitting in our rocking chairs in the old-age home. You'll do your best to keep your promise to me that you won't get hurt again in your job for MI5, and I'll pretend that your job doesn't scare the crap out of me. We'll buy a pretty house wherever we want to live, and I'll get pregnant right away. This is forever love, Connor James Thorne. We'll fight and make up, and love and laugh and raise our family, and grow old together . . ."

"You haven't said you love me."

"I say I love you every time I touch you, every time I look at you. You fill me up, Connor. You fill me up with love and light and unspeakable joy." She tugged his T-shirt over his head. "Grab that oil," she whispered thickly. "Make love with me. Let's make our first baby right here."

"Your every wish, my bossy darling, is my command."

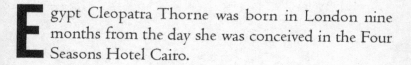 EPILOGUE

Egypt Cleopatra Thorne was born in London nine months from the day she was conceived in the Four Seasons Hotel Cairo.

Want a thrill?

Pick up a bestselling romantic suspense novel
from Pocket Books!

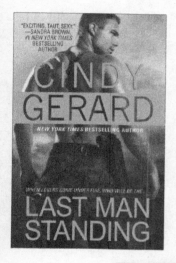

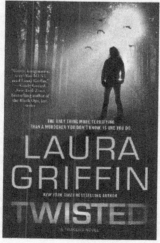